This is a work of fiction. Names, character, places, and incidents
either are the product of the author's imagination or are used fictitiously.
Any resemblance to actual persons, living or dead, events, or
locales is entirely coincidental.

Published by Giraffix Media
Knoxville, Tennessee
www.giraffix.com

First Edition

THE LAST MOTLEY

BY

DJ EDWARDSON

To my cousin Jacob, who was once a boy.

S.D.G.

CONTENTS

To all the poets I have known
You built a kingdom out of sea and sand
You conquered armies with a marching band
You carved a galaxy in stone
You built an altar out of bread
And spent your soul to see the children fed
You wove your heart in every story read
Thank God for poets I have known

You turned your tears into a string of pearls
You held your sorrow high to light the world
When I thought I was alone
In every man you saw the boy
The hidden heart the dark could not destroy
Slipped past the dragons with a tale of joy
Thank God for poets I have known

—Andrew Peterson, *To All the Poets I Have Known*

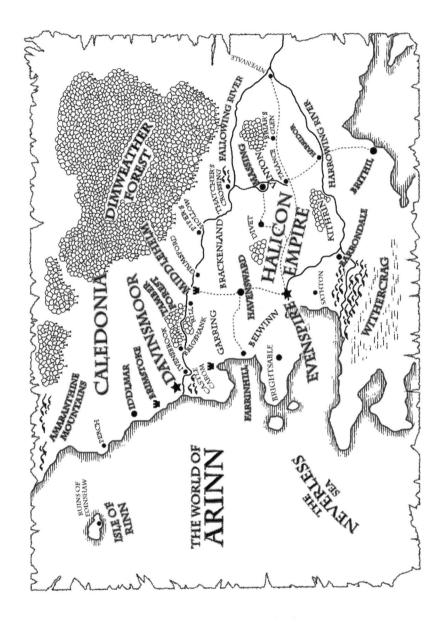

WELCOME TO THE
WORLD of ARINN

OUR STORY BEGINS ON THE
8TH DAY OF AUTUMN'S DUSK,
YEAR 576 H.R. (HELM'S RECKONING)

1

THE FALLEN APPLE

The half-eaten apple hit the dirt and rolled under the cart.

"Eck! Rotten." The well-dressed man who had tossed it squeezed his face into pleated wrinkles.

Standing across from him, Roderick the tailor could hardly believe his eyes. Rotten or not, apples had been scarce that season due to the late frosts and that piece of fruit cost half a day's wages. This traveler must have been even richer than he looked.

"I should have known that hawker wouldn't have anything fresh," the man said with a huff.

Roderick nodded politely, hoping the man's ill humor would not affect his buying habits when it came to clothing. The market would be closing soon and so far Roderick had only managed to sell a wool scarf for a handful of silver miras.

The late autumnal sun labored to warm the empty market square. Lined by mortared stalls with open roofs, thin patches of grass clung to the open ground like faded doilies set out for dinner guests who had failed to come. Though potential customers had begun trickling in over the past half hour, most passed by without so much as a glance, intent on making their way home or to one of the two inns which served the tiny village of Briar's Glen.

The wealthy gentleman at Roderick's stall fingered a pair of black trousers while dabbing the corners of his mouth with an embroidered kerchief. "To top it all off, I soiled my knickers. Ruined a perfectly good execution. How much for these?"

Roderick was tempted to overcharge him. A few extra miras would hardly be missed by someone of such obvious resources. The velvet doublet he sported was worth ten of Roderick's best pieces.

"Thirty," Roderick said. He could almost hear his wife say, *a fair price is its own reward.*

The man guffawed, spewing flecks of apple onto Roderick's cart.

"Really? No wonder the people in this province live little better than paupers. Here—" The man slapped three ten-mira coins onto the counter. Then he swiped the knickers off the rack and trudged off through the commons.

Roderick picked up the coins and let them fall into his money box with a lonesome clink. It wasn't much, but it was honest coin. Besides, there was still that apple the man had tossed under the cart. If Roderick could cut out the rotten bits and wash it off, there might still be enough to bring home to his wife and daughter.

He knelt in the dirt and craned his neck under the cart. The apple was nowhere in sight.

"Oh, buttons," he muttered.

He stood up to see if it had rolled to the side and caught a bit of movement out of the corner of his eye—a flash of color in the midst of the otherwise drab selection of cloaks.

Not another pinch-purse! Where could this one have come from? No matter. He knew how to deal with this sort. Quietly, he reached for the little knife he kept fastened underneath the counter.

The cloaks ruffled slightly. He was almost certain there was someone in there now. His hand shot out and he flung one of the cloaks off the rack and onto the counter.

"Ha!" he shouted, brandishing his knife at a small figure hiding amongst the apparel. From his size, he could not have been much more than seven or eight years old, but his hood was pulled down tightly over his face, obscuring his features in shadow, and making him look more dangerous than perhaps he was.

The figure bolted straight at him, dashing between Roderick's legs and racing past the cart. He would have gotten away, too, if he hadn't tripped and fallen headlong into the dirt.

Roderick was on him in a single stride, grabbing him by the arm and yanking him to his feet.

"Gotcha!" His quarry bagged, he took a step back. Within the hooded shadows, tears glistened on the boy's cheeks.

"I'm sorry, sir," came a little fluted voice, quivering with fear. "I didn't know you wanted it."

The child held out the remains of the apple in his small, gloved hand. The tips of his fingers poked through the threadbare cloth like tender shoots through spring ground.

He's just a boy, Roderick thought to himself. *And he looks to be freezing.*

The child's fingers were as blue as the bachelor's buttons in his wife's garden.

"You're not one of the lollygaggers I usually see running through the market. Where are your parents?" Roderick asked.

The child lowered his hooded head and said nothing.

Roderick bent down, trying to get a look at his face, but the boy turned away, whimpering softly.

"You can keep the apple. I'm sure you need it more than I do," Roderick said.

The child raised his head. His eyes flashed wide from within the shadows. He looked at Roderick as if he had just doubled in size or sprouted wings. "Thank you," he said between sniffles.

"Are you lost?"

The boy shrugged weakly and looked away again.

"It's quite chilly today. Let's see about getting you a better pair of gloves, shall we?"

The boy shot Roderick a look that was a mix of fear and desperate need.

"It's all right. I know you meant no harm. Come, I have some rather nice ones here in this basket. Made from good, Vinyon wool."

The boy allowed himself to be led to the selection of gloves by the counter.

"Take any pair you like," Roderick said.

The child was hesitant. After Roderick insisted several more times he relented and sheepishly picked out a black pair similar to the ones he had on, though much thicker and in much better condition. As he put them on, he turned his back towards Roderick. This rekindled Roderick's suspicions. He peered over the boy's shoulder as he slipped off his glove. The child's hand was completely covered in motley patches of skin, diamond-shaped and brightly colored like the pattern on a bolt of cloth: alternating patches of blue, green, yellow, and red, each shape about the size of a thumb print. It didn't look like paint or even a tattoo. It was so natural it had to be the actual color of his skin. The strange sight jogged something deep in the recesses of Roderick's memory. Could it be...?

He gasped.

"Who are you?"

The boy bolted through a rack of shirts, sending clothes flying everywhere.

Roderick darted around the mess, but slipped and went crashing into a pile of his wares. Shirts and scarves flew everywhere. He recovered his wits just in time to see the boy's foot slide over the seven foot high stone wall at the back of his stall. Roderick heard the lithe creature thump to the ground on the other side, followed by the pounding of his receding footfalls.

"He's quick, that one." A shudder danced through Roderick's shoulders. "Unnaturally quick."

A moment later, the only sign anyone had been there were the soiled clothes and the remains of the apple, fallen and bruised in the dirt.

Roderick tapped his knuckles on the front door with his familiar seven beat rhythm. He could have simply opened it, but he relished the sound of the pattering footsteps of Aisha's approach. Seeing her face, he knew, would take his mind off his troubling encounter in the market.

"Daddy, you're back!" His little girl flung open the door, arms stretched wide. He swept her off her feet and buried his bearded face in her neck, giving her ticklish kisses. She squirmed and giggled in his arms, her dark curly hair bouncing in all directions.

"And how is my sweetness?" he asked.

"Good," Aisha said, drawing the word out, as if the longer she took to say it, the more goodness she would express. Then she launched into a breathless description of all the adventures she had experienced that day: chasing squirrels from the garden, building a house out of twigs, and the discovery of some rainbow-colored beetles under the stepping stones in the walk.

Roderick delighted in the music of her voice. He never grew tired of her endless energy and irrepressible spirit. The sun never stopped shining in her world. She was the happiest child he knew.

"Evening, my love," he said, porting his little girl into the cottage and over towards his wife who stooped over the hearth.

Rich smells of cabbages and leeks and fresh yams and spices from the garden clamored for his attention, as if radiating from Bethany herself, and not the pot she was stirring. He embraced his wife and planted a kiss on her rosy cheeks. Her skin, though naturally fair, was often ruddy. The cottage was only four rooms, three on the ground floor and one above, but cleaning, chopping and hauling wood, fixing leaks in the roof, and running after little Aisha kept Bethany busy enough for two people. And tending the massive garden out back might have been sufficient work for a third, but she wouldn't have had it any other way.

"So good to have you back, Derick. You're home early," she said, her eyes smiling in lovely creases to the sides.

Roderick wrapped his arm around her shoulder. "Aye, there didn't seem to be much point in staying 'til dark today. Business was dead from dawn to dusk. Everyone was over at the execution. The few who did come by weren't buying."

The motley-skinned child played back through his memory. Should he tell her? He didn't want to trouble her. Surely his eyes had been playing tricks on him. Between the failing light and the strain of another fruitless day at the market, he might have gotten it wrong.

He planted another kiss on top of Aisha's head and hung his hat on a hook by the hearth. Letting Aisha down to the floor, he eased into one of the rickety chairs at the table and sat for a moment, staring into the fire. The glow flickered along the cedar walls, looking for one of the many chinks between the boards through which to escape. Outside the wind rustled its way through the thatched roof, making a scratching sound.

"Is something wrong?" Bethany asked. "You look worried."

"I don't know. It's just—"

Aisha leapt into his lap before he could finish and thrust a wilted daffodil into his face.

"Smell the pretty flower, Daddy," she said, "I picked it just for you."

"Why, thank you, honey-eyes." He kissed her. "Oh, I almost forgot. I have something for you, too." He pulled out a scrap of cloth from his pocket and unwrapped it. Aisha's face lit up when she laid eyes on the remains of the apple, cleaned and peeled. There was only enough for two small slices, but the pungent aroma filled the room.

"Oh, yummy!" Aisha bounced up and down with excitement.

"Oh, Derick, you shouldn't have," Bethany said.

"Don't worry, I didn't pay for it. A customer left it. I almost didn't bring it, though. There was a..." He had to tell her, he knew. Bethany would have a way of explaining it. "There was a boy who wanted it...a very strange boy." Was it a boy...or something else? Oh, how he hoped he was wrong about that.

He motioned for Aisha to take one of the pieces to her mother. She plopped one slice in her pillowy cheek and skipped over to Bethany. She placed the other slice in her mother's hand, all the while mashing her own tiny bit over and over again to get out all the sweetness out of it she could.

"A boy? What was so unusual about him?" Bethany bit into her slice. Both girls made pleasant noises as they munched on the unexpected treat. Aisha did a little dance, traipsing around the table, her last bit of apple held high and triumphant like a trophy.

"He had colors on his skin, in a motley, checkered pattern like a piece of cloth. He ran away when I asked about them." He stared intently at her, wondering if she'd pick up on the words 'motley, checkered pattern.'

"That is odd." Bethany's delicate eyebrows climbed with curiosity. "Perhaps he was playing with dyes."

"No, the pattern was perfect—no child could have made it. It would have been quite beautiful if it had not been so..."

His eyes locked with Bethany's. In an instant she knew.

"A motley, Roderick? That's what you're thinking, isn't it? A motley in Briar's Glen!" She wagged her head kindly at the musings of her impressionable husband. "Those are just stories, love. No one's ever actually seen one. For all we know they don't exist."

"Well, he did look more like a boy than a monster, I'll grant you that. Still, you didn't see that skin. It wasn't natural, Beth. I'm straight on that point."

"A motley..." Beth chuckled softly. "Oh, Roderick, you ought to try your hand at story time with Aisha tonight. Would you like that Eesh? If Daddy tells you the story tonight?"

7

"Umm…" Aisha's eyes scanned the ceiling. She loved her daddy, but… "Can't Mama do it?" she asked with a hopeful smile.

Now it was Roderick's turn to chuckle. "Ah, don't worry, Eesh. Mama will do it like always. My stories would probably only scare you." He took Beth's good natured ribbing with a sigh. He may have had the more active imagination when it came to listening to stories, but it did him no good when it came to telling them.

"I'm curious though," Bethany said. "If he's just a boy, I mean *since* he's just a boy, where did he come from? Who are his parents?"

Roderick shook his head. "Didn't have any. He was dressed like one of the street children, but I've never seen him before."

"Well, if he's lost we should tell the magistrate. His parents must be looking for him, especially if he's not from Briar's Glen." Bethany brought out the bowls from the cupboard and set them on the table. The cottage had a single cupboard with two shelves above and two below and a drawer in between. Like the house itself and everything in it, it had been made by Roderick's father, who was almost as fine a carpenter as he was a woodsman.

"What if he hasn't got any?" Roderick asked. Was Bethany right? Had Roderick simply let his imagination get the better of him? "He did look awful lonely and sad."

"Well, if you see him again, ask him," Bethany said.

Maybe he *was* just a lonely child lost in the market. But all those stories about motleys Roderick had heard since he was young were not easy to shake. They lingered on the threshold of his imagination.

"And if he doesn't have any, we could always take him in here." Bethany watched Aisha slide the last bit of apple between her lips, oblivious to what her parents were saying. "And give him a nice good bath," she added teasingly with a poke of her wooden spoon.

"Oh, Beth," he said, his mind wandering and missing the

joke. His eyes strayed to Aisha. "How could we possibly take in another…"

Aisha, still munching on the apple, ran off to grab her wooden ball in the corner. Adopting their daughter had been the best decision they had ever made. She was the fire in the hearth of their home, the warming light that chased away the shadows. He had no doubt his wife would take in another child in a heartbeat, even if the family's coin had been tighter than a varlet's vest of late.

"Children are a blessing. And Adonai has never failed to provide for us." Bethany placed a hand on his shoulder.

"Aye, love. That is true. And maybe you're right about the skin. It's just that the pattern was so distinct."

"Stories, my love, that's all the motleys are, stories." Bethany gave his shoulder a gentle squeeze. "Now let's eat. Soup's ready."

Ah, how he loved that woman. He still found it hard to believe he'd ever worked up the courage to ask her to marry him, and even harder to believe that she'd said yes.

"Aisha," Roderick called. "Come to the table, my sweet."

Aisha leapt into the chair between her mother and father and placed her tiny hands in theirs. Bethany and Roderick held hands as well, completing the circle.

"All right, then," Roderick said, leaning over the table as he held onto those precious hands. "Let us pray."

2

CALLINGS AT THE COTTAGE

A jarring bang on the cottage door broke the stillness of the night.

"Who could it be at this hour?" Bethany whispered in the dark. She and Roderick had just gotten into their nightgowns. Visitors were rare enough during the day. If someone was stopping by at this hour, they must have been lost or in some kind of trouble.

"I don't know. I'll go see," Roderick said.

He left the bedroom, hurrying down the steps and over to the kitchen table. He fumbled around, trying to light the lantern. More knocking shook the door.

The lantern switch finally struck. The resulting glow bathed the walls in soft, ginger light. Roderick crossed the packed dirt floor, wincing as the chill from the ground shot up through his bare feet. In five quick steps he made it to the oasis which was the tired old rug by the front door.

He peeked through the window, but storm clouds had all but strangled the moon. Rain streaked the thick panes. He couldn't see a thing.

"Who is it?" he asked.

"The town watch!" shouted a voice from the other side.

The town watch?

Roderick's cabin was a mile outside of town. He had never been visited by the watch in all the years he'd lived in Briar's Glen. He gulped a spoonful of worry that was bitter all the way down. *Relax, Devinson. It's nothing.* Roderick had never so much as harmed a sparrow or stolen a blade of grass, but he couldn't shake the feeling that he was in some sort of trouble. "Open up," the voice insisted. "We need to speak with the master of the house."

Snapping on his courage, he unbolted the door and undid the lock. With clammy palms he pulled the latch. Four men stood on the stoop wearing kettle helmets and the livery of the township: green and white checkered tunics which looked so faded they could have been sewn by Roderick's grandmother. One of them had a spear. This also was a bit out of the ordinary. The watch normally only used such weapons for parades.

Rain poured down relentlessly on the stoop and runnels of water collected in the grooves of the watchmen's helmets.

"Good evening, sirs. What brings you out at this hour?" Roderick asked, as politely and normally as he could.

"Begging your pardon, but are you Roderick Devinson, the tailor?" asked the man in front. Though Roderick knew most of the men who served on the watch, he didn't recognize the voice, nor any of the shadowed faces on his stoop.

"Yes, yes I am." Roderick said.

"We're on the lookout for a runaway—an orphan boy. Some folk at the market said they saw him around your stall. Do you know anything about him?"

Roderick faltered. *It had to be the one with the motley skin. Perhaps they're just pretending it's a boy to avoid sending the town into a panic.* More spoonfuls of worry slipped down inside him.

The man went on. "His parents died in the execution this morning and he was to be taken up to Massing and consigned to the orphanage, but when we went to the migrant fields he was not to be found."

Oh, how awful. So this was a boy after all? Were those really his parents that died? The fear churned into sadness in his gut. Roderick knew what it was like to lose your parents.

"His parents were migrants?" Roderick asked.

"Yes."

Hmm…migrants were not usually afforded public executions. They must have done something exceedingly horrible to have suffered such a punishment.

"Do you know what they were killed for?"

"All I know is that they got what they deserved. Now, if you please, do you have any information as to the whereabouts of the boy? The higher-ups have got their knickers all up in a wad over this, if you take my meaning." The guard coughed and ruffled his tunic in a vain effort to keep his uniform from becoming even more soaked than it already was.

"Perhaps. Could you tell me what he looked like though—to make sure we're talking about the same one?"

The guard snorted. "Well, baste my brisket, I plum forgot that part, didn't I? The description they gave us was of a lad about yay high dressed head to toe in a cloak and gloves as if winter were coming on early."

Still no mention of the skin. Were they hiding something?

"Ah, I see." Whole dollops of dread and sadness mingled together inside Roderick, but he wasn't sure which emotion he was supposed to feel. Either this was an orphan boy who'd just lost his parents in the most horrible way imaginable or it was one of the nightmarish motleys from the stories, a candy-colored creature with dark powers to drain the souls of men. "Yes, I did see him—briefly. I gave him a pair of gloves, but then he ran off."

The two in the back mumbled something, but Roderick couldn't make it out. The guard in front shot them a look over his shoulder and they promptly went silent.

"New gloves, eh?" The man rubbed his ear absentmindedly. "Did you see which way he went?"

"I'm sorry, but he slipped over the back wall and I honestly don't know what happened to him after that."

"Very well," the guard said, sounding relieved. "Pardon the interruption. We'll leave you to enjoy the rest of the evening, then."

The guards turned to go, but Roderick spoke up.

"Sir, may I ask one last question before you go? You said that 'higher-ups' were involved. You mean the magistrate?"

The man shook his head. He leaned in close and whispered in Roderick's ear.

"It's foreigners. Don't know where they're from, but some say the *Thaumaturge* is behind it." The last part of the sentence was barely audible above the clattering rain, but it went off like a thunderclap inside Roderick's brain. He almost gagged, but the man's expression was serious. First motleys and now thaumaturges? Would nothing stay put in stories where it belonged?

"But I thought the Thau—the Th—" his tongue refused to say the word, "—that he was just a legend. You haven't actually seen him, have you?" Roderick's throat tightened. He had grown up hearing tales of the Thaumaturge, all of them wild and terrible—almost as terrible as the ones about the motleys, but he had never met anyone who claimed the stories had any basis in fact. The prospect of one of these evil wizards meddling in the affairs of Briar's Glen had to be a terrible mistake.

"No, but they're recruiting extra jokers for the town watch just to find this boy. And everyone, including the magistrate himself, is running belfry to basement looking for him. Don't know why, but I've learned it's best not to ask questions." He pulled back, straightened himself, and said in a normal tone, "I'm sure you'll let us know if you find out anything. Just report it to the town hall if you do."

He tipped his helmet cordially. The gesture sent a waterfall of wetness onto Roderick's nightgown. Oblivious to the state of Roderick's sleepwear, the guard and his fellows stepped off the stoop and trudged back towards the road. Roderick was left standing in the doorway, damp robe and all, wondering what exactly was going on in the otherwise unremarkable little town of Briar's Glen.

A few days later another knock rattled Roderick's front door. The sound caught him in mid-gulp as he was downing his evening soup. He, Bethany, and Aisha all looked up from the table to the door. The noise was such a surprise that a bean from the soup went down the wrong way and lodged in Roderick's throat.

He sputtered for a moment, breathless, and then chucked it loose. It launched straight into the hearth where it sizzled and died in the fire in dramatic fashion. As dramatic as a bean's death can be, at any rate.

"I'll see who it is," Roderick said, clearing his throat and getting up from the table.

He pulled open the door to the welcome sight of Farmer Tullum on the stoop.

"Good evening to you, Roderick," he said in his slow, country drawl. He was a short, broad man with a lifetime of weather etched across his features. He was twenty years Roderick's senior, but twice as strong.

"Good evening, Farmer Tullum," Roderick said, giving him a hearty nod and pounding his chest. His throat still tickled from the ill-fated bean.

"Sorry to disturb you. Didn't know you were eating." He held his straw hat in his hands respectfully. His grimy skin showed that he had come straight from the field.

"That's quite all right," Roderick said. "Would you like to join us? You look like you've had a long day."

"Well, that's awful kind of you, but Missy'll be expecting me." Tullum stared up into Roderick's eyes expectantly.

Roderick slapped his forehead. "Ah, you've come for the work clothes! How could I be so forgetful? I have them in the back room. Come in and wait if you like."

"Thank you, but I'll just stay on the stoop if you don't mind. I've yet to clean up and wouldn't want to sully Miss Bethany's fine swept floor."

"Nice to see you again, Mr. Tullum." Bethany rose from the kitchen table as Roderick ducked into his work room.

"How's Missy?"

"Oh, fine as flour," Tullum said.

Roderick thumbed through a pile of brown shirts and jackets while Bethany and Tullum chatted on the stoop. At length he found the farmer's work clothes and returned to the main room.

"That Aisha is looking pretty as a petunia," Tullum remarked.

"And she's growing about as fast as one too." Roderick handed Tullum the clothing. "I can make more for you whenever you like. You gave me enough miras to make two or three shirts, you know."

"That's what neighbors are for," Tullum said, donning his hat. "You do fine work. A craftsman should be rewarded for his efforts."

"I'm sorry that you were made to come all this way. I ought to have brought them to you days ago."

"No need to worry, son. You've got your family to think of. If I had children I'd have a hard time keeping my plow lines straight, too."

"You're a true friend, Mr. Tullum," Roderick said, shaking the man's large, calloused hand.

"You and Miss Bethany thinking of adding to the crop anytime soon?" Tullum asked. "If you don't mind my asking."

Roderick let out a little laugh and put his arm around his wife. Bethany grinned up at him.

"Well...perhaps," Bethany said. "We're thinking about it anyway."

Roderick gave a start. Was Bethany serious? Was she talking about the motley? But that skin...What if the legends were true?

"You know what they say, children are a blessing from heaven," Tullum said. "And I know any child raised in this cottage will be twice blessed at that." He tipped his hat and turned to go.

"Thank you, Mr. Tullum." Roderick flushed, not knowing how to respond to the compliment. Mr. Tullum was fine folk.

He always spoke in that same respectful way.

"Give our regards to Mrs. Tullum," Bethany said.

"That I will. And don't you hesitate to let us know if you need anything. There's plenty to go around."

Roderick returned the man's parting wave and closed the door.

"Such a kind man," Bethany said as she and Roderick returned to the table.

"Are we going to start a farm, daddy?" Aisha asked.

"What?"

"Farmer Tullum said we're going to get a crop, right?"

Roderick chuckled softly. "Well, I think Farmer Tullum was actually talking about something else."

Bethany smiled at Aisha's innocence. "There is another kind of crop, Aisha. And that is when children come to bless a home. I think that's what Farmer Tullum meant."

"Oh, boy," Aisha said, her eyes dancing. "Will I get a brother or a sister crop?"

Roderick's laughter shook down through his shoulders, melting away all his worries.

"I don't know, Aisha," he said. "We'll just have to wait and see."

3

KNUCKLES AND BONES

ld Tim the cobbler's stall was as dead as Roderick's. As often happened on such days (and all too frequently of late), the two forlorn craftsmen found themselves trading in conversation rather than clothes and shoes.

"You feel that Derick? There's something in the air," Old Tim said.

Tim leaned against the front of the wall between their two stalls, staring out at the listless square. His thick gray hair hung down to his shoulders like a faded cloak. His hunched shoulders and skinny arms were unimpressive, but when it came to the making of shoes his nimble hands and sharp eye were more than sufficient to the task. What mattered most to Roderick wasn't Tim's outside though. Tim was as grounded as Farmer Tullum and even more learned. He trusted Old Tim's judgement on things almost as much as he trusted Bethany's.

"Well, winter does seem to be coming on a bit early again," Roderick said, eyeing the overcast sky. "I just hope we're not in for another long one like last year."

"It's not that, my friend." Tim turned back and spoke in husky, conspiratorial tones quite unlike his usual manner. "It's the Thaumaturge."

Roderick scooted forward on his stool and nearly fell off. "The what?" he said in the lightest tone he could muster. "Oh, Tim, you're not going in for those rumors, are you?"

"I know, I know. Until a few days ago, I would have

laughed at the idea, too. Tom foolery and invention, that's what my wife says. 'Might as well believe in fairies or the man on the moon.' But I'm starting to think there's something to it."

Tim's face was the picture of solemnity. He wasn't talking slippers and socks, to use a saying popular in The Glen. This was boots and bare feet.

"But those are just tales," Roderick said. "There's no such thing as wizards. And no one lives out in the Withercrag. The whole land south of the Harrowing is one big desert."

"Or so they say. You and I have never been there, have we? All we've got is the word of the merchants to go by."

Roderick was surprised at Old Tim's tone. What could make a man as sober and no-nonsense as Tim go in for such things? It was usually Roderick taken in by wild yarns, not Old Tim. He was solid, he was sound. He'd lived through twice as many winters as Roderick and worse ones, too, but Roderick had never heard him talk like this.

"Now, Tim, listen. Do you really think a man has the power to disappear from one place and reappear in another, a dozen leagues away? Or to freeze men where they stand with a wave of his hand, or blind his enemies with a word, or wither forests with a look? They're just tales, nothing more."

Roderick crossed his arms conclusively, but, *"You're one to talk, Devinson!"* was what he was thinking. But the motley was different. He'd *seen* that.

Probably.

The look of certainty in Tim's eyes only deepened and his voice grew lower still. "I'm not saying he's all that, Derick. But that doesn't mean he's not real all the same. All tales start somewhere. Where are all these new watchmen coming from? And why are people keeping to their homes so much? No one goes out unless they have to. Have you ever seen the market this dead?"

He did have a point there. Besides the four guards posted at the two entrances—who had only been assigned there three days ago—there were less than two dozen people

18

between the sixteen stalls. Of those who weren't selling their wares, most were just milling about in the common area, talking in low voices like Old Tim and Roderick. They had little interest in buying.

"And Roderick." Tim turned to face him. His clouded brow and wrinkled frown formed a muddy footprint on his face. "They say he's looking for that boy, the one that was in your stall a few days ago."

A stone sank in the superstitious well of Roderick's stomach. So Old Tim had heard about him too. It was one thing to hear about thaumaturges and motleys from some watchmen he'd never met before, but quite another to hear it from his friend's lips. Roderick wondered how many of the townsfolk in Briar's Glen knew about Roderick's little visitor.

At least Tim hadn't called him a motley.

"And why's that?" Roderick asked, attempting nonchalance. "What's so important about one child?"

"Now that I don't know. I'm only telling you what I've heard. Be careful, Roderick. That's all I'm saying. There's change in the wind."

Roderick's eyes gazed across the thatched roofs surrounding the market, a sea of brown blankets covering a town asleep in the middle of the day. The curling tendrils of smoke from the chimneys were the visible snores. Was the motley out there somewhere? Was he still as hungry as he'd been on the day they'd met? Where did he sleep at night? Could his touch really claim a man's soul? That at least would explain why the watch, and maybe the Thaumaturge—if he existed—were so keen on finding him.

Whatever the truth of it was, with each passing day Roderick felt in his heart that he wouldn't know any peace until he found out some answers. For now, though, all he could do was wait and see if the motley would reappear. In the meantime, he had his own worries. With so little coin to bring home for the week, he might have to borrow a little milk and flour from Farmer Tullum again. He hated to do it, but that late frost had crippled Bethany's garden and Roderick couldn't hunt in the forest for game like his father. He couldn't shoot an arrow into the river if he was drowning. Of course he could always promise to pay Tullum with more clothes, but Tullum already had all the coats, shirts, and knickers he would ever need.

Only half an hour remained before the market closed. Roderick's hopes of making a sale ran as low as the ruts in the market roads.

He nibbled on his fingernails. His worries over the motley, the Thaumaturge, and his family balled together inside him in a tangled knot.

"It'll be all right," he told Old Tim, though he scarcely believed the words. "Adonai will provide."

Old Tim drifted back into his stall. "That he will, my friend. And just in time. Looks like you've got a customer."

Sure enough, a newly arrived fellow was headed his way. The stranger was well dressed, which was not a good sign. His tastes might run above what Roderick could offer, but at least he came inside the stall. He began picking, albeit disinterestedly, through some of the cloaks hanging on the outer racks.

"May I help you, sir?" Roderick was not usually so forward, preferring to let his customers browse at their leisure, but he was desperate.

The man was slightly shorter than Roderick and had a cropped black beard sprinkled with gray. Though his cloak had seen heavy wear, it was made of good, undyed Haliconian linen and was thicker than anything Roderick had to offer. The man's dark brown pants and russet shirt were of equal quality. The strangest thing about his attire was the cloth skullcap he wore. It was forest green and embroidered with silver thread around the edges. Such hats were certainly not in style anywhere in Vinyon Province, which meant he must have traveled quite some distance. Overall, he definitely had the look of a scholar about him. Roderick sighed. A scholar was not likely to find anything of interest among the plain, simple patterns Roderick had to offer.

"Do you have anything…*colorful?*" the man asked in a low voice.

The emphasis he put on that last word caught Roderick's attention.

"What colors suit your fancy?" Roderick asked. "Blues and blacks are a fine choice with winter just around the corner, but brown is good for any season." He tried his best to make it sound like his collection was more varied than it actually was, but dyes were terribly expensive and available only in the capital. He only ever made such items on special order and then only when the order was placed months or weeks in advance, since he could only afford to travel to the capital but once a year.

"I'm not sure," the man said, stroking his bristly beard. "What about this coat? May I try it on?" The man pointed towards a beige one on the rack beside him. It had long, draped sleeves and clever gray stitching around the buttons. It was one of the more elegant (and expensive) items in Roderick's stall. Though it did not really go with the man's current apparel, who was to say what other items he possessed in his wardrobe?

"Yes, of course. Try on anything you like." Roderick straightened like a soldier called to attention. A nervous thrill ran through him at the prospect of a desperately needed sale, especially an item of such value.

"Would you pull it off the rack for me?"

The rack was right next to him. Roderick wondered why he did not simply pull it off himself, but he stepped over and obliged the man. Anything to make a sale.

"You're being watched," the man whispered as Roderick handed him the coat. Then he added in a normal voice, "It's certainly fine workmanship."

He was being watched?

The man's comment stole the breath right out of Roderick's lungs.

"You do fine work here, master tailor," the man added.

"Thank you," Roderick mumbled mechanically, recovering

his voice. He scanned the market furtively to see if he could tell who was watching him. None of the handful of people gathered in the commons appeared to be paying any undue attention to him and his stall. Was one of the guards looking his way? It was hard to tell with that helmet shading his eyes. Other than that, he saw nothing to back up what this stranger said.

"This is just what I was looking for. How much do you want for it?" the man asked.

"Um, one hundred," Roderick stammered.

"Fair prices. I like that. I knew you were a man I could trust," the stranger said with a twinkle in his eye.

Roderick was dying to know just who this mysterious person was, but if he was being watched, he dared not ask. Instead, he simply took the man's money.

"Until we meet again, my friend," the stranger said with a slight nod of his head. He folded the coat under his arm and marched towards the southern exit to the square.

Roderick looked down at the money he'd been given. He'd been so out of sorts, he hadn't even bothered to check it before the man left. Instead of silver miras, a gold valin, a coin worth five hundred miras, shimmered in his hand like a desert mirage. But this was no illusion, it was real. Relief and joy surged through him. Oh, mercy! A week's worth of coin in one day!

Roderick had little time to savor the unexpected blessing. The next moment his gaze fell upon a piece of paper tucked away under his money box. It most definitely had not been there before.

On thick vellum was a drawing of some sort, a hill or a mountain with an opening at the base. Below it were written words in fine, flowing script, words which Roderick unfortunately could not understand.

"Oh, buttons," he mumbled. What did it say? He had no choice but to take it to Old Tim to find out. The cobbler was one of the few people in Briar's Glen who could read, at least one of the few people who could read and be trusted to keep a secret. Given the mysterious warning of the stranger who'd left the note, Roderick had no intention of sharing it contents with the rest of The Glen.

Tim had already started tearing down his shop, but he stopped and gave Roderick a ready smile.

"So you sold something after all?" Tim asked brightly. "Or do you just need a new pair of clogs for the little one?"

"No, Tim, I mean yes—yes, I did make a sale!" Roderick checked his enthusiasm. Now it was his turn to look over his shoulder and speak in a low voice. "Tim, did you—did you overhear anything that man said?" Between the thick walls and Tim's weak hearing he doubted his friend had, but he wanted to check.

"No, Derick. Did he say something troubling? There was something odd about him," Tim said.

"Well, I suppose you could say that. He said—well, it's not so important what he said, it's just that he left me this note. Promise you won't tell anyone about it?" Roderick approached Tim and produced the parchment as surreptitiously as possible.

Old Tim raised his bushy eyebrows and his jovial expression faded. "Of course not, Roderick. You know I'd sooner step on a nail than betray a friend's confidence. Let's have a look and see what this mysterious customer of yours left you." Tapping a finger on his cheek, he scanned the words in front of him. "Hmm, fine hand-writing...There's that drawing of course of a hill with...maybe a cave in it. And then it says, 'B. H.,' and below that 'In adversity, we know our friends.' That's it. Doesn't mean much, does it?"

"No, I'd say not. Still, you have my thanks all the same." Roderick snatched back the note. Something was not right. "I —I've got to go now. I'll see you in the morning."

Old Tim scratched the back of his head, a concerned look on his face. "Very well, my friend. Give my regards to Miss Beth."

Roderick rushed back over to his stall and began collecting his things. He shoved the note and the precious gold coin into a secret pocket in the inner lining of his cloak. Scurrying about, he packed the clothes into the cart in half the usual time and with half the usual care. He felt a powerful urge to get home as quickly as possible. He needed to tell all this to Bethany. Surely she would be able to help him make sense of it all.

A group of unsavory looking men had been following Roderick since Crumpet Street. Once he passed the row of yew hedges which marked the outskirts of town, they didn't even bother concealing their presence. They moved from the trees and undergrowth on the side of the road out into the middle of the well-worn path. Their brisk pace and long strides left no doubt as to their intentions. They meant to rob him, plain and simple.

Roderick began pushing his sartorial cart at a light trot. The men quickly matched his pace and then surpassed it. He worked his way up to a full run, but there was no way he could keep up that pace. The cart was too heavy and the men coming after him were under no such burden.

If I could just get to farmer Tullum's. With his pitchfork and his old dog Rivet we might stand a chance…

But he knew he'd never get that far. The Tullums' home was a mile away, just past his own cottage. Perhaps he should abandon his wagon, but the entire welfare of his family was packed up inside those wooden slats. He couldn't just give it up without a fight.

Oh, Adonai, what should I do?

He slowed and let the ruffians overtake him, hoping to have at least a little strength left for when he faced them. Not that it would matter. There were six of them—as roughly dressed and unkempt as any group of scoundrels from Briar's Glen to Talance. Yet the collars of their shirts and the cut of their pants showed that they were not from either of those towns, nor anywhere else in Vinyon province. The style was too angular, more reminiscent of the kind worn in the southern parts of the empire.

As they caught up to him, three of the men circled around front, blocking his way, while the other three came up behind.

Roderick stopped the cart in the middle of the road.

"A moment of your time, stitcher?" asked the big man in the middle. His torso was nearly twice as thick as Roderick's. He had a large nose reminiscent of an onion.

"I'm sorry, but I'm in a terrible rush," Roderick said.

"Well, we're in a bit of a hurry too, mister," the onion-nosed man said, a surly grin wriggling onto his face.

Roderick eyed the lock on the lid of the cart. His knife was inside. He would never be able to get it out in time.

"Um, what do you want?" he asked, gripping the edge of his cart protectively.

"Not what, sirrah, but *who*." The big man took a step closer.

Another of the thugs standing next to the leader chimed in.

"We heard you might've made yourself a little friend, recently."

"I—I'm not sure what you mean." Roderick pressed against the cart so as to keep as much distance between himself and the ruffians as possible. Something rustled in the bushes running along the road. Perhaps there were even more of them there. There was no way Roderick was getting out of this.

"Ah, now don't play daft." The big man wagged his finger. "You know the boy we're looking for."

"If you're talking about the one I gave the gloves to, that was three days ago, and I haven't seen him since."

"Haven't seen him, eh? That don't square with what we've heard. Five or six bumpkins said they saw him lurking around your cart this morning."

"Well, if that's so, it's news to me. What do you want with him anyway?" Roderick peered longingly down the road in both directions, wishing that either the town watch or Farmer Tullum might chance along.

"Ah, now don't you worry your fancy hat. We just want to see that he's properly taken care of. We're representatives of…an orphanage from down the road that's come to take him home." The sneer on the thug's face betrayed his lie.

"But there are no orphanages in these parts. You'd have to go all the way to Massing to find one," Roderick said.

The man's sneer threatened to become a snarl. "Enough games! You've seen the kid. You know what we're talking about. Now tell us where the little firework face is!"

Dull as this man was, it was obvious he knew about the motley's skin as well. He was looking for him, just like the watch. But why?

Roderick took a deep breath to steady himself. Motley or no, these men were up to no good, of that he was sure. "Even if I did know where he was, I wouldn't tell you. He's no business of yours."

The ruffian's eyes lit up in anger. Roderick's arm went up to ward off the impending blow, but at that same moment one of the other thugs tugged on the lock to his cart, mercifully diverting the big man's attention.

"Eh? Lugdrum! What do you think you're doing?" shouted the man who was interrogating Roderick.

"Just lookin' for clues, Dart," the man said with a snicker.

"Eck! Get your paws off," Dart said. "You know we're supposed to talk first and save the fingering for later!"

Lugdrum backed off, spitting on the ground in protest.

"Look, chump," one of the other men addressed Roderick. "Just rat the kid out and we'll leave you and your little diaper wagon be. But if we have to beat it outta ya, we will."

Roderick guessed from the violent look in the man's eyes that he was going to 'beat it out' of him whether he knew anything or not.

"So we're giving you one last chance, sirrah. Hard or easy, what'll it be?" The enormous bruiser called Dart clenched his fists and took one step closer.

"I'm just a simple tailor…" Roderick mumbled, not bothering to try and sound brave or undaunted anymore.

The big man shook his head and placed his beefy hand on Roderick's shoulder.

"That wasn't the answer we were looking for."

The man's thick arm jerked back like a sling and flew into Roderick's face. The snap of knuckles against bone rang out along the road as the world exploded. Roderick's one saving grace was that he did not last long. Two more blows and he crumpled like a rag. He braced himself to hit the road, but the impact never came.

4

CHARITY AND ITS FRUITS

pair of worried eyes stared down at Roderick as he awoke. Shadows shrouded the face they belonged to, but Roderick could just make out the faint checkered pattern on the skin. It took a moment for him to realize that he wasn't dreaming. He cried out in fright and the noise turned his head into a big bass drum, beating a painful rhythm.

All the old tales of the motley chasing down children and turning them into dark, inky ghosts rushed back into Roderick's fuzzy thinking. His fears mastered him once more, for in the darkness, with his face all but shrouded inside his hood, the motley looked more monstrous than ever. Roderick waited for his mouth to sprout fangs or his eyes to light up with sparks, but instead they gazed down at him with childlike concern. His little hand dabbed Roderick's forehead with a damp rag. Roderick flinched each time he did so, waiting for the chilling touch. He wanted to run, but the pounding pain warned against it. He groaned and grabbed his down-stuffed head.

"Please don't hurt me," Roderick mumbled. The words thundered inside his ears, amplified by the cloud of pain hovering over him.

Imposing shadows and dark patches of moss loomed in every direction. Light from a half moon dribbled across the vegetation like spilled paint. Had he been dragged off to the creature's lair?

The motley pulled away with a heavy sigh. The unexpected

withdrawal checked Roderick's fears. For the first time he noticed just how small and thin the motley was inside that tattered cloak of his.

"W-where am I?" Roderick asked, sitting up. He immediately regretted the movement. It set off an even worse throbbing in his head, like it was being squeezed repeatedly in a vice. Running was definitely out of the question.

"The woods by the road," the motley whispered.

Each moment that passed without a threatening gesture cracked a little chink in the armor guarding Roderick's heart. He took several deep breaths and calmed himself. Perhaps Bethany was right. The motley certainly didn't act like a monster.

"How did I get here?" Roderick asked as the encounter with the ruffians came rushing back. "And where's my cart?"

"They took it," the motley said, still whispering. He gestured towards the trees behind him. "They dragged you off the road and into these bushes and then they took your cart and went away."

At this news Roderick forgot all about the danger of being in the presence of a motley. His chest convulsed. For a moment he found it hard to breathe. His father had crafted that cart with his own hands forty years ago, before Roderick had even been born. Now it was gone, along with hundreds of hours of sartorial labor. He could try and replace what he'd lost during his annual trip to Evenspire, but where would he ever get enough coin to do so?

He swallowed hard and tried not to think about what would happen to his family. Then he remembered the coin the man in the skullcap had given him. He felt inside his cloak to see if it was still there in the secret pocket. His spirits rose when his fingers clasped the cold, smooth metal. At least they would have something to get by on for a little while. The note was still there as well.

"You saw it happen?" Roderick asked.

The motley nodded. "It wasn't right what they did to you."

"Have you been with me all this time?"

"Yes." The motley's eyes flashed in a ray of moonlight. For the first time Roderick noticed how beautiful and brilliant they were. Green as sunlight on the grass, and full of gentle kindness.

Suddenly it struck Roderick like a blow from a ruffian's fist how wrong he'd been. This was no motley. It may have been dark, but Roderick was seeing more clearly than he had all day. This was a lonely little boy in danger. Whatever was wrong with his skin, he was in trouble. Who knew if and when those ruffians might come back or what they'd do to him if they found him?

"How was it that you happened to be in the woods when they attacked me?" Roderick asked.

The boy shrugged and lowered his head.

"Those toughs said you were hanging about my cart this morning. Is that true?"

"Maybe." The boy ran his fingers distractedly along the leaves of a nearby bush.

"So you followed me from the market?"

There was a long painful pause. Painful for the boy as he shifted anxiously under the weight of Roderick's questions, and painful for Roderick as his throbbing head reasserted itself to the forefront of his awareness.

"I saw those bad men going after you," the boy said finally. "I knew they wanted to hurt you because of me. I didn't know what to do, so I followed you."

Roderick's pain subsided momentarily with this admission. Here was a boy, orphaned from his parents, living on the streets, with no place to go, and yet he was concerned enough about Roderick to risk following him out into the countryside when he knew him to be in trouble.

"Well, it was a brave thing you did," Roderick said. "Thank you."

"You'd do the same for me," the boy replied matter-of-factly.

"I…well, I suppose I would," Roderick felt his face flush in the darkness, embarrassed he had ever considered this child a threat. "I'm curious, though. Why were you hanging about my cart in the first place? And why didn't you show yourself? You must be very good at hiding since I never saw you."

"I ripped my cloak, sir. I thought maybe you could give me a new one, like the gloves." The boy held up a fold of his cloak, but it was too dark to see the extent of the damage. "But the men kept watching you, so I didn't think it would be safe."

"I'd be more than happy to give you a new cloak, but as you can see, I've lost my cart. I could sew up the one you've got, though, once I get to feeling a bit better."

The boy nodded and the beginnings of a smile crept into the corners of his mouth.

"What's your name, child?"

"Jacob," he said, barely above a whisper, as if it were a deep dark secret he was confiding.

"Well, Jacob, my name is Roderick. Pleased to meet you." He tried to lift his hand to greet him properly, but the effort made him wince and pull back in pain. He took several deep breaths and waited for the throbbing to die down. After a few moments he asked, "Is it true that you don't have any parents?"

Jacob quivered in response. Roderick had seen his daughter do the same thing countless times when she was hurt or frightened. Forgetting his broken body and all his old fears, Roderick reached up and put his arms around the boy, gritting his teeth and fighting through the fire knifing into his skull. Jacob melted in his embrace, weeping softly.

"There, there," Roderick said, patting his shoulder. "It'll be all right. We'll find a way to take care of you." After Jacob had spent most of his tears, Roderick said, "You know, I have a home and a family just up the road here. My wife makes the most delicious lentil soup. Would you like to come visit?"

"Do you have any fruit?" Jacob asked, sniffling.

"Oh, so you want another apple, eh? I'm sorry, but they're hard to come by these days. And we don't have any other kind of fruit either."

31

"It's okay. I can find some winterberries."

"I'm sure we can find something you like, though. Besides, I want you to meet my family. And the needle and thread I need to fix your cloak are there as well."

Jacob's eyes shifted nervously, retreating behind a sudden wall of modesty and propriety.

"And another thing—who's going to save me from the bullies if they come back?" Roderick asked, trying to coax a response out of him.

Jacob cracked a grin, a real genuine smile this time. His teeth shone like white glow-stones in the darkness.

"Okay," Jacob said.

"Wonderful." Roderick rose to his feet, steadying himself with a nearby tree. It took a moment for things to stop spinning.

"Well, I suppose we'd best be off. My dear Bethany—that's my wife—must be worried sick."

Roderick gingerly took a few steps, following Jacob through the shadowy woods.

"The road is this way," Jacob said.

"You're sure I can't persuade you to try some lentil soup?" Roderick asked when they reached the road.

Jacob sighed, as if he were the adult and Roderick the child, a child who was not capable of understanding something no matter how many times he had it explained to him.

"Fruit. Only fruit."

The Thaumaturge glowered at the mewling idiots before him. He would have used his own men to ferret out the motley, but he didn't want to cause more alarm in the town than he already had.

"You have breached the terms of our agreement," the

Thaumaturge said icily. "And therefore you will receive no payment."

Dart, the thug with the bulbous nose, twisted the toe of his boot in the dirt as if to assure himself that the ground had not yet begun to sink beneath his feet.

"When I said, 'stay with him until the boy comes,' I meant for you to *stay with him until the boy came*, not rough him up and leave him beside the road half dead," the Thaumaturge went on.

"But those merchants showed up and—"

"I did not give you permission to speak. And those were not merchants. They were scholars from another part of the province. They are looking for the boy as well. If you see them again, I will pay you extra if you make sure they never find him." The leader of the ruffians nodded his head vigorously and raised his hand ever so cautiously. "You may speak," said the Thaumaturge.

"Thank you, m'lord." Dart's legs started to wiggle. He grabbed hold of them, but failed to corral them. The effort made him look like he was in desperate need of attending to certain bodily necessities (which may well have been the case). "We promise not to mess up any more. We'll get that nasty little motley for ya' sure as daylight. Just tell us what your needin'. The lads and I'll be on it right quick. We—We're, We're willin' to do whatever it takes to…to prove ourselves, m'lord."

The Thaumaturge feigned as if he were considering the man's words. "You do at least remember where the tailor's house is, don't you?"

The big man's head bobbed up and down. Stupidity and enthusiasm often went hand in hand, the Thaumaturge had discovered.

"Very well. If he's still alive you may want to interrogate him at his house this time. Perhaps threatening his wife and child will prove more effective than a beating. Every man has his weakness."

The brigands stared at him dumbfounded, either from

33

terror or because they did not grasp what he was getting at.

"Well? What are you waiting for?" the Thaumaturge bellowed. "Go!"

The men gave a start, like they had just woken up by falling out of bed.

"And remember that if by some miracle you do find the boy, you are not to harm him. If you do, it will not go well for you," the Thaumaturge warned.

The band of thugs scattered like leaves blown on the wind. The Thaumaturge doubted he would ever see them again, but he did not care. They were a mere distraction, a feint meant to flush his quarry out from the bushes. The real trap lay elsewhere, hidden in plain sight.

Roderick sat with Bethany as the two children played in front of the hearth. He adjusted the poultice she had made from one side of his face to the other. The comfrey compound inside the wet rag had already reduced the swelling considerably. Though she had added lavender and pine to mask the smell, it still had a strong stench of decay about it, but this was a small price to pay for the relief it brought.

"So the stories are true, after all," Bethany said, shaking her head. She had been too overwhelmed by Roderick's injuries when he first came in to pay much attention to Jacob's skin, but in time the awareness had leapt onto her face with wide eyes and raised eyebrows. She and Roderick exchanged looks, but a shake of Roderick's head told her he'd had a change of heart about the whole motley business.

"True and yet not true at the same time," Roderick said.

"What does it all mean?" she asked.

"That I do not know, love. That I do not know."

Aisha's ball came bouncing over to his feet. For a moment Roderick forgot his soreness and shuffled his feet this way and that, keeping her from retrieving it.

"Daddy," Aisha protested with a smile. "Let us play!"

He kicked the ball away and into the corner and Aisha squealed after it. She was too young to go very far from the house by herself and she rarely got to play with other children. For this reason she was soaking up every moment with her newfound friend. And around Aisha, Jacob's shyness melted away. He cracked a little grin as she pounced on the ball triumphantly. His skin was even more beautiful when he smiled, the same way a basket is more beautiful when it's filled with flowers than when it's empty.

"What's to become of him?" Bethany asked, lowering her voice. "Those ruffians are not the only ones looking for him."

"The world won't understand that he's just a boy," Roderick answered in equally soft tones. "They'll just see his skin, like I did."

Roderick felt a pang of remorse at how he'd let his imagination run off with him after that first encounter.

"Now don't be too hard on yourself. You only got a glimpse of him," Bethany said. "Most people would have thought the same thing."

She touched his arm gently and rose to go dry the dishes. Ever graceful, ever grounded. That was his Beth.

Since they had no fruit to give him and Jacob politely declined to eat anything else, he had gone out back with Aisha before dinner and found some bright purple winterberries in the thicket behind the cottage. Roderick was surprised there was anything edible at all out there after the frost, but then again they were probably called winterberries for a reason, he supposed. He knew precious little about the surrounding woods for someone who'd lived in them all his life. Home was where Roderick's heart was, and his body seemed to rather prefer it as well.

The berries were a paltry meal in comparison to the hot, thick soup Bethany served, but Jacob offered no complaints. He was the picture of manners, never speaking with his mouth full and never missing his "please's" and "thank you's".

Roderick closed his eyes and tried—without success—to rest and let the pain go away. His daughter's laughter, normally the music he cherished above all others, stung his head to listen to, but he was not about to ruin her fun by asking her to quiet down.

Bethany eventually returned from the dishes and took her place beside her husband. "Roderick, I've been wondering," she said. "How do you think his parents got into trouble? Do you think they were falsely accused or that they were actual criminals?"

"Hmm…criminals…Ordinarily, I'd say we could go to the magistrate to find out, but I don't think we can trust him in this. If he found out Jacob was here he'd treat him little better than those ruffians, I shouldn't wonder."

The two of them gazed at the children for a time without speaking, mesmerized by their antics in front of the fire. They were flicking Aisha's multi-colored ball through a little maze they had fashioned from walnut shells and pebbles, giggling whenever it left the path or they made an exceptionally fine shot.

"What are we going to do, Derick?" Bethany asked at length.

"I don't know, Beth. We could take him in, I suppose, but with all the people looking for him, we couldn't hide him here for long."

And how would we feed him if we could? Roderick thought to himself. With the cart lost, they were in for a lean winter by any stretch. The boy couldn't live off winterberries.

"We have to do something," Beth said. "If whoever wants him was willing to beat you like that, I hate to think what they'd do to poor little Jacob."

"You're right. I suppose we'll just have to protect him for now until we can find a safe place for him. But if those men were bold enough to throttle me in broad daylight, I worry about leaving the rest of you here all day alone."

Bethany crossed her arms in motherly fashion and leaned

back in her chair.

"Don't worry, my love. Adonai will protect us. It's the right thing to do."

But Roderick couldn't help but worry. It was in his nature, unfortunately. He worried about every little sniffle or sign that Aisha might be getting sick, about his dwindling sales in the market, about Bethany's hundred daily chores and the way her beautiful hands had grown so rough over the years. None of this he could control, he knew, and he couldn't stop those thugs from coming back again either, but that did not keep him from worrying all the same.

At least I have the gold valin, he reminded himself, patting the coin in his secret pocket.

Oh! In all the commotion he had forgotten to tell his wife about the mysterious man from the market! He opened his mouth to do just that when Aisha's ball came towards him once again. He picked it up on the bounce. This time Jacob reached out to take it.

"Ah, you want the ball, eh?" Roderick said, pulling it back. With sleight of hand, he made the ball appear to vanish.

"Daddy!" Aisha's mouth was a fountain of giggles. She loved it when he did his tricks.

Jacob stared up at Roderick, a curious look on his face.

"You know magic?" Jacob asked.

"A little," Roderick's said. He reached behind Jacob's ear and pulled the ball out from behind it. He dropped it into Jacob's hand.

Jacob's eyes went wide. "Can you teach me?" he asked.

"Of course. But not tonight. It's getting late and my next trick will be getting the both of you into bed."

"Oh, Daddy!" Aisha cried, this time with far less delight.

"You heard your father," Bethany said.

Aisha stuck out a pouting lip, but Jacob asked in a quiet voice, "Where do I sleep?"

"Well, I think we can roll out the extra blankets on the floor of Aisha's room. Will that be all right, Eesh?"

Aisha's mood changed in an instant. She jumped up and

clapped her hands together. "Oh yes! Come on, Jacob, I'll show you where it is,"

"Ah, ah, ah. Not so fast," her mother said. "You have to get your gown on and brush your hair first."

Aisha sighed dramatically and managed a begrudging, "Yes, mother," before clunking off towards the bedroom.

Bethany bent down to Jacob's level. "I have some night clothes for you, too, if you'd like."

"Thank you, ma'am, but I'll sleep in these."

"You know, I can sew a new pocket inside your cloak for you, if you'd like," Roderick said. He pulled open his own to show him how it worked. It was on the inside on the left, just over his heart. It looked like nothing more than a fold in the cloth, one among many, until Roderick showed him how to open it. "It's secret, you see? No one can tell it's there if they don't know. It's another kind of magic, I suppose. You can keep whatever you like in there. Maybe even a bit of apple if you ever find another one."

Jacob's eyes lit up and he nodded enthusiastically.

"You're welcome to stay as long as you like, Jacob," Bethany said, hugging him gently.

Jacob flashed another of his rare smiles and his checkered cheeks caught the firelight for a moment. Since Roderick had realized that Jacob was not a motley, the strange skin made an odd impression on him each time he saw it. On the one hand, the brightly colored pattern made Jacob appear otherworldly, like he didn't quite belong on the same plane as that of mere mortal men. It did look an awful lot like the way those stories of the motley described. On the other hand, it made him look oh, so terribly vulnerable, like it wasn't something he was supposed to have, and he was all the more in need of help because of it.

"Heaven willing, we'll keep you safe." Roderick placed his hand on top of Jacob's head, his words as much a prayer as they were a promise.

5

SMOKE AND LIGHTS

The door to Roderick's bedroom creaked open, shaking him from sleep.

"We need to go," said a small voice in the darkness. Moonlight crept in through the window, but Roderick's blurry vision made it impossible to tell who the little head in the doorway belonged to.

"What?" Roderick asked, still not altogether awake.

"They're coming."

He recognized Jacob's voice this time. It had a lump-in-the-throat sort of panic to it.

"Who? Who's coming?" Roderick sat up. Bethany stirred beneath the sheets, but did not awake.

"The bullies," Jacob said.

At those words the pain and soreness in Roderick's head flared to life, banishing the last vestiges of sleep. He threw off the sheets and put his bare feet on the chill midnight floor.

"Are you sure? How do you know? It's the dead of night."

"I just know...I always know," Jacob said.

Their conversation at last woke Bethany.

"What's going on, Roderick?" she asked.

"I'll go and maybe they will leave you alone," Jacob said, his voice weak with fear.

"No, wait. Bethany, Jacob thinks the men from yesterday are coming. I don't know how he knows, but I'd better go have a look just in case."

Bethany sat bolt upright.

"Here? They're coming here?" she asked.

"That's what I'm going to find out." He hoped Jacob was just having a nightmare. A shiver ran through him, but not from the chilly floor.

Bethany touched his arm before he started out.

"I'll go and gather Aisha," she said. "If it is them, maybe we can hide out back." Her words lent a measure of calm to Roderick's pounding heart. She was always the level-headed one.

"Jacob, you go with Bethany," Roderick instructed, brushing past him down the steps.

"Hurry, please. They'll be here soon." Jacob said.

Roderick rushed downstairs and over to the window beside the front door and pushed away the curtain just enough to get a look at the road. The smooth dirt lane ran about two hundred feet from the cottage. It went past the Tullum's off to the left and, off to the right, it wound around a stand of oaks five hundred feet or so from the front door. While it was a good sign that no one was visible, even the ruffians were probably not dimwitted enough to approach along the open road.

"Well, buttons. What to do now?" Roderick whispered to himself.

Jacob and Bethany, carrying a still sleeping Aisha, appeared behind him.

"Can you see anyone?" Bethany asked.

"No." Roderick stepped away from the window.

Jacob gave him a desperate look which said, *if you don't do something quick they'll find me.*

First his cart and now his home. Was any place in The Glen safe anymore? Roderick's peaceful little life was unraveling at the seams. But then he thought of Jacob. Who would protect him? At least Roderick, Bethany, and Aisha had each other.

"After what happened yesterday," Roderick said, "we can't be too cautious. Let's go to the cellar out back. If they do come to the cottage I doubt they'll think to look there. And we should be able to hear them and slip off into the woods if

40

they do."

"Right," Bethany said, and headed for the back door.

Roderick flung on his cloak and opened the door slowly, thankful Bethany had oiled the hinges a few weeks ago and gotten rid of that nasty squeak. The cellar was about a dozen steps away and the back of the house was well shielded by surrounding trees. Roderick pulled the door closed behind him, locking it shut and heading for the cellar.

He fumbled with the cellar lock several times before he got it open, finally shoving the key into the hole and springing it. Unlike the house, the door here creaked like a mouse caught in a trap. Roderick could only hope the ruffians were not close enough to hear it. Or better yet that there weren't any ruffians at all.

They descended the dirt steps into the gloom, squeezing up against the earthen walls reinforced with wooden beams. A few stacks of empty jars and some garden tools lurked in the back, but that was all. In his parent's day the jars had been filled with preserves and there had been extra wood and bolts of cloth, but the years since his mother's death had not been so kind. For once Roderick was glad of the hard times for it meant there was enough room for the four of them to fit inside.

He was also thankful that Aisha was such a sound sleeper. She wheezed softly in the darkness, but otherwise made no sound.

Jacob clung to Roderick's arm as if he thought he would fall into a pit if he let go. Roderick stared through the gaps between the slats in the cellar door. The quiet around the cottage was only broken by the sighs of the night breeze through the trees.

Shattered glass cut through the stillness, followed closely by muttered voices and clunky footsteps inside the cottage.

Roderick flinched as if cold air had blown in his face.

"It's them," Jacob whispered in Roderick's ear.

Them. Roderick had never known that word could evoke so much fear.

Once inside the house, the burglars abandoned all pretense of stealth. The sound of doors opening, mixed with low talking, simmered through the night. It was only a matter of time before they boiled over.

"I don't think we're safe here," Bethany whispered. "Maybe we should make a break for it before they decide to check out back."

Roderick's mouth cottoned up. He doubted those toughs were smart enough to check out back, and in the weak moonlight the cellar door blended in with the surrounding underbrush. Still, if they did find it, there'd be no way to escape.

"You're right," he croaked the words out. "Into the woods. Maybe we can make it to the Tullums."

"But we'll have to cross the open field. What if they see us? I don't think farmer Tullum and you together would be able to stand against that band of ruffians."

Bethany was right again. They'd be spotted for sure and getting Farmer Tullum up would take too much time. The way that big one Dart hit, it probably wouldn't make any difference either.

"Where else can we go?" he asked.

"There's the cave at Bald Hill where I used to go when I was a little girl."

The words 'cave at Bald Hill' shot like a lightning stroke through his memory. The drawing of the cave. The note. The man from the market. Maybe that's what he was trying to tell him—to meet him there! Hope glimmered to life inside him. Would that mysterious stranger be able to help? Would he even be there? Whatever the case, the cave was their only hope. It lay through the woods and even if the man wasn't there, the tunnels inside were many and twisting. They might be able to lose the ruffians inside the endless warren even if they somehow managed to track them there.

"Beth, you're amazing," he whispered.

Gingerly, he pushed open the cellar door and stepped outside. A loud crash reverberated from inside the cottage, mercifully obscuring the loud creak. The crash was followed by more loud voices and curses from Dart. Roderick stared at the window to the back yard in utter fear. If the ruffians glanced out back, they would be on Roderick and his family in a flash.

Please, let us get through this night alive, he prayed.

Jacob came out next and latched on to Roderick's arm. Finally, Bethany and Aisha emerged. At that moment a stiff breeze blew through the yard and whipped through Aisha's hair. Her eyes flicked open.

"What are we doing out—" Bethany's hand clamped over Aisha's mouth too late. At that exact moment the house had gone dead quiet. It did not stay that way.

"Did you hear that?" someone inside the cottage exclaimed. "Out back! Quick!"

There was nothing for it but to run. Leaving the cellar door flung wide open Roderick grabbed Aisha from Bethany's arms and tore off into the woods. Bethany grabbed Jacob by the hand, a step behind.

They blundered in and out of the dense forest. Layers of leaves rustled as they passed, making an awful racket, but it couldn't be helped.

Roderick was out of breath almost before he started. Between his fright and his throbbing head, he barely had enough strength to keep hold of Aisha.

Behind them, their pursuers made enough noise to drown out a pack of wild dogs. Their shouts, and the swoosh and crunch of their stampede made it sound like an army had invaded the woods.

Everywhere Roderick looked he saw menace and misgivings. The shadows seemed to take on a life of their own. He was forced to slow down to avoid tripping on the tangled roots and underbrush. At this rate they would never make it to the cave in time.

Roderick shot a glance over his shoulder. Dark figures blundered through the trees. He spit out the bile rising in the back of his throat, forcing himself to run harder, heedless of the searing in his chest, the entangling roots, and the growing weight of Aisha in his arms.

Bethany was panting just as deep and heavy as he was.

The ruffian's shouts rang out through the trees.

"There! Over there!"

"Hurry boys! We've got 'em now!" one of them cried gleefully. Bulky mounds of darkness smothered the gaps between the trees.

Roderick didn't know how much longer he could go. Fear was the only thing keeping him on his feet. He lost all sense of direction. It didn't help that he hadn't been to Bald Hill in years. But Bethany barreled confidently ahead. All he could do was follow her now.

In front of him, Jacob faltered, but Beth quickly pulled him back to his feet.

"Come, Jacob," she said breathlessly.

Please, just let us hold out a little further.

Hot-headed shouts poured after them like an avalanche overtaking the woods.

"Where are we going, Daddy?" Aisha asked as they rushed out of the woods. Of the four of them, she was the only one who showed no signs of panic. They might as well have been out for a midnight romp for all the levity in her voice.

"It's...an...adventure." Roderick whispered between molten gulps of air.

The dark mound of Bald Hill loomed before them in the center of a wide, grassy clearing. The craggy hill shone stark in the moonlight, a silent fortress offering the promise of protection.

"Just...ahead." He pointed towards the hill across the meadow. The entrance to the cave was nowhere in sight, but Aisha murmured a submissive, "okay" in his ear.

Jacob faltered again, this time tumbling to the ground.

"He can't keep up," Bethany cried, helping him back to his feet.

Roderick passed Aisha into his wife's arms just before the first of the dark figures burst out of the woods.

His arms enjoyed a moment of relief before scooping

Jacob up. "I'll take him," Roderick said. Grunting and chugging under the new weight, he staggered off in the direction of the cave.

It was hard to judge the distance in the dark. At times the cave seemed only a few dozen feet away, at other times a hundred yards. Roderick risked a backward glance. The moonlight shone cold and mercilessly upon the meadow and the six men loping across the wet ground. The large figure of Dart was impossible to miss. His massive fists pummeled the air as he ran. No doubt they would soon be pummeling Roderick's face again.

Roderick grew even more winded, falling further behind Bethany. He was only halfway to the cave. The ruffians, unencumbered, surged forward like a pack of wolves after a wounded doe. Roderick's head swam at the thought of what would happen to his wife and the children when they were caught.

"I'm scared," Jacob whispered, but Roderick was too busy gasping for air to reply. Instead he held Jacob tighter and pressed forward with the last bit of strength he possessed.

It was not enough. As they entered the scraggy terrain near the base of the hill, Roderick tripped on some of the loose rocks underfoot. He and Jacob went tumbling to the ground. Somehow, Roderick managed to shield Jacob from the worst of the fall, but he lost his hold on him as he collided with the hard packed dirt and moss.

Dazed and disoriented, he scrambled to his feet. Dart and the ruffians came charging up, closing the last few steps between them, screaming "The boy! Get the boy!"

Without warning, the clearing burst into light. The air shimmered in a dazzling, multi-colored display. It could not have been more colorful if Roderick had fallen inside a rainbow. Eruptions of light blistered the darkness. Dozens of colors consumed the meadow in prismatic rays. The woods and the hill disappeared in the effulgent light. The brigands' shouts filled the air, but the men behind them were invisible now, lost in the overwhelming light. Roderick not only lost sight of the brigands, but Jacob as well. He pawed the grass and rocks, calling out to him while shielding his eyes.

"Jacob! Jacob, where are you?"

"Here," came the nearby answer.

Roderick fumbled towards the voice on his hands and knees, scraping them on the rocky dirt. At last he stumbled upon a tiny arm. Grasping it tightly, he rose and tried to guess which direction the cave entrance lay.

The ruffians screamed and cursed the light. As if called into existence by their bitter invective, a horrible black smoke spewed across the ground, quickly consuming the brightness. It came from all directions at once. Everything went black as coal. Besides the resulting blindness, the smoke had a horrible, acrid stench that made Roderick's eyes water.

None of that mattered, though. Now was their chance to escape. He plunged forward with Jacob through the inky clouds, not knowing where he was going. As he stumbled through the dark mist, an awful realization hit him. Bethany and Aisha were gone. He couldn't remember the last time he'd seen them.

"Beth! Aisha? Where are you? Can you hear me?"

"Here, Roderick," Bethany cried from up ahead. "We're over here!"

Her voice mingled with the cries of the thugs. "It's a curse!" they screamed.

"Black sorcery!"

"It's the motley! He'll kill us all!"

"Run! Run!"

Bethany kept calling out while Roderick lurched forward, following the sound of her voice. The smoke began to thin. A vague, white figure materialized out of the mists. It looked otherworldly, a being made out of moonlight and smoke.

"Bethany?" Roderick ventured, though it looked nothing like her.

In response came a familiar voice. "Master tailor, well met," said the man from the market, then added, in a tone of mild surprise, "Ah! I see you've brought the motley."

6

THE SAVANTS

How Roderick and Jacob arrived at the cave at Bald Hill, they were not exactly sure, but Bethany and Aisha were there too, and four other men, all dressed in dark green cloaks and skullcaps. The man who had bought the coat from Roderick the day before was among them.

The fear and tension Roderick had felt during his flight slowly faded, along with the echoes of the ruffians fleeing into the night. They were safe at last.

The mouth of the cave was at least eight feet tall and the inside rose even higher. A damp, sulfuric scent filled the air, but it was mostly clear of the black smoke which still covered the ground outside. A few greasy tendrils from a brass lantern drifted up to the ceiling. The lantern hung on a metal pole held by one of the men. Its flickering light colored the surrounding rock with amber hues which melded into the darkness at the back of the cave.

Roderick wiped the sweat from his brow.

"You—you're the man from the market," he said.

"Yes. I'm sorry I was not able to properly introduce myself before. My name is Jareth. And these are my companions, Master Kendall, and our apprentices Evan and Rand."

Jareth's companions nodded deferentially. The last two were younger than the others by ten or fifteen years. They could have been picked from any of the younger folk around Briar's Glen but for their unusual garb. The other man was the one holding the pole with the lantern. He appeared older than Jareth, though in good health for his age. His hair was mostly white, though a few streaks of gray persisted. He sported a beard as straight as a ruler and neatly trimmed. He studied Roderick and Jacob intently, as if he knew something about them which they themselves did not.

"I took a great risk in approaching you yesterday," Jareth said. "Not all of us were in agreement about it." His eyes shifted between the men beside him.

Roderick coughed, clearing the last of the black smoke from his lungs. "Begging your pardon, but if you wanted me to come here why didn't you just ask?"

"Things are not always that simple. The Thaumaturge's men were watching me as well as you. If I had lingered too long in your shop and one of them overheard me, the Thaumaturge may have found us out and killed us all. He has more than mere thugs at his disposal."

Roderick's sense of relief cooled at the mention of the Thaumaturge. So these men believed in him too? If anyone knew whether or not such a man actually existed, it was probably someone like these folks. Still, as yet they had shown nothing to back that claim.

Roderick drew close to Bethany. Her face was pale, but her eyes were alert and her expression guarded. Aisha, who shifted restlessly in her mother's arms stared at the men in wide-eyed fascination, showing no more apprehension than if these strangers had been her newly arrived uncles and cousins.

Jacob, on the other hand, had not yet calmed down from their near capture by the ruffians. He gripped Roderick's hand fiercely. It was obvious he did not trust these men any more than the ones they had just escaped from, despite the fact that they had probably saved their lives. Of course, Roderick wasn't entirely sure these men had caused the lights and smoke, but it seemed the most likely conclusion.

"You think the Thaumaturge is real, then?" Roderick asked.

"Oh yes, he is very real," Jareth said. "Which is more, he's not the only one. There are Thaumaturges in many lands, though we only know a few by name. We think the one who has come to Vinyon is called Mekthelion, though we know little else about him beyond that."

"And by now, perhaps you have guessed why it is that he has come," Kendall spoke up. His grizzled voice sounded ominous in the close confines of the cave.

"He wants Jacob," Bethany said. "And you want him too, don't you?"

"To be honest, yes." Kendall regarded Jacob with pity, as though he were sick and in need of treatment. Jacob tugged on the cowl of his cloak, adjusting it so that the strangers would not be able to get a good look at him.

"But our intentions are not anything like those of the Thaumaturges," Jareth assured them. "We want to save the motley—to take him to a place where he can be free of the curse which is upon him."

"You think he's a motley? I thought that, too, but I was wrong. He may have the skin, but all the rest is fibs and fables," Roderick said resolutely. "He's just a boy."

"Do you know why my skin is this way?" Jacob asked, his voice atremble.

"That's just part of his clothes, isn't it Daddy?" Aisha piped up from her nest in her mother's arms.

"Yes, we know about your skin," Kendall said. "You have been cursed by magic—a very dangerous and uncontrollable magic."

"Cursed by who?" Bethany asked. "And how do we know you're telling us the truth? How do we know you're not dangerous, too?"

"Those are very good questions," Jareth said. "And you have every right to ask them after what you've been through. But we did save you from the ruffians. Perhaps that counts for something. In the end, though, we cannot force any of you to trust us. All we ask is that you allow us to tell you the truth about the danger he is in."

"Can you get rid of the curse?" Jacob asked. Not only his voice was shaking now, but his hands fluttered in anticipation of their answer.

Jareth smiled affably. "Yes. In fact that is why we have come. We belong to an order known as the Sanctum. Our members are called Savants. Though we are an ancient order, our enemies the Thaumaturges are just as ancient. They have hunted us down through the ages until there are few of us left. But that is no matter, for in a short while, our hope is that we will no longer be needed."

"Needed for what?" Bethany asked.

"To protect the world from the curse of the motleys. A wild magic runs inside the boy's veins. The only way to protect him, as well as the rest of the world, from it, is to use the Null Stone, an ancient and powerful artifact crafted, some say, by the hand of Adonai himself."

Adonai? Of course His hand would be in this as in all things, but Roderick had never heard of such a stone. "What do you mean, 'magic'? Are you saying that magic actually exists somewhere in the world?"

"Most definitely," Kendall said.

Now that Roderick thought about it, both Kendall and Jareth, with their skull caps, weather-stained robes, and apprentices in tow, did have something of the air of wizards about them.

"Was the smoke and lights—that stuff that chased away the ruffians—was that magic?"

"No, not real magic," Jareth said. "Only an effect produced through the mixing together of various powders. Anyone can learn that sort of craft. No, what we are speaking of is the real sort, the mysterious, invisible energy that courses through the heart of our world and which no one can control."

Here his gaze lingered on Jacob who looked at him expectantly. Whatever Roderick thought of all this talk, it was clear that Jacob hung on every word. He was desperate for answers.

Kendall strode forward, meeting Jacob's gaze. Every fiber of his long green robes seemed infused with wisdom and secrets. "Every generation or so, the magic comes to dwell inside a human child. So it has always been, but the origin of the curse is lost to us. Now the stories of the motley have dissolved into tales, things told to frighten impressionable people." Here he glanced at Roderick with a glimmer in his eyes. "But this much about the legends is true. That when the magic takes hold of a motley, it will unleash terrible things upon the world."

Jacob's whole body trembled now.

Roderick spoke up. "I've never seen him perform any kind of magic. But even if he does have it, what makes you think the magic would be bad? Wouldn't a little magic be a good thing?"

"No, gentle tailor," Jareth said, stepping beside Kendall. "There you would be mistaken." He motioned to one of the apprentices, who opened a canister he had slung over his shoulder. From inside of it, he produced a vellum parchment that looked as if it might fall apart at any moment. The Savant did not bother to unroll it, but it would not have mattered if he had since neither Roderick nor Bethany knew how to read.

"This is all we have left from the knowledge contained within the pages of a book known as the *Emerald Grimoire*," Jareth said. "These are copies of notes taken long ago of the book's contents, but they tell of things long forgotten, of the terrible events surrounding the Night of Ten Thousand Shadows and the appearance of the first motley. His powers called forth dark things from beyond, evil things which plunged the world into darkness and nearly destroyed it."

Jareth returned the scroll carefully to its casing.

"Look at the child," Bethany said. "He's no threat to anyone. Surely your legends are mistaken."

"I would that they were. But I would sooner doubt my own eyes and ears than I would the *Grimoire*. The child is a danger, not only to you, but to himself and to all of Arinn. The magic must be dealt with. The curse must be lifted."

Jacob swayed on his feet. Roderick hoisted him up into his arms, fearing he might faint. Darkness or no, he did not like the way these men referred to Jacob as a problem to be dealt with, as if he were a mere thing and not a child in need of shelter and protection.

"You don't sound a whole lot different than those ruffians," he said. "Why can't you just let him be?"

"We mean him no harm. Quite the opposite." Jareth said. "For within the *Grimoire* lies the way to break the magic's curse."

Something about these words made the air feel heavier. Perhaps it was just Roderick's imagination, but the lanterns appeared to flicker and grow weak.

"The notes from the *Grimoire* speak of the Null Stone. This is the artifact I spoke of before. For hundreds of years it remained lost, but it has been found at last." Jareth placed a hand on Kendall's shoulder. "It was Kendall's diligent study that unearthed it. But for him, its location would remain a mystery."

"And how is a stone supposed to help Jacob?" Roderick asked, more intimidated than ever by all this talk of magic and stones and old tomes.

"The stone has the power to absorb magic," Kendall said. "It can trap the motley's magic inside, to never threaten the world of Arinn again. And with the curse lifted, the boy will become normal again. He would be the last motley."

"Then just use the stone and be done with it, if that's all it takes," Bethany said.

"I wish it were that easy," Jareth said wistfully. "But we do not have it in our possession. The reason it remained lost for so long is because it is in an extremely remote location, far out across the Neverless Sea, near the edge of the world."

"How long have you known about it?" Bethany asked.

"It's been two years since I discovered its location," Kendall said.

"Well, if you know where it is, why don't you have it yet?" Bethany put her free hand on her hip the way she did when Roderick said something silly.

"Because the stone cannot be moved," Kendall explained.

His eyes drifted towards the entrance to the cave as if watching for the ruffians to return, or the arrival of the Thaumaturge himself. "It is trapped in a tower far from here, on the Isle of Rinn, beyond the northern lands and the western shores; placed there by Tronas the Mad, a rogue Savant of considerable power, but very inconsiderable sanity."

"Not all of us believe he was as mad as they say," Jareth offered in a corrective tone, but Kendall brushed off his statement.

"Be that as it may, he was so determined to protect the stone that he took it to the most remote place possible. There he fused it into the rock of a tower he built. He used alchemy to ensure that the rocks and mortar were well nigh indestructible. There is no way for us to use the stone unless we travel to the island."

"You must understand," Jareth said, "that if you do not let us take the child there, all you hold dear will be lost. The magic inside him is simply too powerful. No matter how good and innocent he is, he will not be able to control it once it comes forth."

Magic, curses, stones, old books. It was all too much for Roderick. The only thing he was certain of was that Jacob was in trouble. He needed protecting. Half the town was looking for him. And that dreaded Thaumaturge as well, who it looked like was turning out to be a real person after all. Jacob's skin was the sort of thing that was certain to cause more problems down the road. Unnatural, unexpected, and unavoidable problems if these Savants were to be believed. Perhaps unnatural problems called for unnatural solutions.

It certainly seemed like far too much for a simple tailor and his wife to handle.

7

CARMINE CRYSTALS

oderick tapped his foot unconsciously. Somehow he could not give up just yet. Not until he was sure it was the right thing to do.

"So maybe Jacob is under some sort of curse." He straightened to his full height and put on his "market face", the one he used when haggling with customers who didn't want to pay an honest price. "But you still haven't given us any proof that all this magic business is real, or that you're the men to save him if it is. You yourselves even said you can't do *real* magic."

"Your concern is understandable," Jareth said. "True magic has not been seen in our land for many long years, after all. But I can assure you that, though we ourselves cannot perform it, we have studied it enough to recognize it when we find it. Perhaps you'd like to show them, Master Kendall?"

Kendall handed his pole to one of the apprentices. The lantern swayed, causing the light to flicker wildly back and forth across the walls.

"Though we do not possess the Null Stone itself, on my journey to find it I did not come back entirely empty-handed." He reached into the folds of his robe and pulled out two fantastically large gemstones. Together they nearly covered his palm. Each stone was set in a golden frame. The stones looked like rubies. Their polished surfaces glimmered invitingly, far more brightly than they should have in the dim confines of the cave.

The presence of this finery gave Roderick pause. These

stones were worth more than all the clothes he could sell in a lifetime.

"These are carmine crystals," Kendall said. He had his back to the lantern, but his face glowed crimson in the light of the precious stones. "Legends say such things were made by creatures long since forgotten, in the great underhalls beneath the world. These two are paired. They will grow brighter when they are near to each other, but without genuine magic to augment them, that light will be but faint, as it is now. If the boy will take one, you shall see their true power."

Jacob's eyes had not left the scintillating stones since Kendall had drawn them forth from his robe. Now he looked to Roderick for assurance. Roderick nodded his approval and Jacob stretched out his hand to accept one of the crystals. A flash of light burst from both of them. The light sparkled and danced across the stones like sparks from a fire trapped inside a bottle.

As Kendall withdrew to the other side of the chamber, taking one of the stones with him, the light from both of them dimmed slightly.

"Oh, can I touch it?" Aisha asked.

"In a moment." Kendall pointed his stone towards Jacob. It pulsed brighter again, with that strange reddish, inner light. He then pointed it off to his right at one of the novices and the light faded. "You see that it knows its mate. But it is only able to sense the other stone at a distance because of the motley's own, innate magic giving it power. Pass it to the girl now."

Jacob gave the scarlet gem to Aisha. Her eyes twinkled with delight, but the light inside the stone dimmed to almost nothing when she took it. Kendall's stone did the same.

"Did I do something to it?" she asked. "What happened to the light?"

Kendall pointed his stone towards her, but no pulsing light came in answer.

"Do you believe the boy has magic now?"

Roderick rubbed his beard, pondering. It was certainly

more impressive than any trick he had ever seen.

"What do you think?" he asked Bethany.

A settled look came over her face, resolve mixed with sadness.

"I believe they speak the truth. We are only country folk, Derick. It's obvious that Jacob is a special sort of child. It may be that they can help him better than us."

"The journey is long," Kendall said, soberly. "But I promise that we will do everything in our power to ensure he arrives safely at the Isle of Rinn."

Roderick imagined an immense road stretching out from the entrance to the cave. It ran over hills, along rivers, through woods, and across great, waving plains, ending in an immense tower, black and tall and imposing, like an undertaker waiting for a body. If they let Jacob go, there was little hope they would ever see him again. Was Roderick prepared to do that? Was it the right thing to do?

He hunched down before this dear little boy and took both of his gloved hands in his own.

"Well, Jacob," he said, letting out a long sigh. "We are not your parents, so we cannot keep you from going with these men if you choose to. If you want to stay with us, you can. And I promise that we will do everything in our power to protect you. But you heard what they said about the magic. They may be able to help you in ways that Bethany and I cannot."

Jacob shook his head vigorously. "I don't want to go."

"But they can help you. Are you sure?" Bethany asked, kneeling down beside them.

Jacob's lips turned into a quivering line as he struggled not to cry. "Maybe they do know how to change me, but I still don't want to go with them. I want to stay with you."

Roderick rose, moved by Jacob's tender plea. He thought about the first time he'd seen him in the market and been spooked by the stories about the motley. He supposed most people would have had the same reaction. They'd heard the stories, too. But the stories had turned out to be wrong, or at least only half true. Jacob was a motley, but he wasn't a monster. There was good in this boy. And he needed someone to protect him now that his parents were gone. Perhaps those someones were Roderick and Bethany after all.

Roderick looked defiantly towards Jareth and Kendall.

"Well, there's your answer," he said.

Dismay and frustration spread across the Savants' faces. Kendall adjusted his skull cap testily and fixed his eyes on Jacob.

"You have no idea what will happen if the magic is not dealt with," Kendall said. "You place all our lives in danger if you do not go to the tower. We are offering you the only way to save yourself, and not just you, but the world of Arinn entire."

"You know that we cannot make their decision for them," Jareth said, placing a hand on his companion's shoulder. The tension in the older Savant's body drained, but not entirely. Jareth addressed Roderick and Bethany. "Excuse us for a moment while we discuss this matter in private."

"I may not be able to stand up to you any more than I could those ruffians, but you'll have to knock me out, too, if you want to take him," Roderick said, surprising himself with his boldness.

"Understood." Jareth nodded and even Kendall gave him a look of begrudging respect.

The Savants withdrew to the back of the cave. For long moments they conferred amongst themselves in whispered voices. Every cloistered syllable seemed to turn into a bead of sweat on Roderick's forehead. By the time they finished, he was wishing he could take a long walk in the evening air.

At length Kendall addressed them once more.

"Any attempt to force the motley to the tower might awaken the magic within him. If it rose up to protect him, sooner or later it would take complete hold of him. Such a course of action would bring about the very thing we seek to prevent." His words were calm and even, but Roderick sensed he would not merely let it go at that. Sure enough, the old

Savant added, "So we have settled upon a different plan. If the motley will not come with us alone, perhaps he will come with you. If he is willing, would you accompany him to the tower?"

If Kendall had tossed cold water in his face, Roderick could not have been more startled. "Y-you must be joking. I —I don't even…I don't even know where it is," he sputtered, utterly flummoxed.

"But if the boy were willing, would you go?" Kendall pressed him.

Roderick hemmed and hawed, but had no idea how to respond. He felt the eyes of every person in the cave upon him. He felt the weight of Jacob's eyes heaviest of all. Looking into them, they seemed half full of innocence, half full of fear. It reminded Roderick of the look in Aisha's eyes the night she'd heard a wolf howling in the distance and run to him for protection.

"Oh, Derick," Bethany said. "I suppose he has no one else in all the wide world to help him outside of the people in this cave."

Roderick gazed into his beloved wife's face. Love radiated behind her strong, clear eyes, but what these men were asking would take him from her and Aisha for a very long time. And even if he could bear to be apart, who would provide for them, with winter coming on and their stores laid bare?

"But, Beth…how will you get by? It sounds like a frightfully long distance."

"The hands that hold us have never failed before," she said, placing her hand in his.

He drew strength from her touch. He knew she was right. The death of his mother, the harsh winter last year, and that terrible infection Aisha had suffered through the year before that: he had seen the hand of Providence working in his life enough to know that his family would not be abandoned when trials came. Still…

"We've always managed just fine on your trips to Evenspire. Perhaps we can stay with the Tullums some. They

58

have a big house and they both adore Aisha." Bethany said.

Roderick admired her faith, but a journey to the capital was nothing like what these men were asking. The lands to the North were wild and full of danger, and hadn't they said this tower was on an island? He had never set foot on a boat in his life!

"But my business, I've got nothing left," Roderick protested, thinking of his missing cart and all he had lost to the ruffians. "Even if you do make it through the winter, what will become of us when I get back?"

"My good man," Jareth said. "we may appear as if we are little more than wandering scholars, but we have considerable resources at our disposal. If you tell us what needs to be bought, we can send someone off to Evenspire and purchase cloth enough for ten years of stitching. We shall have it all ready and waiting for you upon your return."

Roderick eyed the man with a sudden sense of awe. Through his words, it was as if Adonai reached down at that moment to calm his fretful soul. His wife gave his hand a comforting squeeze, and yet...he wavered.

"That is a generous offer, sir, and I don't take it lightly, but what about those toughs who gave me a thrashing in the woods and chased us out of our home? Our neighbor is a stout man, but I doubt even he would be able to stand against that band of thugs if they came calling again."

"I will remain to watch over your family until you return," Jareth said. "The apprentices as well. You have seen tonight that simple ruffians are no match for the power of the Savants. I pledge to you on my life that your wife and daughter shall remain safe under my protective care."

Roderick, still standing there in his nightgown and cloak, felt a chill air pass through him. This was not how he had expected his day to end up when he headed off to market that morning.

After all was said and done, though, it wasn't the Savants' offer of protection or the buying of cloth from Evenspire which swayed him. It was the tender echoes of those gentle

59

eyes staring into his in the darkness, in the woods beside Old Cottage road, the eyes of a little boy who had risked a pummeling at the hands of ruffians to follow after Roderick and pick him up when by all rights he should have fled to safety. That was when he first saw the child behind the skin, and that moment resounded afresh within the chamber of Roderick's heart and that was all he really needed to know.

"Jacob." He knelt again. "I will do whatever I can to protect you. Will you go with me to the tower?"

Roderick could almost see the surge of joy bubbling up inside. "Yes!" Jacob flung his arms around Roderick's neck. "Thank you," The gratitude in his voice resonated through his slender frame.

Kendall drew near. "We can help you. We can take away those colors from your skin and the men will stop chasing you. You can live like a normal boy again."

The child lifted up his eyes and they briefly met Kendall's. In that moment, the Savant had a grandfatherly look about him. All those dusty tomes and piles of words he must have read did not make him appear as indifferent as he had at first. It was clear that this man wanted to lift Jacob's curse as much as anyone.

Jacob nodded, an uncomplicated trust gracing his face.

The tension in Jareth's face fled and he breathed a long sigh of relief.

"Our prayers have been answered, then."

Roderick put his arms around his wife and the two children.

"It's the right thing to do," Bethany whispered.

Roderick stared into Jacob's mystical face, wondering what he would look like if that strange pattern on his skin was no more.

"Very well," Roderick said. "Tell us what we must do."

8

THE RIGHT THING TO DO

The Savants had either counted on Jacob coming with them or were very seasoned travelers, probably both. After the decision had been made, they went into the tunnel at the back of the cave and brought forth the supplies they needed for the journey. They carried out satchels, blankets, and foodstuffs. About half of their provender was in the form of dried fruit. Jacob's tastes for such fare were quite well-known to them. His preferences were not, as Roderick had supposed, mere childish predilection. Though no one knew why, fruit was all a motley could eat. Anything else would make them terribly ill.

Since they could not be sure if the Thaumaturge was watching Roderick's house, Roderick could not return to gather any of his own things. He had his traveling cloak with him, but beneath that, nothing more than a nightgown. The Savants helped out here as well, giving him a solid, if rather plain, linen tunic and a thick pair of burlap pants. Along with these they provided a thick wool vest to keep him warm during the upcoming winter, and a well-made pair of leather boots finer than any Roderick had ever owned, though they had seen a fair amount of use. The pants were cinched with an equally fine belt which had a sheathed knife on the side. The little blade was nothing impressive, but larger than the one he kept in his cart.

While Roderick was dressing, the Savants took the opportunity to sew the rip in Jacob's cloak. They did a poor job by Roderick's estimation, but they were scholars, not

61

tailors, after all.

Small satchels with blankets tied upon them were given to both Roderick and Jacob so that Kendall did not have to carry everything, but Jacob's bag was half the size of the others.

"As I promised, we will keep your wife and daughter safe until your return," Jareth assured him once they had finished outfitting the travelers.

"I will hold you to your word," Roderick said. He looked upon his wife and daughter for the hundredth time. He knew this was the right thing to do, but such knowledge did little to abate the cold, gnawing sensation in his stomach. It threatened to rob him of his will for the journey before it ever began.

"So, is Kendall going to lead them to the tower by himself?" Bethany asked.

"He is the only one who has been there before," Jareth said. "He is also the most skilled amongst us in the alchemical arts. His knowledge in that area will prove quite useful if the Thaumaturge gets hold of your trail again."

Kendall stepped forward, gripping his metal pole. The lantern had been tied off onto his satchel.

"We will stick to the wilderness. The Thaumaturge has spies in all the major cities and in dozens of towns. The fewer people we meet on our journey, the better."

"So it's just the three of us?" Roderick asked. "No offense, I mean, you did fend off those ruffians and all, but what if it's the Thaumaturge himself next time? Can he do real magic? And if so, wouldn't it do to hire a man-at-arms or two?"

"Like the Savants, the Thaumaturges also know the secrets of alchemy, but possess no more magic than we do. Their greatest power is fear. The tales surrounding them only play into their designs. Even so, the one seeking the motley is not to be trifled with. He has more power than the Emperor himself in some ways. His vessels float upon many waters. We dare not trust anyone outside this cave with this task."

The cold pit in Roderick's stomach got colder. He adjusted the belt they had given him. It did not fit as well as it had first seemed.

"Just how far is this tower we're going to?" Roderick asked, anxious to talk of other things. Aisha would be turning five soon. Would he be gone so long he would miss her birthday?

"The tower lies in the far northwest, beyond the shores of Caledonia. In fact, it is as far west as anyone can travel. Few maps even show it anymore for the days have long passed since any dwelt there."

Outside the mouth of the cave, the moon shone its mystical light across the meadow. The disrobed woods beyond glimmered like a great bristly rug coating the land. Roderick had been to Evenspire many times and that was a long enough journey as it was, but he had never set foot in Caledonia to the north, never even dreamed he would come close to it.

"The land of the Iddlglim," Roderick muttered under his breath.

"Who are they?" Jacob asked.

"The wolf lords, they are also called," Bethany said. "My father traded with them once near the shores of the Fallowing. He barely came out alive. They are a savage lot."

"Indeed, you will need to stay close to the river to avoid their hunting parties," Jareth said. He motioned to one of the apprentices, who produced a piece of vellum from a scroll case and unfurled it so that Jareth could see what was written there. Though Roderick could appreciate the skill of the lines and shapes, it was so much chicken scratch to him.

"This is the river. You will travel along its norther banks all the way west to the Neverless Sea," Jareth ran his finger along a squiggly line which covered most of the paper.

"Is it really necessary to pass through Caledonia?" Roderick asked. "I mean, Evenspire has a fine enough harbor. I'm sure we can hire a ship there to take us to this Isle of Rinn you spoke of."

"The road to Evenspire is too well-traveled," Kendall said.

"We can be certain it is being watched. And the forests and bramble off the road are a haven of bandits and other slit-throats. It would be safest if we traveled through the northern plains where both bandits and the Emperor's men fear to tread. The fear of the Iddlglim will be our defense and the River Fallowing our road until we reach Davinsmoor. We can charter a ship from there."

"Davinsmoor? The Caledonian capital? Surely that will be a thousand times worse than facing all the bandits in the Five Helms?" Though Roderick knew very little about Davinsmoor, he imagined going there would like walking into one big, continuous brawl. Anyone brave or foolish enough to stray into such a place was practically asking to be relieved of their coin or have their bones broken or both.

"Not all the inhabitants of Caledonia are as wild as those who dwell on the plains. Gold is the universal tongue, and the Iddlglim speak it as well as anyone," Kendall said. "Their port may not be as well run or as inviting as that of Evenspire, but there are still ship captains to be had there for the right price."

"If anyone can get you there, it is Master Kendall," Jareth said. He signaled for the apprentice to return the map to its case.

"Very well," Roderick mumbled. All this talk made his clothes itch. *Honestly, how in The Glen did I end up in all this?* he wondered, scratching underneath his arm.

"And now the time has come," Kendall said. "We must be off."

"Yes, best not to tarry in this cave any longer," Jareth said. "The Thaumaturge and his men are sure to return eventually."

And now at last the dreaded moment had come.

"Oh, Beth." Roderick threw his arms around her and Aisha, holding onto them as though clinging to a rock on the edge of a swiftly flowing river. He hid his face in Bethany's hair, drinking in that singular blend of lavender soap and garden spices one last time.

"Have faith," Bethany whispered.

Roderick slipped the gold valin from his cloak into her hand. "Here, my love. For the coming winter."

Bethany's eyes went almost as large as the coin. A question formed on her lips, but Aisha stole it away as she nestled in between them. She patted her father quietly on the back, the same way she used to when he rocked her to sleep as a baby. Roderick kissed her cheeks and forehead a dozen times over.

With one last, tender kiss to his beloved, he forced himself to pull away. He was slipping into the water with no idea how to swim.

Bethany leaned down and embraced Jacob.

"We'll find you some apples when you get back," she said.

Jacob nodded shyly, but politely. "Thank you, ma'am."

"Aw, does he have to go?" Aisha puffed out her lips. "He only got to stay one night."

She thinks I'm just going away for one of my trips. Oh, if only that were true.

"Yes, Eesh," Roderick said. "But when we get back, he can stay as long as he wants."

Oh, Adonai, may it be so.

Aisha smiled, the only bright face in all that gloomy cave. Roderick ran his fingers through her curly hair one last time.

The four of them huddled close as Roderick prayed aloud for their journey. "If it be your will, Adonai, see us safely to the tower and back home. Give us your strength in our weakness. And keep my dear girls safe from harm during this long time away."

"So be it," Bethany said.

Roderick and Jacob followed Kendall out into the night. The old Savant's long strides carried them away all too quickly. Roderick, working to keep up, looked back for as long as he could and waved, until his family was swallowed up by the looming dark of the forest.

65

9

FIRST MANIFESTATION

hey broke camp the following morning after a miserable night of trudging through the woods and the briefest of rests. Roderick awoke to find he had rolled onto a large and particularly knobby root at the base of a beech tree during the night. This served to add a terrible back pain to all the various and sundry aches and sores he had already accumulated from his encounter with the ruffians. And it was cold on top of that. If the light had been a little stronger, Roderick was certain he would have been able to see his breath.

He rubbed his arms and stamped his feet as they set off again. He wasn't even out of The Glen and he was already bone tired. As he walked along he kept saying to himself, *What was Bethany thinking when she allowed me to go away like this?*

But the light of the new day warmed his tired bones and the going got a bit easier. Plodding through the syrupy undergrowth of moss and silvan decay, he stared at the little boy kicking up leaves in front of him.

That's why you're here, Roderick Devinson, and don't you forget it.

A fresh sense of purpose quickened Roderick's step. He moved up alongside the enigmatic Savant. Kendall walked with a measured step that did not waver nor vary no matter the conditions of the trail. Rough or smooth, firm or slippery, he marched like a soldier to some inner drum.

"How did ever you come to join the, um, Sanctum was it called?" Roderick asked as they passed beneath a great, gnarled rattlin tree. The dappled bark looked like it had been

66

sprinkled with salt and pepper. Such trees were supposed to be rather common in the Mithrin Woods north of The Glen, but as rattlins generally grew only in the deep woods, Roderick had only ever seen a few of them in his life.

"Ah, well, that is a tale in itself," Kendall said, narrowing those insightful eyes of his. "Many years ago, I was a mere librarian working in the royal archives of Evenspire. Then one day, Master Jareth arrived. He was looking for information about certain powders and their properties. This piqued my interest, for I had made such things a matter of personal study for many years. We struck up a friendship. As he returned to the library over the years our friendship grew. Eventually he confided in me that his interest in such things was not merely academic. He sought knowledge about the alchemical arts in order to combat the terrible influence of the Thaumaturges across the land."

"So Jareth invited you to join the Sanctum when you were in the library?" Roderick had never been inside the great library himself, but had walked past it a few times. It was not far from the cloth market. It was a giant, seven-tiered structure with more columns and windows than any other building in Evenspire. It looked more like a waterfall frozen in stone than an actual building. Roderick had tried to imagine what it was like inside, but only nobles, scholars, and the very wealthy were allowed to enter.

"Yes. I left my position and took up his quest to search for the motleys and oppose the schemes of the Thaumaturges wherever possible."

Roderick moved closer to Kendall, speaking in low tones, "So have you ever met one of these...Thaumaturges?" Though they were deep in the woods, he still did not feel entirely safe talking about such things in the open.

Troubled lines wrinkled the old man's face. "Once, but at the time, I did not know his true nature. They do not like to reveal themselves to people unless it serves their interests. For the most part they keep themselves shrouded in mystery."

"Well, whoever they are, I do wish I knew what they

wanted with Jacob."

"The Thaumaturges fear the motley's power," Kendall said dourly. "They do not wish that any real wizard should arise to supplant them. And they have studied the histories as well as we have. They know of the disaster which the first motley rained down upon this land. To keep the magic from running wild, they seek to capture the motleys and starve them to death before the magic takes hold. They have done so with others in the past. If they were to attempt to actively harm a motley, the magic would rise up to protect him."

The hair on Roderick's neck prickled in anger. "Starve a child to death? Who would do such a thing? Why not just use the tower?"

"I do not believe that they know of its existence. That is why Tronas built it out at the edge of the world. And a good thing, too. For if they knew of it they might attempt to use the stone to take the motley's magic for themselves."

"I thought the stone was supposed to get rid of it forever. Could they do that? Could the tower—or this stone give the magic to someone else?"

"It is possible. No one truly knows. For a motley has never been brought to it before."

"Well, I'm grateful the Savants found him, then," Roderick said.

"As well you should be. We will end this curse once and for all."

Roderick glanced at Jacob, wondering just how much he understood about the forces at work in his life, drawing him inexorably to that distant tower. Why such a kind and gentle child would be cursed was beyond Roderick.

At the moment, the curse seemed the furthest thing from Jacob's thoughts. He was enjoying the woods, fascinated by the squirrels and rabbits darting amongst the trees. He never took his eyes off one when he spotted it, his face shining with delight at their quick, tiny movements and furry quiverings.

As midday drew near, they heard what Roderick thought

must be an animal caught in a trap. It sounded like the clinking and scraping of metal. Then came another sound just like it, then another. Kendall's eyes darted amongst the trees. He motioned for a stop. The metallic rustling was muted and still far away, but it was getting closer. And it was no animal trap.

"Is it the ruffians again?" Roderick asked in a whisper. If it was, there were a lot more of them this time.

"Let us hope we do not have to find out," Kendall whispered back. "Follow me—quickly."

Roderick and Jacob ran after Kendall, who skittered down a slope towards a massive oak which lay fallen on the ground. The decaying husk stretched across a depression in the woods. The tree was hollowed out at one end and large enough so that someone of Roderick's size could fit in hunched over. Kendall waved them inside.

Jacob crawled to the back and Roderick wedged himself in the middle. Kendall stayed just inside the lip, peering out into the woods. His body blocked most of the opening. The clinking sounds got closer and closer. Soon, they were joined by the sound of trampling feet.

"What are we—?" Roderick began.

Kendall silenced him with a raised hand. After a minute or two the unmistakable sounds of armor-clad men rang through the clearing. If they passed by the end of the trunk they could not fail to notice Kendall. Roderick wished he would retreat further into the shadows, but he dared not say anything for fear of giving away their hiding place.

The approaching sounds reverberated inside the trunk. Shuffling, clinking, stomping noises. Were the soldiers in the depression now? Had they seen Kendall yet?

Kendall drew Roderick close and whispered in his ear.

"They are going to pass this way. I must go and find out who they are. If they're provincial or imperial troops we should be fine. If not, I'll try to draw them off. If I do not return within ten minutes, head north to the Fallowing River and follow it west. I will catch up to you as soon as I can."

He leapt from the log and charged into the forest. Roderick

stayed back from the opening to make sure he wasn't spotted. No! They were losing their guide already? The journey had barely begun!

A cry rose up and the sounds of armored men stampeding away from the depression echoed through the woods.

"Oh, Adonai, protect that brave old man," Roderick whispered in the hollow dark.

Jacob was so still and quiet Roderick could only tell he was there by his death grip on Roderick's arm.

A few shuffling footfalls and clinking sounds remained. They grew closer by the moment.

Roderick could not take his eyes off the dreaded opening at the end of the tree. The longer he looked at it, the larger it got and the closer it seemed.

Suddenly, a helmeted head appeared in the hole. Roderick's heart lurched like he'd been shot with an arrow.

"There! In the log!" the soldier cried, pointing.

Another soldier's head appeared beside the first.

"Get out of there—now!" he ordered.

"No, please," Jacob whispered, yanking on Roderick's arm. But there was nowhere for them to go.

"Stay here," Roderick said, but Jacob would not let go.

"Don't leave me," he begged.

"Come on, hurry up!" the soldier shouted.

They had no choice. Roderick dragged the terrified Jacob out with him into the clearing. Before they came out, Roderick had considered running, but he gave up all thought of that once he got out. Twenty armed soldiers pressed in around them, brandishing spears and swords, all pointed in their direction.

"The captain will be back any minute," said one of the soldiers. He waved his sword threateningly at the prisoners, but kept his distance.

"Hold steady," added another under his breath.

Jacob's fingers dug into Roderick's arm. The fear written on his face sapped what little courage Roderick had left. But the longer they stood there without the soldiers binding them or carrying Jacob off, the more Roderick began to suspect that he and Jacob were not the only frightened ones in the forest. The furtive glances and shifting stances of the soldiers betrayed their unease. Why a troop of armed men would fear a tailor and a small boy was beyond Roderick. Perhaps Jacob's skin made them nervous. Or perhaps they knew about the magic.

Roderick studied them, desperate to think of a way out. Their black livery covered dark leather armor and chain shirts. The livery was embroidered with a field of white and black diamonds on the shoulders and a field of white angular lines across the chest which looked vaguely like mountains. The designs certainly did not belong to any of the provinces of the Halicon Empire. Their helmets sported long flaps on either side and another flap running down the nose. Their darker skin betrayed them as coming from the south, somewhere beyond Vinyon province.

At length another group of soldiers came marching through the woods. This new contingent fanned out amongst their fellows around the hollow log. To Roderick's dismay, Kendall was among them.

It had been Roderick's one hope that somehow the Savant would come back to rescue them. His smoke and lights were the only real chance they had. But the grim look on Kendall's face snuffed out Roderick's hopes.

As Kendall passed through the circle of guards surrounding them, Jacob mumbled, "Please keep me safe."

"I'll protect you," Roderick promised, holding him all the tighter. "No matter what."

"Well, my friends," Kendall said. "It looks as if the motley has been—"

He never finished.

"He's gone!" One of the guards cut him off, gesturing towards Roderick.

For a brief moment, Roderick had no idea what he meant. Then he grasped for Jacob and his arms found empty air. Where Jacob had been was nothing but bare forest floor.

10

NIGHTMARES

A tide of caustic smoke bloomed up from the ground, engulfing the clearing in the wake of Jacob's disappearance. As at Bald Hill, it stung Roderick's eyes terribly. He could barely keep them open inside the dark, oily cloud. Shuffling and shouting and clanking noises broke out all around him. Cries from the soldiers erupted like firecrackers amidst the smoke. Bodies bumped against him in the dark.

"Where's the boy?"

"Have you got him?"

"Fool, stop grabbing me, I'm not one of them!"

"Agh! My eyes! It burns!"

Roderick crouched low to avoid the worst of the burning fumes and somehow stumbled his way out of the hazy cloud. He was about to take off when someone grabbed him by the arm and pulled him to the side, yanking him up the hill in a different direction. He fought against the grip, but he was off balance and had no leverage. Coughing and wiping his tear-filled eyes, Roderick was finally able to make out the figure who was dragging him.

It was Kendall!

The sounds of soldiers running and crashing into each other reverberated through the woods, but as yet none of them had slipped outside the smoky expanse, at least on Roderick's side.

"Come," Kendall said in a low voice. "We must be away before the Thaumaturge's soldiers discover we have escaped."

The Thaumaturge! He was on their trail already? Oh, buttons…

"What about Jacob?" Roderick's eyes flitted about the woods for any sign of him. Thick pillars of bark covered in moss stared back at him, silent witnesses to the chaos erupting in the woods and inside Roderick's heart.

"He is no longer here. It has begun. His powers have started to manifest themselves. The magic has awakened." Kendall turned and flung a handful of silt onto the ground. Another smoke cloud rose up from the forest floor behind them as he darted up the slope with Roderick following. On the other side of the rise, Kendall pulled out one of the amulets with the fabulous crimson gems. As in the cave, scarlet flashes glinted inside of it.

"He has gone north," Kendall said, building up to a run. Roderick blundered after him, straining to keep up. It was a harrowing dash through the woods. Weaving in and out of the dense thicket, twigs and branches slapped Roderick in the face a dozen times over. Half an hour later, his poor face, crisscrossed with scratches, must have looked like a madwoman's quilt.

They slowed beside a gurgling brook for a short rest and water. Roderick took solace in the fact that there were no sounds of pursuit.

"You think the magic allowed Jacob to escape?" Roderick asked once he caught his breath. He clutched the stitch in his side, but it didn't help.

"I am sure of it," Kendall said, wiping his sweaty beard into his sleeve. "A motley can travel great distances in a single moment with his magic. But the powers are just beginning; he cannot have gone more than a few miles."

"A few miles? He could be anywhere then. Are you sure this is the way he went?"

"The crystal does not lie," Kendall said.

The amulet's light had certainly grown brighter since they started out.

"So you gave the other one to Jacob," Roderick said.

"Yes, I pinned it inside the folds of his cloak while he slept."

"Why didn't you tell me that before?" He gave Kendall a cross look, perhaps crosser than he intended, due to the pain in his side. Though it had turned out to be a wise decision, he didn't like the fact that their guide had given the crystal to Jacob without telling him.

"I did not tell him for fear he might take it off and lose it, but you are right, I should have told him," Kendall said.

Roderick forced a smile through the pain, embarrassed at having questioned his traveling companion's judgment. This whole business had him confuzzled. It looked like magic was real enough all right, but he still had little idea what it all meant.

"Well, if it helps us find him, that's what matters. We'd best get going, don't you think?"

Kendall studied the glinting amulet. "Yes, this way."

They resumed their mad dash, sloshing through the brook. Sweat stung the cuts on Roderick's face, but the further on he went, the less the pain bothered him. Panic crowded out any thought of his own sufferings.

The forest thinned and gave way to a broad moor of scraggly grass. The air grew crisper. It was good to be out under the open sky again. It might give them a better chance at spotting Jacob.

Kendall checked the amulet more frequently now. Roderick could tell from his demeanor that they were close.

As they topped another hill, a stagnant black pond opened up before them. There, sitting on a large flat rock near the shore was a small figure, his cloak wrapped tightly around him.

"Jacob!" Roderick cried out.

Jacob shot up and bolted towards him. Roderick gathered him in his arms.

"I thought I'd lost you." Roderick pressed his face against Jacob's. The motley skin felt like any other sort of skin, save that it was unusually warm.

"I'm sorry." Jacob's voice quivered. "I didn't want them to get me. I don't really know how it happened. I just wanted to get away and this is where I ended up."

"Whatever happens, we have to stay together from here on out," Roderick said.

Jacob nodded fiercely. "Yes. I don't want to be alone ever again." He trembled quietly in Roderick's arms. For a moment Roderick imagined they were back in the cottage and that Jacob had run upstairs to him after a bad dream.

"You won't be," Roderick said. "Not if I can help it."

Kendall did not look nearly as relieved to find Jacob as Roderick was. His bristly eyebrows bunched together in the inverse of his crumpled frown. He looked Jacob up and down. At first Roderick thought he was just being stern. The Savant seemed to have mastered that particular emotion. Then Roderick noticed that one of the diamond shapes on Jacob's forehead, a yellow one, gave off a subtle glow. It was easy to miss in the daylight, but it was impossible to ignore once he spotted it.

Roderick shot a questioning glance at Kendall.

The Savant only shook his head disapprovingly. "We must not let this happen again."

Fortunately Jacob had teleported in a mostly northern direction. Not exactly the path Kendall meant to take, but close enough that they lost hardly any time along their journey that day.

The forest was all but out of sight by the time they arrived at the Fallowing River about mid-afternoon. They stopped at the edge of the slow moving, grayish waterway and sat down for a short meal before crossing. The smooth, straight channel looked more like a stream than a river. It flowed by with barely a bubble or ripple. It was certainly not the watery thoroughfare and paragon of flowing power which the traveling merchants made it out to be. Then again, few of them ventured along it this late in the year. The fact that the Fallowing was less of a river than Roderick had hoped was certainly a disappointment, but given the circumstances, also a boon; it would be much easier to cross this way.

Jacob finished eating and went over to the edge of the river. He picked up a handful of stones and began skipping them across the water. His first few throws were not all that successful, but with each toss the number of skips increased.

Kendall gazed down the length of the water. The hour was growing late and a frigid wind whipped across the river.

"In ancient times this was known as the Vescent River and the great forest of Dimweather grew right up to its northern banks. In those days it never ran this low, even in winter. It would have been twice as deep and three times as wide back then. But since the Scathen Night, the Night of Ten Thousand Shadows, the world is much changed. Though the shadows did eventually pass, the land never fully healed."

"This night you mention, what exactly took place then?" Roderick asked, bracing against the deepening chill.

"No one knows for sure. All we have are fragments, and those differ in what they say. This much we do know— kingdoms were consumed and dark creatures roamed the world. Arinn became a waking nightmare, and all because of the motley."

Roderick suppressed a shudder, unsettled by the nature of Kendall's story and yet at the same time fascinated to learn of its conclusion. He had never heard this version of the motley legend before. "How did it all end?"

"Again, the legends disagree. Some say a great prophet rose up and defeated the motley, others say warriors from heaven descended on the land like a great trumpet blast and scattered the shadows into the far corners of the world. Personally, I believe the darkness turned in upon itself and the creatures the motley had summoned turned on their master. But who can say for sure?"

"It will be different this time," Jacob said, surprising Roderick, who thought he hadn't been paying attention to their conversation.

"We still have many miles to go before I would say that," Kendall said.

"He means that stone. We'll stop the curse this time because we've got that, right, Jacob?" Roderick asked.

"No," Jacob said solemnly, "it's because of you."

At those words every ounce of heaviness in Roderick's body floated right out through the top of his head. If Jacob had asked him to leap the Fallowing in a single bound at that moment he would have done so. He returned Jacob's earnest look with a heartfelt smile.

Kendall grunted skeptically and pointed downstream. "We'll follow the river all the way to the coast, but here is where we shall cross. The waters deepen and the current picks up beyond Thatcher's Crossing."

Fording the river also meant they would be passing into Caledonian lands.

"You're sure the wildmen won't come down to the river?" Roderick asked.

"It is doubtful. They are a superstitious lot. They are fearful of the water and only cross it at great need. It is the river, more than all the great castles and armies of the Empire which keeps the northmen at bay."

"I've never been in the water before," Jacob said, tossing one last stone that made it nearly halfway across before sinking.

"Don't worry," Roderick said, coming alongside him. "I'll carry you. That would be best, don't you think, Master Kendall?"

Though Roderick couldn't swim, he hoped it would be shallow enough to wade across.

"Yes. In a few places, it will likely be over his head. It would be best to keep him as dry as possible in any case."

The two men took off their cloaks and wrapped them around their shoulders. Roderick hoisted Jacob up onto a little padded nest he made with his vest. Kendall was the tallest, so he waded in first to spy out where any deep spots might be lurking. His quick breaths told Roderick he was in for a shock once he hit the water. The Fallowing did not fail to deliver on this promise. The moment he set foot in the icy bath, chills ran through his body like a clapper striking a wintry bell. His shoulders did an involuntary dance, nearly spilling Jacob into the drink.

He pushed forward as fast as he could, both to keep himself warm and to get through it as soon as possible. The river barely went past his shins at first. About a quarter of the way across, it deepened precipitously. Soon it lapped his waist and not long after, his chest. Jacob, safe and dry up top, dragged his shoes in the water, as if carried along by his own personal river raft on a lazy summer afternoon.

Roderick tried to keep his shivering to a minimum so as not to cause him to fall.

Just when they drew near the shore and he thought the misery would be over, Kendall veered west and continued along in the riverbed.

"W-w-why aren't we getting out?" Roderick's teeth chattered against each other.

"We don't want to make it any easier for the soldiers to pick up our trail," Kendall said.

When they stepped out of the water a few hundred yards later, Roderick's frosty woes were far from over. A new misery was added to the first, that of dampness. His clothes clung to him like patches of old, baggy skin, begging to be scraped off.

"It will not do to stay wet with evening coming on," Kendall said. "There is a stand of trees a mile or so off to the northwest. We shall make for that. There we can make camp and warm ourselves."

"I don't s-see how we'll quit this chill once it g-gets dark. We c-can't light a f-fire. Th-that would draw attention." Roderick wrung the water out of his soaking pants and shirt, but his hands were so frozen through he could barely get a grip. The breeze along the shore went right through his skin to his bones.

"There are other ways to warm oneself in this world besides fire," Kendall said.

"And what w-would that be?"

"You shall see soon enough." Kendall cocked one eyebrow enigmatically.

By the time they arrived at the copse of trees, Jacob was shivering as well. Roderick's teeth were chattering like a flock of woodpeckers. He was so desperately cold he would have risked a fire if Kendall had not promised to provide warmth by some other means.

The Savant pulled out three black reeds from his satchel. Placing them on the ground, one by one he began to peel the outer layer from each individual stalk, revealing the golden under-skin beneath. A pleasing yellow-orange glow issued from the reeds the moment they were exposed to the open air. The light provided was about equal to that of a candle. It took a few minutes, but the glow began to radiate a healthy amount of heat as well. They made a sort of tent with their damp cloaks and huddled around the stalks to trap the heat and keep the light from escaping their little circle.

"Flameroot," Kendall said. "It grows only in the far south in the most inhospitable places. Not many know of its existence. I first learned of it from *Griven's Herbal Essays,* the definitive work on southern verdure."

"It's marvelous," Roderick said, basking in the inviting glow. The Savants claimed they didn't know any real magic, but as far as Roderick was concerned, this was just as good. "You certainly are the cleverest man I've ever met, Master Kendall, that's for sure."

Jacob huddled near the heat, stretching his gloved hands towards the reeds.

"Thank you, sir," he told the Savant, who returned his gratitude with a nod.

A serene look fell over Jacob's face as he gazed upon the incandescent stalks. Though he was barely wet at all, he sat closer to the glow than either of the others. The light brought out the motley colors of his skin like the glaze on a clay pot.

The flameroot blazed long into the night and, once the travelers got fully dry, it was the most pleasant time they'd had on the journey thus far. Jacob munched on a bit of dried fruit, sitting in Roderick's lap, while Kendall regaled them with legends and tales from faraway lands and times long forgotten. Kendall kept his voice low which made the tales all the more dramatic. Roderick and Jacob listened intently, caught up in the spell he wove with his words.

"Where did you learn so many marvelous stories, Master Kendall?" Roderick asked him at one point.

"Why from books, my good tailor. Where else?" answered the scholar.

Though he was unable to read himself, Roderick did love a good tale. Few people could read in Briar's Glen, but truth be told there was little need for it. Books were a luxury that only the wealthiest could afford; he had never seen more than a handful of them throughout his entire life. But Bethany always had more than enough stories to keep him and Aisha entertained, though they were usually of her own invention.

As he sat and listened to the tales with Jacob nodding off to sleep in his arms, he imagined he was back sitting by the fire in his little cottage, together with his wife and daughter. Perhaps if he made it back he might have a tale or two to tell of his own.

For two days after the crossing, they followed the gentle river as it wound its way across the rolling hills and scraggly plains south of Dimweather Forest. The great wood was far to the north, but Roderick caught a glimpse of it once when they crested a barren hill. It was little more than a dark line on the horizon, the hem of a blanket whose fabric was the sky.

As far as Roderick knew, no proper kingdom lay claim to these lands. The only signs of civilization were the occasional remnants from the camps of river traders on the southern banks. Kendall assured him that until the spring rains came, there would be little traffic along this stretch of the Fallowing, making this the most inconspicuous time of the year to travel alongside it.

Eventually they left the river bank and worked their way further north. The hills grew rugged and steep, the undergrowth thicker, and copses of trees larger and more frequent. Though it slowed their progress, they traveled through the wooded areas whenever they could. The trees consisted mostly of hawthorns and blackthorns, the latter a tree which Roderick had never seen before. Kendall informed him that they yielded beautiful white blossoms in the spring, but the long spikes on their branches gave them an imposing look now.

Jacob found winterberry bushes growing near the trees from time to time and these were used to save their precious supply of fruit and supplement their humdrum rations. Roderick was not fond of the bitter taste, but they had far more flavor than the wooden wafers of hard tack which the Savants had supplied, so he was always grateful when Jacob offered him a handful. The taste was dreadfully sour, but the winsome smiles Jacob flashed whenever Roderick squinted his eyes and wrinkled his nose were more than worth the unpleasant experience of forcing down the tiny bursts of tartness.

They passed the village of Thatcher's Crossing on the fifth day and Piper's Hollow by the seventh. At least according to Kendall, for they never actually got close enough to see those places. Roderick would not have minded passing through the towns themselves, but it was far too dangerous according to their guide. Both Thatcher's Crossing and Piper's Hollow were independent trading towns so perhaps he had a point. Places like that had a reputation for not being the most upstanding of locations.

On their eighth night together, a scream startled Roderick from sleep. He turned over and spotted Jacob writhing restlessly, half uncovered by his blanket. Tears ran freely down his patterned cheeks and his brow bunched together in a clump of anguish.

"Jacob?" Roderick drew the blanket over him. "Jacob, are you all right?"

"He's just having a bad dream," Kendall said from behind them. The Savant sat with his back against a tree, his cloak wrapped tightly around him, studying his map in the frigid moonlight. On his lap rested a little notebook. He had a quill in hand.

"Master Kendall, I didn't know you were still awake," Roderick said.

"He's had these nightmares every night, you just haven't noticed. Though this looks to be a particularly bad one."

"Poor boy." Roderick grabbed Jacob's shoulder to try and wake him.

"I would let him sleep if I were you," Kendall advised in a grave tone.

"But he must be afraid. Shouldn't I comfort him?"

"There is no comfort you can give him from the things that chase him in his dreams. And if you wake him now, it may very well be that some of his nightmares will follow him into the waking world. No, you must let him fight those monsters on his own. There is nothing you can do for him this side of his dreams."

Kendall's tone drained what little strength Roderick had recovered from sleep.

"Surely there must be something we can do. It's that cursed magic that is doing this to him, isn't it?"

"It is hard to say. There is some connection between the motleys and the lands beyond this world. There is a reason the first motley's reign was called the Night of Ten Thousand Shadows."

Creatures inside Jacob's dreams? Was Kendall serious?

Roderick stared up at the starry sky in desperation. So little light and so much darkness. He missed Bethany now more than ever. How could he protect the child from his own dreams? If only she were here to give him advice.

I should pray for him. That was what Bethany would have told him to do. It was so obvious, he didn't know why he hadn't thought of it before. At that moment he felt his wife's presence very near. He imagined her standing before him, cradling Aisha in her arms, some of her sumptuous lentil soup steaming on the hearth.

"Aye, I will pray for him," he whispered into the night. "That I can do, my love."

He bowed his head and lifted up his voice to the heavens. Long into the night he went, pouring out his heart in tender supplication for this precious child. The words came freely, as naturally as breathing. And in some unfathomable way they drew him close to his Creator and Maker while at the same time drawing him closer to Jacob.

Somewhere past midnight, his prayers were answered. A look of blessed relief settled across Jacob's face and he slept peacefully for the first time that night.

"Thank you," Roderick whispered. By then his strength, along with his prayers, was all but spent. And in the cold quiet of the night he dropped off into dream lands of his own.

II

DAMP AND DREARY

The next few days saw a change in the countryside. The lands west of Piper's Hollow were dominated by the Woaden Heath, a vast open plain of rolling hills with bright yellow foliage woven into the fabric of the land. This brilliant tapestry made it seem as if the sun was ever shining, even on cloudy days. That far south the woad was not dominant, but patches of it could be seen peppering the landscape, each outbreak a bright breadcrumb dropped from heaven, letting them know that they were on the right path.

The blue dye produced from the woad plant was one of the few items the wildmen traded with foreigners. Highly prized by the cloth merchants of the Halicon Empire, Roderick had seen bolts of indigo cloth made from woaden dye in the capital go for as high as three hundred miras, far too expensive for him to afford. The first time they passed through a patch of the plant, he imagined what beautiful things he could make if only he had a way to bring enough of it back home. Aisha would look so lovely in a bright blue spring dress. Bethany, too, for that matter.

Aside from the patches of woad, the occasional rabbit, deer, or flock of birds were the only interruptions to the long, unending trek through that vast unpeopled country. Several times they came across tracks which, according to Kendall belonged to wildmen or wolves (and those tracks were often together), but they saw no signs of human habitation.

Still, this failed to put Roderick at ease. He secretly suspected the wildmen were just waiting for the right moment to strike, and lived in perpetual fear they would come sweeping across the plains and fall upon them when he least expected it.

They were a couple day's journey from Grimsford, another river town, when Jacob began to walk with something of a limp. Though he maintained it was nothing, that night when they made camp Roderick asked him to remove his shoes. It took a great deal of coaxing to get him to comply, but Jacob gave in on the condition that Master Kendall stand behind a tree with his back turned. Kendall kindly remarked that he needed to study his map and went off to do just that. Once he was gone, Jacob sat down on a log and allowed Roderick to tug off his shoes.

The soles had cracked in several spots and pebbles and grass had wedged their way inside. On the side of one shoe was a hole as big as Jacob's thumb. Roderick set the battered old shoes down and took a look at Jacob's feet. Jacob averted his eyes, but did nothing to keep Roderick from touching them.

As expected, his feet had the same motley pattern as the rest of his skin. Besides that, he had three small blisters on one of them, like little colored kernels of corn. Jacob winced whenever Roderick touched them. On the other side of the foot, the skin had been rubbed raw in a few places. Roderick did not doubt the blisters would soon begin to form there as well.

"We should have gotten you some new shoes before we left," Roderick said. "These are worn to nothing. How long have you had these, Jacob?"

Jacob's head drooped and he mumbled in wilted tones, "My mother and father gave them to me."

The way he said the words 'mother' and 'father' sent little pricks of pain into Roderick's heart. He doubted Jacob would be willing to part with those reminders of them even if he were offered another pair.

"Ah, I see. I'll tell you what then. If you'll let me borrow them for the night, I'll try to fix them for you so they won't hurt so much."

Jacob perked up at that. He covered his feet with the hem of his cloak and gingerly handed Roderick the shoes.

"I bet you can fix anything," Jacob said.

Roderick chuckled. He was no cobbler, but he had learned enough from Old Tim to have an idea of what needed to be done.

Jacob watched the ensuing repair work with fascination. First Roderick cut some material from one of the leather flaps on his satchel. Then he fetched his tin cup and went into the woods. He wandered about for several minutes before finding a suitable pine tree. He set to work on it with his knife, cutting off a section of bark and carving a few v-shaped channels for the sap to flow into. Then he took off his belt and strapped the cup to the tree at the bottom of the runnels he had carved.

Leaving the cup, he headed back to camp. As he arrived, Kendall met him and handed him a small black bag.

"Here, this *almamenth* will help his feet to heal," the Savant said.

Roderick nodded. "Ah, wonderful. Thank you, Master Kendall."

He returned to Jacob, who was building some sort of tower out of sticks.

"Maybe this is what the tower we're going to will look like," he said brightly.

Roderick eyed the rickety structure with a smile. "Perhaps. We shall see soon enough. Look what master Kendall gave me for your feet. It's supposed to help them feel better."

He opened the pouch, and a wonderful, aromatic smell wafted from it. Inside was a clumpy, green powder. As Roderick set to applying it to Jacob's feet, he explained what he had done out in the woods.

"We'll have to wait until morning to see if enough sap flows into the cup," he said.

A look of wonderment filled Jacob's eyes.

"You know so much," he said.

"Ah, only a trick or two I learned here and there. I'll let you help me fix the shoes tomorrow, if you like."

Delight flashed onto Jacob's face like sunlight hitting a patch of woad. "Oh, yes, please, I'd like that very much."

As they lay down to sleep that night, Jacob nestled in close to Roderick.

"Are you going to pray for me again?" he asked.

"Yes, but how did you know I've been doing that?" Roderick asked. He had always waited for Jacob to fall asleep before beginning his prayers.

"I hear you in my dreams," Jacob whispered.

"You do?" Jacob's head nodded against his side. "Tell me, Jacob. Are they bad dreams?"

"Terrible." Jacob snuggled in closer.

"But you know I'm always here, don't you?"

"Yes," Jacob rolled over so that the two of them were face to face. Though it was dark, the colors on his skin shone out unmistakably, especially the yellow diamond on his forehead which glowed with its own inner light. "Thank you," he whispered before rolling back over. Those quiet words, so simple, and yet spoken so earnestly, endeared him to Roderick all the more.

Oh, please let me bring him safely home, Roderick prayed, his heart as full and warm as a pot of Bethany's lentil soup.

That night, for the first time since Roderick started praying, the nightmares did not come.

Roderick got up extra early to collect the sap. The cup was barely a quarter full, but that was enough.

He let Jacob help him when he got back. After heating up the sap, they mixed it with the ashen remains from one of

Kendall's flameroot stalks. Once that cooled a bit, they slathered around the sap mixture with a few leaves and covered the sides of the shoes with the slats. They both managed to get their fingers rather sticky and Roderick was sure Old Tim would cringe if he saw the way the shoes turned out, but the repair was solid enough once the sap hardened. Jacob's blisters had completely disappeared in the night thanks to Kendall's wondrous powder and, pleased to no end with his "new" shoes, Jacob fairly bounced along as they set off again. Kendall even had to caution him a few times when his enthusiasm got the better of him and he ranged out too far ahead.

Jacob asked Roderick all sorts of questions that day, about all the trees, plants, birds, and animals they passed. He wanted to know about everything. Though Roderick had to defer to Kendall on many of the questions, it was a delight to see Jacob so chipper.

Even when the rain came in the early afternoon, it did not dampen Jacob's spirits. He plowed on ahead like a little mote of light, guiding them on to sunlit lands. Roderick on the other hand was fairly miserable by the third or fourth hour of the deluge and could do little more than retreat further and further into the hood of his cloak.

That evening, it was Roderick's turn to peel off his boots and give his aching feet some relief. His footwear was in far better shape than Jacob's, but the dampness amplified every irritation. If Bethany had been there, she'd have offered him a hot and salty foot soak.

They camped under the shelter of a few meager striplings, but the trees were so thin and scraggly they did little to shelter them from the never-ending showers. Despite the soggy conditions, Jacob drifted off to sleep straight away. Roderick waited to see if his dreams would trouble him, but his face was placid, with nary a line to trouble it. The long slog through the rain must have knocked the stuffing clean out of him. He slept the blessed sleep of contented exhaustion. Hopefully that would mean another peaceful night.

When Roderick looked up from his prayers a little while later, Kendall was sitting on the ground nearby. The old scholar never turned in when they did and, predictably, was still awake.

"So, Master Kendall," Roderick said. "What do you make of this rain? Think it'll let up anytime soon? I don't know how much more of this dreary slush I can take." Even the patches of woad had eluded them that day. Roderick missed the sun at that moment almost as much as he missed his family. The land had given way to more and more stretches of weather beaten stone and craggy hills against an ever paling sky. These were cold gray days. Winter was coming on with haste, no two ways about it.

"No, I'm afraid the rain will be with us off and on from here on out," Kendall said. "Especially the closer we get to the coast."

Yet another reason to dread the sea.

"Did you travel through the north lands the last time you went to the tower?" Roderick asked.

"No, but I have passed through them many times." Kendall had wrapped himself up in his voluminous green cloak, the rain rolling off his hood in channels like the bars of some watery prison. Roderick had to believe the old Savant must be just as miserable as he was, but his face remained resolute as always.

"I would think librarians would pretty much stay holed up with their books."

"I was not always a librarian. For many years I worked as a scribe in the service of a great lord. He was something of an explorer and I followed him wherever he went. It was through him that I first learned about the motley. It was just a story back then. I never dreamed I'd be caught up in it myself one day."

Nor did I. Roderick shivered and kept talking in order to keep his mind off his misery.

"A part of me—the wet part—wishes I wasn't part of this story. But then when I look at Jacob, I don't know, something tells me that I was meant to do this, that this is where I'm supposed to be. I can't imagine what it must be like to live the life he does—chased by men he doesn't know, no home, no family. Sometimes I wonder about his parents, though. I heard they died, that they were executed even, but that seems hard to figure. He doesn't seem like the child of criminals."

"They were executed the day you found him, I can tell you that much. Dimitrius and Lisel were their names, if memory serves."

Roderick sat up and got a great big drop of rain in the eye for his troubles. "Someone told me they were migrant workers. I don't usually pay attention to what happens with the executions, but that day I wish I had."

"Best not to dwell on what is beyond your power to do anything about. Regret has swallowed more men than the sea." Kendall's somber words carved a chasm of silence in the night between them.

"It was Jacob wasn't it?" Roderick said, the thought suddenly occurring to him. "The magistrate had them killed because of Jacob, didn't he? Why else would they bother with a public execution for migrant workers?"

"That may very well be true. Unfortunately, we will probably never know."

"I wonder if the Thaumaturge wasn't behind it somehow. Sounds like his handiwork." Roderick spit into the mud, wishing there were no such things as Thaumaturges and executions and rain that wouldn't quit. But since wishing was for whistlers, as his father used to say, he consoled himself by imagining that the Thaumaturge, wherever he was, was as soaked and miserable as himself at that moment.

"The machinations of the Thaumaturges range far and wide. Even the members of the Sanctum know little about them."

"Well, they're an awful lot if they think murdering a boy's parents a thing worth doing." Roderick turned to look at Jacob, lying calmly beside him. He wondered if the death of his parents might not be the real cause of his nightmares. "I don't suppose there's any chance I'll sleep tonight, now that I've got to thinking about what happened to those poor folk."

"Shall I make you some tea?" Kendall offered. "I have a recipe that often helps to soothe one's troubles."

Roderick sat up again, trying in vain to wipe his brow from all the rain dripping down upon him. "Yes, I suppose that would do. If you think you can manage it in this infernal drench."

Kendall often made tea at night to share with his companions, though Jacob would only drink it if mixed with berries. The old scholar kept a quaint little kettle in his satchel for such purposes, an ingenious brass contraption. It had a little tray inside it for storing the pouches of tea and the clever metal cups which collapsed flat when Kendall was done using them. Like many of the Savant's possessions, it had the look of foreign lands about it, with clever etchings on the surface depicting designs both exotic and mysterious.

Kendall produced more flameroot from his pouch; a single stalk was all that he needed for a cup of tea. It flared up even in the rain, yet another of its advantages over fire. Kendall inserted it into the ground and propped his kettle over it by means of a long willowy branch. Once the water began to steam, the rain hissed against the kettle, producing little flashes of smoke. Kendall poured the cup and sprinkled a bit of powder into it, and then stirred it in with the end of a twig.

"There you go." Kendall handed the cup to Roderick.

"That's very kind of you. What did you put in it?"

"It's called *sarance*, a mixture of crag roots and desert spices. It will help you sleep."

"It tastes like mint," Roderick said, savoring the sweet liquid. It was the best-tasting thing he'd had since the journey began. The steamy substance went down smooth, warming him from the inside out. His eyelids grew heavier with each sip. Soon he set down the cup and curled up near Jacob. Even the ground didn't feel as wet with the toasty tea flowing inside him. He relaxed and made himself comfortable, as if he were stretched out in front of the hearth in his cottage and not out amidst these craggy plains. Thoughts of the execution and Jacob's nightmares faded from his thoughts. He drifted off to sleep, visions of Aisha playing with her ball near the hearth slipping into his thoughts, wrapped in the aroma of his wife's cooking wafting from the kitchen. The air grew sweet and homey, infused with the sort of enduring warmth that comes from happy memories.

12

HOWLING ON THE HEATH

oderick awoke to the sound of distant howling across the plains. The morning glimmered on the horizon like a fuse set to alight the day. The rain had mercifully died away in the night, but the winds were picking up, their whistling notes melding with the mournful baying in an unsettling harmony.

Jacob remained fast asleep, but Kendall stirred in the dim half light.

"Ah, good, you're awake," Kendall said.

"Those are wolves, aren't they?" Roderick shivered, half from the blustering winds, half from the haunting strains.

"Yes," Kendall said. "And that can mean no good." He rose and donned his skullcap and began fastening his cloak.

"Do you think they're on the hunt?" Roderick knew little of wolves except what he'd heard from the trappers and hunters who passed through Briar's Glen. They mostly painted a grisly picture, and the howling on the heath brought back afresh all their horrible stories.

"We have little fear of wolves on their own," Kendall said. "It is the company they may keep which gives me cause for concern."

"You think the Thaumaturge is using wolves to track us down?" Roderick asked, hoping this was not what Kendall meant.

"I would not put anything past him. If anyone could harness the Iddlglim and their blood wolves to do his bidding it would be a Thaumaturge. But it may be they are hunting on

93

their own. Either way, we do not want to run afoul of them. Rouse the boy. He does not appear to be having any nightmares. It should be safe to wake him."

All it took was a light touch from Roderick to stir Jacob, though he only rolled over lethargically and stared up at the early morning stars, spread across the heavens like spilled salt on a midnight blue tablecloth.

"Is it time to go already?" Jacob rubbed the sleep from his eyes with the backs of his two little fists. "What's that sound?"

"Wolves," Roderick said. "Now up, up, it's time for a quick bite and we're off."

"We're having wolves for breakfast?" Jacob asked.

Roderick ruffled the top of Jacob's head. "No, sleepy, that's wolves howling off in the distance."

Kendall thrust a wooden vial into Roderick's hand.

"Sprinkle this on yourself and the boy," he instructed. "Make sure you cover every bit of you, especially your skin."

"What's it for?" Roderick removed the stopper and sniffed the container. Whatever was inside had no odor whatsoever.

"It is *invios*," Kendall said. "A concoction used by the Savants to throw enemies off our trail. It will mask our scent from the wolves."

Roderick set about applying the powder inside the vial. Jacob was not overly happy with the procedure, but Roderick handed him a piece of fruit and assured him that it was necessary. The powder dissolved a few seconds after it hit their skin and clothing so that, once applied, it was entirely invisible.

"How long will it last?" Roderick asked. The light was warming its way up the sky, rapidly dissolving the salty stars.

"Long enough," was Kendall's brusk reply.

The three travelers gathered their things and set off, munching their breakfast as they went.

Wolves for breakfast. Roderick shuddered at the thought.

Spurred on by the unsettling howls, they went faster than usual, but not as fast as they might have; the recent rains made the rocks slippery and traversing the endless rise and fall of the hills sapped their strength. The crumpled, dingy sky hung over them as close as breath. There was enough light to see by, but it was a hollow, empty luster which failed to cheer the soul.

Thankfully, the rolling hills kept the wolves out of sight and eventually, the baying died away. By noon the sun made a feeble attempt to push through the soggy rag which was gagging the sky. It wasn't much, but enough to dry Roderick's slumping spirits a touch.

"I think that powder of yours worked," Roderick said.

"Do not be so sure," Kendall replied. "We're not out of the woad yet, as they say. Blood wolves are cunning, often stalking their prey in silence when led by their Iddlglim masters."

Oh, buttons. Didn't he ever have good news?

Ill at ease again, Roderick pressed on across the rocky plains. But the climbing terrain and a stiff headwind made the going harder than ever. When it became clear that Jacob was at the end of his strength, they found a hollow amongst a few scattered rocks to shelter themselves from the "blusteries," as Jacob called the unrelenting winds. They huddled together in silence, listening for any sign of the wolves, but nothing could be heard above the whistling gales.

After a lunch of flavorless hard tack for the adults and dried fruit for Jacob, they unstiffened and set out again. They did not press themselves much though, for even Kendall and Roderick were dragging their feet by then.

"I don't like wolves," Jacob said as night came on.

"Nor do I," Roderick said. "Though I hear they make for a lovely breakfast."

The comment failed to draw a smile from Jacob. "They remind me of the things that chase me in my dreams."

Ah, those cursed dreams again.

"One day, you'll be free of them," Roderick said. "One day soon."

The rain started up again. Between that and the oncoming

night, traveling the heath was like walking around in a room surrounded by foggy windows. Jacob stared out into the encroaching dark as if fearing that something was out there.

Roderick put his hand on Jacob's shoulder. His small muscles were tight as a string. "Did you have more dreams last night?"

"Yes. I thought they couldn't find me when I was awake, but maybe they can."

"I know dreams can seem very real when you're having them, but in the morning, you always wake up and they lose their power. They can only affect us if we dwell on them."

Jacob's wet hood rippled across his face in the wind. "But these aren't regular dreams; they're different."

Roderick tugged at his ear, as if trying to coax a wise proverb out of his head, one which would soothe Jacob's fears. He had hoped Kendall was wrong about the nature of the dreams.

"They tell me they'll find me," Jacob went on. "They say I took something from them, something that belongs to them."

"Now don't you fear, Jacob," Roderick said. "I will protect you." *Was that the best he could do?* If only Beth were here. She was the one who had the way with words.

He wished just then that he could carry Jacob on these northern winds, riding all the way to the end of their journey, outdistancing all the nightmares and Thaumaturges and wolves of the world.

Jacob gripped Roderick's arm, but he kept staring out into the darkness, his eyes shifting from shadow to shadow.

"The feyglimmer, that's what they said it was called. They said I took it, but I don't remember taking anything. I wish they would leave me alone."

"Oh, Jacob, so do I. So do I."

Jacob began to cry softly. Though Roderick was exhausted, he picked him up and carried him for a while, Jacob's tears mixing with the steady, falling rain.

For the next two days they heard no more from the wolves, but the rain had plenty to say. It pittered and pattered and splunked and sloshed, over, under, and all around them. At times it was little more than a drizzle, but the sheer incessantness of it drained the little company of their resolve drop by persistent drop.

They were now a few miles north of Grimsford. Since it was officially part of the Halicon Empire, under normal circumstances it would have been a safe place to stop and lodge for the night, but they were afforded no such luxury on this occasion. Instead of a warm fire and a cooked meal at a cozy inn, they spent another night out on the rain-soaked Caledonian heath.

The heavens poured out their abundance all afternoon. Though the landscape transformed from scraggly, rocky steppes into some of the greenest, most luscious grasslands Roderick had ever seen, the eternal damp made it difficult to enjoy.

"Is there any way you can conjure up something to keep us dry?" Roderick asked as they made camp that night. Jacob passed out under one of the trees almost as soon as they stopped moving. Little feet were not meant to cover such distances day after day.

"I'm afraid alchemy affords very little mastery over things like rain. I can make you some more *sarance* tea, though, if you like," Kendall said.

"No, thank you. I've an inkling Jacob might need me tonight and that tea of yours makes me sleep a little too sound."

Kendall answered with an indifferent lift of his eyebrows and went on preparing the pot.

"So this alchemy stuff is only good for smoke, then? No chance of conjuring us up a little shelter or at least some decent food?" Roderick was still unsure how such things worked. "I think if I have to eat another bit of that hard tack, my tongue will fall out of my mouth." Beth and her wonderful cooking seemed further than ever at that moment.

"No, it cannot do any of that either."

"Well, I suggest you work on that in the future, as part of your scholarly pursuits."

"I'll take that into consideration." Though Kendall's expression did not change, Roderick could hear the smile in his voice.

Maybe the old scholar had a sense of humor after all.

"How did you learn that smoke trick of yours though?" Roderick asked. If he couldn't sleep, he might as well pass the time in conversation. Though they'd been together for more than a week now, Kendall was still more mystery than not. With no formal education himself, Roderick was frankly intimidated by the man's superior knowledge. He had always had that problem with learned men. He knew the limits of his small mind. He knew he'd never attain the Savant's level of learning, but he didn't let that keep him from asking questions, even if he didn't always understand the answers.

"It's a skill that's been passed down over hundreds of years. I learned it like you would learn most things, from living teachers and dead writers who recorded what they knew in books. To be honest, most of my learning has come from the latter. Books are much more patient with their students than men."

"I should like to see the inside of the great library of Evenspire one day," Roderick said. "Even if it would be just to wander amongst the shelves and take in the smell of the place."

"The tales do not do it justice. I believe only the great archives of Zantium would have surpassed it." Kendall's eyes glinted with faraway longing.

"Zantium? That jiggles something in my memory, but I can't quite place it," Roderick said, scratching his forehead.

"The ancient city, the one which was destroyed."

"Ah..." something finally clicked in the back of Roderick's mind. "But wasn't that just an old legend? You're not saying it was a real city are you?"

"Oh yes, very real. I've been to the ruins."

Roderick was beginning to believe there were fewer places the old Savant hadn't been than ones he had.

"What happened to it?" His eyes locked in on Kendall. All thoughts of sleep fled. The thirst for the pith of the story was upon him.

"You remember when we spoke of the Night of Ten Thousand Shadows?"

"Partly. I'm no good for remembering details, though. You'd best remind me."

"The first motley's magic brought forth hordes of creatures from the shadow realm. Scathen, they were called in the old books, shades of pure darkness sprung to life out of the nightmares of men. Zantium was where they struck first. It was the jewel of Arinn, the star which burned brightest, and so they hated it more than all other places. Darkness descended upon the city and from there it spread across the land. The places where we now walk were not as deeply affected, but Zantium still bears the taint after all these years. If the magic of the motley returns, I do not believe our world will be able to recover this time. It is far easier to tear down a world than it is to build it back up."

"I suppose so. Still, things aren't all that bad yet, are they? And even if this darkness you're talking about does come back, couldn't Jacob use the magic against it? Or at least pop away to safety like he did before?"

"It takes far too much knowledge to control the magic; a mere child could never hope to master it. And down through the centuries, all the motleys who have ever been have always been children. The magic never comes to the learned and the wise."

"Then how does it choose who will be a motley? And for that matter, who caused the curse to begin with?"

"That I do not know, for none of the legends speak of it.

Nor do they tell what the connection is between the motleys, though one theory is that they are all descendants of the first motley, though there again, no records have survived to bear that out."

In that moment Jacob let out a painful cry in his sleep. He began to toss and turn in ways that had become all too familiar. Roderick reached down and stroked his face.

"It's all right Jacob," he muttered.

"Perhaps it would be best if we do not speak of such things, especially not in the hours of darkness." Kendall sipped his tea grimly, as if it were the last cup he would take before some terrible battle.

All this talk of Zantium and magic and creatures from other realms played with Roderick's imagination. With each passing day, it seemed like the old tales threatened to cross into this world, but in ways that were hard to predict.

Fighting off the shivers such thoughts gave him, Roderick wrapped his arms around Jacob and prayed that all those fantastical things would stay trapped in the stories where they belonged.

The rain let up around midday the following day, but the respite was short-lived. As they took their rest and suffered through yet another bland lunch, the overcast sky told them it was only a temporary pardon from their eternal sentence of sogginess.

Still, they tried to enjoy it while it lasted.

Master Kendall took the opportunity to scribble down some notes in his book while Jacob played hopscotch on six large flat stones nearby.

"May I ask what you're writing?" Roderick inquired.

"Oh, it's just an old habit of mine," Kendall replied from the weathered rock upon which he sat. "Wherever I travel I write down the conditions, descriptions of the land, personal observations, those sorts of things—in case I should ever need to refer to them in the future."

"So that helps you in your studies?"

"Yes. You can learn much from books and other men, but when you've been there yourself—well, that is a lens twice polished."

Jacob left off his game and started munching on a bit of fruit. While Kendall scratched away at his paper, Jacob stole quietly up behind him. He eyed Kendall's handiwork, trying not to let on what he was doing.

"Jacob," Roderick said, "are you curious about what Master Kendall is writing? Would you like him to read you a bit of it?"

Jacob froze where he stood, a slice of fruit dangling halfway in his mouth and halfway out. He shook his head emphatically.

"I don't need to read it to you, do I?" Kendall looked back over his shoulder. "You already know how to do that yourself, don't you?"

The fruit started to slide down an ever-increasing trickle of drool.

"Is that true, Jacob?" Roderick asked, coming over. "Do you know how to read?"

Jacob shrugged and Roderick knelt down in front of him. He wiped Jacob's chin gently and looked him in the eye.

"It's nothing to be ashamed of. Why, I'd love to be able to read myself, but I've never had anyone to teach me."

Jacob shoved the fruit back in his mouth. He chewed on it for a few more moments before answering.

"It's not that hard," he mumbled at length.

"Well, perhaps you could teach me one day, then," Roderick said.

Jacob nodded, dropping his gaze to stare at the tips of his shoes poking out from beneath his cloak.

"And who taught you to read, Jacob? Where did you learn?" Roderick asked.

Jacob shrugged again and bounced nervously back and forth on his feet.

"You learned from your parents, didn't you?" Kendall rose and slipped his notebook back into his satchel.

"Jacob, is that true?" Roderick asked.

Jacob's head bobbed up and down a single time.

"But I thought they were field workers?" Roderick regretted the question the moment it left his lips. A look of terrible sorrow came over Jacob's face. He pulled his cloak tight and turned his back towards them. He wandered back over to the hopscotch rocks and hunkered down. His little body began to shake as he fought not to give into tears.

"Best not to talk of them, I think," Kendall said in a low voice. "We've tarried here long enough, anyway. We should be off."

Roderick started towards Jacob, but he must have heard Master Kendall's words. He sauntered over and gathered his things. Roderick and Kendall shouldered their own burdens wordlessly.

Words did more harm than good sometimes. Oh, that he could reel in the castings of his careless tongue.

He was actually grateful for the aches and pains of the road as they set off again. They took his mind off the pain he'd caused Jacob by bringing up his parents. It hadn't been two weeks since they were killed. How hard it must be for him to bear such loss.

They trekked across the rolling heath in a heavy silence all through the morning and into the afternoon. To make matters worse, the rain resumed its relentless assault on the land and Roderick's spirits. In the midst of all that gray, misty, onslaught he lost track of time. At one point he felt the night must surely have come, but everything had been so dark and bleak for so long he couldn't be sure.

The angry rain continued to cavil until it broke out into a full blown storm. Thunder and lightning erupted on the heath, but there was no place to find shelter, so on they marched. As the weary companions crested a hill they caught sight of several figures heading up the slope. They looked to be on horseback.

"Is that armor they're wearing?" Roderick asked after staring at them for some time. Shimmers of light peeked out from beneath their clothing whenever the lightning flashed.

"Yes," Kendall said.

His answer sent a quiver of fear down Roderick's back. "Do you think those are more of the Thaumaturge's men?"

"Whoever they are, it looks like they've spotted us," Kendall said.

The rain continued to hammer the heath. Roderick kept his eyes trained on the men while holding tightly to Jacob's hand. On horseback there could be no thought of outrunning these men. The three miserable travelers could do nothing but wait and see what the intentions of these mounted strangers were, whether for good or evil.

13

UNWANTED SHELTER

endall's face mirrored the darkening gloom of the sky. The armor of the approaching soldiers sparked in the lightning as the brimming storm asserted its dominance over the heath. Memories of the soldiers from the Mithrin woods rose like a shadow in Roderick's mind.

I wonder whether or not Kendall's black smoke would work in this downpour?

"Let's hope they're from Middlehelm," Kendall said. "It's not too far from here. They occasionally patrol the few scattered sheep folds who venture over to this side of the Fallowing, though I've never heard of them coming this far out."

Ten horsemen picked their way up the grassy ridge with skill and care. Their mounts did not stamp or skitter, even as lightning lanced down from the heavens all across the heath. At last they came to a stop and fanned out to either side.

"Greetings in the name of the High Lord Emperor," the lead soldier shouted over the pealing thunder. The rain fell even harder at his words, as if the Emperor himself had commanded it.

The man wore a dark gray tabard over his finely crafted plate armor. The symbol on his livery blustered in the wind, unrecognizable, but his round shield was clearly marked with the trappings of the Haliconian Empire: five small silver stars at the points of one large golden one, set in a field of blue. The man raised the visor of his helm, revealing a solemn face framed by black hair and a full mustache. He was of slighter build than his companions, but his gaze was imposing.

Roderick had only ever seen imperial soldiers in Evenspire and had never been stopped by one. Jacob shivered at his side, perhaps from the driving rain, perhaps from fear of the men, perhaps both.

"Greetings," Kendall said. "I was not aware these lands belonged to the Empire."

"Not officially, but the Duke of Middlehelm extends his protection when possible to those of the Emperor's subjects who travel these lands. You don't look like Caledonians. I take it you are citizens of the Empire?"

"We are," Kendall said.

"And what business have you north of the Fallowing?"

"We are traveling west," Kendall said. "We have business to attend to further up-river."

The soldier's eyes narrowed. "Well, it looks like your business will have to wait. Within a day, these lands will be overrun by Iddlglim hordes."

Kendall inclined his head deferentially. "We are grateful for the warning. We shall quit these lands with all due haste."

"Don't the wolf men usually attack unawares?" Roderick addressed the soldier. "How can you be sure they're coming now?"

"The Iddlglim are not capable of pulling off a true invasion," Kendall said confidently. "The tribes are too scattered and they possess no engines of war capable of breaching Middlehelm's walls. The castle can easily repel whatever force they send at it."

"Something's changed." The soldier edged his mount closer so he did not have to speak so forcefully over the rain and thunder. "Our scouts have seen them. They've reported a great host—ten to fifteen thousand strong, coming this way. I doubt even the Fallowing will hold an army of that size back. We suspect they are being organized by some outside force, someone with an interest in sacking the city. We are under orders to escort any Haliconian citizens we come across to

105

Castle Middlehelm by order of the Helm of Brackenland."

"But we are traveling from Vinyon. We are not from Brackenland," Roderick put in, earning an ill-tempered look from Kendall, who clearly did not appreciate his loose tongue.

"You will perish if you stay on this side of the Fallowing and Middlehelm is not the only city in danger. There are rumors of a second force headed for Rill, further west where you're headed.," the soldier said.

"We shall leave these lands ere long. Have no fear," Kendall said. Lightning struck out across the hills to the west. The thunder's raucous reply came close behind it, causing Jacob to jump.

"I'm afraid I cannot allow that." The soldier motioned towards his men. Three of them dismounted and brought their animals forward. The spooled muscles of the horses flexed as they pranced forward in sudden excitement. For a moment Roderick feared they might charge, but their riders quickly reined them in. Still, unmounted the beasts appeared far less tame than before.

"You can come willingly or we can take you by force, but my orders are to bring all Haliconians into the safety of the keep, and that is what I mean to do." The leader allowed his gauntleted hand to rest upon the hilt of his sword.

Kendall glared at the soldier intensely. Roderick wasn't sure who looked more intimidating, the soldier with his nine armored men behind him or the old scholar. A fierce wind blew across the heath and Kendall's cloak flew open, revealing the myriad of pouches and compartments he wore on his vest and belt. His hands moved quickly to pull his cloak tight. Roderick tensed, prepared to fly if the Savant decided to defy the Lord Helm's orders.

"Very well, we shall go with you to the castle," Kendall said.

Roderick let out a grateful sigh, not realizing he'd been holding his breath for some time. Defying the Emperor's men would only have led to trouble. There were no woods to hide in this time. As long as this was not some trick of the Thaumaturge, they could survive a day or two in Middlehelm, especially if an invasion really was on the way.

The three dismounted soldiers stepped forward to help them mount the steeds, but Jacob clung to Roderick's arm and would not let go.

"It'll be okay," Roderick assured him. "They just want us to go to Middlehelm."

"Don't let them take me," Jacob begged. His eyes shone out like beacons of warning in the darkness.

"Are you afraid of the horses?" Roderick asked.

"Hurry along, you little mawker," grumbled the soldier trying to grab hold of Jacob. Jacob darted to the other side of Roderick.

The man was half a head taller, but Roderick looked him in the eye and said in as firm a voice as he could muster. "Just one moment, sir. I'll handle this."

The soldier gave him a cross look and opened his mouth to reply, but the leader of the patrol spoke first.

"Let them sort it out, fenrik. We're already soaked to the bone. Another minute or two won't make any difference."

Knowing this man was a mere fenrik, the lowest rank in the Haliconian army, made it easier for Roderick to excuse his rudeness. Perhaps he had been pressed into service and was merely taking out his frustrations. Roderick decided to give him the benefit of the doubt.

"I'm terribly sorry," Roderick said. "I won't be long."

The soldier backed off and Roderick leaned down to whisper to Jacob. "We have to go with these men. But they're going to take us to a big castle; it will be warm there and we'll be out of the rain and—and maybe we can even find a bed to sleep in."

"You won't let them see my skin?" Jacob whispered back.

"Not a stitch, I promise." Roderick reached down and, after a brief hesitation, Jacob allowed Roderick to lead him to the horse before turning to address the lead soldier. "Sir, if I may ask one favor. The boy is frightfully scared of strangers.

Would it be possible if we rode together?"

"Can you manage a horse?" the leader of the men asked.

Roderick nodded. The only horse he'd ever ridden in his life was farmer Tullum's old work horse, Blandy, and that had not turned out well, but he didn't trust Jacob with these soldiers.

The leader motioned to the man glaring at Jacob. "You will ride with one of the other fenriks."

The soldier did as he was told, but stamped in the loam next to Roderick when he passed, spraying his cloak with mud.

Roderick's doubt was looking less and less beneficial, but he held his tongue. He led Jacob to the horse. Getting him mounted was not difficult, but getting himself up on the monstrous beast in the slippery rain proved to be quite another matter. He fell off not once, but twice. He was now covered in mud and certain the commander would call him out for his lack of horsemanship.

The soldiers chuckled, the surly fenrik most of all, but the lead soldier said nothing, letting Roderick flounder on his own. Roderick's ears went redder than Bethany's radishes. On the third attempt, though, he managed to scramble on top of the beast through sheer desperation. It may have been a small thing in the grand history of the world, but he felt as if he had conquered an army when he finally sat astride the massive beast. He raised his shoulders with what little pride he had left.

The journey thus far had been none too pleasant, but the lofty perch on which he now sat was the epitome of discomfort. His thighs straddled the great beast like a wishbone being pulled apart for the holidays. He slid about in the saddle and wondered how he would ever stay mounted all the way to Middlehelm. But when the leader gave the order, his horse, along with the other destriers, trotted off dutifully down the hill. Roderick had no control whatsoever over the powerful beast beneath him, but the animal was so well-trained that riding it was more like sitting atop a horse of stone than one of flesh.

"You're a good deal better bred than some of these soldiers," Roderick whispered into the animal's ear.

Though Roderick's nerves began to settle somewhat, Jacob still trembled in front of him.

"What's wrong?" Roderick asked.

Jacob jumped again at a monstrous, many-forked bolt which lit up the countryside. Night would be coming on soon and the rain showed no signs of letting up.

"Is it the soldiers?" Roderick pressed him. "Remember what I promised. I won't let them see your skin."

A shudder ran through Jacob's body. "It isn't them. It's the things in the night. They're coming for me. I can feel them drawing close."

"What do you mean?" Roderick leaned in, hoping he had misheard.

But Jacob buried his head in Roderick's cloak and would say no more.

During the journey on horseback, Roderick tried to think as little as possible about Jacob's "things in the night." Perhaps passing a day or two in a fortified castle like Middlehelm would help Jacob feel safe, though Roderick doubted this change in plans sat well with Master Kendall.

They traveled through the long, soppy night and arrived along the southern bank of the Fallowing via ferry just after dawn. After disembarking, Roderick roused the sleeping Jacob so that he would not miss the sight of the great city as they cantered towards the outbreak of walls and towers along the bank of the river. The coal black outer ramparts were ten feet thick and three times as high. A second wall stood a hundred paces beyond the first, just as high and almost as thick.

Beyond the walls a wide paved street stretched all the way into the center of the city. There the castle proper arose in the center like a great mound of mausoleums piled on top of each other. There was something ancient and ponderous about the stonework. The thick, rounded columns, massive buttresses, and stout towers formed a living architectural mountain which felt like it must have been there since the dawn of time.

A central tower rose defiantly, its five thin spires piercing the sky like giant bodkins, daring the wooly clouds to come and rip themselves open should they pass too close. They kept vigilance over the burgundy rooftops of the long lateral buildings surrounding the castle. Not only the castle, but the city walls, pavement, and surrounding buildings looked to all have been cut from the same dark, basalt stone. Mercifully, the rain had ceased an hour before they arrived and now everything still glistened in the post-dawn light.

Jacob yawned, unimpressed with the massive city, as if he had seen it all before. Perhaps he was just too sleepy.

The early risers were already busy making the rounds of the shops. One group of customers banged on the doors of a bakery, grumbling about why the poor proprietor was still in bed. Most of the people they saw were dressed in black. At first Roderick wondered if that were simply the fashion in Middlehelm, but then he remembered that the festival of Winter's Rest must have arrived. He had forgotten all about it in their timeless march through the wilderness. That was just as well, for Winter's Rest was the most depressing holiday of the year as far as he was concerned. It was a time centered around the remembrance of loved ones who had passed on into the Shining Lands, a time of somber faces and dirge-like songs sung into the night. It was customary to light a candle in the window and keep it burning all through the night, each of the six nights of the festival. If the candle went out, it meant bad luck. Roderick thought it was all a load of rubbish. The loss of his parents was hard enough without having to revisit the pain each and every year. It was like reopening closed wounds and he saw little point to it.

"Let the dead rest in peace," he always told Bethany when this time rolled around each year.

The soldiers led them off the main thoroughfare and down a cobblestone road to a wide square in the shadow of the city's inner wall. Everywhere Roderick looked, tents had been erected. Some of them were little more than pieces of canvas propped up on rickety poles. From the sheer number of them there must have been hundreds of refugees. Sickly smoke lilted through the air, as did the foul smells of the inhabitants in this overcrowded section of the city. Despite the vast number of tents, only a handful of folk were up and stirring here. Of those present, few except the children gave the newly arrived party more than a passing glance. A hushed pall hung over the place, making Roderick miss the noise and bustle of the main streets.

The soldiers helped them off their horses and told them to find what space they could amongst the refugees. The commander informed them that bread would be brought in at noon and a clerk would visit in the afternoon to address any grievances or issues they might have, but that no one was to go beyond the castle walls on pain of death.

"So to protect us from getting killed by barbarians you'll kill us yourselves if you have to? That makes perfect sense," Kendall quipped.

The soldier clamped shut his visor and spurred his horse away from the throngs and the offal-scented square without reply.

Kendall waited until the soldiers had gone before informing Roderick of what he planned to do next.

"I'll have us out of here by nightfall," he promised.

"But you saw how many guards were at the gates. If they aren't letting anyone leave then I don't see what chance we have," Roderick said.

"I have a few contacts in the city from my exploring days." Kendall's eyes scanned the castle off in the distance.

"Well, I trust you know what you're doing. You've gotten

us this far in one piece. Only just—be careful is all I'm saying." Roderick had never knowingly defied the authorities in his life and was not looking to get into the habit.

"A good scholar knows how to conduct his research. And no scholar is anything without his sources," Kendall said, pulling out a kerchief to cover his mouth in order to blunt the awful stench around them.

Roderick took his cue from the Savant and did the same. Jacob, now wide awake and leery of the great mass of humanity surrounding them, was the only one who appeared not to be bothered by the smell.

"This camp is no place for us. It's too out in the open, too exposed," Kendall said.

"And the smell doesn't do it any favors," Roderick said. "Do you think the Thaumaturge has men in this city?"

"It is likely, though I've never heard anything definite about his influence in Middlehelm. It would be best to assume that to be the case, however. We need a place to ourselves. There is an inn I stayed at once on Capstone Street where we should be able to find lodging. The owner is a close-lipped man and owes me a favor. We should be safe there."

They shuffled off through the congested tents, strewn haphazardly about the courtyard as if they'd been dropped there by the recent storm

"What's this inn called?" Roderick asked.

"*The Executioner's Corner,*" Kendall said.

Roderick grimaced at the Savant's words. What a terrible name for an inn.

14

CTHE EXECUTIONER'S CORNER

he Executioner's Corner was not nearly as grim on the outside as its name implied. It had brightly painted blue and teal wood paneling and decorative floral carvings on the four stone columns embedded into the façade. Another stone carving rested above the entry transom, this one on a semi-circular slab, depicting a portly executioner sharpening his axe. It was not exactly an appealing picture, but far enough removed from the real thing so as not to jar with the rest of the inn's otherwise pleasing appearance.

Besides the carving above the door, another reason for the inn's unfortunate name was obviously its location. It sat in the corner of what was clearly a square for public executions. It was one of the few grassy areas they had seen inside the city walls. A stony path framed the edge of the square. The customary raised platform and chopping block occupied the center, ensuring a good view of the proceedings. It looked predictably similar to the one in Briar's Glen aside from the close cropped grass and the higher platform. Such places invited little originality. Executions, like most human rituals, thrived on sameness.

Jacob liked the sight even less than Roderick. His head drooped and he turned away, refusing to look at the terrible engine of death.

He's remembering his parents. Oh, dear, why did Kendall have to bring them here of all places?

Though no execution was taking place at the moment, the

square was flooded with people. In fact, aside from the platform and the greenery, it was nearly as packed as the refugee compound. Judging from the quality of the dress and the makeshift habitations of those gathered, it appeared that these people were significantly better-off than those in the first camp. The tents had fewer patches and there were even a few covered wagons. Several of the men sported brass buttons, studded doublets with herringbone stitching, and the sort of billowing pants Roderick often sold to the wealthier merchants who passed through the Glen. If not actual nobility, they were certainly well off. Several even appeared to be attended by servants. Though not entirely wholesome, the smell which pervaded the air here was not nearly as nauseating as their last stop.

Roderick and his companions received quite a few stares here. More than one muffled comment floated their way, along with a few spoken more openly, questioning what right "people like that" had in this area. When Kendall marched up and knocked on the door to the inn, the chiding and scoffing grew even more pronounced. Well-dressed arms folded in judgment and well-groomed mustaches sneered in derision.

Kendall ignored the grumbling and the asides and kept knocking.

"It's closed, street rat!" jeered one of the nearby men, a fellow with a green and yellow doublet made of Evenspire velvet. "*All* the inns in Middlehelm are closed. Full up, you hear?"

Kendall gave him nary a glance, but persisted in his knocking. Jacob ducked behind Roderick.

"And from the looks of you, you wouldn't have the miras to stay at an establishment like the *Corner* even if it was open. So why don't you just skitter on your merry way? That racket is starting to grate on me." Other folk inched closer, anticipating the inevitable outcome of the confrontation.

The next time Kendall set his knuckles to the door, the stranger exploded in a fit of anger. "I thought I told you to quit your bloomin' knocking! I've half a mind to call in the watch. You should be thankful I haven't done so already."

"Maybe we should go," Roderick whispered to Kendall. "He's right. This place is obviously closed."

"I know what I'm about," Kendall said in hushed tones. "The owner will come eventually." He resumed his knocking.

"Come on, Brandon," the well-to-do man snarled, motioning to a lumbering tough standing nearby. Roderick had assumed he was just a part of the crowd. The man was several inches taller even than Kendall and his shirt strained to contain his massive arms and chest.

As the giantish fellow advanced, Kendall finally took his attention off the door and stepped in front of Roderick.

"Gentlemen, I do not wish to make a scene," he said.

But the tough kept coming.

"Ah, now he's all lace and tears!" The wealthy man scoffed, stepping in behind his overgrown bruiser.

Roderick hoped this man did not hit as hard as the Briar's Glen ruffians, but it did not look promising.

Jacob tugged at Roderick's cloak. "Let's go," he said.

Roderick gave Kendall an imploring look, but the old man had his eyes locked on the two men.

The wealthy man cracked his knuckles as if he were the one about to lay into the travelers. "I'll teach you how to answer your betters. Ol' Brandon here'll give you a box that'll set you back a tooth or two and *then* we'll call the watch and have you carted off to where you belong."

Before the men could take another step, Kendall stepped forward and flicked a handful of white powder in their faces. A sweet, mildly sickening odor filled the air. When no smoke came along with it Roderick froze, expecting a fight, but the men barely had time to give a start of surprise before their eyes rolled back in their heads and they crashed to the ground, landing hard on the cobblestones.

Kendall glanced around at the crowd. Half the square must have seen the men go down. Within moments the whole area was a-flutter. One man ran off down a side street.

"Quickly, we must leave this place at once—" Kendall

began. The next moment, clicks and clacks came from behind them and a man with a bushy beard jutted his head through a crack in the inn's door.

"Ah, Kendall—" came the voice of the bearded figure. "If I'd have known it was you, I'd have come sooner. Now hurry inside before the watch shows up."

With the murmuring chatter growing louder by the moment, and every eye in the square upon them, the three travelers disappeared through the entrance to the inn.

"This is Merrill, the owner of the inn," Kendall introduced their rescuer. He looked as if he had partaken a little too much of his own fare over the years for he had a sizable paunch and jowls and chubby hands to match.

"Welcome to *The Executioner's Corner*," Merrill said, his friendly grin out of place with the awful name of his establishment. Behind him, coming through the foyer door, drifted rumbling conversations and clinking plates and mugs.

"I have need of a room, Merrill," Kendall answered before Roderick could reply to the greeting. "But first there is the matter of our little squabble on the stoop. Would you see my companions to a safe place while I make arrangements to deal with the matter?"

"Of course, Master Kendall. Anything for you," Merrill answered energetically, perhaps a bit too energetically, betraying a touch of nerves. "All I've got left is the spare room. Don't like to rent that one out, it's rather small, but I suppose it'll have to do."

"That will be fine."

The innkeep escorted Roderick and Jacob into the crowded common room. Roderick did not return the countless stares he received, but he felt every one of them. There must have been fifty people packed inside, all of them dressed even better than those from the square.

Merrill led them briskly up a short flight of stairs to a small room on the second floor. He showed them inside and muttered a brisk farewell. Then he slammed the door before Roderick could turn around. So much for hospitality.

But if the service was less than exemplary, the room, small though it was, was nicer than anything Roderick would have been able to afford on his own. The wooden walls had a deep russet hue and none of the chinks and cracks of Roderick's cottage. Two beds and a nightstand with a lantern were lined up against the wall to his left and a window hung opposite the door, though its panes were clouded and let in very little light.

As tired as he was, Roderick was too high-strung to lie down and enjoy the inviting beds. He sat on the edge of one and held Jacob, trying to warm him from their long damp journey.

"Do you think Master Kendall's powder will get us into trouble?" Jacob asked.

"We'll be fine," Roderick said. "He knows how to handle himself, no doubt."

Though Roderick certainly meant the words, as time wore on and Kendall did not return, doubt did set in. Jacob drifted off to sleep in his arms. An hour later, Roderick's confidence in Kendall's return had worn down to a thread, but it was just then that the door opened wide.

"Oh, Master Kendall, I'm so glad to see you!" Roderick said as their guide stepped inside and shut the door. Jacob awoke amidst the commotion. "Is everything all right?"

"Nothing a little coin and some greased palms couldn't handle," Kendall said. "Though it took a visit to the garrison. The Duke certainly has his men on a tight rein."

"Did the watch come and investigate the disturbance, then?"

"Yes, not long after we came into the inn."

"And you...you bribed them, I take it?" Roderick asked. He felt bad accusing Kendall of using such a shady tactic, but the Savant had already said as much.

"Naturally," Kendall said. Noting Roderick's look of disapproval, he added, "I realize you have not traveled much, but in most places in this world I think you will find that justice still goes to the highest bidder. So it is in Middlehelm at any rate."

Roderick's frown deepened. "That doesn't mean it's the right thing to do," he said quietly.

"Wither and woe, I'm in no mood to endure a lecture from you," Kendall snapped, looking testier than Roderick had seen him in many days. "Not today or any other for that matter. I got us out of trouble and that is all that need concern you."

Roderick cleared his throat. If Kendall meant to do things his own way, there was probably not much Roderick could do, but the prospect saddened him all the same. He did not like to think less of this man who had done so much for them.

"And the two men?" Roderick asked, changing the subject. "I forgot to ask how you knocked them down."

"Just a bit of alchemy," Kendall said. "I used *sarance* on them, the same substance I put in your tea, only more concentrated."

"Oh, my," Roderick said, greatly relieved. "I was worried you might have…"

"Killed them? What do you take me for? The Savants do not shed blood unless absolutely necessary. But we have been noticed and that damage cannot be undone. People will talk and that is what I had most hoped to avoid."

"But no one here knows who Jacob is."

"Can you be sure? And even if that were true, the news of two able-bodied men knocked to the pavement by an old traveler will not go unnoticed. It may eventually find its way to the ears of the Thaumaturge even if he is not in Middlehelm and he will recognize it as the work of the Sanctum. Our need to escape this city is greater than ever. We cannot afford to let him sniff out our trail."

"So what's your plan?" Roderick was hoping they would get to spend at least one night in a decent bed.

"I shall leave at once in order to begin looking for a way out of the city. You stay with the boy. Do not open the door to anyone save myself or Merrill. I will instruct him to bring you food at midday and at supper."

"Does he have any fruit?" Jacob asked. He'd been sitting on the bed staring vaguely about the room, but he perked up at the mention of food.

"I'll be sure and have him get some," Kendall said. "I hope to be back long before dark, but if I'm not, you two bed down for the night without me. Only make sure you're packed and ready to go. If I have to wake you, there'll be no time for preparing your things."

"Very well," Roderick said. "We'll be ready."

Kendall went to the door. "Get some rest while you can," he said. Then he stepped out into the hallway, locking the door with a robust click.

The inn, despite being filled to capacity, was a terribly quiet place. Neither sound nor sign of another living soul could be detected while they remained inside the room. Roderick wondered at the silence, but in the end decided it was a good thing. If they couldn't hear the other guests, hopefully that meant the guests couldn't hear them either. The sound of the occasional bird fluttering by outside was the only interruption.

After getting sufficiently dry, Roderick and Jacob lay down and let the weariness of the road sink into the soft cotton sheets covering the pillowy beds. They were just dozing off a short time later when Merrill and a young lad of about twelve or thirteen opened the door and came in bearing two large trays laden with all manner of tantalizing victuals.

"I know it's Winter's Rest and all, but I thought you might enjoy something a little more scrumptious than date cakes and milk," the innkeep said brightly. He appeared to have calmed down from when they first met.

Roderick thanked him profusely and he and Merrill chatted while the serving boy laid out the trays. Merrill spoke in a warm and friendly manner, going on about his inn—how it had grown, its prime location, and the increasing number of nobility and wealthy merchants who had come to stay there in recent years. He professed to know little of the coming invasion and brushed it off as an overreaction by the rulers of the city.

"But I'll not complain. It's been a wonder for business!"

Jacob hid between the two beds as soon as the visitors arrived, only peeking out around the edge of the bed posts once or twice to catch a glimpse of the young fellow doing all the work while Merrill talked.

Though Roderick enjoyed the innkeep's conversation, he was not at all sad when he left. At last he could turn his attention to the sumptuous provisions. It was a feast fit for a king, especially compared to the paltry meals he had eaten of late. It even surpassed what he might have gotten in his own cottage. Bethany was a wonderful cook, but she could only do so much with the humble gleanings from their garden and such foodstuffs as Roderick could afford to bring home from the market. Merrill had brought in trays brimming with such things as Roderick had only heard about from merchants and other wealthy folk.

There were two hay-yellow peaches, a cluster of the darkest grapes, and even an orange, or as it was more commonly called in Vinyon province, a "golden apple." Though Roderick had never tried any such delicacies and would have dearly loved to have done so then, Jacob needed the fruit more than he did. But Roderick was hardly left wanting. In addition to the fruit, there was also a fresh loaf of herb bread that fairly glowed with aroma and savoriness, a great hunk of goat cheese, and a steaming bowl of white bean soup. To top it all off, several jelly cookies were spread invitingly upon one of the earthenware plates.

The two famished travelers settled into their meal, taking their time, and enjoying every bit of the innkeep's sumptuous provender. They spoke very little until towards the end when all that remained of the fruit were skins and seeds and one slice of orange. That is when Jacob leaned back against his pillow and said, "Do you think that boy who brought us this gets to eat fruit every day?"

"I should say not," Roderick said. "He's just a servant. This kind of food is likely reserved for the innkeep's paying customers."

"But it must be nice to have a bed like this to sleep in every night." Jacob fingered the last section of orange.

"Yes, now that is certainly true," Roderick said. "Would you like to work in an inn like this some day?"

Jacob let out a long sigh. "I just want to be normal. I don't care what I do when I grow up as long as I can just be like everybody else." He rolled over on his side and bit into the orange.

Roderick smoothed the back of Jacob's cloak. "You will be," he promised. "Very soon." A powerful longing for his family overtook him once again. The thought of Jacob, normal and safe, returning home with him to become a part of that family melted away all the tired, lonesome weight of the road.

Jacob eased into Roderick's arms and soon fell fast asleep. After laying his head on the pillow, Roderick found that he could not join him in that longed-for release. He was too worried about Master Kendall.

Dinner came and went and still the Savant had not returned. Jacob remained fast asleep, thankfully with no nightmares.

How Roderick would have loved to have joined him, but his worries would not allow it.

The evening meal was much more modest, though it did feature a fine turnip soup and more cheese and bread. More fruit was brought in for Jacob, but he slept so peacefully Roderick did not have the heart to wake him.

In the end, the weariness of the road surmounted Roderick's worries and, with no one else to talk to and keep him awake, he slipped off into a deep and lovely sleep. And yet, as the night wore on, his dreams were increasingly tinged by darkness and shadow.

15

AWAKENED

midst the press and gaggle of humanity which swelled the city of Middlehelm, amongst all the fret and wringing of hands which accompanied the looming threat of war, one man trembled more than any other. But not out of fear of the Iddlglim and the coming invasion. The threat Lord Bryne faced was far more imminent.

The overdressed nobleman sat rubbing his jeweled signet ring as though it were a talisman which might protect him from the shadowy figure before him. A fine meal of venison and minted squash sat in front of Bryne, cold and untouched. The Thaumaturge's plate, by way of contrast, looked clean enough to have already been washed.

"I assure you my men have ranged all across the province looking for the motley," said the aristocrat.

"That is of no consequence." The Thaumaturge leaned forward threateningly. "He is here—now—in Middlehelm, you fool."

"Oh, well, that is a different matter." Bryne fetched a white, silken kerchief from his vest and mopped his brow. "Tell me where he is and I'll dispatch my men at once."

"It won't be that simple," The Thaumaturge said in low, unnerving tones.

"Y-you're worried about the Duke's men?"

"You think I care one jot about the Duke and his pathetic army?" the Thaumaturge asked.

"Well, no. Of course not. It's just that—"

"Stop your gabbling and let me finish." The Thaumaturge rose from the table and loomed like a tombstone at midnight. The poor fellow gave a start and his mouth flew open, but his words died in his throat.

The Thaumaturge glowered at the tweed before him. He was nothing more than a tin and copper merchant whose family had bought its way into a title. A real nobleman might have had some upbringing, some training, perhaps even experience serving in the Haliconian army, but not this man. With lace at his neck and a peacock feathered vest cradling his ample belly, he had all the reek of new wealth about him. But that meant he could more easily be manipulated, for he knew what would happen to him if that wealth were suddenly taken away.

"The magic has now awakened within him. Even if your soldiers were to capture the child—which is highly doubtful —they would not be able to hold him for long."

The nobleman nodded so deeply and slowly it might as well have been a bow. He stared up at the Thaumaturge, blinking compulsively, his bejeweled hands quaking.

"His capture is no longer your concern," The Thaumaturge continued. "You have proven yourself utterly useless in that regard. I will see to his capture personally, but once I have him I will need safe passage out of the city. This is where I offer you a chance to redeem yourself."

The man's shaking hand reached for a glass of nectar-sweet, but instead of taking a drink as he had intended, he inadvertently knocked the pewter goblet to the floor where it hit with a loud clank. The nobleman did not even bother to look at the mess, so transfixed was he by the Thaumaturge's stare.

"Well? Can you get me passage out of the city or not?"

"Oh, I beg your mercy, but—but—" the man stammered. His lips shriveled around his faltering mouth.

"What is it? Out with it, or I'll pull your tongue from your mouth and make it speak on its own. Perhaps if it were disconnected from your vaporous brain it would prove more intelligent." A ghastly light issued forth from the Thaumaturge's sleeves, licking his gnarled fingers with a phantom flickering.

"The Duke—" the man cried out, fanning himself with the white kerchief as if waving a flag of surrender. "The Duke has given orders—"

"I know that, you prawn. That's why I've come to you." The Thaumaturge raised his glowing hands, no doubt to make good on his threat of relieving the hapless noble of his tongue.

"But—but he won't take bribes, not this one—he's too loyal to the Emperor."

"I don't care if you have to bribe the Emperor himself," the Thaumaturge threatened in rumbling tones. "You will get me passage out of Middlehelm or I'll send this food away and dine on your innards instead!"

The Thaumaturge's ghostly fingers curled into fists and banged on the table. The utensils and settings jumped in the air, but quickly fell back into place. One thing did not, however—the Lord Bryne. He slumped in his chair, passed out from sheer terror.

The Thaumaturge rolled his eyes. Nobles. They were as useless as brigands.

As usual, he would be forced to take matters into his own hands.

An explosion of broken glass shattered Roderick's dreams, jarring him awake. Feeling no draft, his first thought was that he must have dreamt it, but shouts from outside the building made him think otherwise. A window must have broken somewhere in the neighborhood. Roderick thought he heard a woman scream. Merrill had mentioned an alleyway running behind the inn; it sounded like it was coming from some building along that street.

"It's here."

It was Jacob who spoke, but he remained invisible in the darkness. Roderick fumbled about on the nightstand, groping for the lamp. "Jacob, what do you mean?"

Jacob's ragged breathing was so loud it seemed to come from every side.

"What's going on? Speak to me," Roderick said.

"It's coming," Jacob whispered.

At last Roderick found the lamp and pressed down on the flint switch to light it. After several frustrating attempts the flame took. The light revealed Jacob, sitting up in bed, his patchwork face glistening with sweat, trembling in fear like a kite stuck in a tree. The sounds outside ceased, but Roderick doubted they were the source of Jacob's concern.

"Oh, child." Roderick wrapped his arms around him. "You've had another bad dream."

"No. It's not a dream this time. It got out. It got out."

Though Roderick did not fully understand his words, their breathless tone bristled down his neck.

"What got out? What are you talking about?"

Jacob kept shaking his head and repeating, "I'm sorry," over and over again, his voice growing quieter each time until he was only mouthing the words.

Roderick's mind flitted this way and that, trying to think how he could console Jacob. He had never seen him this distressed.

"Now calm down, Jacob," he said. "I've got you. Remember my promise? I won't let any of those monsters from your dreams get you."

Roderick tightened his embrace, but Jacob did not stop trembling.

"Not this time," he said. "You can't stop it. It's too powerful."

No sooner had the words left his lips than the door clicked open. In the dim recesses of his mind Roderick recalled that Kendall was long overdue, but something told him this was not the return of their guide.

His hair stood on end. He couldn't say how he knew it, but there was something *otherly* on the far side of that door, something not of this world, something that was not supposed to be there.

The door flew open. A stiff breeze rushed in and blew out the lamp, plunging the room into darkness save for a small snatch of light coming in from the hallway. Silhouetted in the opening stood the terrible thing which Roderick had feared, the thing which Roderick had somehow known must exist and yet should not. Barely rising above the bedpost, it had no clear shape or definition; haze and shadow wrapped themselves about it like an ever-shifting muslin. A terrible coldness radiated from it. The chill sank through Roderick's skin and went straight to his heart.

Its two eyes, simmering crucibles of crimson wrath, floated in the pitch of night. They gave off a pale, sickly glow, like old coals in a dying fire. The malevolent power behind them struck Roderick with tangible force, knocking the breath clean out of him.

Dread of the shadow overcame him. He froze, helpless to resist as the gauzy blackness enveloped Jacob and dragged him from Roderick's arms. The next thing he knew, Jacob's limp form, muzzled in darkness, was drifting through the doorway. Though Jacob did not stir or resist or cry out, his eyes were wide with terror.

Roderick's mind raced after him, but his body remained helplessly chained to the bed. And then, just like that, Jacob was gone, whisked away into the shadows, leaving Roderick frozen where he lay, staring at the empty doorway in abject horror.

16

DESCENT INTO DARKNESS

oderick wasn't sure how much time he lost staring at the empty doorway, but when at last he came to his senses it was still swaying on its hinges.

He shoved on his shoes and snatched his knife off the night stand, but didn't bother with his coat or anything else. He bolted into the hallway and flew down the steps, rattling against the banisters, careening his way to the ground floor.

A single flickering lamp hung from the ceiling of the common room. He started for the front door, but a thick plank barred it shut. It would take too much time to remove, and the door was probably locked. Roderick plunged through the only other door in the room, the one to the kitchen. He smashed into a table, sending pots and pans and all manner of metal things crashing to the floor. Objects hanging on the walls and from the ceiling swung threateningly in the unlit room, like jagged warning signs left by the dark creature which had kidnapped Jacob. Roderick picked himself up and took a moment to shake off his fears.

Hurry, Devinson, he could be anywhere by now!

He glimpsed another open doorway at the far end of the long, rectangular room. Avoiding the other tables and the shadowy cooking instruments, he picked his way to the exit, at last coming out into the narrow alleyway at the back of the inn.

Nothing stirred along the desolate backstreet. A few rancid barrels and a hay wagon next to the door offered possible hiding spots, but he doubted what he was hunting had any need to hide. The recollection of that dark creature made Roderick wonder just what he planned on doing if he found it, but he pushed the thought out of his mind and dashed off down the stretch of alley that looked the longest, the one to his left.

He shot out into an intersection with another alleyway, this one even narrower than the first. His eyes darted down the new pathways, with no sign of Jacob or the creature in any direction, only cold, empty moonlight shining puddles of ink on the wet stones. Off in the distance, the nighttime hymns of Winter's Rest drifted through the air like ghosts haunting the city.

Roderick stamped around the intersection like an animal caught in a cage. In the midst of his aimless pacing he stumbled and nearly fell when a part of the street wobbled beneath him. At his feet lay a stone sewer cover that was not quite flush with the edges.

The sewers. Yes, that was just where a creature like that might live.

He whipped out his knife and pried the lid up far enough to get his fingers underneath. Heaving the unwieldy disc to the side, he let it clatter onto the street. Warm fetid air wafted up from below. A set of rungs, barely visible, clung to the edges of the hole. He shoved his knife into his belt and grabbed the first rung. Ignoring the shock of the grimy, cold metal, he swung himself down into the darkness.

Roderick fumbled down the rungs with all the grace of a fish out of water and splashed into the standing murk below. Little streams trickled off down tunnels in each direction, following the pattern of the streets above. The passage was wide enough that he could not touch both walls with his arms and tall enough for him to walk upright. Slivers of moonlight pierced through the sewer covers ahead, but off to his right one of the tunnels dissolved into darkness. He plunged into the black hole, guessing that whatever took Jacob would go where the darkness was deepest.

Racing blindly down the passage, he stumbled over the

slippery stones, but refused to fall. He never once stopped to consider the hopelessness of his search. Each time he came to a branch or an intersection, he took whichever tunnel looked darkest.

At about the fourth or fifth turn he spotted it—there, shuddering down the center of the tunnel, even darker than the blackness surrounding it—the shadow. Jacob floated along behind it, just above the murky water, pulled by a dark mercurial cord. The semi-transparent leash rippled and billowed like smoke in a bottle.

Roderick lurched towards it, cold sweat pouring down his brow. If the dark thing noticed him, it gave no indication, shambling steadily onwards. Soon Roderick was almost on top of Jacob. Just as he was about to dive on him, the creature's baleful eyes flickered his way and he faltered. The monster's otherworldliness washed over him and his strength failed. His legs gave in and he fell headlong in the muck at Jacob's feet.

At that moment, the creature's path strayed into a beam of moonlight shining down from a crack in the ceiling and it, too, stalled. Mustering all the courage he had, Roderick grabbed onto Jacob's dangling foot. He held fast to it and for a moment the darkness shivered, its eyes burning bright in a fresh wave of fury. With supernatural strength, the shadow pulled Jacob forward, dragging Roderick through the filth.

He was about to lose his grip when the beam of moonlight burst into a glowing column, flooding the sewer with light. The creature shuddered, the light landing on it like a stone. A loud scraping noise rang out from above, followed by the snap of a sewer cover. The moonlight vanished, but another wave of light cascaded down from above, this time orange and flickering.

The dark thing shifted and trembled, unable to bear the tremendous gravity of the light weighing down upon it. A startled cry came hurtling down along with the light. A cloaked figure landed with tremendous force beside Roderick, thundering into the shallow water and rolling on top of him.

Painfully, Roderick squirmed out from under this new arrival and turned to see who it was.

A man lay groaning in the muck. A blazing torch now rested on the raised lip next to the tunnel wall. It was impossible to say exactly what the man looked like beneath his sludge-covered face, but there was no time to study him or guess what had brought him down into the sewers in the middle of the night; the creature was on the move again. It gave a violent shake and Roderick seized Jacob with both hands, determined to fight the shadow to the end. To his astonishment, the thing let go, recoiling against the side of the tunnel. The shimmering cord shrank away, vanishing into the darkness. Jacob dropped to the floor with a splash.

The creature's terrible appearance changed. It ceased to billow and foam like an inky cloud. It looked more like black paper now—thin and whispery and brittle, though still transparent like a shadow. Its eyes no longer blazed with hatred, dimming to a sickly yellow. Even the shivers of terror which had first seized Roderick when he looked at it began to fade.

The man who had fallen from above groaned as he groped about for the torch. At the same time, Roderick gathered Jacob in his arms and pulled him away from the creature.

Jacob's eyes fluttered open. "Is the dream over?"

Roderick shook his head and Jacob turned and regarded the shadow. He set his feet down and stood on the stony edge of the muck.

"Jacob, we have to run." Roderick pulled him by the hand.

"Wait."

Jacob stood fast. His skin began to glow. Barely noticeable at first, its luster grew by the moment. Red, green, blue, and yellow diamonds lit up alternately across his face and hands in a beautiful, pulsating pattern, like ripples of sunlight passing through a stained-glass window. As the intensity mounted, so did the light from the torch. It flared as bright as a summer's midday. A faint melody, like the tinkling of bells drifted through the tunnel. The notes spoke like a whisper in the ear, bidding the sleeper to awake.

Jacob's eyes bore into the dark mass shivering against the wall. The creature sank in upon itself. The once terrifying apparition grew weak and pathetic in the surging torchlight, its amorphous body shuddering in what Roderick took for pain or fear, though it was such an alien thing he could not be sure. The dark shape contorted into what looked like arms and legs and perhaps even a head, then coalesced into an animal shape with terrible fangs and claws. The one thing that stayed constant were the eyes, which shook with a mixture of torment and desperation as the dark thing shrank back against the wall, moving as far away as it could from the torch's brightness, clinging to every snatch of shadow it could find.

But the creature found no sanctuary, even in the dismal sewers. The bell chimes grew louder, and the torchlight grew ever brighter, until Roderick had to shield his eyes. Still the light blazed on, brighter and brighter until the creature seeped into the mortar like water flowing down a drain. The eyes were the last to go, fading until they were no more than two motes of pathetic light. Then they, too, disappeared and the creature with it, leaving behind a black stain on the wall like wet ashes. The torchlight dwindled, the effulgence dying until it went back to what it was before. The song of the bells faded as well, into nothing more than the echo of a memory.

The glow from Jacob's skin was the last to go, though some of it lingered on the yellow diamond on his forehead. And now that spot was joined by a green diamond on one cheek and a blue one on the other.

"Jacob, are you okay?" Roderick asked, embracing him tightly. His clothes were damp and his skin was cold to the touch, but he was unharmed.

"I think so," Jacob said. "I couldn't feel anything when it was holding me. It was like I was dead, or in a dream. But I feel better now."

"That was the oddest thing I ever saw," mumbled the newly arrived stranger in open-mouthed astonishment. "That knock to the head on the way down must have been nastier than I thought."

Roderick surveyed the bedraggled man before them. He appeared fairly young and might have even looked handsome if he were cleaner and there was better light. As it was, his tanned skin was mostly covered in mire and his longish locks slopped over half his face in a stringy net.

"Nagan's the name," he said, holding out a grimy hand. "At least if memory serves."

Roderick had no qualms about shaking his hand for his own was just as dirty. "I'm Roderick. And this is Jacob."

"A pleasure, I'm sure," Nagan said, flashing a smile. The white teeth shone out all the brighter against his filthy skin. "Taking your son out for a stroll in the sewers in the middle of the night, are we? It's always best to acquaint them with the, um…foundations of Middlehelm, don't you think? Or is this just your way of celebrating Winter's Rest? Find some dark, secluded spot like this to weep over your lost loved ones, is that it?"

While a part of Roderick remained in shock over having nearly lost Jacob, something about this man's tone took the edge off of his fears. He spoke as if their meeting here in the sewers, and even the presence of the shadow, were some private joke or game they had been playing at.

"Well, he's not actually my son," Roderick said. "His parents are gone. And I've been taking care of him."

Jacob clung to Roderick's soiled clothes, regarding the stranger uneasily.

"Ah, I see," Nagan said. "Or rather, I don't. But what does it matter? If the apple cart tips, then you just have fruit with rolls, as my ol' mum used to say. Now, the real confusion I have is about that nasty black puffer I saw—looked like sin itself, it did—and the way the light livened up there for a moment, and…oh my goodness, what in the Wither happened to your skin, boy? At first, I thought I was just seeing stars, but that's your honest to goodness flesh, isn't it? Or have I gone completely tom-twaddle after all?"

Jacob shrank back, seeking refuge in Roderick's shadow.

"He's sort of sensitive about that," Roderick said hastily.

"Oh, sorry," Nagan said. "I suppose he would be. It's just with the light show and the ding to my noggin and all the stench down here and whatnot, I thought my mind might be playing a little shell game with me. No offense, little one. Your skin is as lovely as anything hanging in Castle Middlehelm—any painting, I mean, or tapestry, or, well, you know what I mean."

"You're not going to hurt him, are you?" Roderick asked, suddenly reminded that he had no idea who this person was. Nagan's torch light may have been the happy providence which saved them from the shadow, but what in heaven's name was he doing down in the sewers in the first place?

"Hurt a child? Me? Do I really look so callous and ill-mannered as that?" He gazed down at his soaked trousers and grime-covered sleeves. "Well...apart from my...you know... present condition, I assure you that I am the picture of gentlemanliness. They don't let just *anyone* into the Duke's castle, you know."

He gave Roderick an odd wink. Or perhaps he was just dealing with the muck running down his brow.

Jacob peeked out from behind Roderick, sizing up the stranger with a concerned expression.

"You've been to the castle?" Roderick asked.

"Oh, yes, on many an occasion. The Duke Regent gives the most splendid parties."

"So then, you must be nobility," Roderick said, though at the moment Nagan hardly looked it. "If so, you might be able to help us. You see, we need to get out of Middlehelm, but currently no one is allowed to—"

"Leave the city? Yes, of course I know all about the edict. Unfortunately, I'm no nobleman—far from it, actually. But even if I were, it would do me no good in a case like this. The Duke's got this place so battened down, he won't let the sunshine sally forth at the behest of the dawn."

"Ah, well, that's a pity..." Roderick said, crestfallen. "We have an urgent need to leave—"

"Don't we all? But I never said I couldn't get you out," Nagan's muddy cheeks swelled in a smile. "As a matter of fact, I'll let you in on a little secret." He leaned in close as if someone might possibly be listening to their conversation down in the sewers. "I was on my way out of the city myself when we had our little collision. If you want, I can take you to a secret exit I know about. It's not far from here."

Roderick perked up instantly, but then checked himself. Could he trust this person? Should he? "Oh, but we have a friend. I almost forgot about him. We can't leave him behind."

"Are you referring to that little shadowy tagalong with the beady eyes? If so, I think you'd do well to seek better company. He hardly seemed the amiable sort."

"Oh no, no, not that...thing. I'm talking about Master Ken —about our leader, our guide, I suppose you could say. He's taking us...north for some...important business." Roderick wondered if even that vague description had been too much. This man certainly appeared harmless enough and his reaction to Jacob made it doubtful he was a servant of the Thaumaturge, but how could Roderick be sure?

"Master Ken, you say? Well, bring him along, I have no qualms about making new acquaintances."

"But he's back at the Inn, I'm afraid—or at least I hope he's back by now."

"Ah, that is a bit of a quandary isn't it? I hadn't thought of that. I myself have never quite managed the art of being in two places at once, though I've been in plenty of situations where that would have proven immensely practical. I'll tell you what. Since I'm in a bit of a hurry and there isn't time to go back for him, I'll just show you the way out and then we'll part company and you can go back and meet up with your friend and show him yourselves."

"Well..." Roderick hesitated. If this was a chance to find a way out of the city wouldn't it be foolish not to take it? For once he might actually be able to do something to help further their little journey along instead of always having to rely on Master Kendall. Who knows, the old Savant might even thank him for it. Besides, if this man turned out to be the unsavory sort, Roderick still had his knife and this man looked to be unarmed. At any rate, he judged it a risk worth taking. "You're sure it won't take long? I wouldn't want our friend to get worried."

"Pshaw!" Nagan waved his hand, the one with the torch, sending smoke zig-zagging up to the ceiling. "With old Nagan as your guide, I'll have you out of here before you can roast a rat."

Roderick had to admit that he liked this fellow. Jacob, on the other hand, studied Nagan with a furrowed brow.

"What do you think, Jacob?" Roderick asked.

Jacob's narrowed eyes did not bode well for the stranger.

"It shouldn't take long," Roderick said. "We'll head back to the inn as soon as Mr. Nagan here shows us the way out."

"I suppose it's all right. For now," Jacob said. "But he has to promise not to tell anyone about my skin."

"Oh, you're secret's safe as raisins in a cookie jar," Nagan said. Noting Jacob's puzzled look, he added. "That's another thing my ol' mum used to say. You see everyone prefers the cookies to the raisins. So raisins, though normally quite delicious, can be kept very safe if you put them in with something much tastier."

"I prefer raisins," Jacob said.

Nagan crossed his arms and raised his eyebrows.

"All right, Mr. Nagan," Roderick said, not really understanding the analogy, but anxious to find the exit and return triumphantly to Master Kendall with his accomplishment. "Show us the way."

Nagan thrust his cloak back dramatically over his shoulder like a magician about to introduce his next trick. The gesture sent a spray of mud spattering against the wall. "Very well, then. Hold your noses, mind the rats, and let old Nagan show you the best of what the city's nethers have to offer!"

17

THE LOST GUIDE

he three grimy travelers trudged on in the same direction the shadow had been heading. Now that it was gone, the regular, everyday awfulness of the sewers reasserted itself. The stench and filth assaulted Roderick's senses. Covering his mouth and nose with his sleeve helped a little, but the dank, fetid air pursued him at every turn. Sad, colorless stones enclosed them like a tomb. In the flickering torchlight, frightful shapes drifted by in the water. Shadowy rodents went scurrying along the edges of his vision, their scarlet eyes reminiscent of the creature that had brought them here.

Jacob dragged his feet, still shaken by his brush with the shadow. He kept his eyes on their guide with unmasked suspicion, as if he suspected there might be some connection between Nagan and that dark monster.

Roderick was about to ask about this when Nagan spoke up.

"All right, I can tell you've got something floating around in that multi-colored mind of yours. What is it boy? Don't worry, I won't bite. I'm only half-rodent." He bared his two front teeth and gave Jacob a wink.

Nagan's pleasant air failed to break through Jacob's skeptical defenses. "How do you know your way around these sewers?" he asked with all the pluck and perk of a seasoned haggler at the market. Roderick didn't quite know what to make of his odd behavior towards the stranger.

"Well, now…" Nagan stroked his grimy chin. "That's a

137

very good question. Doubting my qualifications as a guide, are we? Before I answer, however, you tell me: what do *you* think the answer is?" he asked impishly.

"You're a burglar," Jacob said.

"Ah, well, I never! A burglar? I know I'm a bit muddied up, but is that really what you take me for?"

Jacob stared at him all the harder. "It seems like only burglars would know their way around places like this."

"Now, Jacob, you ought not to talk like that," Roderick came to Nagan's defense. "Mr. Nagan is doing us the courtesy of showing us a way out of the city. You shouldn't accuse him of such things."

Jacob's bravado cracked a hair. "I'm sorry. He asked me what I thought."

"Ah, no offense taken, lad. I'm the least offensible man you'll ever meet. I've certainly been called worse at any rate."

Nagan blew a stray lock of hair out of his face as if he had just passed an important test. He stopped in the middle of the four-way intersection they had just entered. He licked his finger and made a disgusting face, having forgotten it had recently been dipped in sewer muck. Holding up the filthy digit towards each of the three new directions, he tested the air. In his other hand, he held the torch, but it did not shine far enough for him to see where the other tunnels led.

"It's been so long since I came this way. Ah, this is the direction, I think," he said, marching off to the right.

The tunnel he chose looked exactly like all the others in the dim light, but Nagan picked up his step, growing more and more confident the further along they went. Occasionally he would stop and scrape some gunk off one of the flagstones to scrutinize what looked like engravings. He would then nod enthusiastically, assuring them that they were on the right path.

"What do those symbols mean?" Roderick asked.

"Oh, why the names of the tunnels, of course," Nagan said breezily. "I suppose they help the workers find their way around when they have need of venturing down in the muck."

Jacob shook his head like a physik whose patient had taken a turn for the worse.

"Fine, cast your aspersions," Nagan said in wounded fashion. "Old Nagan is used to the scorn and scurvy of this world's opinion. But no matter what you think of me, I assure you that I am no burglar, though I am a thief of sorts. I steal hearts, at least that's how some describe it. But it's not my fault I was born with these rakish good looks and clever wit. To be strictly honest, it's done me more harm than good."

"That still doesn't explain how you know your way around the sewers," Jacob insisted. "Or why you're even down here in the first place."

"I was getting to that, lad. Give a fellow half a moment." Nagan held up his hand. "Patience is a virtue, but gout is a disease, as my ol' mum used to say (though I never quite understood what she meant with that one). It was my heart-stealing that forced me underground, you see. There was a certain lady who was just mad for me, but she was a fifth cousin of the duchess or some such nonsense and I'm afraid the rest of the nobility rather frown upon commoners mixing it up with high stock."

"They executed a man once back in...in my province for that very thing," Roderick said, only just catching himself. *Master Kendall would have been proud.* He had to remember that Nagan, as harmless as he appeared to be, was still a stranger.

"You see what I mean? Dreadful practices," Nagan said. "The sewers were the way we kept everything secret. One must often stoop rather low to attain the heights, I'm afraid."

"So then why are you trying to leave?" Jacob asked.

"Full of questions, aren't we? I'd forgotten how inquisitive young people can be. Well, if you must know, I broke it off. She really lacked the character and moral fortitude I had at first esteemed in her. She was a bit of a shrew to put it bluntly. Needless to say she didn't take the news all that swimmingly."

"She got mad at you?" Jacob continued with his questions.

"Mad at me? You're about fifty nicks shy of a shave, my young friend. To say she was mad would be the statement under the understatement. Imagine the worst tongue-lashing your mother ever gave you and then imagine that tongue had spikes and poison and acid and was made of rusty, jagged metal and you'd be half approaching the truth. The poor woman turned purple, started crowing like a rooster, and roaring like a tiger all at the same time. Why, she threatened to send me to the gallows if I left her!"

"I'm sorry to hear of your troubles," Roderick said, though he thought Nagan's claims a bit much. "I can certainly see why you would want to be getting out of the city."

"Her screams nearly tore my coat asunder, and they brought those awful bodyguards of hers storming in. Pure brutes, those fellows—oxen in uniform. I had to make a mad dash for it. I flew through the window and shimmied down the trellis like an otter diving into the river."

The memory of the shattering glass which had awoken Roderick in the middle of the night came rushing back. And hadn't there been a scream as well? Could that have been Nagan and this Duchess?

"The nobility can be so tyrannical," Nagan went on with a great and rather self-important harrumph. "They think they own us."

Poor fellow. Despite the obvious embellishments, he was clearly in a tight spot.

But Jacob did not share in Roderick's compassion for the star-crossed young man. He scrunched up his nose so that the diamonds on his face turned into jagged stripes.

"What? It's the truth," Nagan said defensively.

"He's just not used to trusting strangers," Roderick said.

"Ah…" Nagan, nodded sagely. "That's understandable. I myself was the same way as a boy. 'Contrary as the moon,' my mum always said."

"Did you grow up in Middlehelm?" Roderick asked, hoping to steer the conversation in a friendlier vein.

"No. My father was a river trader. I grew up on the Fallowing, floating from town to town. It was a fine life for a young boy, I suppose, all things considered."

"Is that where you're headed, then, back to your family?"

"Well, Mum and Da died when I was young, so I've no family left to speak of."

"I'm sorry to hear that," Roderick said. Even Jacob's expression softened.

Here Nagan stopped again, for they had wandered into the middle of another intersection. He shone his torch down each passage, but as before, they all looked the same.

"Ah, yes. I do believe this is the way." Nagan traipsed off down the tunnel on their left, holding his torch and head up high, looking for all the world as if he were leading them into some grand gala and not trudging through the sludge below Middlehelm.

"We already went that way," Jacob said, freezing Nagan in mid-stride. Their guide regarded the boy with unmitigated shock, as one might regard an opponent in a game of traitor's chips who counters your every move.

"It seems I can do nothing right in your eyes, my diminutive friend. Perhaps *you* would like to lead us?" He bowed in mock surrender with a great flourish.

"I don't know where we're going," Jacob said.

Nagan placed a hand smugly on his hip. "Precisely my point. Now if you'll just keep quiet and let me do the guiding, I'll have you full and found in a lick and a half, no longer." Then, spinning on his heel he slogged off in the same direction he'd been heading before.

Twenty minutes later, they still had not found the exit.

Though Roderick didn't see how Jacob could tell one section from another, the longer they wandered, the more sympathetic he became to his questioning of Nagan's guidance. Still, they followed along dutifully and Jacob, for his part, did not openly challenge Nagan further, though his pursed lips showed how he felt about the situation.

At last Nagan began to lose his confident air. He'd

sometimes start off down a passage, get about halfway down, and then double back the other way. After he had done this several times, Roderick concluded that Nagan was indeed truly lost.

"You know, Nagan," Roderick said. "Master Ken—our friend—might be wondering what happened to us. We've been down here over an hour by my guess. Perhaps we should return to the surface and see if—"

"Middlehelm's a large city." Nagan shook off his defeated-looking expression and wagged his finger. "Its sewer system is one of the most complex in all the Empire. It took me months to master it."

"Are we close to finding the exit, then?" Roderick asked.

Nagan cleared his throat, "Five minutes, I'd say—fifteen at the absolute most." His suppressed grimace betrayed the fact that he was really just asking them to be patient while he kept hunting.

"It's just that Jacob needs his sleep. If it were only me, I'd be more than happy to—"

"I know the way out now," Jacob said, causing both men to stop and regard him with puzzled expressions.

"Excuse me?" Nagan said.

"It's back that way." Jacob pointed.

"You've never been in these tunnels your whole life and you think you know the way to the secret exit after tromping around for an hour? Not even the city watch know about it," Nagan said.

A sort of mischievous pride flashed in Jacob's eyes. If Roderick didn't know better he would have said that Jacob was enjoying this.

"And how did you come by this marvelous knowledge, oh master of grime and slime?" Nagan asked.

Jacob's amused expression passed as quickly as it came. He was all business now. "It's the only passage you haven't taken."

"Well, then, there we have it! The little genius has mapped out the entire sewer system of Middlehelm in one pass."

Nagan flung his free hand in the air.

"Jacob, are you sure about what you're saying?" Roderick asked.

Jacob nodded with quiet calm.

"You know what?" Nagan said, licking his lips and leveling his gaze at this strange, multi-colored lad who claimed to know so much. "Just to show you I'm the sporting type, let's go your way—just to see. I don't doubt it'll lose us another half an hour down here in this stench, but why not spend the time exploring together? 'Pleasant company is never remembered', as my old mum used to say. Have at it, my boy."

"He doesn't mean any harm, sir," Roderick said, feeling sorry for the poor man despite his obvious failure at finding the way out. "I know it might seem far-fetched that he would have noticed something you might have missed, but I've never known the boy to lie."

"An expert guide, and a paragon of virtue as well! What more could one hope for?" Nagan said. "Fine, fine; lead on little one. I care not."

Now it was Nagan's turn to sulk. As the two grown men followed after Jacob, Nagan let out long sighs, rolled his eyes, dragged his feet, and generally let his disapproval be made known every step of the way. He even puffed on his torch once or twice as if in a half-hearted attempt to blow it out. Despite these misgivings, about ten minutes after Jacob started guiding them, the air grew noticeably cooler and fresher and the tunnels even began to grow somewhat less filthy.

With the change in atmosphere, Nagan's perturbations became gradually more subdued until at one point he stopped and exclaimed, "This is it! I recognize it now!"

Their erstwhile guide dropped his head, shaking it from side to side. "Well, I'm sorry I doubted you. I don't know how you found it, but your prow floated higher than mine this time around, I must admit. Well done, my brilliant friend, well done."

Jacob stared at the folds in his cloak. If his patchwork skin had been capable of blushing it most certainly would have.

"Well, Nagan, if you really do recognize this place, then perhaps we should let you take the lead again," Roderick suggested, smiling approvingly at Nagan's deference towards Jacob. He may not have been a stellar guide, but he at least had the character to admit when he was wrong.

"That's ever so kind of you, my friend, but there will be no further need of a guide from here on out. The exit is at the end of this tunnel." With a magnanimous gesture, Nagan invited the others to go before him and the little party resumed their journey.

The waters soon dried up along this new tunnel. The stones were of much newer construction. The air grew less and less foul and Roderick took in his first real whiff of honest air in some time.

Their high spirits ended a short time later, however, when the tunnel stopped abruptly, barricaded by a pile of rocks which rose floor to ceiling. The torchlight could not penetrate the rubble clogging the passageway.

"How are we supposed to get past that?" Roderick wondered aloud.

"Well, they weren't here before, but these rocks are nothing for two strapping men like ourselves. We'll gnaw through it like beavers on a willow branch," Nagan said.

"But how can you be sure?" Roderick asked.

Nagan gave a rueful grin. "Another soldier to swell the ranks of the doubters? I may have gotten us lost in the sewers, but these rocks are not as many as they look. Why, I'm quite sure I felt a slight breeze coming through a crack somewhere up near the top. Did you feel it as well?" Nagan groped around in the rocks, trying to locate the spot he had mentioned, but Roderick felt nothing. "Well, I can't seem to feel it just at the moment," Nagan admitted. "But believe me, it was there. And the sooner we start moving these rocks, the sooner we'll see the other side."

Nagan set to work at once. Roderick sighed and pitched in.

Whether he believed Nagan or not, Jacob did his part as well, picking out whatever small rocks he could, even though Roderick told him he could rest if he wanted to.

The breadth of the tunnel allowed all of them to work at once. They labored at it for the better part of a half hour with little to show for their efforts when Jacob pulled on Roderick's sleeve and gestured for him to stop.

"I hear someone coming," he whispered.

Roderick put down the rock he had in his hand and listened. Muted footfalls echoed through the tunnel from somewhere off in the darkness.

"Nagan, are you sure no one else knows about this exit?" Roderick asked.

Nagan halted his work and listened for the footsteps, clearer now, and closer.

"I've never encountered anyone down here in all my weeks of running the sewers. We've got to get out of this tunnel."

Abandoning the rocks, they fled down the passage. But Roderick sensed the approaching sounds were already too close for them to escape.

18

VERIS, VERILY

leeing the mound of rock behind them, Nagan, Roderick, and Jacob rushed towards the oncoming sounds, desperate to reach the junction before the interloper. Roderick expected a soldier, or a burglar, or some other unsavory character to appear at any moment. Indeed he did not have to wait long. A figure bearing a small, metal lantern attached to the top of his staff materialized out of the darkness. Such lanterns were commonly used by the night watch in Evenspire. It seemed only natural that the guards in Middlehelm must use them as well.

The cloaked figure had long passed through the intersection. Roderick struggled to think what reason he could give the guard for why they were down here in the middle of the night. As the stranger drew nearer, the details of his face coalesced out of the shadows and the telltale beard and sharp eyes at last gave away his identity.

"Master Kendall!" Roderick cried. "Ah, you're a stitch in time, you are! How ever did you find us?"

Kendall regarded the three of them sternly, especially Nagan. "I have my ways." He pulled on the chain around his neck belonging to the carmine crystal.

The Savant had Roderick and Jacob's gear slung on his back in addition to his own. Roderick happily relieved him of the extra burdens.

Free of the weight, Kendall straightened to his full height. "Now what in the Wither brought you into the sewers in the dark of night? And who is this Gitano you've got tagging along with you?"

Nagan a gypsy? Master Kendall may have been well-traveled, but surely this was one occasion where the man's aged eyes or the vagaries of the torchlight must have gotten the better of him. Roderick had seen Gitanos pass through Briar's Glen on many occasions. Certainly Nagan's skin and hair were dark like a gypsy's, but his dress was nothing like that worn by those flamboyant hucksters.

"Oh, Nagan is no Gitano. He's showing us a way out of the city. We planned on coming back for you as soon as we found the exit."

"I beg your pardon, Master...Kendall is it? Just because my skin is a little darker than the rest of you doesn't mean I'm a Gitano. I am nothing but a poor, honest boatswain, fallen on hard times."

A sour stew simmered on the old Savant's face. "Spoken like a true Gitano. My friend here may be too naïve to recognize it, but I've associated with too many of your ilk not to know one when I see one. Still, I am curious as to what you're about down here and how you came upon my friends. If you were sent by the Thaumaturge, I warn you, it will not end well for you."

"Thaw my—what kind of urge? I have no idea what you're —" Nagan objected.

"You cannot keep the truth from me, Gitano. I shall have words with you in a moment. But first," here he pulled Roderick and Jacob aside and a little way down the passage. "I must have a word with my friends."

Nagan puffed himself up and clearly meant to give a retort, but at a look from Roderick, he checked himself.

"We'll only be a moment," Roderick promised. "Sorry."

Kendall's eyes burned in the darkness and his nostrils spread in a permanent flare. He spoke as quietly as possible, considering his level of vexation. "The sewers? And with a cutpurse? How in the three realms are we ever going to finish our quest if you run off into messes like this?"

"Now, now, Master Kendall—"

"And please refrain from referring to me by name in front of the Gitano!"

"Oh, my. So sorry, Master, um, sorry—I wasn't thinking. But Nagan is no threat, honestly he's not. And as for our being down here, I can assure you it was the last place I ever wanted to come."

Roderick then launched into a rundown of the events spanning the past few hours, doing his best to explain how he and Jacob had been startled awake in the middle of the night by a broken window and of Jacob's ensuing abduction and rescue. When he mentioned the shadow, Kendall's face clouded over, but he waited for Roderick to finish his tale.

"So, they are loose once again," Kendall said once Roderick was through.

Roderick did not like the sound of that. *They?* He had hoped the appearance of the creature was a one-time event, never to be repeated and that the shadow had been truly and finally defeated.

"What's loose? You're not saying it will come back, are you?" Roderick asked.

"Not only will it come back, but it may not be alone the next time."

"Do you know what it was?" Visions of the awful, otherworldly creature shuddered back through Roderick's memory.

"Based on your description, there is little doubt in my mind but that it was a scathen, one of the ancient spirits called out of the nether by the first motley's magic. They were banished when the Scathen Night ended. Only the magic of a motley could bring one back."

"But I didn't want it to come," Jacob said. "It wasn't me, I promise."

"I know," Kendall said. "But now you see why the magic is so dangerous. It has a way of working on its own. And now that the scathen have re-established a connection to this world, it is only a matter of time before they break through again. Your nightmares will cover all of Arinn if we do not lift the curse."

"Are you sure, Master Kendall? What if it appeared because of our, um, well, you know—because of where we're headed." Roderick looked askance at Nagan who maintained a respectful distance, but it was difficult to know exactly how sound carried down in a place like this.

"It said it knew what I was up to," Jacob said in a quivering voice.

Kendall pressed down on his skullcap and kept his words close. "I have no doubt the creatures will do everything in their power to keep us from getting to where we need to go. But if we turned back now we would only be delaying the inevitable. The shadows will always come if the magic is not dealt with."

"It is getting late, isn't it?" Nagan said, at last growing weary of Kendall's exile and finding his way back over towards them.

Roderick, noting the harsh look Kendall gave Nagan, spoke up quickly. "Yes, indeed. I think it's high time we left Middlehelm. Nagan's exit is just down this tunnel."

Nagan scowled. "I wouldn't be surprised if that creature blocked it up, somehow. But with so many hands, we'll clear it up soon enough. I don't know what dark news you've brought, but I can see from the boy's shivering that you've nearly driven him to tears," he scolded the Savant. "Roderick, are you sure this is the same fellow you were talking about before? It might be a master of disguise sent by the Duchess to hunt me down."

"Enough of your prattling," Kendall snapped. "Do you know of an exit or not? I highly doubt it as none of my contacts could tell me anything."

Ignoring the Savant's tone, Nagan bowed in exaggerated fashion and said, "'The seal isn't proven 'til the barrel's in the river,' as my dear mum used to say. Right this way, oh, cantankerous one."

Kendall stifled a grunt and allowed Nagan to lead them to

where the rocks filled up the passageway.

"This is your exit? I might have known."

"Only a few feet more and then we're through," Nagan said defensively.

"Come, let's be going," Kendall said. "Enough time has been wasted this night already. We'll leave this gypsy to his thieving and be on our way."

"I think he's right," Jacob spoke up unexpectedly. His voice was meek, but steady.

"What?" Roderick asked.

"The tunnel continues on the other side. There aren't that many rocks left until we'll be able to see through."

"And how do you know that?" Roderick asked.

Jacob gave a half-shrug. "Maybe we should take out a few more rocks and see."

"Well, there you have it!" Nagan thrust his torch playfully in Kendall's direction. "Absolved by my greatest critic. I'd say that is irrefutable testimony, your Grumpiness—though it makes little difference to me whether you stay or go. I'll be here slaving away in any case. I dare not show my lovely face in Middlehelm 'til the Duchess is dead and gone and they've dedicated a statue to her memory."

"Very well," Kendall said. "We shall help each other out— for now. If the passage truly continues on the other side we will need all the help we can get in clearing it. The sooner we're away from Middlehelm, the safer we'll be from the scathen and certain other unpleasantries." He fixed his eyes on Nagan.

Nagan turned his nose up at the insult and trotted up to the rocks.

Though each stone seemed heavier than the one before, bits of fresh air soon wafted through the little chinks they opened up in the rocky barricade. After several minutes of diligent work, Kendall judged the space on top to be large enough for Jacob to fit through. Roderick stood wringing his hands while Jacob clambered over the rocks, cringing at every jostle and shift in the sharp-edged pile of rubble, but Jacob made it through with little trouble. Taking Kendall's lantern, he reported that the tunnel did indeed continue on the other side.

By the time they cleared away enough rocks for the rest of them to get through, they were thoroughly sapped. They sat down to rest on the other side. Kendall suggested they take some water to quench their thirst before going on and, surprisingly, even offered some to Nagan, who readily took it.

The other side of the tunnel was much like the previous one, save for the even fresher air. It ran ahead, long and straight, and their lights did not reach the end of it.

As they sat recovering their strength, Kendall addressed Nagan in a different sort of tone. He was less suspicious of him than before. Nagan's tone changed as well. The conversation quickly took on the air of old friends catching up after a long absence. Roderick found the change encouraging. He did not think Nagan deserved the harsh treatment he'd been given by the Savant and was glad to see the softer, gentler side of Kendall return.

"So, how long have you been in Middlehelm?" Kendall asked.

"Oh, far too long. I'll be glad to be rid of this place. I never did get used to the city life," Nagan said wistfully.

"And you swear to me on your mother's name that you are not working for the Thaumaturge?"

"You mean the ones from the old scary tales? You're pulling my teeth, aren't you?"

"Just answer the question."

"Well, how could I be working for someone who doesn't exist, hmm?" Nagan said. "No, sir, I've got enough holes in my net already to be working for some figment of my imagination."

"You mentioned something about a duchess," Kendall continued. "Tell me about her."

"Oh, she was just one of the ones on my list to pilfer. The last one, thank heavens," Nagan said.

Roderick sat up at this, hoping he had not heard right.

"There were other nobles you stole from? How many, might I ask?" Kendall pressed him.

"Eight of them all told. The Anciano said I only needed to get seven, but I figured I'd better stiff another one for good measure since he's not an easy one to please. Some of the nobles were harder than others, but they get so carried away at their parties sometimes they practically throw their jewels at your feet," Nagan said with a sly look.

"I knew it," Jacob mumbled, shaking his head at Nagan.

Roderick glanced back and forth between Nagan and Kendall. "What's going on?" he asked. "Nagan, you told us you were involved with the Duchess romantically. You said nothing about stealing."

Nagan snickered. "Well, I wasn't being strictly honest…but then again, I hardly knew you at the time."

"Gitanos never want you to know what they are about. It's the way they're taught to work," Kendall said.

"Precisely." Nagan's face glowed with pride at this admission.

"So you really are a Gitano?" Roderick asked.

"Oh, I wasn't born into it like most, but yes, after my mother and father died—or were killed by the Gitanos (I never could get clear on what happened there)—they raised me up as one of their own. Awfully kind of them, don't you think, considering the circumstances?" Nagan gave a half-hearted smile.

"So you lied to us," Roderick said.

Nagan shrugged whimsically. "Terribly sorry. It's part of my upbringing. Can't really be helped."

"So is Barillio still the Anciano of the Gitanos?" Kendall asked, ignoring Roderick's comments and certainly sharing none of his shock at these revelations. Jacob plopped down with his back against the wall and arms crossed, scowling at the newly revealed thief.

Such an insightful boy. How did he know? Roderick resolved to listen better to Jacob's suspicions in the future.

"Of course Barillio's still riding on top of the barrel, who else?" Nagan said. "The man has the skin of an iron kettle and the constitution of an oak. They've tried to gutter him a dozen times over, but he always manages to survive and string up the would-be cutthroats along the river."

"You're headed back to Tamber Forest, then?" Kendall asked.

Nagan nodded. "I hope Barillio will take me back into his good graces, but that's hardly a given."

"And how do you plan on proving yourself to the Anciano?"

Nagan's face swelled with a conspiratorial grin. He withdrew a brilliant diamond necklace from a pouch he had on his belt. At least a dozen stones glittered in its golden settings, none of which were smaller than a mira coin. It sparkled even in the poorly lit tunnel. Roderick's eyes went wide. He had never seen such finery in all his life.

"I think this should be sufficient." Nagan beamed. "The first seven heists were mere trifles, a diamond here, a gold bracelet there." He patted another pouch on his belt. "But this...this is something special. Truly a prize worthy of the old wrinkled one, don't you think?"

"The Hapshire Necklace..." Even the wizened old Savant looked impressed. "You're a better burglar than you look. May I examine it?"

"Of course." Nagan handed it to him nonchalantly. "But I'm not really that much of a thief. It took me six months to get it. And even then, I woke up the Duchess in the middle of lifting it. It's only a matter of time before her guards find out I'm down here. Don't you think we'd best be moving along?"

Kendall nodded and Roderick pulled him aside as they rose, waving Jacob and Nagan on. Nagan attempted to engage Jacob in conversation, but he tromped resolutely forward, ignoring the Gitano.

"What's going on?" Roderick asked. "If he lied to us before, why is he telling you the truth now? It doesn't make sense."

"I slipped a little something into his drink," Kendall

answered in low tones. "And I've had a change of heart about him. I think it might be best to retain the services of this Nagan fellow a bit longer. Once the Iddlglim pour into Halicon, the Gitano forest will be one of the few safe havens left in these lands. The wildmen have no more love of the blaizewoods than they do the river. They believe them to be haunted. If we can reach the Gitano lands, perhaps we can hire them to ferry us to Davinsmoor. Their leader, the Anciano, is very particular about those he will meet with face to face, but if Nagan can get us to him, the Gitanos may be able to help us."

Roderick stared at Nagan from behind. "Well, buttons. And he seemed so genuine. Are you sure this is a good idea?"

"Desperate times make for desperate alliances," Kendall said. "The timing of this war could not be worse. These Iddlglim will be the death of us all if we can't find a way through. If I knew of another way, believe me, I would try it. Your running into Nagan may prove to be the stroke that saves us all."

Roderick shook his head, deeply troubled by Nagan's deception and the fact that he'd been so easily taken in by it.

Kendall waved his pole in Nagan's direction. "The *veris* powder will not last long," he warned. "Once Nagan returns to normal, he won't remember anything he's told us. If we're to use him as our guide, it would be best if he remained ignorant of how much we know. For now, let's just keep this between the two of us; make sure Jacob doesn't let on anything either."

"All right, then," Roderick said and the two of them caught up to the others.

"You know, all of a sudden I've got the worst headache," Nagan said. "It must be the air in these tunnels. I've been down here far too long. Let's be rid of this dank dungeon once and for all, my friends, eh?"

"Yes, indeed," Kendall said. "Lead the way."

"Right. Now, where were we off to?" Nagan muttered to himself. "Ah yes, the exit! How could I forget? Away from the clutches of Lady Shrew once and for all! May she live to shriek another day."

The colored pattern on Jacob's face bunched into a worried tangle.

Roderick whispered in his ear, "We must keep things to ourselves for now. The time will come for the truth soon enough, I'm sure."

But Roderick did not like this new arrangement one bit.

19

STRANGE PASSAGES

ot far beyond the rocky barricade, the tunnel began to change. At first the stonework grew rough and uncut. Soon all trace of masonry vanished. Then the passage began to narrow. Just when it looked like the tunnel might end altogether or whittle down into an impassible, natural crevice, it changed again.

It widened suddenly and also became entirely round. Tree roots infiltrated the walls, thick and black and terribly ancient. They grew in such an organized, uniform way it was as if they were holding the tunnel together and not the rock in between. After a certain point, the rock disappeared completely and the passage turned into nothing but thick roots braided together.

The air changed. It was not just that it was fresher, but that it was too fresh for something underground. A sense of foreboding pressed in upon Roderick, as if they were somewhere they shouldn't be. Jacob stepped gingerly along the roots, staring anxiously at the strange walls. Nagan was noticeably subdued, though that may have had more to do with the headache he claimed to be suffering.

"This is not the same tunnel I was talking about," he muttered.

"What is this place?" Roderick asked. "It doesn't look like anything made by the hands of men."

"You spoke rightly there," Kendall said. "These have nothing to do with Middlehelm. They are much, much older."

"The shadows made these," Jacob said.

Roderick looked about, half expecting the inky creature to seep back in through the root walls.

"Slivers and thorns, don't say that," Nagan said. "We're not walking into that black thing's lair are we?"

"Can you sense any nearby?" Kendall asked Jacob. The group stopped. All eyes fell upon the child.

His gaze flitted behind them. "No," he said. "Strath is sleeping now."

"Strath?" Roderick asked.

"That's the name of the shadow who tried to take me," Jacob whispered, as if afraid of waking his sleeping enemy.

"Did the creature speak to you?" Kendall asked.

"I could hear his thoughts. He said I was going to help him free the rest of the shadows."

"It is an ill destiny that has led us to this place," Kendall said. "We must be far away from here before the scathen return." He headed off down the passage, picking up the pace.

Soon the tunnel branched off in three different directions. They stayed on the main branch, passing several more offshoots as they went. Eventually, they came to a place where the tunnel split off to the left and the right and they were forced to make a decision.

"Shouldn't we be out of this place by now? Middlehelm is not nearly this big," Nagan remarked. "Unless we're walking in circles..."

"For once, I think you are right," Kendall said. "We must be well beyond the city's boundaries by now. Have you noticed, though, that the tunnel has been gradually sloping downwards ever since we entered?"

"I wondered about that," Roderick said. "I was hoping I was wrong."

"We might wander around down here for hours before we ever find a way out." Nagan eyed the root-filled walls anxiously.

"There may not be a way out," Kendall said. "Legends tell of the fabled underhalls deep below the surface of Arinn, crafted through magic long ago."

"In all honesty, the longer I stay in this place, the more tempted I am to head back and face the Duchess and her goons," Nagan said. "But if the netherworld really is going to be raining down on our heads at any moment, don't you think we ought to be choosing a path instead of standing here yapping? I'm for the right. 'Right's always right', as my mum used to say. An eminently practical woman."

"If there isn't any exit, there isn't any point in going any further, we'll just go deeper and deeper underground. The only way out is up." Kendall pointed above his head.

"Well, last I checked, none of us were wood mites," Nagan shot back. "So I don't believe we'll have much luck there."

"If we have passed beyond the walls of Middlehelm, we may be able to break through to the surface and out again into the open air. And while it's true that there is no way to dig through such a thick tangle of roots, I do have my lantern."

Nagan let out a hearty laugh. "That little tiny flame you've got? Look at these roots—they're alive or I'm the Lord Helm of Brackenland. And even if they weren't, they're so thick we'd all die of hunger by the time your little flicker burned through. Roderick, I thought you said this man was a scholar."

Ignoring the Gitano, Kendall set off back down the passage. "We'll fare better if we try to penetrate from further back."

"Back?" Nagan let out a groan.

Roderick put a hand on his shoulder. "He knows what he's doing."

Nagan rolled his eyes, but said no more as they followed after the Savant.

When they reached the place that Master Kendall had chosen, he warned them to stand back. He reached inside his pouch and tossed some glittering powder up towards the roof of the tunnel where it stuck fast to the roots. The golden dust twinkled enchantingly, like a crowd of flaxen stars. Removing the cover from his lantern, Kendall waved the open flame so that it licked the sparkling wood. The roots burst into flames and everyone but Kendall gave a start.

The fire burned bright yellow, unlike any sort of fire Roderick had ever seen. The flame had no tongues to it. It was more like liquid light. It ate through the wood several times faster than normal fire, but the glow quickly began to die out. Kendall hurled more and more sparkling powder onto the wood. Each time he did so, the glow blazed forth with renewed intensity.

"It's so beautiful," Jacob said with openmouthed wonder.

"That's top shelf, that's what that is," Nagan said. "I take back what I said about you not being a fine scholar, Master Kendall."

The thick roots curled up like burnt leaves. They fell in embers and soot to the floor. In little time at all, there was a hole wide enough for them to push through. Beyond it lay blackened soil mixed with rocks.

"How will we get through the rest?" Roderick asked.

"I'm afraid that will take common digging." Kendall removed the lantern from the top of his pole. "Fortunately, the dirt is quite soft in this part of the province."

The pole made a clicking sound and a long, thin knife shot out from the base. The edges glinted in the dim light. Kendall raised the shaft and began prying the rocks loose from above.

"My, he's just full of tricks, isn't he?" Nagan said. "A regular magician."

"Here, let me do that for you," Roderick offered.

"No, that's quite all right," Kendall said. "I'm not as old as I look. Just stay where you are. This won't take long."

Indeed Kendall was right. The first few chunks of rock and dirt took some effort to knock loose, but with each new bit, the work got easier and easier. Kendall was careful to avoid letting the larger rocks fall on his head. A pile of dirt and debris soon lay in the middle of the tunnel and the first timid shafts of moonlight poked through the turf above.

"I say—you're handy with that spade, old man," Nagan

said. "If I ever get thrown into some nobleman's dungeon, I'll know who to call on to dig me out."

Once Kendall finished, Roderick and Nagan helped the Savant up on their shoulders and pushed him through. Jacob went next, followed by Nagan, who slipped twice and fell back down while trying to get a grip on the edge of the hole, but eventually made it through. Last came Roderick, pulled easily up by Kendall and Nagan.

The spot where they emerged lay a few hundred yards beyond the castle walls.

Nagan took in a deep breath of cool night air. "Ah, 'free as empty pockets', as my mum used to say."

"Not as free as you might think," Kendall said. "We have no way of covering up that hole and I've no doubt Middlehelm's soldiers will see it come sunrise. If they do and they decide to track us, they'll have little difficulty doing so over this rain-soaked ground."

"And there's still the shadows," Roderick said. Jacob moved further away from the gaping hole at the reminder.

"Right. Well," Nagan said, brushing off some of the caked on muck from his clothing. "As much as I've enjoyed this midnight romp through the dregs and swill, I'm sure the three of you are more than capable of avoiding the guards and those shadows. After all, you've got Kendall's sprinkling things and the boy's...whatever it is he has about him. Regrettably, I must take my leave. I swear I shall never forget you gentle folk—or your smell—but my feet are calling me home."

"And where would that be?" Kendall asked.

Nagan hesitated, scanning the horizon in several directions as if attempting to get his bearings.

"That's an interesting question," he said finally. "You know I've lived in many places during my short life, but the one I'm most particularly fond of at the moment I would have to say is Rill. Yes, Rill is where I'm headed. And I've such a longing for it that I dare not delay."

Nagan started forward, but Kendall barred his way with his

staff, the blade still jutting conspicuously from the end. "Actually, we're headed in the exact same direction," he said. "We'll pass right by Rill on our way to the Tamber Forest."

At the words 'Tamber Forest' the young Gitano's eyes shifted nervously. "Ah, lovely." His expression quickly reverted back to something more congenial. "It's quite beautiful this time of year. The blaizewoods are enchanting in the early winter."

"So you've been to the Tamber then?" Kendall pressed him. "But how did you manage to avoid the notice of the Gitanos? They have a reputation for killing anyone who sets foot inside their forest, or at the very least robbing them and leaving them penniless on the edge of the woods. How did you manage not to get caught?"

"I never said I'd been *into* the forest. Oh, no, no, no. I've only seen it from the outside—nature walks, afternoon picnics, that sort of thing. I've heard stories about the Gitanos like everyone else, but I've never actually seen any. Do you really think they exist?"

"You've lived in Rill and have never seen Gitanos? I find that hard to believe. They pass through there quite often."

"Well, I've led a sheltered life. A sheltered life that is calling to me rather strongly at the moment. And it would be bad manners to keep it waiting. 'When the dinner bell rings' my mum always said, 'you'd best act like you're hungry.'"

Nagan gave a curt nod and once more made to go, but Kendall did not withdraw his staff.

"But I *have* dealt with Gitanos," Kendall said. "And at present, I am in need of their services once again."

Nagan's face wore a mixture of feigned shock and nervousness. "You, Master Scholar? But what could someone as upstanding as yourself have to do with assassins and sharpers—if they exist, that is?"

"With war about to break forth all across the north, the woods of the Gitanos will be one of the few safe places left if one seeks to travel in this area. The Iddlglim believe the Tamber to be haunted, you see. Besides that, the Gitanos are also experts at moving their wares undetected along the Fallowing. My hope is to bargain with the leader of the Gitanos, Anciano Barillio, for safe passage west."

"But what makes you think I could help you travel through the Tamber? I'm just a common fisherman from Rill," Nagan said. Even Roderick could see through him at this point. Nagan was losing his touch.

"You mean, boatswain," Roderick corrected him.

"Eh? What's that?" Nagan asked.

"A boatswain. Before, you said that you were a boatswain," Roderick said.

"Oh, did I? Well, yes I did. Fisherman, boatswain—I've done it all. I'm a man of the river. If it has to do with the water, I've had a turn at it one time or another!"

"Like most Gitanos," Kendall commented.

"Oh, now see—there you go again," Nagan said.

Jacob regarded the Gitano with pity.

"It's no use, Nagan—I know who you are," Kendall said. "Your parents were killed by Gitanos and you were taken in and raised by them. It's a typical practice of theirs to kidnap the young children of the people they rob from, especially boys. That business with the Duchess was all wink and nod and you know it. So let's cut through the misdirection and get to the point."

"But—"

"We need someone to get us to Barillio. And you're heading there anyway so it will hardly be an imposition for us to accompany you."

"Now wait half a moment. I never said—"

"Oh, you've said plenty. And if you ever want to see *this* again, you'll say yes to guiding us through the forest." Kendall reached inside his cloak and pulled out the glittering Hapshire Necklace, allowing it to dangle before him. The stones sparkled in the moonlight. Nagan gasped.

"Why you common thief!" he cried, "How did you—" He reached out for it, but Kendall deftly yanked it back.

"Let's just say my 'sprinkling things' can do far more than

produce fire. Now what will it be?"

Jacob folded his arms solemnly. "You shouldn't have lied to us."

Nagan grimaced and shot a trapped look towards Roderick who only shrugged in reply. Nagan had been dishonest with them from the start and Roderick saw no reason why he shouldn't make up for it in the way Kendall suggested. Perhaps if he kept better company for a while he might even rethink his ways.

"Never fear," Kendall said. "All you have to do is get us to the Anciano. Then, if all goes well, I promise to return your stolen necklace."

Nagan kicked at the dirt and gazed longingly back at the hole.

"Barillio's going to kill me."

20

A New Kind of Shadow

he Iddlglim attacked Middlehelm at dawn. By that time, Roderick and the others were at least two miles away from the castle, but the fires of the barbarian host could be seen dotting the plains. It looked like so much of Kendall's sparkling dust cast upon the land. The fires unveiled a mass of humanity stretching along the far side of the river. The vast army swallowed up the land, churning and frothing on the riverbank, a mighty swell building up to burst forth over the castle walls.

The wildmen attacked without warning or fanfare. No time was given for parley or an opportunity for surrender. The invaders only slowed long enough to hurl their rafts into the river and then themselves onto the rafts. In moments they were plunging across the Fallowing, rushing straight for the castle.

"Do they not fear the river?" Roderick asked.

Kendall, standing on top of a hillock with the others, surveyed the battle through an ornate brass spyglass. "There is some dark purpose behind this attack. Something drives them. Something which they fear even more than the river."

Waves of arrows rained down on the the Iddlglim vanguard. Countless wildmen fell into the river, but the rafts were so thick, others rushed from behind and took their place almost immediately.

The invaders were half-way across when blazing orbs streaked forth from the far bank. The spheres flew through the night like shooting stars, careening into the basalt

164

defenses. Chunks from the castle's crenellations crumbled and fell into the narrow stretch of land between the city and the river. Half a dozen balls of flame lit into the castle on the first volley. Twice as many flew with the second. The massive walls were slowly disintegrating onto the riverbank. By the fourth wave, which consisted of fifteen shots, a gap near the gate had opened up. The Iddlglim let loose another volley, concentrating their fire on the castle's open wound.

No counterattack came from within other than the arrows, and those were fewer with each volley, as those manning the crenellations fled to safety amidst the fiery orbs and crumbling stone. For what could be done against an army of such size, wielding, as it were, the power of the sun?

Roderick had never witnessed a battle before. Though he had heard tales of the great wars of the past, he never imagined they would be so frightening to behold.

"This is the work of the Thaumaturge," Kendall said. "He is the one behind this attack."

"But why? What does he have to gain by attacking Middlehelm?" Roderick asked.

"That I do not know," Kendall said. "Perhaps he is aware that we are abroad and wishes to make our journey north as difficult as possible. But this is a bold stroke, even for a Thaumaturge."

Jacob turned away and dropped his eyes to the ground.

"Such a strange fire, a bit like…" Nagan said.

"Yes, it is a form of *flintfire*, the dust I used to free us from the tunnels, but in much larger amounts and mixed with some sort of catalyst to spread it when it impacts the walls. This more than anything betrays the hand of the Thaumaturge."

"I wish we could go," Jacob said quietly.

Kendall lowered his glass. "Yes, I think we have seen enough. There is nothing we can do but fly to the Tamber and hope the Gitanos do not kill us on sight. It is the only path we have left."

Jacob pulled on Roderick's sleeve as they turned to go. "Is that battle really because of me?" he asked.

"No, Jacob. Men have their own reasons for war. It's in our blood, I'm afraid. No one person is to blame, especially not you," Roderick said, but the look in Kendall's eyes made him doubt his own words.

They soon passed out of view of the battle, winding their way along a little gully whose stream fed into the Fallowing. They did not follow it long, passing over to the other side after a few miles. They traversed the trickling waters by stepping on the exposed stones in the stream bed.

Kendall walked in the lead, with Nagan a few steps behind. Roderick and Jacob followed after him, further back.

"I still don't trust Mr. Nagan," Jacob said in a low voice. "Are you sure we should be going with him?"

"Have you ever seen gypsies before?" Roderick asked. "They're mostly just petty thieves and entertainers. I like our odds with them a lot more than I do with the Iddlglim."

"Yes. I've even met some kind ones. But I still don't trust them."

And why should he? I suppose I wouldn't trust anyone either if I were in his place.

No one said much after that until they broke for lunch. Roderick collapsed, exhausted, and would have gone to sleep right then and there had Kendall allowed it. As famished as he was, the tasteless hard tack was blander than ever after the sumptuous food of *The Executioner's Corner.*

"Is this really all you've got?" Nagan complained as he bit into one of the crumbling wafers. "How come the little master gets dried fruit while us grown men starve?"

"That's all he can eat," Roderick said.

"A likely story," Nagan said. "Don't you know he's just a whiffin' in your miskit? All children are like that. Why as a boy, I had my mum convinced that my stomach could tolerate nothing but wheat pudding and sweet yams. And I've scarcely eaten any better since those gentle days. This little muncher is taking a page out of old Nagan's book, I'll wager."

Jacob turned so he didn't have to look at Nagan as he continued to chew on his fruit.

"Enough talk," Kendall said. "We must reach Rill by tomorrow night. Up, up! These miles won't walk themselves."

Nagan groused loudly as the journey resumed. He protested that the break had been precious little. Though Roderick was inclined to agree, he did not join in the grumbling. But with every step he fought not to lay down. In this he was greatly helped by forcing himself to think of the terrible Iddlglim army swarming across the Fallowing. That was enough to keep any man trudging forward.

"This will have to do," Kendall told them as they stopped in the middle of a field. They had walked all that day and it was well past dark and there was simply no cover to be found.

Roderick had been carrying the sleeping Jacob for the last hour. The little fellow was so tuckered out, Roderick didn't even bother waking him for dinner. He chomped down his food, eager to join him.

"You and I will have to stay up and keep an eye on the Gitano," Kendall said to Roderick in confidence. "I'll take the first watch."

Roderick would normally have offered to take that duty, but he did not believe himself physically capable of staying awake more than a few minutes longer.

"Well, you're a stouter man than myself. Just wake me when you need to rest," Roderick said, unable to stifle a yawn.

"You're wasting your time, friends," Nagan said, curling up in the tall grass. "I couldn't move a mustard seed with a sneeze right now. The Incomparable Nagan is not long for the waking world. You'll get no trouble out of me tonight. Tomorrow? Well, that's another story."

Despite Nagan's words, he didn't sound quite as tired as he was attempting to come off, but Roderick didn't care. His worldly concerns, like his strength, vanished with a yawn and a wink.

Kendall's cold hand on his shoulder woke him.

"Master Kendall? Oh, right. It's my turn…Thank you for waking me," Roderick mumbled.

He forced himself to his feet though his body begged him to remain on the hard ground. Kendall wandered off into the grass and stretched out. Nagan lay sprawled out on the opposite side of the camp, a contented smile on his face as if he was enjoying his own private joke.

He's no doubt dreaming of diamond necklaces. Roderick sighed, envying him.

Jacob moved restlessly next to him. From the expression on his face, he was struggling to overcome the evil things which plagued his dreams. Roderick held him close and began to pray.

He soon forgot all about keeping watch. He wanted to be strong for Jacob and remain awake and pray, but found himself nodding off only to wake up again with a start every few seconds, or was it minutes? He was no longer even aware of what he was praying. He was too far gone.

At some point he must have given in completely for, after what seemed only a moment of dozing, he awoke to find Jacob wide awake and standing over him.

"The shadows are back. There are more this time. We have to run," he said, his eyes two trembling pools of warning.

Cold terror shattered Roderick's weariness in an instant. He dashed over to where Kendall lay and gave him a shake. Kendall's sharp eyes flashed open.

"What is it?" he asked.

"Jacob says the shadows are coming."

Kendall jerked to his feet. "Where?"

Jacob pointed into the darkness, back from the way they came.

"Grab what you can and run," Kendall ordered, but then caught himself. "Where is the Gitano?"

Roderick looked around and let out a groan. Nagan was gone.

168

"Oh no…"

"They're close now," Jacob said.

"Never mind the Gitano," Kendall cried. "To the river!"

Roderick and Jacob raced after him, struggling to keep up as they plowed through the tall grass.

They ran headlong in the dark until breathing air was like drinking liquid fire. They hardly even slowed when they reached the banks of the Fallowing. The icy shock of the midnight waters shot through Roderick's veins. He barely had the presence of mind to turn and hoist Jacob's trembling body into his arms.

The river was mercifully narrow there, even narrower than the last time they crossed. Roderick kept looking back over his shoulder, but there was no sign of the shadows. The waters came up above his chest, but went down almost as quickly. Huffing and wheezing, they achieved the far bank. Here they stopped to catch their breath and shake off the chill.

They hadn't taken five gulps of air when the hollow lights of a shadow's eyes winked into existence across the water. The burning red lamps lanced through Roderick's heart and drained his courage even at this distance. He found himself unable to move, frozen amongst the short grass which grew along the bank. His breath came in short, pathetic gasps.

At first only one pair of eyes glared at them, but before long two more appeared, then more after that. In moments six shadows menaced them from across the water. Their smoldering stares sapped Roderick's strength to the point that he forgot all about protecting Jacob, or even fleeing. Dark thoughts wrapped themselves around him in a cocoon of fear. Why was he even here, so cold and far from home in the middle of the night? Why even bother fleeing the shadows? He had no way of resisting them.

Kendall seized him by the arm. "Do not look at them," he warned. Kendall's tenacious grip dragged Roderick back to reality. "It is as I had hoped. I do not think they are solid enough yet to cross the water. We must go on before they find some means to pass."

Strength returned to Roderick's limbs. He started up the bank. He resisted the urge to look back, but felt the shadows' glare on the back of his neck like a prickly wind.

They had not quite achieved the top of the bank when a chilling scream ripped through the plains. Roderick could not help but turn back then. The six inky shadows slithered in rage and frustration along the opposite bank, but the scream had not come from them. It had come from much further away. The scream came again, louder. This time the words, "Save me!" could be made out inside the cry.

"That's the thief," Jacob said. Roderick recognized the voice as well. "A shadow got him."

"Then we have to save him," Roderick said. "We must go back—"

"No," Kendall said. "We cannot risk the boy."

"All right. You stay here. I'll go myself." Roderick could only imagine what a creature like that was capable of, but whatever it was doing, Nagan would not last long.

"You have no way of standing against those creatures. They will only take you as well," Kendall said.

"But—" Roderick was cut off by another series of screams. Nagan's strangled pleas cut straight through Roderick's heart.

"Please!" he screamed. "Someone help me! Please!"

"We can't just leave him to those fiends," Roderick cried, starting off back towards the river. Kendall grabbed him and jerked him back.

"There is nothing we can do." Kendall's voice rang out hard and dire. "We must keep moving."

The screams ceased in mid-cry. The shadows bristled expectantly. Their eyes flared with fresh wrath. Surely Nagan had met his end.

As much as it sickened Roderick, Kendall was right. He would only be throwing his life away if he went after Nagan now. Roderick turned and followed Kendall, assisting Jacob up the bank. With each step, his chest tightened at the thought of the poor, helpless Gitano in the grasp of the shadows. Had they killed him? Or done something even worse?

Jacob pointed beyond the far bank to the plains. There, a new set of eyes appeared. Unlike the shadows slinking along the river, it moved above the tall grass with incredible swiftness, floating across the plains at the height of a man.

"What is it?" Roderick's heart froze with dread at what the answer might be.

"It's him," Jacob said. "Nagan is one of the shadows now."

21

STAND BY THE RIVER

Jacob's words smote Roderick like a hammer.

Though the inky black shape rushing towards them had the same, shifting dark haze clinging to it as the others, it stood upright like a man. It did not float like the rest either, but ran on two legs. The arms, chest, and head were those of a shadowy person, stepping out of some awful nightmare. Its face was a blackened parody of Nagan's. Pitch black locks floated about its head with a life of their own. The cruel mouth was frozen wide in a silent scream. And the eyes, the eyes were the least human thing of all. The same baleful embers floating inside the other apparitions blazed inside this new creature, ardent points of hatred which drained the will of all who looked upon them.

The shadowy Nagan plunged into the river, his feet skimming the surface of the water like some ghostly insect. He was across in a shuddering heartbeat.

"Oh, Nagan, may Adonai have mercy on your soul," Roderick whispered under his breath.

The only sensible thing was to run, but Jacob and Kendall remained where they were.

"What's going on? We can't fight that," Roderick said. The idea was pure madness.

"Nor can we outrun it," Kendall said.

"Take out your knife," Jacob told Roderick. "And ready your staff," he instructed Kendall. The note of finality in his voice made him sound far older than he was.

"Please, child, no—not the magic," Kendall said. "It will

only make things worse."

But if Jacob heard what Kendall said he gave no indication. His skin began to pulse with light as in the sewers of Middlehelm. The diamonds blinked in and out with a fierce rhythm, washing away the darkness surrounding them. A song of deep notes arose on the plains, filled with foreboding, and terrible resolution, a song of fell deeds in a desperate hour.

Roderick pulled his knife from its sheath. He was as doubtful as Kendall about the prospect of using Jacob's magic, but there was no time to think of anything else. Nagan's shadow swept up the bank, but then, halfway up, it hesitated.

Roderick's knife shone with a subtle, mysterious light. Kendall's staff shimmered with the same sort of glimmer. Kendall dropped his satchel and gripped the metal shaft with both hands. The glow brightened, surrounding both weapons with shining ribbons which undulated like moonlight on the water.

The music of the night delved deeper into the scale, dropping great bass vibrations into Roderick's bones, notes heard as well as felt.

"Hurry. Attack it. I don't know how long it will last," Jacob told them.

Kendall rushed forward, but the shadow was too quick. It darted around and past him and came at Roderick.

Roderick made the mistake of locking eyes with the horrible creature. His knife grew heavy in his hands as his strength drained from him. His hand began shaking so fiercely he feared he would drop the weapon. The light intensified, but the creature tumbled along the ground to his left, avoiding the luminous glow.

Before Roderick knew what was happening, the shadow's icy grip closed around his neck from behind. It was not constricting, like human hands would have been, but it numbed his skin and sapped his strength even further. He could not shake the shadow's hold for all he tried. The numbness crept down his back. Roderick waved his knife wildly over his shoulder. He was as likely to stab himself as the shadow, but he was desperate. The numbness swept past his waist and into his legs. His knees gave way and folded to the ground. The knife fell from his insensate hands.

"Adonai, help me!" Roderick cried out, but he could no longer hear the night song, nor see the river bank. A curtain of darkness closed in upon him.

"You are mine," a windy, soulless voice whispered into his thoughts. "Your ember dims. Come dwell with Strath—"

From somewhere far away drifted the echoes of Jacob's scream. "No! You can't have him!"

The numbness swept down into Roderick's feet. He felt himself slipping from the world. Just before the deadness overtook him completely, a terrible blow from behind jarred him back to consciousness. Roderick cried out and rolled over, writhing in pain. The bent form of Kendall loomed over him, holding his glimmering staff with an uncharacteristic look of astonishment on his face.

"What happened?" Roderick asked.

"The shadow is gone," Kendall answered. The sheen surrounding his staff began to fade. The music, which briefly returned, drifted away once more, like some forgotten dream which slips away upon waking. "It was as the child said, the light from the weapon scattered the creature to nothing. I am sorry that my blow had to hit you as well. It was the only way I could be sure of striking it. Are you all right?"

"I feel a bit numb, but the feeling is starting to return," Roderick said, rubbing his neck. It was still deathly cold to the touch.

Jacob ran up to him and threw his arms around him. "I thought the shadow was going to take you." he said, his voice thick with emotion.

"I'm safe now," Roderick said. "Your magic saved me."

A red diamond now glimmered on Jacob's face near his right eye to go along with the other three.

"This is no time for sentimentality," Kendall said curtly.

174

"There are still six more of those creatures across the river. They may find another way across at any moment." As he spoke, the creatures dispersed, half heading west, the other half heading east.

"They won't catch us today," Jacob said.

"How do you know?" Roderick asked.

"The sun's coming up soon," he said, pointing to a small glimmer on the horizon. "They aren't strong enough to endure the day. At least not yet."

"And Nagan?" Roderick asked, unable to get the twisted, shadowy version of the Gitano out of his mind. "Is he...?"

"Dead?" Kendall finished Roderick's question. "I do not think so. He was not in the shadow's grasp long enough for that."

"Oh, thank heaven! So what happened to him?" Roderick wondered if he would be permanently changed or marred in some way.

"That numbing you felt—it reminded me of a passage in the *Grimoire*," Kendall said. "According to what I read the scathen can pull a person into their world if they grab hold of him long enough, distancing his own soul from his body. Then they can assume his form while also becoming more solid, more real."

"The dream world," Jacob said. "That's where they take you."

Kendall reached down to help Roderick up. His limbs tingled, as if they had fallen asleep, but he could move well enough. He thanked the Savant and tried to walk off the numbness.

"If we can find Nagan, he may be able return to this world," Kendall said. "While I have little desire to hear his jabbering again, we are still in need of his services. We will wait until the sun rises and then cross the river to search for him."

"I know he's not an honest fellow, but the fact that he might still be alive, well, that lightens my heart. I feared..." Roderick found his knife in the grass and picked it up. The mysterious glow was gone. "Thank you, Jacob. You saved us all."

"It was the magic. I don't know if I could do it again," Jacob said.

"It would be best if you didn't," Kendall said gravely.

Roderick was inclined to agree. This magic business was certainly not something he would ever get used to. If that was the last he ever saw of it, he'd live a happy man to the end of his days.

After a chilly trek back across the river Roderick grew numb all over again, this time from the frosty winter morning. The sun's light shone hollow and cheerless across the plains. Until they found Nagan, Roderick doubted anything would absolve him of the terrible cold which he felt down to the very marrow of his bones.

Kendall had a fair guess as to the direction Nagan had fled, and, sure enough, about an hour later, they found the Gitano's body curled up in the grass half a mile west of their camp. As Kendall had suspected, Nagan fled in the direction of the Tamber Forest. His eyes were shut and his skin was several shades paler.

"You're sure he's not dead?" Roderick asked, loath to touch him and confirm his fears.

"No, he but sleeps." Kendall felt inside Nagan's jerkin. A moment later he pulled out the Hapshire necklace the Gitano had stuffed inside one of his pockets. "He is quite the determined cutpurse."

Jacob shook his head disapprovingly.

Unexpectedly, Kendall handed the piece of jewelry to Roderick. "Here. It might be safer with you this time."

"All right. If you say so." Roderick had no desire to possess such finery. It was stolen goods. He felt guilty just touching it, but he slipped it into the secret compartment inside his coat for safe keeping while Kendall roused Nagan.

Nagan awoke with a start, his chest heaving as if he had just come up out of the water for air.

"Is the shadow gone? Is it safe? Where am I?" he blathered. His eyes darted about erratically. "Oh, Roderick, I had the most awful dream about you. You had stolen something from me and I was trying to get it back. I had my hands around your throat and I was—oh, it was all so real."

"It wasn't a dream. It was the shadow creatures," Roderick said. "One of them got you and made you chase after us—or something that looked like you anyway."

"And you—" Nagan pointed at Jacob. "You were there too. But you were shining and awful and impossible to look at."

"The light is what saved you," Jacob said.

"You should not have fled like that," Kendall said. "I warn you; we may not be able to save you if you run off again."

"I thought the shadows were keen after Jacob, not me." Nagan rubbed his face and arms. He looked even colder than Roderick felt.

"If we do not help this child get to where he has to go, the shadows will imprison everyone in Arinn just as they did with you."

"Please don't talk like that, Master Scholar," Nagan implored. "There are children present and you don't want to frighten them."

But Jacob had turned his attention to the horizon, watching the sun's imperceptible ascent into the heavens. "I'm more afraid of them in my dreams," he said. "I don't know how to fight them there. The only thing that helps is the prayers." Jacob squeezed Roderick's hand in silent gratitude. He was as soaked as Roderick, but his skin was surprisingly warm.

"The point is that there are things at work in this world far more dangerous than Barillio and your petty ring of thieves," Kendall said. "You must decide quickly which side you are on."

"Oh, on your side, of course, Master Scholar, on your side.

Last night was an aberration, I assure you. I was wrong to wander off; I see that now. No, your dear, sweet Nagan pledges to be ever faithful and true from here on out. I'll take you to Barillio strapped on my back if I have to." His face had a gravity to it that had not been there before. Perhaps he really meant his words this time.

"We're all just glad you're still alive," Roderick said. "But Master Kendall is right. No more false promises."

Nagan's face wore a doleful look. "I know, Roderick; I'm a dreadful person. It's just, well, my past is an awful burden to bear; you can't expect me to just throw my rudder against the stream and turn the whole boat around all in one day, can you?"

Roderick clapped his hand on the Gitano's shoulder. His color was returning and a new day lay ahead. Perhaps the wayward burglar would sober some after his brush with the shadows.

"Well, Master Kendall," Roderick said. "It seems as though we have our guide back, such as he is."

Nagan was unusually quiet as they resumed their journey. Kendall was quite content with the change, but Roderick worried the shadow's touch might have had some sort of lasting effect. The further they went, the more he withdrew into himself. Roderick tried to get him to open up when they stopped for a rest at midday, but Nagan would only say that he had, "a lot on his mind," and preferred not to talk at the moment.

They journeyed on, gloom overshadowing Roderick's heart despite the sun poking through the clouds now and then.

Smoke appeared on the horizon just past midday. As usual, Jacob saw it first and pointed it out to the others.

"What could it be? Iddlglim?" Roderick asked.

They all stopped and stared at it for some time.

"It's too large for a campfire," Roderick said. "And with the recent rains, I don't see how it could be a grass fire."

"It's Rill," Kendall said. "The Iddlglim must have razed it."

"Oh, those poor people," Roderick murmured. Images of the burning blasts which brought down the walls of castle Middlehelm blazed through his thoughts.

Rill was not a large town, but it was part of the empire. It rested along the southern banks of the Fallowing River. The invading army at Middlehelm could not have reached Rill by now. That imperial captain's warning about other Iddlglim forces had proven right.

"Rill was no fortress," Nagan said hotly. "There could not have been two hundred men of fighting age in all the village. A pox on these mangy wolf lords and their cursed war."

"The tendrils of smoke are weak and few," Kendall said. "It looks as if the fires there are dying. Let us hope the invaders have already passed on to the south. We must be doubly cautious from here on out."

And so to the chill and gloom were added wariness and fear. The smoke did indeed thin as they drew nearer, but that did nothing to better Roderick's mood. The tall grass rippled in the wind as if the plains themselves were trying to warn them not to pass this way. Roderick imagined Iddlglim warriors lying in wait for them within every clump of bending grass, but if they were there, they remained hidden.

They traveled well south of Rill and the sun was slipping past the horizon by the time they caught their first sight of the Tamber forest. It appeared as a dark smudge across the horizon.

"I would prefer to enter into the woods by day," Kendall said. "But with the Iddlglim on the move, we have no choice but to press on."

They were still a few miles from the edge of the forest when the wolves began to howl. The cries came from several directions. Kendall broke out his *invios* powder once again. Once the four of them had been thoroughly doused, they

179

started back off, pushing their weary feet on to the forest.

The farther they went, the louder the howling grew. At last Kendall brought the group to a halt. They stood listening as the wolves drew ever closer. It was too dark to see much of anything. Kendall made them lie down in the tall grass and warned them not to speak a word.

They lay there in dread of the approaching sounds: growling mixed with the occasional shouts and cries of men. They were closing in from the south and the west. Roderick held onto Jacob and prayed silently. He tried desperately not to think of the wolves and their terrible fangs and the wild-eyed warriors who were running with them.

Then came a new sound. Horns blasted through the darkness from far away to the south. After that, the sounds of wolves and men moved in that direction, away from the group. Kendall waited until the sounds died away completely before daring to rise from the grass. After a few moments of surveying the countryside he signaled that it was safe for the others to rise as well.

Roderick stared out across the swiftly darkening plains. There were no signs of the Iddlglim.

"I reckon we slipped the hangman's noose there, fellows," Nagan whispered.

"Perhaps," Kendall said grimly. "Perhaps."

They resumed their march west towards the Tamber. They moved even more swiftly now, the sight of the forest quickening their steps. The dark mass grew ever closer until at last they found themselves passing beneath the first of the outlying trees.

Tall, thin trunks shone pale in the moonlight. As the night closed in, their ghostly bark made it look like a forest of bones. Myriad leaves coated the ground with a rustling carpet that surely must have announced their presence to every Gitano in the forest. Only Jacob seemed to tread lightly enough to avoid the murmuring of the fallen leaves.

Roderick had heard many tales about these woods growing up in Briar's Glen. Most claimed that spirits haunted the forest, leading travelers astray by false lights at night and with haze and fog during the day. He'd never actually met anyone who'd been to the Tamber, though, and he'd always assumed the tales to be mostly untrue. Seeing it now, he understood why people would think it haunted.

The land grew quiet as the grave. The blowing of the wind was the only sound and even that was a mournful moan.

"The trees look strange, but I don't think they're enchanted," Jacob said, wandering over to one of the trunks and running his hand over the bark.

"They look that way now," Kendall said. "In the day they glow with a golden light."

"It's the most beautiful sight in all of Arinn," Nagan said, his voiced tinged with melancholy.

Perhaps Nagan and Kendall were right, but the sun was long gone and the stars poking through the branches overhead gave off a sense of watchful danger. The trees gave some shelter from the wind, but a brooding chill lay upon the woods.

I shall either freeze to death in this place or be frightened out of my knickers. At least if his knees started knocking for the second reason he could say it was the first.

"Are you sure the Iddlglim won't come into the forest?" Roderick asked, hoping that turning his thoughts to a more distant threat would take his mind off the present one.

"No Iddlglim in his right mind would dare set foot in this place," Kendall said. "They believe blaizewood trees are possessed by evil spirits who lure men to their deaths. And the Gitanos have made certain that those beliefs remain alive and well."

"But what about the shadows?" Nagan asked, as if to remind Roderick that there were worse things than Gitanos and eerie trees in the world. "Will they come after us again?

"They will not stop until they have the motley, but I am hopeful we will not be visited by them while we are in the Tamber. According to some of the old legends, the scathen loathe to enter the blaizewoods for some reason as well,

181

though no one is exactly sure why."

"Afraid of trees, eh? I might just have to chop one down and wear it around my neck, then," Nagan said.

Kendall motioned for them to stop in the midst of a small clearing. They could no longer see the edge of the forest.

"Well, I have guided us up to this point," Kendall said. "Now it is your turn, Gitano. This is your land and you are the only one who knows where Barillio might be holed up."

Nagan let out a sigh. "I must confess that—" he began, but stopped short when the wind gusted up, accompanied by another moan that was louder than usual.

"What was that?" Roderick asked, stepping away from the tree he'd been standing next to.

Kendall cocked his head to one side, listening.

"The wind passing through the limbs of the blaizewood trees I shouldn't wonder," Nagan said, but Roderick found it hard to put stock in his words. That cry sounded nothing like the wind.

"Or it could be something else," Kendall said.

The moans were coming from all around them now, growing closer by the moment. Roderick thought he heard a rustling in the leaves, but when he whipped in that direction all he saw were pale trunks, sucking in the surrounding light so that between them was utter darkness.

"Stay close," Kendall said. "Whatever happens—"

Roderick did not catch the rest of his words. At that moment the woods erupted with a loud boom and a cloud of darkness enveloped them, swallowing what little moonlight was left.

22

THE SHIFTING SANDS

oderick's eyes bulged with every cough. Others coughed around him, but no one could be seen. The black smoke of the Savants filled the air, but it was not Kendall's work this time.

"It's the Gitanos! Everyone stay together!" Kendall shouted.

"Jacob, where are you?" Roderick called out, groping.

"I'm here," Jacob cried back. Roderick felt a small body press against his side.

Nagan's voice boomed through the smoke.

"It's me, Nagan! River's blood! Didn't you recognize me?" That was all he got out before an outburst of coughing seized him.

A gang of hands clamped onto Roderick and dragged him forward. He fell, sprawled out on the forest floor beyond the edge of the smoke. Kendall and Jacob lay beside him on a mantel of leaves and moss.

A moment later, Nagan came staggering out of the cloud with four men wearing dark leather jerkins and black scarves covering their faces. Their dagger blades caught the moonlight, and by the cold look in their eyes they were looking for an excuse to use them.

"So, let's see what the river rat dragged up," said the man closest to Nagan, the tallest of the group. All the men had black hair, but this man's was wavy and went down to his chin. He had a short sword and a red sash at his waist, though he was the only one so armed. The others had only the daggers, though they also wore wide belts with numerous leather pouches attached.

Nagan gave the man a nervous smile.

"They don't look like they have much to offer," another Gitano said.

"They're dressed little better than peasants," remarked another. Nagan and the tall man stopped where they were, but the others continued to advance. Roderick grabbed Jacob's hand and said a silent prayer for protection.

"Search the old man," Nagan said. "I think you'll find he's carrying a piece that'll put a glint in the Anciano's eye."

The Gitanos removed Kendall's cloak and opened all his pouches and pockets and rifled through his satchel. The Savant had a dizzying assortment of equipment and contraptions, but all their captors were interested in were the pouches of powder and a huge bag of coins. Upon opening the bag, their expressions soured.

"That's the biggest bag of copper plinks I've ever seen. We couldn't buy two strings for that," said the man directing the search. "But these powders are another matter. Where did you get them?"

"I made them," Kendall said cooly.

"You deal in elements?"

Kendall nodded. "That *ornythite* powder you used on us is one of my specialties. I know the Gitanos are always in need of extra, that is why we risked venturing into your woods. If you allow me to meet with the Anciano, I can offer him a very reasonable price." The way he spoke made it sound as if he were the one in a position to make a bargain and not the other way around.

"Well now, that's something. Can you vouch for this, Nagan?"

"So he knows a thing or two about powders," Nagan said testily. "That doesn't mean he's all whistle and woot on a windy day. Where did you hide that necklace, old man? Tell me!" Nagan took a step towards Kendall, glaring.

"Little you know, Nagan," the Gitano said, stepping

between him and Kendall. "If this man is a powder merchant the Anciano will most definitely want to meet him. The last two shipments we ordered from the coast failed to arrive. With the war coming on we'll need all we can get."

"But he stole my swag!" Nagan said.

"Well, whatever it was, it's gone now. It looks like you'll have to face the Anciano with whatever other trifles you managed to filch. Not that it would have mattered either way. Search the other two and see if they've got any scraps," he directed his men.

The Gitanos searched Roderick and Jacob while Nagan proceeded to pull out the gems, bracelets, and other small trinkets he had stolen besides the necklace.

"Six months away and this is all you have to show for yourself?" the leader scoffed.

The Gitanos searching Roderick found nothing of interest. They made him take off his coat and gave it a thorough patting down, but the clever folds and padding of the secret compartment kept the necklace safe from detection. Unless you knew the trick, the only way to find what was inside would be to rip the fabric apart.

They moved on to Jacob who shrank back. One of the Gitanos seized him by the scruff of the neck and yanked off his hood. Jacob hid his face in his hands, but it was too late. They had seen his skin.

"What in the blaizewoods is this?" exclaimed the astonished Gitano.

"Garamond," another one said. "What do you make of it?"

Garamond, the tall man who had been doing most of the talking, narrowed his eyes. Jacob peeked out at him from between his fingers, but kept his face covered.

"Well, I'll be hanged. That's Dimitrius' boy," he said, moving in closer to examine him.

"But he's dead—" objected the first Gitano.

"Hush!" Garamond cut him off and addressed Jacob. "Do you remember me?"

Jacob replaced his hood, pulling it down as tight as it could go.

Garamond knelt before him. "I knew your father. We met when I was passing through Brackenland. The Gitanos take a cut from some of the farms in that region and the overseer on one of them said your father needed help, that he was in danger. Dimitrius wouldn't let us see you, but he told us about your condition. We helped smuggle your family to Briar's Glen. We're not all bad, you see. At least not all the time."

"I remember you," Jacob said quietly. "Thank you."

Garamond rose, his aspect noticeably softer. "All right, put your things back on, then. Don't worry, we won't kill you. It would be bad luck anyway, what with it being Winter's Rest and all."

The Gitanos sheathed their weapons. Roderick and Kendall donned their cloaks and gear once more.

"Very well," Kendall said, continuing with his business-like air. "I'm anxious to finally meet your infamous leader. I take it the Anciano is still in good health?"

"Never better." Garamond yanked down his scarf to reveal an unshaven, but comely face. "I don't doubt he'll outlive us all. The old man simply refuses to die."

They spent the night in the forest with the Gitanos. Despite their apparent acceptance of Kendall and familiarity with Jacob, they spoke little to the members of Roderick's group. One of them went up into the trees, no doubt to keep watch, though Roderick couldn't spy out exactly where he ended up. It was too dark.

In the morning, four new Gitanos arrived at the camp.

Garamond spoke with them briefly, out of earshot, while Roderick and his companions breakfasted from their own provisions. After a short conversation, the other Gitanos returned the way they came, perhaps to send word on ahead of the arrival of these newcomers to the Tamber.

Nagan looked as sullen as an old broom, worn and frayed and no longer of any use. He eyed Kendall hotly when he wasn't straining to overhear Garamond's conversations. He seemed especially hurt that he was made to stay with Roderick and the others rather than join his fellow Gitanos.

After the brief breakfast, the Gitanos marched them through the woods. Getting moving helped warm Roderick's limbs against the bitter cold. As they journeyed on, the sun brought a welcoming warmth as well, turning the bark of the blaizewoods to brilliant gold. The honeyed forest filled the land with a wondrous hush. Beneath the barren, auric limbs, lay a majestic crimson carpet. Wherever the sunlight hit the forest floor the leaves glistened like cherry crumb cake. Jacob, especially, seemed to forget all about the Gitanos and the scathen and his magical curse as the day wore on. He kicked up the scarlet leaves and even hummed a little tune as they marched through the stunning patchwork of color and light.

"What's that you're humming?" Roderick asked, for he had never heard it before.

"A lullaby, I think," Jacob said. "But I don't know the name."

Somehow Roderick found his spirits lifted by the little song, but Nagan and Kendall seemed not to notice either the beauty of the forest or the soft sweet melody it had inspired.

They reached the Fallowing by mid-morning. It was flowing broad and deep at that point, close to eighty yards across. The Gitanos uncovered a raft near the bank, cleverly camouflaged in a mound of foliage.

There was barely room for the eight of them on the craft, but they managed to get afloat with little difficulty. The Gitanos maneuvered the raft deftly around the eddies and bars as they traveled.

They met a few other rafts on their trip, all of them piloted by Gitanos judging by their dark skin and the friendly manner in which they greeted Garamond and his crew. They were dressed in loose-fitting shirts and trousers. Many had bandanas tied loosely around their necks. All wore black, of course, in honor of Winter's Rest. The gypsies may have operated by their own peculiar laws and compass, but they were greatly committed to the various holidays and feasts celebrated throughout the Haliconian empire, Winter's Rest, coming at the end of autumn, being one of the four major ones.

It was late afternoon by the time the raft turned out of the main body of the Fallowing into one of its smaller tributaries. The forest thinned along the inlet. Roderick was sad to see the beautiful blaizewoods go. Not long after the golden trees disappeared, so did the stream, and the raft could go no further.

The Gitanos dragged the boat onto the banks and slipped it under some more sheets of foliage. Though Roderick watched them hide it, after glancing away for a moment he was at pains to tell where they had stashed it.

"We walk from here," Garamond said. "Don't worry, it's not far."

As they left the trickling stream, the forest sprang up again around them. The scarlet mantel beneath the blaizewoods soon gave way to a well-traveled dirt road, wide enough for two carriages to travel abreast. They had not been on the road for long before it opened into a clearing filled with people. Six large wagons of similar size and appearance, and one singularly enormous wagon, were spread out around the perimeter. The wagons had wooden walls and doors, shingled roofs, and stairs leading up to them so that they were more like moving houses than the open-aired carts typically seen in Vinyon Province. Several horses grazed peacefully nearby.

Many Gitanos milled about, a mix of men, women, and children, dressed after the fashion of the folk they met on the river, save that several of the women wore shawls with threaded patterns woven into them.

A wonderful, spicy smell drifted through the glade. Roderick spotted a few large black pots roasting over fires and could only guess what delicious provender was being prepared within. His stomach rumbled embarrassingly as he passed by.

A pair of Gitanos sat strumming long-necked instruments in the center of the clearing with a dozen or so others gathered around, half-listening to the music and half-focused on their meandering, easy-going conversation. The melodies faded as Roderick's party approached, but the conversation continued, albeit in lower tones. Several of the men stopped what they were doing and studied Garamond and his captives with obvious interest.

"Welcome to the Crescent Meadow," Garamond said. A few of the onlookers grinned mischievously in response.

"Barillio has been expecting you," said one of the musicians, gesturing towards the huge wagon. It was twice as tall and wide, and half again as long as the others. As befitting such a behemoth, it had three sets of large wheels that came up almost to Roderick's shoulder. It had a porch on one end and four windows on the side facing them, all of which were shut. Though all the carts were colorfully painted with circus-like designs, this wagon was the most ornately decorated of all. Its swirling patterns had not only been painted on, but carved into the wood itself. Stars and wave-like dunes dominated the designs. It had large eaves propped up on the sides, though no one lingered beneath them, preferring the warmth of the open meadow and the early winter sun. Brightly colored poles, replete with flags and streamers jutted out from every conceivable angle like an enormous pin cushion.

They followed Garamond up the stairs to the porch. Here they stopped before a thick double door painted and carved with orange and green genies around the frame.

Garamond rapped on the door and a young lady with jet black hair appeared in short order. Unlike the other women they'd seen, she wasn't wearing black, but a gray-green tunic with matching trousers.

"What is it, sharper?" she asked, scowling at a startled Garamond. She had a keen look about her, as if she were thinking up a response even before the Gitano gave his reply.

Garamond cleared his throat and for the first time appeared slightly addled.

"Portia," he replied. "I didn't know—I thought—"

"Yes, I'm back—for now. Don't be surprised you haven't heard. Now what do you want with my grandfather?" she asked brusquely.

"I have some men who have come to pay him a visit. One of them claims to be a dealer in powder."

Portia raised her chin high.

"Out of the question," she said. "He and I have things to discuss—"

She was interrupted by a loud voice from inside. In response she turned back and shouted, "But grandfather, you promised!"

The voice from within drowned her out once again.

"Agh!" she screamed and stamped her foot. "You never have time for me. For all you know, it's another assassin come calling. You don't care half as much for your own flesh and blood as you do for these scoundrels and cutthroats!"

She barreled straight through the men and down the porch stairs. Nagan attempted to address her as she shoved her way through.

"Portia, it's me, Nagan. I'm back and I—" he began, but she pushed him aside and dashed off into the woods.

"Pardon the misunderstanding," Garamond said, watching her go. "Step on into the *Shifting Sands*. The Anciano will see you now."

As they started up the steps, Nagan looked more lost than ever. He remained motionless where he stood, as if he had not heard Garamond's words.

"Is something wrong, Nagan?" Roderick asked.

Nagan's shoulders drooped and the clever sparkle in his eyes dimmed. "No, I suppose everything is just as it's always been," he said. Then, without further explanation, he followed Master Kendall up the stairs into the waiting maw of the giant wagon.

23

THE ANCIANO

he interior of Barillio's wagon was even more elaborate than the outside. Rugs, tapestries, paintings, sculptures, carvings, and other works of art covered the walls and floor in a veritable cultural cavern of wealth. The place was littered with such abundance there was scarcely room to move about.

Four Gitanos, much heavier set than Garamond, rose from a table where they sat. They were armed with swords and daggers. Their studded leather vests and leggings stretched tight against their hulking frames. They placed themselves like a wall of flesh between the newly arrived party and the other Gitano in the room, an old, round man whose white hair came down past his shoulders. His face was so scarred and wrinkled it was difficult to distinguish between his nose, mouth, forehead and cheeks. It reminded Roderick of the back of a cross-stitch. His eyes leapt out from amidst these fleshy scratchings like search lights in a fog, taking in the newcomers with keen interest.

"Anciano, we picked these strangers up on our patrol of the southern woods," Gararamond said.

"So I heard. Welcome, friends, to the *Shifting Sands*," the elder Gitano said, motioning them forward with his right hand. His other one was missing, replaced by a thick-bladed dagger, polished to a mirror sheen. "I don't get many visitors these days. Or rather, most of my visitors don't get to me, I suppose." His voice gargled a bit, like water simmering over a fire.

191

"An honor to finally meet you, Barillio," Kendall said. "You're looking well."

"Indeed, I live to spite my enemies." Barillio smiled, revealing a checkerboard grin alternating between gold teeth and natural ones. "They tell me you go by the name of Kendall and that you're a dealer in elements?"

"Indeed, though not directly. I work with a fellow by the name of Jucket. He sells barrels of *ornythite* out of Rill."

"Ah yes, I've heard of him, though we've never had the pleasure of buying from him," Barillio said, looking Kendall up and down. He turned and, recognizing Nagan, gave the younger man a contemptuous glare. "I see you've drug something up off the river bottom as well, Garamond. I did not think that one was foolish enough to set foot in the Tamber again."

"Greetings, Anciano," Nagan said, giving a half bow that looked more like he stumbled forward. "I've been so anxious to see you again—I did as you asked. In addition, I went above and beyond what you requested. I lifted the Hapshire Necklace. You would already have it in your hands if it were not for this double-crossing knave—"

Barillio waved irritably. "Bah! The Hapshire Diamonds? You expect me to believe that a penny-pinch like yourself could pilfer something of that renown? Humph."

Nagan was visibly crushed by the Anciano's reply. His face went sallow.

Poor Nagan. He'd be better off if he didn't run with these folk.

Roderick touched the spot on his chest where the diamonds lay hidden. Should he reveal them? For half a moment he thought about it, then Barillio started speaking again.

"And these others, who are they?"

"This is Roderick the tailor and his ward," Garamond announced. "The boy was that odd little wisp we helped smuggle into Briar's Glen not too long ago."

Jacob, who had returned to his subdued self upon entering the Gitano camp, kept his face buried beneath the shadows of his hood. At Garamond's words he dropped his head even further, as if he had suddenly fallen asleep.

Roderick stuck out his hand hastily to shake the Anciano's. "A pleasure to meet you Mr. Barillio," he said. Two of the large attendants moved in on either side to block him.

"Calm down, boys," Barillio said. "I'm certain Master Kendall doesn't travel with disreputable folk. And I hope it will take a bit more than a common tailor to do me in. I very much doubt that I shall be stitched to death."

The guards moved aside and Barillio invited Kendall and the others to take a place at the table.

"I see you're not wearing black, so I take it you haven't come to the Tamber for the holidays. But I'm sure you could have easily done business through Jucket if you wanted to sell me something. So what is it that brings you to the *Shifting Sands?*" Barillio fixed the Savant with a stare.

"Have you gotten word of what happened to Rill? The wolfmen have sacked it. It is nothing more than smoldering ruins. I can only hope Jucket made it out alive."

The lines in the Anciano's face twisted and deepened. "This is ill news if you speak true."

"You will know the truth soon enough I am sure. But more to the point for our purposes here, it is my understanding that you are in need of more elements for the defense of the Tamber."

"We can never have enough. And as you know we pay heavy coin for it, too. Unfortunately, with the Iddlglim crawling over the north like ants in the Emperor's larder, our principle supplier has had to halt shipments."

"Located in the north, you say? You are referring to Virinian of Brimstoke, I take it?" Kendall asked.

"We do not discuss our dealings with other clients." Barillio gazed at his reflection in the dagger on the end of his arm, as if to assure himself that no one was sneaking up behind him.

"Fair enough. Regardless, I can see that my arrival is most timely. Your supply of black powder has dried up precisely at the time when it is most needed."

"You're a shrewd man. I like that. War greases all wheels, as they say." Barillio spread wide his checkered grin. "Let's clear the fog, then, shall we? I'm prepared to give you ten valins a barrel and I'll buy out your entire stock, whatever you have. How does that strike you, Master Kendall?"

Kendall returned the smile. "A most generous offer. I can have fifty barrels delivered to you by the middle of Winter's Dawn. And since I am myself also in a bit of a bind, I'll sell you the entire lot for only five valins a barrel if you'll provide me with a much needed favor."

Barrillio's smile widened. "Excellent, name the request."

"I need safe passage to Davinsmoor," Kendall said.

Barillio stared at him for a moment before bursting out laughing. "River's blood! Even innocents and fools know better than to put their head in the jaw of the beast come suppertime. It's smooth enough sailing to Ivensbrook, but if the wildmen capture it—and if they've taken Rill, I don't see why they wouldn't—you'll get no further. And even if you somehow got through before they took it, Davinsmoor is bound to be crawling with Iddlglim now that the war's started. I wouldn't send my best men within twenty leagues of that place. We hold our own in the Tamber, but outside these woods, the wolf lords will skin a Gitano first chance they get."

"My demand still stands. We need to secure passage to Davinsmoor," Kendall said, firmly.

The old Gitano laughed all the louder.

"Master Kendall, are you an elements merchant or a jester? You've certainly lightened this old heart by good measure today."

Roderick fidgeted in his chair. Intuition told him they were wasting their time with this man. And if that was the case, they might be in considerable danger even speaking to him at all. But hadn't the Gitanos helped Jacob before? *Better wait and see what he says before assuming the worst, Devinson. Just stay calm. Adonai will see us through.*

"Very well, I'll part with the powder for two valins a barrel and I'll find a way to get you an extra ten barrels if you'll ferry us to the Caledonian capital. It is little more than a three day trip if the weather holds. Surely a man of your business acumen can recognize how profitable a venture this will be for you."

Barillio's laughter slowly died away. "Master Kendall, you're asking me to lend you something far more precious than anything you have to offer and that is Gitano blood. I may be a cutthroat when it comes to other people, but the Gitanos, we're family. I see you're traveling with a boy there. I'd mind you look to his safety and wait 'til this war blows over because if you try to test the waters of the Fallowing just now, you'll find you're in over your head."

The impatience Roderick had been stuffing inside his chest suddenly swelled to bursting.

"Sir," he said, "it is precisely because we want to protect this boy that we need to reach the coast."

Barillio gave him a puzzled look, as if he had his cloak on backwards or had donned a ridiculous looking hat.

Kendall leaned towards Roderick. "Best to let me do the talking," he said.

"I'm sorry, but shouldn't they know the truth? We'd have a better chance of getting help if they knew what we were about," Roderick said, lowering his voice.

Kendall was about to reply, but Barillio raised his hand.

"With all due respect, Master Kendall. I'd like to hear what this fellow has to say," he said.

"He's not familiar with all the details of our journey, Barillio," Kendall interjected. "If it's all the same to you—"

"He's traveling with you to wherever it is you're headed, is he not? Surely there must be more to him than simple skill with a needle and thread if he's venturing about with the likes of you in a time of war. I desire to hear what he has to say, and here in the *Shifting Sands* I am accustomed to getting my wishes."

Kendall gave Roderick a sour look, but inclined his head,

signaling his approval.

"The boy's name is Jacob," Roderick said.

"Dimitrius' son, Anciano," Garamond put in.

"Yes, yes, I remember," the old man said testily. "I may be old, but I never forget anything when it comes to our business. A family of migrant workers with a mysterious past —in trouble and so forth." Barillio waved his good hand impatiently.

Roderick resumed in breathless fashion, "Yes, sir. But there's more to it than that. You know about his skin I take it? He's, well he's been touched by magic somehow—real magic —the kind that does unexplainable, unpredictable things. And because of this magic there are creatures that have been let loose in the world which don't want him to have it—terrible things, the stuff of nightmares. And if we don't find a way to get him to the Isle of Rinn, they'll soon come for us all."

Barillio glanced slyly at his fellow Gitanos.

"And taking him to the barbarian capital will put all these ghosts to rest?" he asked in thinly veiled mockery.

"Yes, or at least go a long way to that end. Please, we must get there as soon as possible. I know it sounds far-fetched, but it is the truth sir, as I am an honest tailor."

The other Gitanos joined in their leader's laughter this time, with the old gypsy guffawing the loudest.

"Well, it seems I have a jester *and* a storyteller in my house. What is the boy's talent, then? Is he a juggler?"

"I've seen the shadows," Roderick insisted. "They're real. This is no story." He pointed to Nagan. "Ask him. He's one of you. And he's seen the creatures that stalk us. One of them grabbed hold of him and almost...well, perhaps Nagan himself would be the best one to tell you what happened."

"Nagan?" Barillio stared at the young Gitano. "Are you a part of this traveling circus as well? I've always thought you'd make an excellent clown."

The remark drew a fresh round of laughter from the other Gitanos.

"Well..." Nagan grimaced. "I mean they, um, they forced

me to bring them into the Tamber. I got them out of Middlehelm as well, and in return for it, this old leather-bound lifted the necklace I stole for you. There's gratitude for you!"

"Enough about nonexistent jewels. What of this business with the ghosts? What do you have to say about that? Come now, out with it, I've wasted enough time on you already." Barillio began cleaning beneath his fingernails with his dagger. The blade was hardly ideal for such work, being far too thick, but the old man moved it deftly beneath his old, crusted nails without giving himself so much as a nick.

"I—well, it's hard to describe—"

"Have you seen one or not?"

"Um, well, yes. I suppose, in a manner of speaking...Yes, there are such things as the tailor mentioned. That is, if I have not been ensorcelled by this conjurer here."

"Well, Nagan," Barillio said after pausing to consider the matter. "If you weren't such a liar and a fool, I'd almost half believe you."

Nagan's countenance fell even further.

Roderick realized his mistake. It didn't matter that Nagan was a Gitano. Barillio had nothing but contempt for him. There had to be some other way of convincing him.

"Jacob, show these men your magic," Roderick said impulsively.

Jacob looked up at him for a moment. Though his face remained deep inside the hood, the glowing diamonds showed his terrified expression. He could not have looked more frightened if Roderick had been one of the shadows himself. He shook his head vigorously.

"Roderick, no!" Kendall said.

"But how are we going to get them to believe in the curse?" Roderick asked.

Jacob only lowered his head further and shook it again.

Another mistake. *What were you thinking, Devinson? You're meddling with things far beyond you!* Roderick, hung his head in shame, sorry he had spoken at all.

"It matters not whether you believe these stories, Barillio," Kendall said. "The question remains whether or not you intend to help us."

Barillio pointed his dagger at the scholar. "Exactly. And yet, I am sure you see my difficulty in answering. I'm not a philosopher like you, Master Kendall, but from my experience I would have to say that living threats are altogether more dangerous than ghostly ones, wouldn't you?"

"You do not intend to help us, then?"

"Well, taking into account that there are ghosts involved..." Barillio raised a condescending eyebrow. "I'd have to say *no*. We Gitanos may be a superstitious lot, but even we have our limits."

"But sir—" Roderick started to speak again in spite of himself, but a stern look from Kendall silenced him.

The Anciano rose to his feet with obvious stiffness and effort.

"And now, my fine fellows, I do believe our time together has come to an end. You're welcome to stay and take refuge in the Tamber until the end of Winter's Rest—let no one say I'm not a hospitable man—but I am simply not in a position to risk the lives of any of my men, except of course when it comes to the fellow you've already fallen in with. Him, I have no use for. In fact, you'd be doing me a great service if you took him off my hands permanently."

"Anciano, you can't mean that," Nagan said in a pathetic voice. "Don't cast me out—I've changed. I'm not the same man you sent away six months ago—"

"Guards, if you'll escort our guests to the door—all of them." Barillio gave Nagan a withering look.

"But I thought if I stole the Hapshire Necklace—something truly worthy of your collection..." Nagan persisted.

"Truth be told, the only reason I sent you to Middlehelm was because I hoped to be rid of you once and for all. You are of no use to me any longer. Still, if you did actually steal it, I'll gladly take it off your hands."

"That's just it, Anciano—this magpie here," Nagan pointed at Kendall. "He took it from me."

"A likely story." Barillio flipped his hands dismissively. "Now be gone, before I reconsider and send you to join the rest of the rabble who've crossed me, down by the river."

Watching the poor Gitano's life unravel was too much for Roderick. Reaching into the secret pouch where he kept the necklace, he pulled it out and flung it on the table.

"Here," he said. "Nagan is telling the truth. Though you really ought to return that to the lady it belongs to."

Barillio's eyebrows rose like two puffs of smoke above his enflamed eyes as he regarded the magnificent piece of jewelry. The pull of the necklace on him was instantaneous. He picked it up with the point of his dagger and held it out before him like the glorious prize that it was.

"Well, well, well, Nagan," Barillio said, the lines in his face relaxing somewhat. "I must admit I thought this was just another of your feckless boasts." Nagan began to perk up. He even managed a tentative smile. The old Gitano flashed him a steely glare. "Still, there is one thing you have yet to learn."

Barillio made a sudden move and brought the point of his daggered stump up under Nagan's chin. He looked him dead in the eye.

"No one steals from me. No one. The only reason I sent you away before was because Portia begged for your life and because I am growing soft in my old age. So let me be clear this time: I never want to see your wretched face within ten leagues of the Tamber again or I'll gut you no matter what my granddaughter says."

Nagan shrank back, so weak and frail-looking that for half a moment, Roderick wondered if Barillio had not surreptitiously stabbed him with the knife.

"Well," Kendall said, his manner stiff and formal. "I'm afraid the nature of our errand to Davinsmoor does not afford us the opportunity to partake of the legendary Gitano hospitality at this time. If you will allow us to make camp in the safety of the woods for the night, we'll be off and out of your way in the morning."

Barillio smiled broadly once again. "Certainly, Master Kendall. It has been a pleasure doing business with you."

The four massive Gitanos crowded in around them and herded the visitors towards the door. They left the old gypsy behind, his eyes dancing as he drank in the singular wealth and beauty of the majestic jewels dangling from the end of his dagger, like a fisherman admiring the biggest catch of the day.

24

UNEXPECTED HELP

agan bolted for the forest the moment they left the *Shifting Sands*. Roderick could hardly blame him. Thief or not, Barillio had cut him to the quick.

As he disappeared into the trees, Roderick said to Kendall, "Poor Nagan. I wonder if we'll ever see him again."

"I doubt it," Kendall said. "And we'll be better off for it."

Garamond found them an empty section of the clearing where they could sit and mull over their future. The other Gitanos kept their distance, only coming by around suppertime with some date cakes and fresh milk in honor of Winter's Rest. Unfortunately, Kendall would not let Roderick eat the cakes.

"Winter's Rest hospitality or no, I wouldn't put it past them to slip something in it," Kendall said in a low voice. When the Gitanos weren't looking he sprinkled some gray powder from a little vial into the milk. "This at least, should be safe," he said.

The milk was delicious, whether from Kendall's powder or because the milk was especially sweet to begin with, Roderick couldn't tell. So as not to offend their hosts, they pretended to eat the cake, crumbling it into the grass when they weren't looking. They ate of the tasteless hard tack instead. Jacob, of course, had some of his fruit.

As night fell across the camp, the gypsies marched in slow procession around an open fire, singing songs in honor of the dead. These were new songs to Roderick and he liked them better than the ones they sang back at Briar's Glen. But though the words and tunes were not as sorrowful as the ones he knew, they still made him sad. For they brought to mind his deceased parents.

His father, Nigel, had died twenty years ago, from an infected wound he'd suffered while hunting. His mother, Cordelia, had died only five years ago from the quieting fever. They were both good, honest people, raising Roderick without so much as a harsh word or a lifted voice. Though Bethany had been a constant comfort to him since their passing, and later Aisha, he had never felt truly whole since then. The world was a poorer place for their absence, and he doubted the emptiness would ever be filled this side of heaven. Some wounds were just too deep.

Kendall needed no dirges to dampen his mood. His expression was as solemn as a skillet. He kept his thoughts to himself, though, and Roderick had little interest in mining them. He was certain that a good deal of the blame for their failure to secure help from the Gitanos lay upon himself. He wished he had stayed quiet, but he really couldn't help himself.

The old Savant sat brooding in silence, staring at his maps as if he meant to bore a hole in them with his eyes. He fretted over the parchments like wayward children, scribbling in his journal and leafing through old entries until the daylight faded and he finally put them away.

Even Jacob had the doldrums. He played with a little rock, drawing pictures in the dirt of what looked like animals, but he resisted all efforts to engage him in conversation when Roderick asked about them. Roderick knew he had disappointed him back in the wagon by trying to get him to do his magic. It was a foolish idea and he ought to have known better. He only hoped Jacob would forgive him in time.

As the sun went down Roderick stared at the glimmering trees surrounding the clearing. They had lost their amber luster and taken on the pale ghostliness of the moonlight once more. Jacob drifted off to sleep as the last notes of the Gitano's laments faded into the trees. Once all the gypsies retired to their wagons Kendall drew near.

"Get what rest you can," he whispered. "We need to leave while it's still dark."

"But where will we go?" Roderick asked.

"We'll have to attempt to make it to Davinsmoor on foot."

"Will that be safe? What about the Iddlglim?"

"Of course it won't be safe. But nothing is ever truly safe. Some things are just more dangerous than others. Now pack your things and get some sleep. I shall wake you when it's time."

Roderick did as Kendall asked. After arranging his pack he nestled down beside Jacob, who, thankfully, was sleeping peacefully. Roderick had only just closed his eyes when a rustling from the bushes put him on his guard. At first he saw nothing. Then came something like a low hissing sound. Staring into the foliage he could just make out the forms of two shadowy figures crouching low to the ground.

Kendall noticed them as well. He quietly placed a hand on his staff. Roderick was about to unsheathe his knife when a voice whispered from the shadows.

"It's me."

Roderick glanced at Kendall, who motioned for him to stay put while he got up and crept towards the bushes. As he reached the edge of the clearing, he stopped and turned back towards Roderick, signaling for him to come on.

Kendall disappeared into the shadowy foliage. Roderick followed, his eyes adjusting to the low light. As he squirmed through the bushes, finally it dawned on him who had called out to them a moment before.

"Nagan, is that you?" he asked.

"In my skin for the present, yes—though I sometimes half wonder if I've not fallen back into one of those nightmares," Nagan said in hushed tones. "And this is Portia, my partner in nocturnal mischief." He motioned towards a woman standing next to him, but it was too dark to make out much about her.

"Pleased to make your acquaintance," she said. From the sharp, confident way she spoke, Roderick recognized her as the woman from the *Shifting Sands*. She was shorter than he remembered, but Roderick had been standing on the steps looking up at her the last time.

"An honor to meet you," Roderick replied.

"Hurry up and explain yourself, rogue, so that we can get back to sleep. What is this about?" Kendall demanded.

"Well, actually, I'd best let Portia do the talking. This was her plan, really, not mine. I'm not much of a strategist," Nagan said. He did not sound quite as despairing as when he'd left Barillio's wagon, but neither was he back to his old self.

"So we noticed," Kendall said.

"I know we've never met, but Nat has told me about the difficulty you're in and I'd like to help," Portia said.

"What do you mean?" Kendall asked.

"I knew Dimitrius—well, his wife Lisel, mostly. I was the one who convinced Garamond to help them. And Nagan told me what happened in the *Sands* and about Jacob's magic and where you're going. And, well, I'd like to help."

"But if you assist us, you would be going against your grandfather's will," Kendall said, cooly, clearly unhappy that yet another person seemed to know about their quest.

"Ha!" Nagan risked a low chuckle. "You don't know Portia. For her, that's the fig in the pudding."

"Not true," she said, backhanding him lightly on the shoulder. "And mind you keep your voice down. I'm here to save your hide as much as theirs."

"So you do not shy away from defying the Anciano?" Kendall asked.

"He barely knows I exist. And besides, I'm not like the other Gitanos. This may be the life I was born into, but it's not the one I choose. The only reason I keep coming back is out of fear for my grandfather's life and the foolish hope that somehow I might change him. But it's always the same—plots and heists, swindling and throat slitting. I've had enough. It'll take all the wildmen of Woaden Heath to drag me back to this wood."

"That may very well end up being what we have to face," Kendall said.

"Let them come. I'll take you to Davinsmoor, and past the edge of the world if need be. Only let's be rid of talking and gather up your things. I have a raft hidden in the brush not ten minutes' walk from here."

"And Nagan? He's to come with us as well?" Kendall asked.

"I know what a nuisance he can be, but if he stays here, my grandfather will kill him. And if we let him go off alone, he's just as likely to get himself killed—"

"For the record I didn't want to come either," Nagan said. "This was all Portia's idea."

"And I don't see any reason why you should," Kendall said. "We'll go with you, but I have no desire to continue in the company of that rogue."

Portia hesitated. After a long pause she said quietly, "He's my friend. I have to do what I can to protect him."

"Then taking him on this journey is the last thing you would want to do."

"You don't understand. Even though he's taken a wrong turn or two of late, he and I grew up together. I can't leave him behind."

Now it was Kendall's turn to hesitate.

"I think he should come," Roderick spoke up. He could not help but admire Portia's loyalty to her friend. She was the only Gitano who seemed to have any regard for the poor, wayward fellow. "I know he's got his flaws, but if this young lady counts him a friend, I think we'd do well to listen to her. And if she does have a raft as she says, we could always use an extra hand at rowing. Heaven knows I'm no good for anything on the water. It seems a small price to pay for our one chance at reaching Davinsmoor."

Kendall wrung his staff irritably.

"Very well," he said at last. "But at the first sign of

falsehood or foolery, he's to be dumped in the river."

"Understood," Portia said and then turned to Roderick. "Thank you for sticking up for him. It's nice to know I'll be traveling with at least one man of character."

Roderick shrugged, caught off guard by the compliment. He was grateful the forest had already gone dark, for he was sure he must have been blushing.

They collected their things quickly and quietly and stole away from the slumbering Gitano camp. As Portia had promised, a few minutes later they arrived at the hidden raft. The Gitanos uncovered it and loaded it with the travelers' possessions. They also added a large pack of food and other supplies which they'd brought. Once the party was on board, their two rescuers shoved off and the craft slipped into the stream with nary a splash or sprinkle.

This raft was larger than the one the other Gitanos had used. For a while they had difficulty keeping it from drifting into the shallower parts of the little stream, but the waterway soon widened, giving them more room to maneuver.

The moonlight was weak at best and muted by the clouds at worst, but Nagan and Portia rowed steadily downstream, picking out every hazard before Roderick could spot them.

Roderick and Kendall both offered to pitch in, but the Gitanos would have nothing of it.

"Get some rest," Portia said. "You'll need it for the journey."

Jacob had no need of such advice. He had not stirred, even when Roderick gathered him up in his blanket and carried him down to the stream.

But Roderick was too anxious to sleep. Portia seemed nice enough, quite different from the rest of the gypsies, he thought, but he couldn't keep from worrying about what lay ahead. His mind flitted between the Iddlglim armies and Portia's grandfather and the burly Gitanos from the *Shifting Sands*. At every bend in the stream he expected to see the crafty gypsies pop out of the woods or appear on the water to bring back Barillio's granddaughter. And if the Gitanos didn't come after them, the Iddlglim waited beyond the forest edge.

Darker, even more troubling thoughts came as he stared at the black water flowing past. For the shadows must still be out there somewhere, and they were the most frightening of all.

Kendall also remained awake, but from the way he eyed their pilots, Roderick guessed he was more concerned about Nagan and Portia at the moment than he was about the Iddlglim, the Gitanos, or even the shadows.

For all the uncertainty and doubts surrounding their voyage, Roderick eventually gave in to his exhaustion and fell asleep beside Jacob.

When he awoke, the sun was already well above the trees. Jacob and Kendall were awake as well, but Nagan was passed out near the edge of the raft. Kendall was wearing a large black cloak. A similar one had been placed on top of Roderick, covering him like a blanket.

Portia gave him a bright smile. "Welcome back to the land of the living," she said.

The river was so quiet, she barely had to raise her voice to be heard. He could tell they were on the Fallowing itself for the waterway had grown substantially wider while he slept. The trunks of the blaizewoods along either side of the river shone golden in the sun. The ruby red floor of leaves beneath them glistened with dew under a bright, cloudless sky.

"Good morning, and what a fine one it is," Roderick said.

Jacob nibbled happily on a piece of fruit, watching the patterns in the water meander and weave along the silvery surface of the river.

"You're not mad at me anymore?" Roderick asked.

Jacob looked up into his eyes. "Everybody makes mistakes," he said with a shrug.

Ah, the glory of children. Quick to love and quick to forgive.

His heart lightened, Roderick again offered to help Portia row. "Though I've no experience with an oar," he added apologetically.

"I'm fine," she said. "Just grab some breakfast and enjoy the sun while it lasts."

But Roderick felt the need to make himself useful. He surveyed the raft, which he had not had time to examine during the night. It was not a very impressive construction. It dipped dangerously low in the water and the ropes binding it together looked frayed and rotten in several places, but it held together for now.

"What about the raft? Does it need repairing?"

Portia gave a weary shrug.

"We didn't have much time," she said. "The raft may be a bit slipshod, but it'll hold together for a while at least. Now stop your fretting and take a bite. There is some fine Brackenland cheese in that pack over there."

"Brackenland cheese?" Roderick exclaimed. "I haven't had occasion for anything that fine for ages, not since my mother passed."

"It's fitting that you should have some now, then. Something to remember her by on the last day of Winter's Rest," Portia said.

"She was the best mother a son could have asked for," Roderick said wistfully. "It was she who taught me how to sew. I daresay if I live a hundred years, I'll never approach her skill with a needle."

"A man of honor and he respects his mother as well. You've impressed me twice in less than a day, and I am not easily impressed," she said. "The scholar was telling me while you slept how you came to be the boy's protector. It's rare to find your sort walking the Tamber these days, or anywhere else for that matter."

"I'm sure anyone would have done the same," Roderick

said, looking away and pulling a hunk of cheese from the pack.

"I'm not so sure—" Portia stopped mid-sentence, her brow collapsing into a troubled knot. "No," she said in a low voice.

Roderick followed her gaze to the bank alongside the next bend in the river. There, another raft was being pushed into the water by six Gitanos dressed in black.

"Oh, buttons," Roderick muttered under his breath.

"Wake Nagan," Portia said, withdrawing her pole from the water and picking up one of the oars.

"What do you have in mind?" Kendall asked.

"I don't know," Portia said. "Nagan said you're an alchemist. Do you have some powder in that satchel of yours?"

"I have a little *sarance* left," Kendall said. "But not enough to put six men to sleep. And black smoke will do no good on the open water."

While they were talking, Roderick shook the sleeping Nagan.

"What's going on?" he asked in a wobbly voice, vainly attempting to smooth his tousled hair. Roderick pointed towards the incoming raft.

"We have to get off the river." Portia said. "Nagan, help me row."

Nagan grabbed the other oar, but Kendall shook his head.

"They will overtake us either way," he said.

"We have no choice. Nagan and I will hold them off on the bank as long as we can while you flee into the woods."

"No, Portia, look," Nagan said, pointing at the lead figure in the other raft. "That's Garamond or my hair is blue. He's twice the swordsman I never was."

"That fool," Portia said through gritted teeth.

"Though he'll no doubt go gentle on you," Nagan said crossly. "Everyone knows Barillio's best man has your name stitched on his—"

"Hush!" Portia snapped. "Now is not the time, Nat."

Ignoring the conversation, Jacob rose and walked to the

front of the raft, staring at the approaching men. Four of them rowed furiously upstream while the other two drew small crossbows. The Gitano craft was closing in quickly.

"Don't go too near the edge." Roderick hurried over to where Jacob stood.

"I think I can help us get past them," Jacob said quietly.

"What do you mean?" Roderick asked.

"If I can get near their boat, I can use magic to stop them," Jacob said.

"You're sure?"

Jacob nodded.

Magic again. Kendall was not going to like this.

Roderick didn't like it either, but what else could they do?

"Turn the raft back downstream," Roderick said.

Portia regarded him as if she wasn't sure exactly what he'd said and Nagan appeared not to have heard at all. Both continued paddling wildly.

"What are you talking about?" she asked. "They'll be on us any minute."

Roderick pointed at Jacob. "He says he can help us if we can get him close."

"No," Kendall said emphatically. "We don't want him using any more magic. The stronger he gets, the worse off we'll be."

Nagan stopped rowing. "Didn't you say he saved me from those shadows? And I saw that blinky thing he did in the sewers. Portia, if the boy says he can help, we need to let him try. He might be our only chance."

"I will not allow it," Kendall said. He looked considerably more stodgy and old at that moment than usual, far less grandfatherly and far more of a curmudgeon.

"But what chance do we have in the woods?" Roderick asked.

Portia left off rowing as well. "Roderick's right," she said. "Even if we make the bank, Gitanos won't be fooled by black smoke and there's little hope the two of us could hold them off long enough for you to get away, especially with

Garamond among them."

"You do not understand the powers at work here," Kendall said, growing even more forceful with his words.

"I still say—" Portia began, but her words were cut off by the sound of something whistling by the boat and landing with a splash in the water several feet wide and to the right.

"Surrender, Lady Portia, and we won't hurt your friends!" Garamond yelled at them from down river. The man who had fired the crossbow bolt was in the process of reloading.

"Blast it," Portia said. "We're in over our heads."

"We have to surrender," Nagan said. "All I can hope for now is that Garamond won't slit my throat on the banks. I promised my ol' mum that I wouldn't die on the river."

"Nagan's right. If you try to run, they'll just shoot you down. They didn't have to miss with that shot."

"Then, our only chance is with the motley," Kendall said with great difficulty. "Do what you must."

Portia took up her pole once more and began steering them towards the oncoming raft. It did not take long before the two boats were less than fifty yards apart.

"A wise choice, Lady Portia," Garamond called out to them. "Your grandfather is only interested in your safety."

"He's lying," Portia said under her breath. "Nagan, make sure you go down fighting if Jacob's magic fails."

Nagan discreetly loosened the short sword he now wore sheathed at his waist. Roderick had not noticed it last night in the dark. Portia grabbed one from under a cloth as well. Roderick rubbed a clammy hand across the handle of his own small knife.

Jacob stood resolutely at the front of the raft. The Gitanos drew to within about four boat lengths. Jacob closed his eyes and furrowed his motley brow. The colored lights from his skin reflected off the water, as if bright jewels had been cast into the river. Notes from a mischievous melody bubbled up from somewhere under water, a renegade symphony whose music sought to rise above the surface.

"Ah!" a cry went up from the Gitanos. One of the

crossbowmen lost his footing. He slammed onto the surface of the raft. Two of the rowers cried out, teetering on the edge, desperately trying to keep from falling in. The raft shook violently as if a giant fish was ramming into it from below. Soon every last Gitano was gyrating this way and that in a sort of ridiculous-looking dance. Nagan laughed out loud. It was rather comical, Roderick supposed, but at that moment he was too tense to share in Nagan's mirth.

The Gitano raft was about a boat length and a half from them when its beams pulled completely apart. In a matter of moments, the eight thick logs of the raft turned into nothing more than a pile of flotsam, each beam rolling away from the others in a different direction.

Cymbals clashed through the aquatic song as the Gitanos plunged into the river, just before Jacob's raft reached them. Portia threw down her sword and grabbed an oar.

"Row!" she screamed at Nagan, who immediately followed her example.

Most of the Gitanos were too busy floundering around in the river to think about grabbing hold of the escaping raft as it went sailing by. Only Garamond recovered his wits in time to grab hold on Portia's side.

"Portia," he cried, pulling himself halfway onto their raft. "Your grandfather—"

Portia landed him an oar stroke on the side of his head. The blow sent him reeling back into the stream. The river song crescendoed in a flurry of percussion and died away, melding into the trickling, bubbling sounds of the flowing water and the whoosh of the oars.

Garamond floundered with the others briefly before recovering. "You'll regret this, Portia!" he shouted.

Portia just smiled and kept on rowing, never missing a stroke as the raft sped down the river. A satisfied grin burst across Nagan's face.

"Well, that's one way to deal with your would-be suitors, I suppose," he said, beaming.

"No, that's the way I deal with cutthroats and rogues,"

Portia said. "So mind your manners."

"Don't I always?" Nagan replied sheepishly.

Portia turned to look at Jacob who had collapsed into Roderick's arms. The lights on his skin had faded, but a green diamond on his neck had been added to those that refused to dim.

"That's quite a boy, you've got there, Roderick," she said.

"I know." Roderick wiped the sweat from Jacob's brow and kissed him on the forehead. He was glad they'd escaped the Gitanos, but looking down at Jacob's unfocused eyes and lolling head, he wondered if they might not pay a greater price for this small victory at some point down the road. Kendall's disapproving glare told him that such a payment was all but certain.

25

THE FAINTING LADY

After their brush with the Gitanos, they made swift progress down the Fallowing the rest of the day. Nagan and Portia took turns rowing and even Roderick tried his hand when they would let him, giving them a bit of rest, though he got dangerously close to snagging the raft several times. The river seemed to sense their urgency; the farther along they went, the faster it flowed.

No one but Jacob was able to get much sleep during the long day on the river. Neither was there much conversation. All eyes stayed on the river and its banks, anticipating another attack, but they met only two other rafts that day. They were both manned by Gitanos who were apparently unaware of The Anciano's urgent desire to bring his granddaughter back home. They merely waved and continued on upstream.

As Kendall had predicted, they saw no signs of Iddlglim warriors while the river still flowed through the Tamber.

The river widened as they went. By the time they slipped free of the forest in the middle of the night, the moonlit waters were close to two hundred yards in breadth. The waving plains beyond the Tamber looked almost identical to those on the eastern side of the forest. The sight of them brought to mind the smoke at Rill. Roderick couldn't help but think it was only a matter of time before they saw signs of the wolf lords on this side as well. Sleep eluded him through the night as they drifted, exposed and vulnerable, out on the open river.

Despite Roderick's worries, they neither saw nor heard any

sign of the Iddlglim warriors between leaving the Tamber and arriving at the village of Brigshank just before dawn.

Though little of the village was visible from the half a dozen docks, the number of lights off in the distance gave the impression that a fair number of people were already up and about.

Before the outbreak of the war, Kendall would have ordered them to keep sailing right on past, but with the wildmen abroad there was nowhere safe in any of the surrounding lands. This, coupled with their deteriorating raft, contributed to the decision to enter the town and seek a more river-worthy vessel. Nagan and Portia had offered to pitch in and build a better raft, but they had only one axe between them and very little rope. Kendall worried that the second effort would be little better than the first and waste precious time. After Jacob's most recent display of magic, he had a renewed sense of urgency to arrive at Davinsmoor as quickly as possible.

Roderick coaxed the exhausted boy awake and they gathered their things and ventured into town. Jacob followed along dutifully, though he was half in a daze and said little except to ask for a piece of fruit.

"Looks like he slept too much," Portia said from within her hooded cloak.

"He'll be fine," Roderick said, though privately he wondered if Jacob were not coming down with something.

"Just getting his land legs back, I imagine," Nagan said. "Blessed moonbeams, I could use some winks myself. Where's this shack you're taking us to, Portia?"

"On the old dirt road leading to the mill," Portia replied.

"You're sure this friend of yours will be there?" Kendall asked.

"No," Portia said. "But if he isn't, I know where he keeps his key and we can stay there until he returns. Dacton's not the most honorable man you'll ever meet, but if you pay him enough, he'll do what you ask. This won't be the first time he's helped me get out from under my grandfather's thumb."

"You know," Nagan said. "I still say we don't need this fellow's help. I don't like the thought of you consorting with these unsavory types, Portia."

"If it were up to you, I wouldn't consort with anyone, my dear Nagan."

"I'm only looking out for your best interests," Nagan said, but Portia trotted on without reply.

The cobblestone pathways quickly deteriorated into mud roads which had suffered greatly from recent rains. The houses beyond the center of town were made out of flimsy-looking wooden planks with broken roof tiles and boarded up windows. The few people they passed on the road failed to greet them with anything beyond suspicious looks.

They reached Dacton's shack as the first full rays of dawn snuck through the clouded horizon. The weather-beaten wood of the hovel was so old a swift kick might have knocked the whole thing down. A pitiful trail of dark smoke crept out of an opening in the roof indicating that someone was brave enough to risk living inside.

Instead of knocking on the door, Portia went to the window and gave it three raps with the backs of her fingers. After a long silence, the door squeaked open and a scraggly man, with whiskers growing over every part of his face that could grow them, and a few places that shouldn't, glared out at them.

"Dacton, it's good to see you again," Portia said, removing her hood. At the sight of her, his face broke into a surly grin. He looked to be a mixture of Gitano and Haliconian parentage based on the olive color of his skin and dark brown hair.

"Portia, my lovely," he said in a grizzly voice. "Looks like the sun rose double on me this morning. I didn't expect to see you back in these parts, at least not so soon."

"My patience with Grandfather grows a little thinner each time," she said. "And once again I find myself in need of your services."

"Well, come on in, then," Dacton said, waving her inside.

"I see you've brought friends this time, even a little nipper there." He eyed Jacob more than the others, no doubt curious as to why the child kept his face so well hidden when everyone else had removed their hoods.

"Will that be a problem?" she asked.

"Any friend of Portia's is a customer of mine," he said, giving her a bristly smirk.

Dacton stepped aside and they filed into the little shack. Though the structure was little bigger than the size of the raft they had just left, they all managed to crowd in. The place was nice and toasty, but that was about all that could be said for it. The furnishings consisted of nothing more than a rickety bed, a droopy little chair and a table that was slanted and in need of repair.

Their host offered Portia the chair, but she politely refused.

"We don't intend to stay long," she said. "In fact, the quicker we can get back on the river the better. We need safe passage to Davinsmoor."

Dacton's eyes bulged as if he had suddenly choked on some invisible food.

"You're a spitfire, for sure, Portia, but I never took you for a fool," he said once he'd recovered from the shock.

"I know the risks. But I'll pay you five hundred miras in advance and another thousand when we arrive safely at the capital."

"Fifteen hundred?" Dacton spit out his imaginary food. "You're more desperate than usual, my sweet. I don't deny your offer is tempting. If I had any wits about me, I wouldn't even consider it. But, on account of your loveliness and our deep and abiding friendship, I might be able to rig something up for you *if* you'll triple the advance."

"Dacton, you grifter. Even I don't have that kind of—"

"Here," Kendall said, tossing a pouch from his satchel onto the table. It was about to slide off when Dacton's hand shot out and grabbed it with cat-like quickness.

Feeling the heft of it, Dacton smiled. He gave a long, greedy look inside, like a starving man about to sit down to a feast, but then frowned as if all he saw were an empty plate.

"Twenty copper plinks?" Dacton said disgustedly. The pouch was not large. "They may weigh as much as silver miras, but I'm not looking to start a brass band. What sort of sap do you take me for?"

Kendall calmly reached into the bag and handed one of the coins to Roderick.

"If you'd be so kind as to scratch this with your knife," he said.

Roderick fumbled for his blade and obliged the Savant. Dacton's mouth dropped open as the copper paint flaked off, revealing pure gold beneath.

"Gold valins! Well, sir…" Dacton became as giddy as a songbird. That was five hundred more than he'd demanded. "I may not know your name yet, but if the rest of these coins prove as pure as that first, I'm as pleased as ever a man could be to make your acquaintance."

"You may call me Kendall. And I can assure you that every coin in that bag is the same as the first."

"Mr. Kendall, you have bought yourself a river rat. And the finest one this side of the Tamber, if I may be so frank. I can have my barge ready to leave the docks in two hours, sir." Dacton gave the scholar an odd salute that was more like a half wave. "In the meantime, you're welcome to stay and enjoy all the trappings of my modest palazzo whilst I busy myself with the preparations—and skin the rest of those coins for good measure."

"Very well, Dacton," Portia said, regarding Kendall with no small amount of surprise. "If Kendall wants to throw his money away, I can't stop him, but I won't forget you gouging me like this."

"Ah, my lovely, don't pout. It's only this wretched war you have to blame. Business will be few and far between while those wolf lords have their snouts stuck in things. Us water folk are just digging in, preparing for the worst. No telling how long it might last. I promise you, I wouldn't bleed you if it weren't absolutely necessary."

Portia gave him a scathing look, clearly disbelieving every word of what he'd just said.

Dacton's barge was not much more to look at than his shack. It was long and narrow and tapered on both ends. The wood was warped in several places and the prow looked like it had been broken and patched back together in a hurry. It was hopelessly crooked. A small covered compartment near the back was the only aspect in reasonably good shape.

"Behold, my pride and joy—the *Fainting Lady*," Dacton said as they met on the docks. "I know, I know, she's not much to look at, but on the Fallowing, it's best to look poor or you're liable to be poor, no? Appearances are not always what they seem. She's river-worthy, I can assure you, and that's what counts."

Roderick helped Jacob onto the boat first and the others followed. Jacob still moved lethargically, having spent most of the morning asleep on Dacton's bed.

"Do you think Jacob's coming down with something?" Roderick asked.

"It's the magic." Kendall's eyebrows gave him a silent lecture. "Each time he uses it, its effect on him grows stronger. He must not use it again."

"I know," Roderick said. "It's just that there never seems to be any other choice."

"Sometimes giving into the need of the moment threatens the possibility of living another," Kendall warned in a sagely manner.

Roderick knew Kendall was right, as usual, but wondered if they would be able to make it all the way to the island without using it again. They had an awfully long way still to go.

As Dacton and Portia inspected the ship, the rest of the party nestled in amongst the many crates and barrels tied down on deck. The *Fainting Lady* must indeed have been sturdier than she looked to stay afloat with so much cargo, but it remained to be seen how she would fare on the open river. Portia assured them that she'd been on the *Lady* before and had seen her in worse shape than she was in now.

"Where? At the bottom of the river?" Nagan quipped.

"Now don't you go down-talking my lady." Dacton undid the last of the boat's moorings. "You're a Gitano by the look of you. You ought to know better than to show disrespect to a boat while you're on her."

"Oh, this is a boat?" Nagan shot back. "I'm sorry, I mistook it for a giant chunk of driftwood that had floated up near the docks."

"Ah, *Lady*, now don't you pay that wood-worm any mind." Dacton patted the roof of the covered compartment as he passed. "We'll show him what you're made of."

"Here." Portia shoved a long pole in Nagan's chest. "Give your mouth a rest and let your arms have a turn."

Portia took another pole and began pushing the boat away from the docks. Reluctantly, Nagan did the same.

"It usually takes over two days to make it to Davinsmoor from Brigshank. But with this current and my nautical wiles, we're sure to beat that," Dacton said. "Of course, don't hold me to it. There's still the bridge at Ivensbrook we'll have to pass and it's likely under control of the wolf lords unless the Emperor has managed to get his britches pulled back up again."

Dacton steered from the back of the boat while Portia and Nagan propelled the ponderous vessel out into the slate blue flow. The ramshackle docks receded off in the distance as the river curved and cut its way through the wide open heath. The rolling plains to the north unfurled like a sun drenched yellow blanket beneath the cloudless sky. Even the breeze brought a touch of warmth.

"Well, we're on a proper boat now, more or less," Roderick said to Jacob. "And it's good to be out in the open air, though the blaizewoods are something I shan't soon forget."

Jacob seemed to perk up under the fresh breeze.

"I like Lady Portia," he said, his voice still a little sleepy. "She has a kind heart."

"I think you're right, Jacob," Roderick said. "We stitched a fine seam landing her on our side, didn't we?"

Jacob nodded and turned to take in the rolling river.

They creaked and ambled their way further and further from Brigshank. As the afternoon wore on the land slowly began to change. The bright, tawny plains settled into a washed out green. Clouds swept in from the north, crowding the sky with a gray veil, growing darker by the hour. When night dropped across the land, so did the rain. Before long, it was coming down in sheets so thick, the river banks could no longer be seen.

"This storm's going to drink us stem to stern if we don't get to ground and wait it out," Nagan bellowed pessimistically, but Dacton paid him no mind. He grunted, shook the water from his brow and kept the *Lady* moving obstinately forward.

Though Jacob showed no signs of fear at the blustering tempest, the winds and rain gave the *Fainting Lady* such a beating that Roderick took him into the covered compartment to keep him safe. They sat in the dark, praying the storm would let up, but it pounded on for several more hours until eventually Roderick passed into a heavy sleep.

He was awoken when the boat lurched to a stop. He glanced over at Jacob and, seeing he still slept peacefully, was about to open the door to find out what had happened when it swung open on its own. A rain-soaked Kendall appeared, crouching down so he could fit through.

"The ship's taking on water," he said, his voice rising above the pelting winds. "The Gitanos are going to see about making camp for the night along the shore while I help Dacton with the repairs."

"I could help if you need me," Roderick offered.

"No. If the boy awakes, he'll want you close," Kendall said. "You might as well get what rest you can. Perhaps the storm will let up by morning and we can be back on our way."

Roderick nodded, "All right, I'll stay with Jacob. Be careful."

Kendall disappeared into the storm. A few moments later, lightning flashed all around, followed by peals of thunder that sounded as if they were right along the riverbank. The noise startled Jacob awake.

"Is something out there?" he asked in a voice so soft Roderick could barely make it out over the pounding rain.

"Jacob, what's the matter? Were you having another dream?" Roderick asked.

"Yes," Jacob said, "but not about the shadows this time. I saw an old man, even older than Kendall. He was bald and had no beard and terrible eyes. He was coming for me." His hood was down and his hair damp with sweat. He kept his gaze locked on the door.

"Don't be afraid. It was only thunder," Roderick assured him.

"No," Jacob said. "There is someone out there—on the boat. Don't you hear them?"

The words had barely left Jacob's mouth when a loud explosion shattered the night. The force of it rocked the boat and sent Roderick and Jacob crashing into the wall. Shouts arose outside. Roderick wrapped his arm around Jacob and pulled him close so he could get a better look at him in the moonlight which filtered through the cracks in the cabin walls. He did not appear to be injured.

"Are you all right?" Roderick asked.

"Yes, but we need to run—" Jacob said, but at that moment the door burst open and a large dark shape hurled through.

26

TENDING A WOUND

he cabin was too cramped to avoid the lunging figure that burst through the door. Powerful hands seized Roderick and Jacob and dragged them out on deck before they could put up any resistance. Figures in black cloaks pressed in all around them. In a matter of moments they had bound their hands tightly in front of them.

The rain beat against the deck in blinding sheets, obscuring the forms of their captors.

"Who are you?" Roderick addressed the storm-shrouded figures, but they just stared back at him.

Jacob tugged on the cords at his wrist, wild with fright. "I can't let them take me!"

He was going to use the magic. Roderick sensed it.

"Not this time," Roderick said in his ear. "Let's see who they are first, and see if we can find out what happened to the others."

One of the figures grabbed Roderick by the scruff of his collar and jostled him about.

"You shut your trap," he said in a spiteful voice.

"Don't hurt him," Jacob shouted.

"And no lip from you, either!" Their tormentor leaned over Jacob as if he meant to pounce on him.

"Easy with the motley," the voice of a man striding towards them rang out above the storm. He was one of the tallest men Roderick had ever seen. Unlike the others, the hood of his cloak was pulled back, revealing a metal helmet that looked like the open beak of a hawk. "The Baron has gone to a great deal of trouble to find this one. We don't want to deliver him damaged goods."

"Yes, Captain," the gruff soldier said.

High-pitched screams rang out amidst the torrents of rain. They did not come from the boat, but nearby.

"Portia!" Roderick called out, certain it must have been her, but she was nowhere to be seen, on the boat or along the riverbank. The pounding rain and swaying willows were all that was visible.

Please protect her, Adonai, Roderick prayed.

"Bring these two ashore," the captain ordered.

The soldiers marched Roderick and Jacob across the main deck. There, Dacton was engaged in a heated discussion with four of the captain's men.

"But it wasn't my fault!" Dacton protested. "I was only told to bring 'em to Gutter Point. It was up to you to take it from there."

"Your instructions were to bring the boy *and* the old man," one of the men said. "You can take the five thousand, but you'll get no more."

The captain stopped to address Dacton while his soldiers herded Roderick and Jacob to the plank connecting the boat to shore.

"What seems to be the problem here?" the captain asked.

"Captain Gotard, have a care, sir," Dacton addressed him in smoother tones. "Even smugglers have to make a living. Surely ten thousand miras is pocket stuffings to the Baron of Brimstoke."

"If you don't stop your wheedling," Gotard said, "You can leave with nothing."

"But Captain—"

"You've been warned." Gotard peered down at him from inside his imposing helm.

Roderick glanced at Dacton as he stepped onto the plank. The man scowled back, as if it were Roderick's fault he hadn't gotten all the money he'd expected. Roderick shook his head, appalled at the man's treachery, but feeling sorry for him at the same time. He had never known how profoundly greed could control a person, but Dacton had surely been swept off into its currents, which were far deeper and stronger than the Fallowing in the heavy rain.

When they set foot on shore, ten more men emerged from the bushes and trees, dragging Portia and Nagan with them. Portia was doubled over in obvious pain, gripping her side with both hands. Nagan, though not wounded, looked nearly as pale as he had been after his encounter with the shadow.

"Where are the rest of my men?" Gotard asked.

"Harlan's seeing to their wounds," one of them answered. "That she-wolf stuck her fangs in three of our company. I gave her a taste of my blade for good measure."

Gotard gave Portia a scathing look. "She'll get what's coming to her in the Stoke. Leave horses behind for our wounded and let's be off. We cannot wait for them."

"Dacton, you two-faced cur!" Portia screamed at their pilot who stood, miserable and wet, on the edge of the barge.

"Aye, ill met all around I suppose." He gave an indifferent shrug.

"My grandfather will have your—" she yelled, but her words dissolved into a cry of pain when one of the soldiers shoved her from behind.

"Leave her be!" Nagan said, straining against the grip of his captors. One of them yanked him back by the hair. "Agh! That's not a wig, you dullard!"

"I don't intend to be seeing your dear grandfather any time soon, my lovely." Dacton leered at Portia. "And as for you, you little river rat," he added, wagging a finger at Nagan. "The *Fainting Lady* sends her regards."

Their captors bound the wound on Portia's side before Roderick could get a look at it, but the dressing was soon soaked through with blood. She didn't complain about it, but she grimaced and clenched her teeth with the jostling of the wagon over the pitted grasslands and her cheeks and forehead had gone red with fever.

Nagan tried his best to comfort her, but with no supplies and his hands bound, he could do little more than shelter her from the rain, which continued off and on.

"Is Lady Portia going to be okay?" Jacob asked. He was shivering from the wet and the cold, despite being wrapped up in Roderick's arms.

"Wound's deep. And infected, too, or I'm a fish." Nagan said, fidgeting with his bonds, his face still frightfully pale.

"This rain can't help, either," Roderick said. "We need to get her inside, to some place warm, and clean that wound properly."

Portia stifled a grunt as the wagon lurched over a large stone. "I'll be fine," she said, gamely.

Nagan's forehead was a nest of worry. He turned impulsively to Jacob. "What about our little conjurer? Do you have any magic that could help her, little one?"

"Don't be foolish, Nat," Portia said. "I've had worse. It will —" She winced. "It'll heal."

Jacob regarded Portia with a crinkled brow. "Master Kendall doesn't like me using it."

"But he's not here anymore, is he? There must be something you could do," Nagan pleaded.

"I could maybe try…" The glowing diamonds on Jacob's face flickered briefly. "But it might not be safe, the shadows might be listening."

"Jacob's right," Roderick said. "He shouldn't use the magic. It's too dangerous." He wanted to help Portia as much as anyone, but they had to pray she would heal on her own.

Nagan remained silent for a time, studying the soldiers around them. There were two on horseback, riding on either side. Another two sat on a bench at the front, driving the horses through the miserable rain. Water sloshed around inside, seeking its freedom, but the holes and gaps in the boards were not enough to drain it completely. The water running under Roderick's shoes mattered little, however. He was already soaked through.

"It couldn't get much worse than it already is," Nagan said in a desperate whisper. "Maybe the shadows might attack these soldiers and we could get free."

"Don't say such things," Roderick said. "For all we know the shadows are on this Baron's side, whoever he is. Even if they're not, we wouldn't be able to outrun them once they finished with the soldiers. You of all people should know that."

"Oh, please, little master," Nagan begged.

"Nat, don't cause trouble," Portia's feverish glare was more fiery than usual, but Nagan paid no heed to it.

"I've done so many things wrong in my life, but if Portia dies I won't be able to live with myself," he said. The rain made it impossible to tell if Nagan was crying, but his expression had never been more miserable.

Jacob let out a sigh. "All right, I'll help her."

"Jacob, no. You don't know what might happen," Roderick said.

"It will just be a small amount this time," Jacob promised. "I think I can control it. We can't let Lady Portia die."

"Jacob, please, don't—don't worry about me," Portia said, straining to hold her head up.

"Give it time, Jacob," Roderick said. "She may heal on her own."

With a shaking hand, Jacob touched her forehead for a moment and closed his eyes. As he opened them, he shook his head. "No, she won't."

Roderick looked into Jacob's pleading eyes. He was on the verge of tears. Did Jacob really know she wouldn't recover?

Remember the sewers. You promised you'd trust him then.

Roderick looked back at Portia, clenching her teeth bravely against the pain, and remembered the sickness which had taken his mother. She had not been all that old. He would have done anything possible to have prevented her death. And hadn't his father died from an infected wound as well? What if he could have stopped that?

Nagan was right. If Portia ended up not making it, Roderick would not be able to forgive himself.

"Please, Roderick," Nagan said. "I don't care if the shadows take me for good this time. Only let her live."

Master Kendall would not approve, but in the end, Jacob's fate was in Roderick's hands, and now so was Portia's. It would not be right to let her die, no matter the risk.

"Go ahead, then," he said. "Just be careful, Jacob."

"Jacob, you don't have to…" Portia said, but her protest now was weaker than before.

"It's all right, Lady Portia," Jacob said. "You fought for me. Now let me fight for you." He sat up and stopped shivering. "Ask one of those men for a drink," he told Roderick.

Nagan squeezed Jacob's shoulder, his eyes brimming with unspoken gratitude. Portia gazed at him in silent admiration.

"Excuse me, sir, a little water if you please?" Roderick asked.

One of the guards reached in his pack and pulled out a waterskin and handed it to him.

"Here," he said. "A sip or two and that's all."

Roderick thanked him and was about to hand the skin to Jacob, but his eyes were closed again and he was concentrating intensely. His skin began to glow softly in the moonlight, reflecting off Portia and Nagan's faces in multicolored hues.

Roderick moved quickly to hover over Jacob so the soldiers wouldn't notice. Thankfully, the glow faded shortly after it came and none of them gave any indication they had seen the unnatural display.

But then, a fluted melody drifted softly upon the wind. Roderick and Nagan exchanged alarmed glances and both looked to Jacob who merely gazed up in silent wonder.

Nagan suddenly began humming the same high, hopeful

notes of the magical melody. Roderick, though he had little musical talent himself, did his best to follow.

The guards looked at both of them as if they'd begun to question their prisoners' sanity.

Seized by a sudden fit of coughing, Jacob took the waterskin and handed it to Nagan.

"Shall I give her a drink from this?" Nagan asked in a sing-song voice to the same warm, optimistic tune drifting through the air.

Jacob nodded. "All of it," he managed to say between coughs.

With Roderick's help, they eased Portia up and Nagan removed the stopper, the two men humming all the while. A subtle fragrance wafted through the air. It smelled of flowers and herbs and other green, growing things. Portia closed her eyes as she drank. A few drops spilled on her face and shirt. The liquid looked like normal water except for a slight silvery sheen, but that may have just been a trick of the moonlight. Whatever it was, the effect on Portia was dramatic. Even before she had finished, her breathing evened out and the tension in her face eased.

A faint, but furious fiddling joined in with the flutes. Nagan did his best to cover it, but it was hard to hum that fast.

The water was only about halfway gone when the soldier who loaned it to them spoke up.

"Hey, that's enough!" He lunged towards them, but another soldier placed a hand on his shoulder.

"I wouldn't if I were you," he warned. "We have our orders. And that boy's trouble anyway. Best keep your distance."

Portia was allowed to drain the rest of the waterskin. By the time she finished, her normal color had returned, but the drink made her drowsy. The music trickled to a happy conclusion, the bright flutes and joyful fiddles dissipating into the night.

"Thank you," she said, and curled up in the corner and promptly went to sleep.

Roderick thanked the soldier, who took the skin back with a grunt and an ill look.

Jacob nestled himself in Roderick's arms and began to shiver again.

"Are you okay, Jacob?" Roderick asked.

Jacob nodded and Roderick enfolded him in his cloak, but they were both as wet as swamp rats.

"Thank you, Patches," Nagan said, putting his arm around Portia. Roderick had never seen a more serious or sincere look on the Gitano's face.

"Patches?" Roderick asked. "What's that supposed to mean?"

"I don't know." Nagan pointed at Jacob. "His skin, it sort of reminds me of patches on a coat, don't you think? You don't mind if I call you that, do you, little fellow?"

But Jacob, like Portia, was already fast asleep.

The guards gave them materials to redress Portia's wounds the next day. She had a long gash on her left side, but from the fading pink color around the edges, it looked like the infection was dying down. She had yet to stir since drinking the water, but by all appearances she was past the worst of it.

The rain had ceased sometime in the night, but the sky remained filled with charcoal tufts and the sunlight offered little warmth. The guards offered them some hard tack biscuits which tasted even worse than Kendall's. They were along the lines of what Roderick imagined eating tree bark would taste like. Jacob, of course, refused to eat any of it. Though Roderick pleaded with the soldiers, they would not allow him to eat any of the fruit in their bags, which were stored in the wagon trailing behind them.

By the light of day, Roderick counted twenty-seven soldiers on horseback or riding in the wagons. They were traveling north along a barely visible track which meandered through the plains. The grasses and heather bristled in the wind, their lavender buds muted by the overcast sky. Scattered trees peppered the countryside far off in the distance. Not a single soul could be seen wandering that wide, lonely land. It was as if all the north had emptied itself over the Fallowing to join in the Iddlglim invasion.

"Why have we met no wildmen or anyone else for that matter?" Roderick asked.

He and Nagan sat together with their backs up against the side of the wagon.

"Hard to say, isn't it?" Nagan said, keeping his voice down to avoid the soldiers overhearing their conversation. "But my guess is that these fellows are doing their best to go where others are not."

Jacob gazed out across the plains, but the tilt of his head suggested he was listening to their conversation with great interest.

"But aren't the Iddlglim nomads? How would they know where they are and where they aren't?"

"Confound your sound thinking, tailor, what do I know?" Nagan said. "Maybe the Iddlglim are afraid of this road the way they are of the Fallowing. Everyone knows they're a superstitious lot. Or maybe these lads have struck up a deal with the barbarians. It's not unheard of for the Iddlglim to ally with folk from time to time when it suits them."

"I overheard Dacton mention the name 'Brimstoke' when we were on the boat." Roderick said, lowering his voice further. "Does that name mean anything to you?"

Nagan's expression grew suddenly grim. "I've heard stories about a Baron Brimstoke, but never knew if they were true. They say he's a slaver and worse—someone who practices dark magic."

"Like the Thaumaturge?" Roderick asked.

Jacob shifted nervously at the mention of that name.

"Something like that," Nagan said. "They say he burned a whole village to the ground with his sorceries and that he can read men's thoughts or make them go insane just by looking at them."

"That sounds like the stories I've heard about the Thaumaturge, though he's said to dwell in the south, in Withercrag. Kendall said he was looking for Jacob in Briar's Glen." Memories of Bethany and Aisha and their last night together came rushing back.

"We can't let them take us to Brimstoke if that's who they serve," Nagan said. "Even if one tenth of the tales about the Baron are true, we'd best be free long before then."

Roderick surveyed the company of soldiers. Captain Gotard rode at the front of the procession, speaking little. He carried himself like a man familiar with the harsh life of the open plains. Whenever he gave orders his men obeyed unquestioningly. This was no rag-tag band of outriders. They bore themselves like men who had faced far more challenges than transporting four bedraggled prisoners across the plains. All the soldiers were armed with longswords and six of them had yew bows. The only chance Roderick could see for escape was stealing some of the horses without them knowing, but there was little chance of that happening. They were too closely watched.

"At least Master Kendall didn't get captured," Roderick said. "He'll come for us as soon as he gets the chance. I'm sure of it."

Nagan nodded, but did not reply. One of the guards was glancing their way more frequently, so he and Roderick kept quiet after that.

Roderick spent the rest of the day trying to think of how to get away from the soldiers. The only thing he could come up with was Jacob's magic, but that was out of the question. Saving Portia was one thing, but it would likely take a great deal more magic than that to free them of their predicament. If Jacob risked using that much power, bad things were sure to follow. If nothing else, using the magic seemed to be weakening him physically now, so that Roderick worried for Jacob's health.

After driving the horses through night and day, the soldiers finally made camp just after dusk. Roderick and the others were allowed to leave the wagon and stretch their legs briefly, but Portia remained asleep. Nagan frowned and asked why she still had yet to wake, but Jacob only guessed that meant the magic was still doing its work.

Later, Roderick drifted off to sleep alongside the others while gazing into the bright fire the soldiers had lit to cook dinner. He woke in the middle of the night with a splinter digging into his leg. It was difficult to ferret out in the dark, but with some effort he managed to yank it out with a painful grunt.

Jacob sat up wide awake at the noise. He looked around for a moment until his eyes fell upon the horses milling about, near a small copse of trees. They looked skittish, nostrils flaring and heads meandering in the moonlight.

"What are you looking at, Jacob?" Roderick whispered. "You should be asleep."

"The horses. They're scared," Jacob said.

"Hmm...I wonder what for?"

A few of them started to stamp the ground.

A pair of soldiers were standing guard at the end of the wagon and a few more were talking quietly in the center of the camp, but they failed to notice what had gotten into the horses, or if they did, they didn't care. Jacob studied the animals a bit longer and said, "Tell these men we need to go."

"What do you mean, Jacob?"

He gave Roderick that same look he had given him that night in *The Executioner's Corner*. "We have to leave this place. The shadows are coming."

27

IN DARK OF NIGHT

oderick hailed the two soldiers standing guard behind the wagon.

"Sir, excuse me—there's something wrong. We need to get out of here."

The two men, who had been chatting together in low tones, turned and looked at Roderick as if he was talking in his sleep.

"There's not a soul within ten leagues of this place. Now go back to sleep," one of them said.

"But look at the horses, they're frightened," Roderick said.

"Probably a storm coming is all."

"No, listen. You think your master is the only one who wants this child? Well, he's not. And the other things looking for him are far worse." Roderick wished at that moment he had a better way with words. He couldn't just come out and tell them the truth. They would never believe him. But how else was he supposed to get them to listen?

"What's all this about?" Captain Gotard asked, coming over.

"Sorry this fellow's jawing disturbed you, sir," the other soldier said. "It's nothing."

"Captain, there are dark things—enemies that are after us. We must leave before they overtake this camp," Roderick pleaded.

"And you know this, how?" the captain asked.

"They've found us before," Jacob said. "You can't beat them in a fight, but the horses can save us if we leave now."

234

"You see, sir," the guard said, shaking his head. "It's all nonsense—just a ruse, and a pretty poor one at that."

One of the horses reared up and several whinnied loudly. They strained against the ropes binding them to the trees.

"I don't believe them any more than you do," Gotard said. "But it's only another hour 'til dawn. Rouse the rest of the men and we'll start breaking camp. And have someone see to those horses."

But it was too late. As the soldiers began to stir, the first of the shadows burst into the camp. The dark, squat form loped along the ground like some twisted boar mixed with a cat. Shadowy tusks faded and coalesced amid what seemed like a maw. Its flickering eyes fixed themselves on one of the guards who had just risen. A menagerie of black claws and fangs sank themselves into the man's neck and chest. He screamed, struggling to pull the inky creature off him, but his hands passed right through it. The other soldiers stood frozen in a panic, watching as the man slumped to the ground, his skin pale and ashen.

Four more shadows dashed into the clearing. Roderick seized the sleeping Nagan by the shoulder and shook him violently.

"Nagan, we have to get out of here!" he shouted.

The Gitano's eyes flew open. Roderick did not have to tell him the shadows had come; an unnatural chill pervaded the air, as if someone had suddenly opened a door during a blizzard.

"I won't leave Portia." Nagan hovered over her.

Portia had completely slipped Roderick's mind. Nagan was right. They couldn't leave her behind. The horses were their only chance of escape, but they were still tied up and on the other side of the camp. Even if they weren't, getting Portia onto one of them in the state she was in would be next to impossible without getting caught.

Three more shadows descended on the camp.

"Give me something to fight them," Roderick told Jacob. "I still have my knife. Make it change like last time."

"It won't work," Jacob said. "There are too many of them."

Several soldiers drew their swords to attack, but the shadows leapt straight at them. The soldiers' attacks sliced through their dark forms with no effect.

More claws and fangs penetrated into the bodies of their victims. Horrific cries split the night air. In short order, six more men fell to the roving nightmares.

Those who had fallen arose as shadowy imitations of the soldiers they once had been. Their bodies moved like men, but their coal black skin, glowing eyes, and jagged talons erased any thought that they still might be human.

Half a dozen more shadows poured into the camp. Gotard shouted orders bravely, urging his men to stand and fight, but several broke and ran. It was only a matter of time before enough of them fled or were possessed and then the shadows would have a clear shot at the wagon.

"The fire," Jacob said, pointing to the dying embers in the center of the camp. "We have to get it started again. They hate the light."

"It's all but died out," Roderick said. "I have no way to—"

"There." Nagan pointed. "There's a lantern hanging on the side of the other wagon. If you light it and toss it into the embers, it might flare up again."

"But there isn't time—"

"Please try," Jacob said.

Three more men fell to the shadows. Their cries made it impossible to think clearly, but looking into Jacob's eyes, Roderick knew he had to go.

"All right." He touched Nagan's shoulder. "Protect Jacob and Portia."

Roderick flung himself over the side of the wagon and landed in the tall grass. Everywhere, men lay fallen across the camp. No sooner did the shadows transform themselves into the twisted shape of one soldier than they sank their coal black claws into another. With each subsequent victim the shadows grew larger and more solid-looking. The largest one was already eight feet tall. Though the faces of the soldiers remained, the rest of their bodies looked less and less human the bigger they got. They were more like clumps of contorted limbs and distorted faces, bound together by roiling masses of black gauze.

It took every bit of courage Roderick had to head for the fire.

But for all the pandemonium the shadows caused, they appeared to be in as much disarray as Gotard's men. They went from victim to victim, like scavengers looting corpses. Roderick knew what they were looking for. He had to get the fire started before they found Jacob.

Roderick was no more than a dozen steps from the lantern when one of the shadows, fresh from pulling down another soldier, raised itself up and locked eyes with him. The hateful orbs burned like cinders under the blast of a bellows. Roderick's body went stiff. Despair held him in its grip.

If the creature had closed quickly, it would have had him in a moment, but like a cat toying with its prey, it loped after him with a lazy smugness, as if the shadow knew Roderick would be an easy target and wanted to flaunt its superiority.

Jacob needs you, snap out of it, Devinson!

If he was going to do something, it had to be now. A greater fear than that of the shadow shook him free. Roderick gave up his attempts at stealth and sprinted full out for the lantern. He managed to crash into the side of the wagon and yank the lamp loose just as the shadow's chill came up from behind. He turned and swung the unlit lantern in a foolish attempt to force it back, but missed completely and his momentum sent him tumbling to the ground.

Roderick was in such a state of terror he did not feel the impact of his fall. He rolled blindly on the ground, coming to a stop underneath the wagon. The shadow's dark body hunched down, its eyes trained upon him through the spokes of the wheel. But the creature's semi-solidity worked in Roderick's favor. It could not pass straight through the wheel, but was forced to slink around. Its eyes glaring with fresh malice that its prey had temporarily eluded it, the monster rushed around the edge, no longer interested in toying around.

Roderick slid backwards along the ground, moments from meeting the same fate as the soldiers. Then he remembered the lantern. He flicked the flint lever once and it sparked, but failed to light. He flicked it again, and then again, but the worthless device remained dark.

The shadow's numbing claws clasped at his throat. The horrid eyes leered over him in triumph. Roderick screamed and writhed, but could not get free. The lantern slipped from his limp hands. His mind grew dim. He struggled to remember what he was doing there beneath the wagon or why he had ever bothered resisting the shadow.

"Come with me," the creature murmured into Roderick's mind. "I'm so very thirsty and you will make such an excellent —"

"Stop your gorging," commanded another voice from somewhere far off. Roderick couldn't tell exactly where. It sounded like echoes down a long tunnel.

"Strath," shrieked the first voice. "You said we could have our sport—"

"You can feast later," Strath bellowed. "We found the child! Soon we will be free. Come!"

Roderick's body shuddered as the numbness vanished and he awoke once more. Every shadow in sight went racing to Jacob's wagon at the other side of the clearing.

"Jacob!" Roderick cried out. He dove out from under the wagon and sprang to his feet.

Jacob stood in the middle of the prison wagon, a throng of misshapen shadows sweeping towards him. Nothing else moved. All the soldiers lay fallen about the camp.

As the first of the shadows, the largest of all, and the most solid-looking, reached the wagon, Nagan rose up and pulled Jacob back. Interposing himself between Jacob and the scathen, he swung his bound hands bravely to fend it off, but it was no use. The looming figure mauled him with one of its enormous, now quite solid claws. The impact knocked the

Gitano clean out of the wagon. He dropped like a stone and failed to rise.

Jacob stood like a tiny statue on a darkening shore. Black waves threatened to topple him, but he caught Roderick's eye just before the shadows covered him completely.

Use the magic Jacob! If there was ever a time for it, it's now!

Jacob's skin pulsed weakly with colored lights, but it could not penetrate the shroud of shadows. His eyes closed just before the darkness enveloped him.

No! Roderick refused to believe this was the end. He would not let them take Jacob. He had to get the lantern lit.

Roderick flicked the lever again and this time it took. A slippery flame emerged. It was small, but it was enough to hope. He eyed the shadows, wondering if they would notice the light, but they were too far away. They swarmed over the wagon like flies buzzing around a carcass. He ran towards the fire and kicked over the largest log he could find. Sparks and ash went flying into the air. With all his might, Roderick hurled the lantern into the dull glow of the log's inner husk, shattering the glass housing with a crash. For a moment, nothing happened, then the flames leapt up from underneath the log, licking it all around. For a brief moment, the blaze flared brightly. Roderick jumped back, lest his clothes catch fire. Then, just as quickly as it came, the flames began to fade. Soon, a few pathetic tongues of fire were all that remained.

Roderick looked this way and that, desperate to find another lantern. Some nearby movement startled the breath right out of him. A figure rose up from beside one of the fallen soldiers.

"Portia!" Roderick cried out. "How did you...?"

But Portia paid him no attention. She dashed across the camp to where another soldier lay. She knelt beside him, shaking him violently. The man stirred, terror gripping his waking features.

"What are you doing?" Roderick asked, arriving at Portia's side.

"Bringing them back," Portia said. "Hurry, wake as many of

them as you can!" She ran off to another corner of the camp, leaving several soldiers nearby for Roderick to stir.

"But what good—?" his question was cut short by a withering shriek from somewhere near the wagon. One of the shadows pulled out from the pack and fell to the ground, shrinking back to its normal size.

Something was having an effect on the other shadows as well. A moment before they were smothering the wagon in darkness. Now they shivered and pulled away, their flickering eyes darting about in confusion and rage.

Roderick wasted no more time trying to determine the cause of the disruption. He began shaking the first soldier he could find. The man's eyes slowly came open. His face was pale, and he was still in shock, but he was alive. Roderick turned and began to wrench another man from his shadowy slumber. In a short time, he had roused three more, but now the shadows were moving back his way. Whatever had thrown them into confusion, they now fixed their attention on Roderick and the soldiers as they raced back towards the center of the camp. Many of them were noticeably smaller and only a handful still walked on two legs. Most had returned to the amorphous, chaotic shapes from before.

As the first of the shadows reached the waking soldiers, the men began to flee, but most of them were still too dazed and were quickly overtaken.

One of the shadows rushed straight for Roderick.

Roderick turned to run, but tripped over the body of the man he had been trying to wake. He crawled his way off the slumbering soldier, getting back on his feet just as the shadow reached him. Roderick raised his hands to fend off the creature's inky claws, but the fiend never touched him. An explosion of flame and sound burst from behind it, sending it flying into the air. Light surged across the camp in all directions, tossing the creatures aside like crumpled wads of paper while a clamorous song stormed through the night. Heavy stringed instruments reverberated across the clearing, notes falling like boulders onto the ears of those present. It was a battle song, and more than that, a song of victory.

The camp fire was ablaze once more. And this time the flames did not die down. They grew, licking up the night. The fire took on a life of its own, eagerly reaching out with flaming tendrils and scorching the surrounding grass. It was far brighter than any natural fire should have been.

Roderick, so captivated by the surging brightness, failed to realize how close he was to it. The blaze spread too quickly for him to avoid. He buried his face in the ground as the combustion washed over him. Intense heat surrounded him, but miraculously his cloak did not catch fire.

Astonished by his temporary escape from immolation, he scrambled out from underneath the flames, emerging onto a spot of bare ground where the fire had yet to take hold. All around the camp the shadows shrank in upon themselves. Those closest to the fire were knocked flat to the ground, unable to get up. The ones further off rippled and contorted where they stood, as if fighting against a raging wind. The rumbling melody roared like thunder, its powerful peals reverberating in triumph.

The shadowy creatures could not abide the light. Slowly, inevitably, they withered and crumbled into great piles of ash. Soon all that was left were charcoal shavings, swept up by the winds and carried off into the night. The shadows were gone, and with their departure, the fire dwindled back down to nothing and the conquering musical accompaniment marched back into whatever magical, orchestral hall it had come from.

28

BENEATH THE SAGGING ROCK

he scene before Roderick unfolded like the opening of a treasure chest. He took it in with a mixture of bewilderment and wonder. Nagan stood beside the wagon, helping lower Jacob to the ground. To Roderick's amazement, Jacob looked unharmed, though two new diamonds now glimmered on his face. Close to half of it now glowed like some gem encrusted crown caught in the firelight.

Roderick ran and swept him up in his arms. "Oh, Jacob, how did you make it out alive?"

Jacob returned his embrace weakly. His breathing came in shallow rasps. The encounter with the shadows had taken its toll.

"I need to rest," he said. Jacob closed his eyes and leaned his head against Roderick's chest.

A stunned silence settled over the camp. It was as if the soldiers were trying to determine whether they were awake or dreaming. Portia made her way over and gave Nagan a fierce hug. The Gitano was so shocked that his arms simply flailed in the air, unable to return the embrace.

"Thank you, Nat, for standing up for us," Portia said.

"Turns out we both needed saving." Nagan shrugged, though his false modesty fooled no one.

"You were very brave against the shadows," Roderick told him.

"I knew you had some stiffness in that spine of yours somewhere," Portia said. "It was a fine thing you did, even if it did no good in the end." A rare hint of tenderness graced the young woman's face.

One of the soldiers, the one who had loaned them the waterskin, began murmuring nearby amongst his fellows. "It was that boy. He called down those evil spirits on us," he said. His face remained pale from his encounter with the shadows, a sullen, suspicious echo of the creature which had possessed him.

Roderick covered Jacob's ears.

"We knew the child was dangerous when we set out from Brimstoke," came the voice of Captain Gotard from the center of the camp. He pushed forward to the front of his men. "But we survived and every man has been accounted for. So, unless you'd like to face the Baron's wrath as well, I suggest you all gather up your things and secure the prisoners. We still have a long way to go."

Though the men dispersed more sluggishly than usual, they set about striking the camp.

"Bind their legs this time, too," Gotard said. "It's too dangerous to let them roam free."

"Our roaming free saved your lives," Portia shot back.

But their heroics apparently did not impress their captors. As Gotard ordered, their feet were bound as well. None of the soldiers would go near Jacob so they made Roderick bind him instead. He intentionally left the bindings as loose as possible and the soldiers were too wary of Jacob to check his work.

Within the hour they were back moving again. The dawn arrived shortly after that, the sun feathering the horizon with some much needed color, a deep orange sprinkled with canary yellow.

"Do you think those creatures are gone forever this time?" Nagan asked.

"No," Jacob said. With the coming of the sunlight some of his strength seemed to return. "They can't be killed. Only in the dream world, I think, and even there...I'm not sure."

"I still don't understand how Portia woke up just in time,"

Nagan said.

Portia's brow furrowed thoughtfully. "It felt like someone was calling to me right before I woke up. 'Wake up so you can wake the others,' it said. When I first opened my eyes and saw those creatures coming after Jacob, and Nagan getting thrown down, I thought I was still dreaming. Only for a moment though. Then I heard the voice again, "Hurry, wake them before it's too late!" it said. Somehow I never questioned it. I think on my own I would have fought for Jacob, like Nagan, but I sensed that I needed to follow the voice."

"Maybe it was the voice of the magic. It talks to me, too, sometimes," Jacob said, but Roderick wasn't sure. Something was calling these creatures and Kendall seemed to think the magic had something to do with them.

"I don't know," Portia said. "There was certainly something magical about it, but it felt more like the voice of an actual person." She patted Jacob on the head. "Whatever is behind the magic, thank you for using it to heal me. My side feels almost completely better."

"I'm glad." Jacob said.

As the wagon rattled on, Jacob stared vacantly into the sunrise. "It's the color of tangerines," he said after a long silence.

Nagan gave him a bewildered look. "Always fruit with you, eh, Patches? Well, at least Master Kendall didn't have to endure that nightmare. Though we certainly could have used his help."

"His kind of magic doesn't work on the shadows," Jacob said.

"I do wonder what happened to him." Roderick would have eaten a barrel of hard tack to have had Master Kendall back. He had no idea how to get out of this mess on his own. "We've gone so far, I don't see how he'll ever find us now."

"Not where you're going," one of the soldiers riding with them said. It was the same sour fellow as always. "Nobody who goes to Castle Brimstoke ever comes back."

Disturbed by the ominous words and the reminder that the

guards were listening in, they gave up on the conversation.

They rode on in silence, beneath an ever-changing canvas stretched out across the heavens. As Roderick watched it transform from brooding sienna to tarnished ochre and finally dusky blue, an old saying his mother was fond of came to mind.

"Even beggars have the sky."

That was certainly true. And that was no small comfort.

The Thaumaturge stared through the doorway into the face of Savill, his contact in Ivensbrook. Time had not been kind to the old merchant. Since last they'd met, the pockets around his eyes had grown deeper and darker and his hair had gone from gray to white and thinned considerably, but the man's health was of little concern to the Thaumaturge.

"Master Savill, I have need of your services." He brushed past him, not bothering to wait and be invited in.

"Um, yes." Savill smoothed his thin, doubletted sleeves and shut the door as quickly and quietly as possible. "Yes, of course. It's just—well, I didn't expect to see you. You gave no word you were coming."

"I'm looking for someone." The Thaumaturge paced before the merchant, his searching eyes taking in the fine furnishings and tapestries lining the walls of the man's oversized foyer. Savill's business in fabrics and dyes had certainly fared well during the intervening years. "He's been captured by Virinian's men. They're taking him to his castle as we speak."

"Virinian, my Lord? But I've heard nothing of this. Are you quite sure?" Savill punctuated the question with an audible gulp.

"Do you doubt me?" The merchant wilted even more beneath the Thaumaturge's unrelenting glare. "I'll need four horses—fast ones—and a guide who knows the Woaden Heath—a wildman, preferably."

"Oh, but my lord, no wildman would venture out on the Heath in time of war. His people would flay him alive as a coward if they caught sight of him. And I'd advise against it also for your own safety."

"My safety is none of your concern. I am perfectly capable of taking care of myself." The Thaumaturge caressed his staff, as if he meant to call forth a demonstration of his power that very moment.

"Of course, of course," the merchant said. "Who would doubt that? It's just—it's just—"

"Can you get me what I need or not? I have no time for your middling. The trail grows cold as we speak."

"I—I—yes, I will find you a guide, then—somehow. The horses—they won't be a problem, but the guide, well..."

"Well what?"

"It's just that with the war starting, my caravan from Evenspire has yet to return. And in light of the danger, I was forced to hire extra guards this time around. As a result I'm just the tiniest bit low on coin at the moment and a guide of the sort you are requesting—"

"You dare deny me?" The Thaumaturge reached into his cloak.

"No, no—but if I just had a day perhaps I could secure a loan of some sort and then, of course, all would be well," the merchant explained gingerly.

"I want the horses and the guide within the hour or a lack of coin will be the least of your worries." The Thaumaturge brandished his staff in the man's face. He was in his element now. He was almost grateful for the setback which had put him in this predicament.

"But, my lord," the haggard merchant pleaded.

The Thaumaturge flicked his wrist and a drop of something landed on the merchant's fine, mahogany table. The next moment, it began to smoke and burn. Savill quivered in horror as a hole the size of a man's fist formed on the table's surface and bore right through the three inch thick wood.

"That's what you have waiting for you if you should fail me —though it won't be nearly as quick. Have the guide meet me outside the guardhouse on the Blue Road. One hour—or else!" The Thaumaturge strode past the jittery fellow and flung wide the door to his estate.

As the terrible figure marched out and down the flagstone path, Savill fell into one of the chairs around his ruined table. Despite its stoutness, it shook from his quivering. The Thaumaturge had not even reached the end of the lane when the merchant broke down and began to sob like a little child.

Castle Brimstoke loomed in the distance, lonely and defiant on the end of a long, narrow promontory rising high above the sea. The charcoal gray fortress was dominated by a frenzied assortment of serrated spires, like an arsenal of jagged swords thrust into the cliff. The crumbling stonework looked as if it had been chiseled out of the rocks long ago and then forgotten and left to decay.

The narrow land bridge which led to the castle was close to a quarter mile long. Freshly mortared stone walls lined the side of the road, but like the castle in the distance, they were in disrepair. Roderick's caravan passed a crew of workers toiling with shovels and rocks. A grim-faced foreman watched over them. He wore a thick wool coat and sturdy leather boots. He wandered up and down the line, fingering a studded club hanging from his belt. The workers were chained together, with the final link fastened to a post in the ground. Though the air near the coast was not nearly as frigid as that out on the plains, their tattered and threadbare clothing was not adequate enough to shut out the cutting winds. The poorest peasants and migrant workers who came through Briar's Glen were not as frail and wretched as these men and women.

"Slaves," Nagan said. "No doubt that's what we're headed for—or worse."

Just past where the road narrowed, a small steel gate blocked their path. Stationed in front of it stood a contingent of more than a dozen soldiers wearing winged insignias on their livery.

The wagons came to a stop and Gotard, atop his large black destrier, exchanged words with the guards. The gates opened, creaking and groaning on their hinges as if they were just as miserable at having to allow these prisoners inside as Roderick and the others were at being let in.

The two days in the wagon since the scathen attack had not been easy ones. Besides the awful cold, it had rained off and on both days. The soaked cords binding Roderick's ankles and wrists chafed painfully against his skin. Exhausted as he was, he hadn't been able to stay asleep for more than an hour or two without waking.

Jacob fared worst of all. He had gone three days now with nothing but water. Roderick did not know how much longer he would make it. The colors in his skin remained as bright as ever, but his eyes had lost their luster and he kept them half shut most of the time. He barely spoke, even to Roderick.

The horses lurched back into motion, dragging the wagons through the metal gate. Their hooves striking the pavement rang out like the sound of firewood cracking apart in the heat of the flame.

No one spoke as they passed beneath the shadow of the decrepit castle. Even the guards grew quiet as they entered, like pall bearers arriving at an open grave.

They passed beneath a massive, fang-like portcullis and into a bleak courtyard surrounded by arched walkways. A large statue of some sort of bird rose up out of the flagstones. Whatever detail the work may once have possessed had been weathered away by time and the elements. Its beak was missing altogether, and half of one wing, but judging by the size of what remained, it must have been impressive in its day. It was still upwards of twenty feet tall. The wagons halted before the base of the mangled bird. Gotard rode back to speak to the men guarding the prisoners.

"The Baron is not in residence," he announced. "Take them down to the dungeon. Except the boy. He goes to the tower. He's too dangerous to be left with the others."

Roderick's heart sank at these words.

"You craven varlet." Portia gave Gotard a fiery look. "He's just a child!"

"At least see that he gets some fruit," Roderick begged.

"I'll do as I please." Gotard motioned to his men. The soldiers seized Jacob, tearing him from Roderick's arms. Jacob gazed listlessly back at Roderick, offering no resistance as they carried him away. Roderick reached after him, but the soldiers shoved him back.

As Jacob disappeared beneath one of the archways, Roderick's head slumped forward. They had come all this way only to be separated. All of Roderick's promises to protect Jacob rang in his ears, toneless bells sounding a hymn of failure. He had lost him.

The soldiers brought Roderick and the others down out of the cart and unbound their feet. Physically, it was a great relief, but Roderick found no joy in the momentary comfort. His gaze lingered on the walkway where Jacob had been taken away.

The soldiers marched them in the opposite direction. They entered a stairway and descended several flights before stopping at a bloated wooden door. The guards banged on it for a terribly long time until a voice came from the other side, asking them their business.

"New prisoners for the Stoke," the guards said.

After a short pause, locks clicked and bolts clanked and the door swung inward. The stench wafting in from the hallway beyond was almost as terrible as the sewers of Middlehelm. It reeked of moldy food, fetid water, and decaying flesh.

The prison guard on the other side of the door wore a

leather jerkin, but no livery like the soldiers. He was a squat little man with bits of gray flecking his temple and his wispy excuse for a beard. He shuffled along in front of them, leading them down narrow, sagging stone passages. The walls looked as exhausted and bedraggled as Roderick felt, as if supporting the weight of the massive castle above was a burden they could not long continue to bear.

They passed through several twists and turns and down many more flights of stairs, finally arriving at a cell door. Metal plates bolted onto thick wooden beams surrounded a row of thick iron bars which filled a narrow slit near the top. The guards opened the door and trudged further into the bowels of the prison, passing a dozen or more similar doors before reaching the one meant for the prisoners. The jailor unbolted it and sprang the lock with one of seven or eight keys dangling from his belt. He strained to get the door open and the guards thrust the prisoners inside.

The jailor slammed the door behind them and bolted it shut with a metallic clap of thunder.

"You'll get meals twice a day, one mid-morning and the other just before dark, got it?" The jailor's voice sounded like his throat was as swollen as the cell doors, though he didn't look sick.

"What do they intend to do with us?" Nagan asked as the jailor made to leave with the soldiers.

"Boil you and eat you for dinner." The jailor snickered as he made his way down the hall.

"No, really," Nagan shouted after him. "Please tell us!"

"That's for the old Baron to decide," the jailor said, his voice trailing down the passage.

"But, but—" Nagan stammered. "Is he really as bad as they say he is?"

"Ah, no, lad," the jailor replied. "He's much worse!" The echoes of his laughter ricocheted down the hallway, enduring long after he had left.

"If we don't find a way out of here, Jacob will die," Roderick muttered, half to himself, half to the others.

His two cellmates sat on the stone bench across from him, the only furnishing in the cramped chamber. Roderick squatted near the floor. It was covered in so much filth he couldn't bring himself to sit down. It was the last shred of dignity he had to hold onto, the one thing keeping him from giving in completely to despair.

He had often squatted like that while playing with Aisha out behind the cottage. They would flick her little ball across the grass or build little houses out of pebbles, sticks, and leaves. Sometimes he'd just watch her talking to the flowers, her little "circle of beauties" as she called them. The bright orange gazanias were her soldier flowers, set to watch over the great pink dahlia's, her "ladies of the wood". The children were the bachelor's buttons, who could run all day and play whenever they wanted and never had to go to sleep. And then there were the purple lilacs, the grandmothers of the garden who whispered wise things in Aisha's ear. She had names for each individual flower, though Roderick could never keep up with them all. And they had adventures and endured the perils of rainy days and windy ones, and roamed all across The Glen in Aisha's little imagined world, bringing beauty and joy to all the woodland creatures and the various and sundry trees in the deep, deep wood.

But Aisha's bright eyes and the gentle flowers waving in the breeze felt like idle, foolish daydreams in a place like this. The joys of his past life were nothing more than clever inventions here. The only reality was the decay, the stench, and the anticipation of a sure and meaningless death.

"If we don't get out of here. We're *all* going to die," Nagan grumbled.

"We need to come up with a plan—fast," Portia said. "I

don't think they have any intention of feeding Jacob. I think those dastards intend to starve him to death."

"Perhaps when the jailor brings the food we can overpower him," Nagan said.

Portia bit her lower lip in frustration. "Even if we could, we'd still have to find Jacob and probably fight our way through half the castle. There's no telling how many soldiers are holed up in this place."

"Just give me a sword and I'll fight a whole host of these helmet heads if that's what it takes. I wasn't meant to be somebody's bird, trapped in a cage."

"I'm sorry," Roderick said, "but if it comes to fighting, I won't be of much help. I'm a tailor, not a warrior."

"Don't you worry about that," Portia said. "It's the heart of the man that wins the battle. Don't forget what you did when those shadows attacked. I'd take that kind of bravery over skill in fighting any day."

"I'm not really brave. Any man would have done the same for his…" Roderick had been about to say 'son,' when he remembered that Jacob was not his actual son. Inside, though, that is how he felt. He realized now that he had felt that way ever since he saw past the skin into those bright, shining, innocent eyes. Roderick's heart cracked inside him at the thought that he might never get to tuck Jacob in at night, or play with him and Aisha out behind the cottage, or walk into the market holding his hand on a warm summer's day. But all those dreams were powerless against the unyielding stones surrounding him and the cruel men who walked the halls outside of them.

"Maybe Patches will work some of his magic and free us all," Nagan said at length.

Roderick did not reply, but remembering how weak Jacob had been, he doubted very much whether they could expect his magic to save them now. The only thing Roderick could think to do was bow his head and pray.

That indeed is what he did, but it was perhaps the most hopeless and doubt-filled prayer he had ever prayed in his life.

29

THE CONVERSATION ROOM

he jailor did not bring them anything the first night. By the time he came the next morning Roderick and the others were famished. The man came accompanied by two armed guards who stood on either side of the door while the jailor struggled to open it.

"What about the child?" Roderick asked. "Have you seen him? Is he all right?"

"Don't you worry, mister," the jailor said amidst his grunting efforts. "At Brimstoke we treat every prisoner just the same!" He let out a miserable chuckle and the soldiers joined in.

He shoved in a tray with three bowls of gruel and three flagons of water. The watery gruel sloshed about and some spilled onto the pavement. After depositing the tray, the jailor pulled the door shut with a bang.

"It will be all right," Portia said once they were alone again. "We'll get out of here somehow."

Nagan, who had already picked up his bowl and begun to eat, started to sputter and choke. "Ack! This stuff is awful," he exclaimed, making a vinegary expression. "I don't know what these gray bits are, but they taste like moldy sponge."

"It looks to be mostly water," Portia said. "But I don't care. I'm so hungry I could eat the stones in the wall if I had to."

"That would be one way out of this gutter trap, I suppose." Nagan said. He worked up the nerve to try another spoon of the swill, but gagged and made faces as before.

Portia downed hers with a bitter grimace.

Since the soupy gruel apparently tasted as bad as it looked, Roderick tried the water first. Even before he brought it to his lips, the rancid odor spewing from the cup assaulted his senses as rudely as the ruffians on Old Cottage Road. He held his breath as he took a swig, but he was barely able to keep it down.

As hungry as they were, none of them took more than a few sips of the water or a few spoonfuls of the swill. Better to go hungry than get sick, they reasoned.

The three prisoners settled in for a long day of waiting and worrying. Roderick was thankful he had Portia and Nagan to keep him company, but he could not keep his mind off Jacob. If indeed the guards at Brimstoke "treated their prisoners all the same" there was little hope he would survive for more than a day or two in a place like this.

They endured a long, monotonous wait until the jailor returned. When his head at last appeared in the slit, he was visibly disappointed to find the offerings on the tray barely touched.

"Don't like the hashmaster's slop, eh?"

He uncorked the door and his arm snaked in. He dragged the old tray out while shoving a new one in with practiced ease. The new tray was laden with the exact same swill and water. "Well, that's typical, I suppose. But don't you worry. It'll grow on you. In more ways than one, eh boys?"

The guards chortled and guffawed along with the ill humor of the jailor as the door was dragged shut. They marched off again, their rollicking conversation spilling down the hall, punctuated by bouts of laughter.

"Well, those fine fellows certainly seem to enjoy their job, don't they?" Nagan eyed the swill with a mixture of longing and disgust.

"Some people get their enjoyment out of seeing others suffer," Portia said. "You can see it in that jacktwister's eyes. But he's a coward at heart. Give me two minutes alone in the same room with him—we'd see how much he'd laugh then."

"A few more days on this swill and you won't be able to

topple a piece of straw in the wind," Nagan said.

"We've got to try and stay as strong as we can," Roderick put in. "Our chance to break free may come at any moment."

"Oh, really?" Nagan said. "And what makes you think that? The six inch thick door to our cell? Or maybe the hundreds of feet of rock over our heads? Or the fact that we're trapped in the belly of some insane Baron's castle?"

"Hush, Nat," Portia said.

"No offense, Roderick," Nagan rambled on, his eyes bloodshot from hunger and lack of sleep. "But we can't just sit around waiting for the castle to fall down around our ears. We need a plan. And hiding your head in that corner and praying hasn't done us a speck of good as far as I can see—"

"Nat, I said *enough*." Portia treated him to a glare that could have boiled the nastiness right out of their slop.

"I can't take this anymore, Portia," Nagan went on. "Why are we even with these people anyway? This isn't our fight. We don't deserve to be buried alive down here in this dungeon."

"And neither does Jacob. Pull your oar out of your own stream for once, Nagan Casparo. We're talking about a little boy, here." Portia shook her head, disgust written all over her face.

"Drown it all, if I thought there was some way we could save him, I'd try. But for all we know he may be—"

"Hold your tongue or I'll hold it for you," Portia warned.

Her fierce tone and livid disapproval finally registered with the dazed Gitano, who flushed with embarrassment. But Roderick knew what Nagan had meant to say. He had been thinking the same thing.

It was all too much. Roderick dropped to his knees, tears spilling down his face and into the sludge and grime. "I tried to protect him," he mumbled. "I tried..."

Portia came over and put her arm around him.

"I—I'm sorry," Nagan said, plopping down on the bench. He opened his mouth to say more, but words failed him for once.

They sat in silence in the dismal cell until Roderick's tears were spent and dry, more from exhaustion than any relief from sorrow. Shortly after that, he drifted off into a restless, troubled sleep.

He was awakened by the sound of footfalls coming down the hall. His face was still tight from the dried tears on his skin. Portia and Nagan looked as if they had not slept at all.

In his half-aware state, Roderick let himself believe that the footsteps were soft like those of a child, that somehow Jacob had escaped and was stealing back to them. But when the jailor and the two guards slid open the door, he saw through his vain delusion.

"Having a little rest, are we?" The jailor regarded them disapprovingly, begrudging them any respite from their torment. "Well, you'll have to save your dreams for another day. We've had an incident which requires your assistance."

"What are you talking about?" Portia asked.

The jailor pointed at Roderick. "Since you're the oldest, and presumably the most responsible of the lot, I'll take you first."

The guards pushed into the cell, shoving Portia and Nagan aside. They shackled Roderick's hands and dragged him out.

"What's going on?" Portia cried. "Where are you taking him?"

"Ah, now don't you worry your pretty little nodder." The jailor shut and locked the door behind him. "Just need to ask this fellow a few questions is all."

"But why? What happened?" She pressed her face up against the slit in the door. She could just barely reach it.

"It seems we've had an escapee," he said. "A friend of yours, I believe. Little fellow, but very important to the Baron of Brimstoke. Very important indeed."

Roderick stared at the jailor, stunned by his words. Jacob must still be alive! He was allowed one brief moment of elation before the guards shoved him from behind and marched him briskly down the long crooked passage on his way towards the Conversation Room.

They led Roderick down twisting passages and three flights of stairs, deep into the heart of the castle. The steps were half the width of a human foot and as steep as a chapel roof, but the soldiers never missed a step. They kept Roderick from falling more than once. The stairs bottomed out in an expansive room with a high-arched ceiling. Dozens of candles set in wooden rings hung from above and nearly all of them were lit. Puddles of wax dotted the floor like outbreaks of mold on the flagstones. The abundance of light meant that the room's contents were plainly visible, though Roderick wished they weren't. Spiked chains, pincers, and various saw-toothed implements lined the walls. A system of ropes and pulleys hung from the ceiling in one corner with rusty hooks dangling down like a gruesome wind chime. Several thin, vertical cages lay helter-skelter in another corner.

In the center of the room stood a row of three tables, but they were not the typical sort. They had straps and manacles on top. All were positioned at an incline and a conglomeration of winches, gears, and levers peeked out from beneath them. Large cabinets stood at either end of the row.

"Welcome to the Conversation Room." The jailor said. "It used to be a typical torture chamber, back when the previous Baron ruled Brimstoke. To be honest, I rather would have liked to have been around back then. The old implements are all rusted from disuse. It's an awful waste if you ask me."

Roderick relaxed slightly. Good. At least it wasn't going to be torture. What did they have planned, then?

The soldiers lifted him onto one of the tables and held him down while the jailor strapped in his hands and feet. With Roderick bound good and tight, the jailor opened one of the cabinets and pulled out a jar of viscous green liquid.

"This is how we do things nowadays," the jailor said. "It's much tastier than the regular jail water, you'll be glad to know."

"What if I refuse to drink?" Roderick asked, though he doubted he would be given that option.

"Well, I suppose we could always oil up some of the old implements, eh lads?" The jailor gave the guards a wink.

The man cracked open the jar and the smell of green tea wafted up from inside.

"Here you go," the jailor said, tipping it into Roderick's mouth.

After a brief moment of hesitation Roderick swallowed it down. He was pleasantly surprised that it tasted just like it smelled. A warm sensation crept over his body. The lights softened and the room grew more inviting. Even the jailor's face, which had appeared cruel and conniving moments before, took on a gentler appearance.

"Well, how do you like it?" the jailor asked in a neighborly tone. There was something familiar about the way he spoke, slow and steady, like the way Farmer Tullum talked.

"It is rather tasty," Roderick said, licking his lips. In fact, he could not remember the last time he had tasted something so good.

"You know, I'll bet that little boy of yours would love some of this, wouldn't he?" the man said. Who was this again? Farmer Tullum or the jailor? Roderick couldn't remember.

"Oh, I'm sure of it," Roderick replied enthusiastically.

"What was his name again?"

"Jacob. He's a wonderful little boy—noble, caring, everything a father could want in a son," Roderick gushed.

"I should very much like to make his acquaintance," the gentleman said. Was he actually a gentleman? He certainly carried himself like one. And well-dressed too. Roderick wondered if he was in need of any clothing.

"But you must have met him if you've been to the market," Roderick said. "You have been to the market, haven't you? Is that where we met?" Roderick was sure he had seen this man in Briar's Glen, he just wasn't sure when.

"Oh, of course I know the boy. We're good friends, he and I. But he's gone missing, remember?"

"Missing? Oh, buttons," Roderick tried to recall the last time he had seen Jacob. It took a moment, but at last it came to him. "Ah yes, I remember now. He was captured by these men on the river and taken to prison."

"Yes, we're trying to find him—to help him escape," the man said. His face started to shift a bit, becoming less familiar. There was something suspicious-looking about it now.

"Lots of people are looking for Jacob," Roderick said.

"He has some strange powers, doesn't he?" the dubious man asked. "They make it hard to find him."

This man may have been to the market in Briar's Glen, but so had a lot of people. People who were trying to hurt Jacob. How did Roderick know he wasn't one of them? Perhaps he planned on doing something terrible to him. Roderick scrutinized his face, trying in vain to place it.

"Your throat's looking a tad dry there, sir. Why don't you have a bit more tea?" the man offered.

Roderick was thirsty so he took another drink. Warm comfort cascaded over him once more.

"That's better," said the man. "Now where were we? Oh yes, you were telling me about the boy."

"I was?" The lights around the room began to sway hypnotically.

"Yes."

Roderick felt so cozy all of a sudden, like he was curled up before his hearth in the cottage, back in The Glen.

"Yes, I think you're right." Roderick closed his eyes, growing more and more drowsy. "He can do things with light. One time when we were in the sewers he—he made a shadow go away. The shadow was trying to take him away."

"A shadow? Trying to take him away?" the man said. "Interesting. And what else can you tell me about his powers?"

Roderick faltered, trying to remember. Suddenly he recalled the first bit of magic Jacob had ever done.

"He can, um, move from one place to, uh…from one place to another," Roderick replied, his speech slurred.

"And how far could he go with this power? Outside the castle? Does it have some sort of limitation?" The man asked.

"I'm not sure." Roderick was so tired he barely knew what he was saying. "I think—yes, he could go outside the castle… perhaps. He liked playing with Aisha's ball, I do know that."

The other man let out some sort of grunt, but it sounded so far away Roderick couldn't be sure exactly what it was.

"But how do we stop him from using it? Or, let's say he has used it, how do we find him? That's the most important thing." the man said, but the words came out too quickly for Roderick. He was having a hard time following what was said.

"Ah, yes, my home is just outside of town on Old—"

"No, the boy. Tell me how to find the boy." The man raised his voice. "Stay awake, now."

Roderick's mind drifted in a fog. "Ah, yes, Master Kendall," he said. "I see your stone—oh, it's not a stone? It's a crystal, you say? Yes, the lights are pretty. They'll lead us to Jacob, won't they?"

"Yes, this is Master Kendall," the man said. "But where am I and where is my stone?"

"I have no idea," Roderick said, chuckling to himself. "You're a strange man, Master Kendall. I never could quite figure you out. But you're clever, though. You wouldn't let the Baron's men take you. No you wouldn't."

A sense of relief that Master Kendall had returned washed over him. Perhaps everything would work out after all.

"Ah, I'm the one that got away then?" Kendall asked. "Well, that does us no good."

There was some distant muttering after that and Roderick began drifting off to sleep. He heard some clicking and then a shout, which startled him back awake.

"You got it from *that* cabinet?" another voice asked. "But

that's the undiluted mixture. You fool! No wonder he's drooling all over himself."

Then came a crashing sound and Roderick tried to turn and see where it came from, but found he was tied down.

"Fine, then. You'll take full responsibility for this with the Baron," the stern voice went on.

"Oh, please, no," yapped another voice, deeply distressed.

"Bah! Away from me," the harsh voice grumbled. "Go fetch me Aldin. He knows a bit of alchemy and we might as well interrogate him, too, while we're at it."

Roderick drifted off to the sound of retreating footfalls. It felt as if only a moment passed before he was awakened by the sound of chains dragging along the floor. A man shuffled towards him. He was escorted by three other, much larger men, with blurry, indistinct faces. The man in front had a stringy white beard and his skin looked like worn leather. His limbs were all crooked and dangerously thin.

They untied Roderick's hands and feet and pulled him off the table. He tried to stand, but his legs wobbled out from under him. Two men on either side caught him and lifted him up.

"What do you make of him?" a man asked from somewhere nearby.

"Do you like fruit?" the withered fellow asked. Roderick was so startled by the question that he didn't answer.

"What's that got to do with anything?" came the other man's voice, indignant.

"I have some back in my cell," the old stranger added, leaning in close to Roderick. "If you need any—or if you know someone who does."

Roderick stared at him, unable to fathom what he was trying to say.

"Listen, Aldin," came the harsh voice again. "Enough with these meaningless questions. They gave him two jars of *veris* concentrate by accident. Can you help or should I send you back to your cell with a beating for good measure?"

Roderick was terribly drowsy. He began fading back into

sleep.

The old man leaned in close and whispered in Roderick's ear.

"I've seen your boy—he's safe."

The words were almost enough to fend off Roderick's slumber, but he was too far gone. Not far enough to miss the man's final words, however.

"In adversity, we know our friends…"

Roderick watched Aisha's little ball roll down the grass towards the stream. He followed it, curious as to where it might be going. It moved slowly, almost purposefully, as if it had a mind of its own. He wondered whether or not he should pick it up before it fell into the current, but somehow that didn't feel like the right thing to do.

As it neared the water, the colors on the ball began to glow, alternating between the different hues—reds, then blues, then yellows, then greens, and then repeating. Roderick reached out for the ball, but it slipped into the stream and the current took it away. It did not get far before dissolving into ribbons of color, painting the stream in the same primary shades as the ball, though they moved in overlapping strands with no definite pattern.

Roderick sat down on the bank, mesmerized by the vibrant hues. The water was achingly beautiful, like ribbons of glowing, undulating yarn stretching off to forever.

The wind brushed lightly against his face. A choir sang off in the distance. It was some old song, one Roderick knew, but sung in a new way so that he could not quite place it. The harmonies were so beautiful they gave him an ache in his heart just to hear them.

Somewhere on the breeze, quiet as morning, but still strong enough to be heard above the music, a voice whispered.

"He's looking for you."

Roderick looked around, but there was no one there, just a forest of shimmery trees beside the bright, luminous river.

"Who's there?" Roderick asked.

"He can't find you," the voice said. It was old and young at the same time, laughing and full of sorrow, friendly and fell. Whoever it belonged to, Roderick could feel their presence, though he could not see anyone there.

"Who can't find me?"

"The child."

Roderick thought hard, trying to recall. He stared into the stream until it began to shift and change again. The colored strands came together in the familiar checkered pattern from the ball. Then he remembered.

"Jacob? You mean Jacob is looking for me?"

"He needs you. He is afraid."

"Who are you? Are you with him?"

"I've always been with him," came the answer as the wind picked up.

"How can I find him?"

"I've sent someone to help you. I may speak to you again before it is all over. If I do, remember to listen to my voice." The current in the stream began flowing faster. The pattern dissolved again, the colors running together into one giant conduit of white light. The song of the distant choir rippled through the wind.

"Tell me where I can find him," Roderick pleaded, the light washing over him.

The wind blew harder and harder. From the forest, scores of multi-colored leaves tumbled into the river, only to be swallowed up by the light.

"A dark soul comes for him," the voice said. "He is very close now. You must protect him."

The wind surged, along with the music, and the light rushed over him, pulling everything into itself until all that strange land disappeared in a blaze of perfect whiteness.

30

THE AILING PHYSIK

oderick awoke on a bed of fresh straw inside a prison cell. The taste of the green tea was gone, as were the colors and the choir and all that strange, mysterious countryside.

As his senses returned, he realized that he was not in the same cell as before. The pattern of stones in the ceiling was different, and there was far more light. A torch from the hallway bathed the walls in a flickering glow.

Nagan and Portia were not there either. In their place sat a crooked old man on top of a squat barrel. Roderick felt sure he had seen him before. The man had his eyes closed and wasn't moving. In fact, he was so gaunt that at first Roderick wondered whether or not he was dead. But then a soft, hissing snore snuck out from beneath his stringy beard.

A bowl sat on top of a small trunk next to the barrel. Instead of swill, it was filled with a mixture of dried apples, dates, and figs. The sight of them made Roderick's stomach buckle with fresh hunger. He longed to try a piece, but he dared not. No doubt they were for the old man and he was in far worse shape than Roderick. Even if they didn't belong to him, would it not be best to save them in case he found Jacob?

"How odd, that there would be fruit in a place like this," Roderick commented aloud without thinking.

"Eh?" The old man stirred. He let out a long ragged breath, his beard flapping like a threadbare flag. "Ah, you're awake."

"I'm sorry," Roderick said. "I didn't mean to disturb you."

"That's all right." The man sat up stiffly. "I just dozed off for a bit. You took an awfully long time to recover. That jailor has no skill when it comes to alchemy."

The man had a softhearted look about him. His voice was weak, but it had the effect of making him sound even gentler. Whoever he was, Roderick was glad of his company in such a miserable place.

Suddenly he recalled where he had seen him before. "I had the strangest dream. There was someone who was asking me questions. And then you came. And after that there were colored lights and music and a voice on the wind. It was trying to tell me something about Jacob."

"Only the last part was a dream." The man paused to cough. It was a rattling, crackling sound that was painful to hear. "The jailor gave you *veris* serum. It can make things seem like a dream and cloud your senses. That's why it is so effective at getting people to tell the truth. But he gave you too much and it knocked you out instead."

"So you really were there?"

"Yes, they brought me in to try and bring you back, but you were too far gone. I convinced the jailor that I could bring you back eventually if he let me take you to my cell and tend to you. My name is Aldin, by the way."

"I'm Roderick. It's a blessing to meet a friendly face in this dark place."

They shook hands. Aldin's skin felt like a husk of dried corn.

"I know who you are." Aldin's voice brightened. "Jacob told me about you."

"Jacob?" Roderick exclaimed. "You've seen him?"

Aldin nodded. "Yesterday. I like to stay on my feet as much as I can. It's the only thing that helps with the pain in my joints. I was pacing about in my cell when I noticed a shadow flicker past my door. My ears are the only thing that's still good and so I thought it odd that I hadn't heard anyone approaching. I peeked through the slit and that's when I saw this small boy pass by wearing a hooded cloak."

"Yes, that was him!" Roderick leapt up from the bed, sending straw flying, like yellow party streamers. Jacob was still alive! And he had escaped!

Oh, thank you, Adonai.

"I called out to him and when he turned around, I could not believe what I saw—a motley in Castle Brimstoke."

"A motley? So you know about his powers?" Roderick asked, unsettled by this new bit of information. Though Aldin appeared friendly enough, Roderick wondered how he knew about the curse.

"Yes," Aldin said. "I am a member of the Sanctum, or was, I suppose."

"So, you must know Kendall."

"No, that name is not familiar to me. But I have been here many years so there may be some within the order now whom I do not know." Aldin steadied himself against the wall with one hand as he rose to his feet.

"Is Jacob all right, then? You said he talked to you?" Roderick stared through the slit in the door hoping Jacob might somehow still be nearby.

"We talked for some time, until he heard one of the guards coming and had to flee. He looked very sickly when I saw him, but I gave him all of my fruit and I think that helped."

"Oh, thank you, you dear, good, gentle man! Your kindness surely saved his life. How is it that they let you have fruit here though? I've had nothing but the most awful gruel." Roderick eyed the bowl of fruit longingly once again.

"Well, I have some skill as a physik and, in exchange for tending to the soldiers and guards from time to time, they treat me a bit better than the rest of the prisoners. You may have as much as you like. I can always get more." Aldin gestured towards the bowl.

"Thank you." Roderick's mouth began to water.

Aldin passed the bowl to Roderick with a trembling hand. Roderick quickly grabbed it, afraid Aldin might drop it.

The first slice of dried apple that entered his mouth was

better than the best pie he had ever tasted, even the ones his mother used to make growing up. In fact, he could not imagine a pie ever existed which was sweeter or more delicious than that small sliver of fruit. Aldin stared at him pleasantly, as if watching one of his children eat. Though the fruit had been offered freely and Roderick eagerly moved on to his second piece, he felt a bit guilty enjoying such delights while his benefactor sat staring at him.

"If you don't mind my saying, you don't look all that well. You're sure you couldn't use some of this?" Roderick asked.

"I look that bad, do I?" Aldin sighed, his head nodding forward as if it was an effort to hold it up. "Alas, a little fruit will not save me. I've been in this prison too long, suffered too much. It will serve you far better than it would me, I can assure you."

A weary sadness crept into Aldin's smiling eyes. Though Roderick did not know this man, his heart went out to him. He was about to ask what was wrong when Aldin resumed speaking.

"Jacob asked me how to find you. Unfortunately, I could not help him there."

"You gave him food. That was more than enough considering the circumstances," Roderick said, already on his third piece of fruit.

"I think it must have been the magic sustaining him up to that point. The air of it was strong about him."

"We're taking him to the Isle of Rinn—to get rid of the magic." Roderick didn't see any harm in telling Aldin. He seemed as trustworthy as any of the Savants in the cave at Bald Hill.

"He told me about the Null Stone as well, and about the scathen." For the first time, Aldin's expression grew grim. "We have to get him out of here. If they find him and the Baron returns, the curse may never be lifted."

"Do you think the Baron would kill him?" Roderick paused to stare at Aldin, a fig suspended halfway between the bowl and his mouth.

"Without a doubt."

"But why? What could a Baron want with Jacob?"

"Oh, the Baron is not just the Lord of Brimstoke." Aldin's expression hardened. "He is also a Thaumaturge."

Aldin's revelation nearly made Roderick drop his piece of fruit. He wanted to know more, but the sound of booted feet coming down the hall sent all his thoughts scurrying.

"What if they're coming back to interrogate me?" Roderick asked.

"No doubt they are," Aldin said in a low voice. "Let me do the talking."

They sat and listened for a few long, fretful moments as the footsteps drew closer and closer. Roderick's newly eaten fruit pushed fiercely against his insides, unhappy in its new home.

The jailor's face appeared at the window in the door.

"Well, it looks like you've done your work, physik. I've come to take the patient off your hands," he said.

He undid the lock and wrangled the open door.

"I do not think that would be wise. He has not fully recovered," Aldin said.

"Nonsense," the jailor scoffed. "He looks better than when I dragged him out of his own cell."

"Ah, well, that may be," Aldin said. "But you won't be able to use the *veris* on him in his present state. There's too much of it still inside of him. You'd be risking the man's mind at this point. He may very well be driven insane if you—"

"What do I care if he goes crackwaller?" The jailor gestured for his men to lay hold of Roderick. "Besides, we're taking him to the Baron this time. He's half mad himself so he may find it an improvement."

Aldin gave a start at the unexpected news and for a

moment appeared unsure of what to say. "Well, that changes things, then. I'll need to give a full report to the Baron on everything he said while under the influence of the *veris*."

"He talked to you?" The jailor eyed the old man suspiciously while the guards finished shackling Roderick's hands.

"Oh, I think it's fair to say that I could save the Baron a great deal of time by telling him what I know."

Roderick flinched and stared hard at Aldin. Did he mean to betray them? Aldin caught his eye and gave him a look of assurance. Aldin must have had some sort of plan.

The jailor scowled at Aldin as the guards pushed Roderick out into the hall.

"I made some notes," Aldin said, pointing to the trunk at the end of the bed. "I'd let you take them, but I'm afraid my hand writing is no longer legible. The Baron might find it too difficult to decipher and grow frustrated."

The jailor rubbed the back of his neck and let out a gurgling grunt. "Fine. Come on then."

With some difficulty, Aldin bent over and hoisted the small trunk off the ground. It could not have weighed much, but was an obvious burden for the frail old man.

"You'd better not slow us down," the jailor warned as Aldin shuffled out the door.

Aldin nodded respectfully and gave him a pleasant smile. The jailor responded with an irritated look and slammed the door behind them.

"I could carry that for you," Roderick offered, feeling sorry for the old man.

"No, Roderick," Aldin said. "That's very kind of you, but I can manage."

They made their way down a hallway lined with torches. Apart from the smoke, the air was not nearly as foul here as it had been outside Roderick's previous cell.

Aldin's labored breathing grew more and more pronounced as they progressed, but somehow he kept up. His face wore a look of grim resolution, as if he were moving along on borrowed strength and would collapse the moment they got to wherever they were going.

They walked up several flights of steps, the air growing fresher with each stride. The steep climb proved too much for Aldin and he fell behind. One of the guards, went back, grumbling, to accompany him. Fortunately, the stairs ended in a massive door criss-crossed with latches and locks. By the time the jailor had undone them, Aldin was only three or four steps from the top, but the jailor moved on, not bothering to stop and give the poor man a chance to recover. Aldin offered no complaint, but dragged himself forward, desperately clutching his wooden box.

The hallway they emerged into was twice as wide as the narrow passages they had come from. No cells lined the walls, only square columns and lit braziers embedded in the stone. They walked to the end and turned onto another passage of similar construction.

Poor Aldin was wheezing and coughing so badly the jailor ordered one of the guards to carry his trunk for him, but the old man pulled it away and shook his head violently in refusal.

"For a physik, you're not very good at taking care of yourself." The jailor remarked, and the procession went on.

At the end of that passage they emerged into the courtyard with the crumbling avian statue. It was nighttime and the moon was hidden somewhere in the clouds, but many of the guards stationed around the perimeter held torches. The flagstones glistened with moisture, catching the light.

The guards led them across the courtyard and through a sizable archway at the far end. Here they passed down the widest passage yet. A dozen men could have walked abreast and it was tall enough to have ridden through on horseback. Intricate designs graced the stone walls, but the lights were few and it was impossible to tell what they represented.

At the end of the hallway stood a broad, sweeping stairway. Aldin fell behind again as they mounted it. The steps were not as steep and long as the other stairwells had been, but even so, Aldin's eyes were bulging by the time he reached the top. His hair dripped with sweat, his face was pale as moonlight.

"Are you okay, Aldin?" Roderick asked, but the old man shook his head and gave him a sharp look which seemed to say, "best be quiet."

At the top of the steps, a set of four large double doors rose before them, covered in red studded leather. Half a dozen guards stood there at the ready. One of them opened a door as they approached.

"Hurry on inside. The other prisoners have already arrived," the guard informed them. "The Baron should be here at any moment."

The jailor saluted him and pointed towards Aldin. "Sorry for the delay. This old bone bag decided he wanted to tag along."

The guards regarded the old man with a mixture of suspicion and contempt, but said nothing. The group passed through the doorway into a small antechamber supported by thick columns. The marble tiles on the floor were chipped or missing in several places, but it must have been an impressive place in its day.

From the antechamber they passed into a massive room with a high, vaulted ceiling. It was more than a hundred feet wide and three times as long, but it was mostly bare except for a few long tables and several thick, substantial chairs arranged at the base of a dais on the far end. A large piece of furniture rested upon the dais, draped by an even larger piece of burgundy fabric. It was at least six feet tall and almost as wide, rounded at the top, and flat, like some sort of plaque or board was hidden beneath the drape.

A few lit braziers and some small windows high above made a feeble attempt at bringing light, but it was inadequate for such an enormous space. It was enough, though, to spot Nagan and Portia. They sat in two of the chairs, with their feet shackled to the legs and their hands bound in front of them like Roderick's. Six mailed guards armed with swords watched over them.

Roderick's friends looked weak and weary, but greeted him cheerfully. "Welcome to our grand party, master tailor. So glad you could make it," Nagan said.

"It's good to see you both again." Roderick was thankful the time in prison had not squelched their spirits entirely.

"I knew we hadn't seen the last of you," Portia said.

"Enough chatter," the jailor snapped.

Roderick and Aldin were escorted to two massive chairs next to Nagan and Portia. The guards shackled their feet in place. "This meeting isn't meant for any of your benefits. If you've any sense, you'll clap those tongues of yours right shut. Especially you." He pointed at Nagan. "The Baron has no patience for jackanapes."

Nagan let out a petulant puff in response.

The swinging open of all four doors at the other end of the room drew everyone's attention in that direction. A tight formation of armored figures entered. They were in full mail and wore falcon helmets like Captain Gotard's. Judging from the gap in the center of their formation, they were escorting someone, but at first, all that could be seen was a small dark shape.

For a moment Roderick thought it might be one of the shadows and his whole body tensed, ready to flee—as if he could. Then a shaft of cold clear moonlight fell upon the dark shape, revealing a figure dressed in sable robes. His head hung so low his face was not visible, only the top of his head, which was covered by a black, scholar's hat after the fashion of those worn by the nobility in Evenspire. The flat, angular design had flaps on the sides and a pronounced brow which hid the owner's face from a distance.

After they had marched to within a dozen paces, the entire retinue halted, except for the man dressed in sable. He strode forward, his ample robes folded about him in layers like diseased skin. He had no sense of fashion whatsoever.

One of the newly arrived soldiers stepped forward and removed his helmet. It was Captain Gotard. He drew his sword and raised it into the air.

His voice rang throughout the empty chamber. "The falcon has returned to his nest. Hail the Baron of Brimstoke!"

The other soldiers raised their arms in salute. Slowly, as if the weight of it were a tremendous burden, the Baron raised his head and peered out over the assembled prisoners.

31

THE GLISTERING GLASS

The Baron looked less like a hawk and more like a vulture. A very angry and ravenously hungry vulture. His face was long, a veritable slobber of skin, and his nose was hooked and jagged. He was bald like a vulture as well. At least if he had any hair it was hidden by the cap he wore. The flaps covered the sides of his clean shaven face. The most unsettling thing about him, though, was his eyes. They were the darkest Roderick had ever seen, so dark they seemed to absorb the light rather than reflect it, as if night would fall wherever he looked.

He circled the prisoners twice. No sound disturbed the utter silence of the voluminous chamber, apart from the scratching and scraping of the Baron's metal boots upon the flagstones. Each time his gaze fell upon Roderick, a cold wave washed over him. He felt exposed somehow, as if the Baron could read his very thoughts and meant to use them against him.

Baron Brimstoke stopped suddenly and pulled off his long, black leather gloves and tossed them on the table near the jailor. He folded his knobby fingers together in front of him but they did not close fully, as if they were permanently crooked, like the branches of an old tree.

"So you've managed to lose the motley?" The Baron's way of speaking was uncannily similar to Aldin's, though his voice was much deeper.

"My lord, we've looked everywhere." The jailor inched forward, wiping the sweat which sprang from his brow in

274

quivering pools.

"From what I'm told, you also failed to get anything useful out of the prisoners." The Baron turned his midnight gaze upon the jailor, who fidgeted with his collar compulsively.

"If I only had more time, I'm sure I could have gotten something useful from them, but your lordship returned sooner than expected."

"You failed to remember to dilute the *veris* serum." The Baron took a step towards the jailor, who flinched as if he expected to be struck.

"An honest mistake, Baron. It won't happen again."

The Baron's scowl dripped with spite. His hand shook as if he might strike the poor man after all, but he turned on his heel and pointed at Aldin instead.

"And what is he doing here? I did not request his presence."

"Well, um, he tended to one of the prisoners when he got…sick," the jailor stammered, looking to Aldin for salvation. "He said the man confessed something to him— something about the child."

"I said nothing of the sort," Aldin replied. A fresh wave of sweat poured from the jailor's face. "I merely said that he told me some information that might be of interest to the Baron." His words ended in several rasping coughs and the Baron recoiled as though he were contagious, though Aldin was more than half a dozen paces away.

"Can't you see he's deathly ill?" the Baron asked indignantly. "I could have gone down and questioned him in his cell if it was so important."

"I didn't want to waste your time, my lord. I'd half a mind he was lying, but—"

"And just what do you call this—what you're doing right now?" the Baron asked. "Is this not a waste of time? By the primordials, your entire life is a waste of time, Ergot."

"I'm terribly sorry, my lord." The jailor's words came out like the last bit of air to escape from a bag. He was clearly out of excuses.

"Bah! Enough of you." The Baron spat out the words and turned on Aldin. "So what is this great and important news you have for me, corpse? Do you have another of your foolish experiments to show me in that box of yours, or have you come back from the edge of the grave just to fritter away my time as well?"

Aldin met the Baron's gaze without fear. "It is good to see you again, brother."

The Baron swatted at the air. "Ah, spare me your kindness and get to the point or by Athos, I'll be rid of you this time. You are a chain around my neck that I have born too long as it is."

"I had hoped you would return in a better mood this time." Aldin cleared his throat. "But as I can see that you are in a hurry, I'll be direct." He inclined his head towards Roderick. "This man has been traveling with the motley. He's the child's guardian in a manner of speaking."

"Tell me something I do not know. Gotard already gave me a full report."

"But did you know that the motley is being pursued by the scathen?"

The Baron narrowed his eyes, as if his brother had just confessed to being one of the dark creatures himself. "Impossible," he said. "I would have seen such a breech in the glistering glass."

"You've been gone for some time," Aldin said. "Check for yourself if you do not believe me."

The Baron swooped forward and grabbed Aldin by his coarse robe and yanked him halfway out of the chair. Though he was no great physical specimen himself he had little difficulty man-handling the skeletal physik "If you are lying to me—"

"You know me better than that. I've never hidden anything from you." Aldin regarded the Baron with a look of tender sorrow. This only infuriated the Baron further. He shoved the feeble prisoner back into his chair. The side of Aldin's head collided awkwardly with the corner and blood began trickling down his cheek.

Oblivious to his brother's injury, Baron Brimstoke stormed up the dais towards the monolithic object draped in cloth. With a violent tug, the fabric wilted to the ground. Beneath it lay an oval-shaped pane of smooth black stone that glittered with blue, green, red, and yellow motes of light. The lights were not reflections, but appeared to come from within the surface of the stone. The tarnished brass frame had been fashioned into a wreath of stylized leaves supported by two thick feet carved in the likeness of the trunks of trees.

"We shall see whether these are merely more of your delusions, brother. Men see strange things just before they die."

The Baron pressed the palm of his hand onto the center of the stone. After a few moments, his hand began to glow with a shimmering, reddish light. He passed his palm over the surface in ever-widening circles, spreading the glow until the blackness disappeared altogether. The frame was now a window, filled with what looked like rippling liquid. The liquid gradually became less and less opaque until it turned into silver smoke with colored motes floating inside. Through the smoke drifted hints of a vast, otherworldly chamber. Translucent pillars of rose-colored light lined the great, glittering room. Fast moving shadows skittered around the edge of the scene, darting to avoid the brighter areas.

The Baron reached over and touched the edge of the frame, dragging his hand across the scene. The view shifted towards the edge that he touched. Inky shapes floated into view, but fluttered out of view the next instant. He dragged his hands over the window several more times; each time he did so, the shadows would come into view for a moment and then scurry away.

At last the lens settled on a wide plane of shadows, too many to count. These did not flee, for there was nowhere for them to go. They crowded the entire landscape, roiling over and around each other. From their hateful, smoldering eyes, Roderick knew them at once. Scathen. Hundreds upon hundreds of them. They filled the entire frame. The chamber inside the glass radiated with brooding wrath, a hatred that had been boiling for centuries, just waiting for the time when it could vent itself upon humanity. Despair washed over Roderick. Even Jacob's magic could never defeat such a host. If they somehow found their way into this world, all of Arinn would be lost.

Off in the distance, two enormous pillars framed a stretch of yawning darkness, as deep and infinite as the night sky. The shadows churned towards the opening, but were held in check by a gulf of utter darkness. Roderick had mistaken it for more shadows at first, but nothing moved inside of it, not even the sparkling motes which drifted here and there above the scathen.

The jailor and several of the guards let out gasps and shrank back from the dais. Roderick wanted to look away, but could not, for fear the shadows might at any moment come streaming out of the world beyond and into their own.

"You see?" the Baron said smugly. "They are still there, gathered at the edge of the infinite fathom, just as always. The motley's magic is not yet strong enough for them to escape the Dwimmerkell."

Aldin had his eyes closed. It was doubtful he had heard his brother's words or seen anything inside the sparkling glass. His breathing had become shallow. Blood continued to trickle down the side of his face.

The Baron turned from the brass frame and walked down the dais steps towards the prisoners. Behind him the scene continued to play out inside the glistering glass. The sea of shadows parted unexpectedly and a shimmering, translucent bridge appeared before the great portal. In a flash it crossed the wide chasm of darkness. Shadows began pouring across, shrouding the bridge in utter blackness. In their frenzy to reach the portal, some of them fell off the sides of the bridge and went writhing and twisting into the depths. The falling creatures cried out in inhuman voices, something like the sound of a sputtering candle flame consumed in liquid wax.

The Baron wheeled about and stared at the shadow world.

"No," he said, hurrying back to the frame.

Only a handful of shadows had reached the other side, but those which did turned and looked back through the glass towards the Baron and the prisoners as if they could see them.

"You belong to us..." Voices, hissing with hate, whispered into Roderick's mind.

"This—this cannot be," the Baron stammered, his feet rooted on the steps of the dais.

"Ah, but it is, my old friend," came a voice in reply.

Roderick had been so caught up in the scene from the mirror, and the words were so unexpected, that at first he did not recognize to whom they belonged. They came from behind the dais. Until that point, he had not been aware that anyone was even in that part of the room. Two figures emerged from the unlit area beyond the glistering glass, one large and one small.

As the larger shape stepped into the light, Roderick's breath caught in his throat.

"Master Kendall!"

"Greetings," Kendall said. "I see you and the others have held up well. Though I doubt you were shown much hospitality at Virinian's hand."

Kendall looked no different than the day they'd been separated, as serious and as sure of himself as ever. Roderick thought he could not have been happier to see anyone, but a moment later that first happiness was eclipsed by another, far greater one. For when the second figure stepped up beside him, Roderick's joy burst the dike. There stood Jacob. He was wearing his hood so that only some of his face could be seen, but love affords vision far beyond sight and Roderick knew at once that this was his precious little boy.

32

RAIN OF FIRE

oderick strained forward as if the strength swelling in his heart were enough to break his bonds.

"Jacob, you're safe!" he cried.

"I knew Patches would land on his feet," Nagan said.

The Baron glowered at Kendall and Jacob, his chin raised with an air of superiority.

"I see you still remember the back way into the meeting hall," the Baron said. "But your presence here puzzles me. If you have the motley, why bring him here? I do not want to indulge myself by thinking you have returned to your senses. Have you come to strike a bargain, perhaps?"

"I come for your prisoners," Kendall said, never flinching beneath the Baron's dark gaze. "We travel together."

"You expect me to believe you are going soft in your old age?" the Baron scoffed. "But your true purpose matters little. You and I both know the motley must die."

"The motley is no longer your concern." Despite the soldiers surrounding them and whatever dark powers Brimstoke himself might possess, Kendall carried himself as if he were the one who had the upper hand.

"And since when does your word hold sway in Castle Brimstoke? I am lord and master here." The Baron's voice echoed throughout the great hall.

"I am not leaving without them," Kendall said.

"I shall make certain that you never leave at all." The Baron's face cracked into a cold, joyless smile. "Seize them."

With a wave of his crooked hand, the guards surged onto the dais.

Kendall stepped in front of Jacob and reached into his robe. A concussive burst exploded on the steps. Black smoke engulfed the guards. The noise and smoke threw the room into chaos. Booted feet pounded the flagstones. Shouts and cries erupted from within the dark cloud.

Aldin's eyes flicked open and a keen look flashed within them just before the smoke overtook the prisoners. "We must free the motley at all costs," he said.

"Yes." Roderick fought to breathe in the cinder-choked air.

"We've got to get out of these shackles," Portia cried.

Nagan's chains rattled. His chair banged up and down in the darkness. "It's no use, Portia, I'm a fish on a hook," he shouted.

Roderick tried yanking himself free, but in vain. Though the chairs were not fastened to anything, they were far too heavy to attempt an escape while he remained chained to them.

"Leave this to me," Aldin said. Roderick heard him rustling around for something amidst the shouts and cries of Brimstoke and his men.

"Find them!" the Baron's voice boomed.

A sparkling projectile flew up and exploded overhead, so bright it was visible even through the smoke. The after burst showered sparks in every direction which continued to burn even after they hit the floor. The scattered embers made silhouettes all about the room, flickering in and out amidst the haze.

"There." The Baron's hoarse cry rose above the others.

Several dark shapes swept past Roderick. He heard a clicking sound and his bonds fell away.

"You're free. Go. Save the child," Aldin said after him.

Forgetting to even mutter a word of thanks, Roderick rushed off towards the dais, sparks flying all around him.

"Jacob!" All was a blur of dark shapes and eerie lights, like a shadow-puppet play. "Jacob, where are you?"

A soldier barreled into him, knocking him to the floor and running on past. Roderick got to his feet as more smoldering balls crashed to the floor and broke apart around him.

He dodged another soldier and the veil of smoke parted, revealing Kendall and Jacob surrounded by half a dozen guards. The soldiers advanced cautiously. Roderick wondered why they did not charge forward, having the greater numbers, but the three soldiers who lay unconscious at Kendall's feet told the tale.

As Roderick rushed forward, the Savant laced the air with white powder and two more men dropped, but there was not enough powder for them all. The other four lunged over the fallen men and seized Kendall and Jacob.

Jacob's skin flickered wildly, but no magic came to save him this time. He locked eyes with Roderick, sending out a panicked, wordless plea for help.

Roderick rushed forward, wondering how in the world he was going to conquer four armored soldiers, when the Baron appeared on the steps off to his left, clapping slowly as if he had just witnessed the end of a fantastic play.

More guards rushed out of the dissipating smoke and seized Roderick from behind. He looked back at the bottom of the steps, hoping for help from somewhere. The smoke was thinning in places. Nagan and Portia were free from their bonds, but a crowd of soldiers had seized them and were wrestling them to the ground. Aldin was nowhere to be seen.

The Baron ascended the dais to stand before Kendall and Jacob.

"That was all you brought? A little *sarance* powder and some *ornythite*? Did you really think to escape with only that?"

"No, that was not all," Kendall said. Then, still in the grip of the guards, he flicked his wrist and flung some reddish powder in the Baron's face. The Baron grabbed his face and doubled over onto the floor, howling in agony.

Though the pain Kendall inflicted on the Baron sounded excruciating, it did nothing to free him. One of the guards spun him around and yelled in his face.

"You'll pay for that, wizard!"

"It's best not to interfere in matters beyond your ken," Kendall said. He shifted his weight and a glass phial dropped from his waist shattering onto the floor. A thick, shiny liquid poured over the feet of the guard. Kendall pulled the man forward. The guard's foot hit the dark pool and slipped out from under him, causing him to fall into his companion. Both men lost their balance and crashed to the floor, letting go of the Savant in the process.

Before the other soldiers could react, Kendall let another phial shatter on the floor at their feet. The soldiers holding Jacob scrambled to keep their balance, fluttering their arms like flightless birds. Kendall grabbed hold of Jacob in the confusion and lifted him over the dark pool. Reaching after the escaping child, the two men pinwheeled against each other and fell in a great tangled heap. Both landed on their backs in the oily substance like armored beetles flipped upside down.

The Baron, writhing in pain, continued to scream and flail blindly about, but was unable to rise to his feet. "Sound the alarm!" he shouted in the midst of his agony.

Ergot the jailor, all too ready to obey his master's orders if it meant fleeing the scene, sprinted towards the entryway as Kendall and Jacob rushed towards Roderick. More of Kendall's phials hit the floor. The three men holding Roderick were forced to let go, their legs skating out from under them in the black goo. Roderick leapt free as they went crashing to the floor.

Of the half dozen or so soldiers who had fallen, the oily, black ichor and their heavy armor made it impossible to rise. And the ones holding Nagan and Portia seemed paralyzed by indecision as to whether they should charge the crafty Savant or stay with their prisoners.

But their confusion lasted only a moment.

A loud bell tolled from the corner of the room, shattering the Savant's momentary triumph. Across the chamber, the jailor pulled frantically on a long rope hanging in the shadows.

The ringing notes roused the soldiers from their stupor and the others at the base of the dais stormed up the steps towards Roderick, Jacob, and Kendall. Roderick turned to the Savant for salvation, but a shake of his head told him he had no more tricks left. They ran for the back of the platform, but the guards quickly overtook them. In a matter of moments they were prisoners again.

The Baron rose painfully to his feet. He glared at his prisoners with the one good eye he had left. The other was fused shut in a blistering swell of bright red flesh. The rest of his face was barely recognizable, covered in streaks of black and red like a charred apple pulled from the fire. His single, good eye blazed with wrath, fixing itself upon Kendall.

"I taught you everything you know and this is how you repay me?" He spat out hate in every syllable.

For the first time since he had arrived in the chamber, doubt plagued Kendall's face.

Baron Brimstoke tore at his mangled face. "I'll make you drink this cursed *brenwick*!" His shrieking voice seemed loud enough to shatter glass. "But first, there is the matter of the motley to be dealt with. Bring the child to me," he commanded his men.

"Yes, my lord." One of the men began dragging Jacob towards his master.

"No," Jacob pleaded, reaching out for Roderick.

Roderick strained against the mail-clad men, but he might as well have been back in his prison cell.

"I won't let them take me." Jacob's skin glowed as fireworks of color went off inside him, but Brimstoke, whether from being down to one good eye or because his mind was consumed by rage, failed to notice.

"You will not be able to kill him, Virinian," Kendall warned. "The magic won't let you. It's too strong now. If you force him to use it again, you will only make it stronger."

"Silence! I know what I am doing!" The Baron's single, bulging eye, roved wildly about. His neck twitched at odd angles. Bright white flecks of foam and spittle coated his lips and chin. Whatever sanity he might have once had, it had clearly left him. His spinning gaze finally came to a stop on Jacob. "The boy must die! And since he escaped his cell by magic, it is clear that starvation will no longer work. Therefore, by the primordials, I'll kill him myself!"

The Baron reached into his robe and pulled out a small cylinder wrapped in dark paper. His arm quivering in pain, he hurled it at Jacob. It exploded in front of him, filling the air with molten shards which slammed into the child as well as the guards around him. By some special grace the fiery missiles missed Roderick and Kendall, but the two guards holding Jacob fell backwards with smoldering holes in their chest plates.

"Jacob!" Roderick shouted.

The dais burst into light. At first Roderick thought it was another blast, but then he saw that it was coming from Jacob. Instead of falling to the ground in a wave of fire like the soldiers, Jacob's body had transformed into one of pure, translucent light. He looked like Roderick's knife or Kendall's staff that night they'd faced the shadowy Nagan on the river, only ten times brighter. The light soon grew so bright Jacob was impossible to look at.

A haunting hum filled the room, like fingers rubbing the rim of a glass. The sound and the light both grew in intensity, but then faded in a sudden crescendo almost as quickly as they came.

As the light and sound vanished, Jacob collapsed to the ground, no longer glowing, apart from the diamonds on his skin.

The doors of the entryway flew open and more soldiers came pouring in, close to twenty men. They marched to a halt at the base of the steps. "You called for aid, my lord?" one of them said.

The Baron stood shaking as he looked at Jacob, unable to speak. Though Jacob no longer appeared to be a threat, the Baron stared at him, transfixed, as if he'd seen a ghost.

His mouth hung open. A spindle of drool crept out of one side. "What have I done?" he muttered to himself.

An icy wave swept up Roderick's back. Instinctively, his eyes flitted to the glistering glass. It had gone dark. Unnaturally dark. The darkness inside it sucked in the light surrounding it so that the frame was little more than a whispery outline, as faint as chalk on dark pavement.

Wind blew through the chamber and the guards stopped, glancing around in confusion. Somehow Roderick knew the wind was coming from the glass. The gusts whistled over the braziers lining the walls, causing their lights to flicker. The soldiers who had escaped Brimstoke's molten blast grabbed Jacob and the other prisoners and moved away from the glass like men on the side of a mountain who have just heard the first rumblings of an avalanche.

The wind sent Kendall's and the Baron's robes flying about. One by one it snuffed out the braziers. The feeble moonlight from the high windows left the room a chiaroscuro of darkness and light.

"You…" came a strangled whisper from the glistering glass. "You cannot have him."

"It cannot be…" Brimstoke's carbuncular eye darted towards the magical window.

The winds swirled ever fiercer. Even the guards in their armor had to fight to keep their balance.

"He has the feyglimmer." The murmuring voice grew louder.

"Don't listen to it," Brimstoke commanded his men. "Get the motley out of here, now!"

"We won't let you take it away," more dark voices joined the first, rising upon the wind.

Dark beings streamed along the currents. The lightless, gossamer creatures snaked through the chamber, their ghostly, open-mouthed screams sounding in Roderick's mind. Shadowy tendrils poured out from the dark portal to the scathen world.

"The feyglimmer was promised to us," the tortured voices

wailed.

A tremble that went down to his very bones shook Roderick from within. He had no doubt that the creatures inside the dark winds had come to claim him, had come to claim them all.

"It is witchery!" cried one of the soldiers before breaking and sprinting for the doors.

More guards followed, their terrified shouts rippling along the wind.

"It's the devils from the Woaden Heath!"

"No man can face them and live!"

Gotard shouted for them to stand firm, but no one listened. The men abandoned the prisoners, scattering and bolting for the exit. The one holding Jacob dropped him to the ground without so much as a glance.

"No!" the Baron screamed. "We must not let them take the motley! Don't you fools see? That will be the end of us all!"

A furious insanity frothed inside Brimstoke's broken face. He flung back his outer cloak, revealing row upon row of bulging pouches. He hurled something at the dark, sinewy winds. A glassy globule burst to pieces, releasing dozens of streaks of molten fire. Some of the jets landed on the escaping guards. They cried out in pain, but kept on running, now fleeing the fire as well as the wind.

Brimstoke hurled more burning spheres at the shadowy winds, but the currents whipped around them and all the fire did was pelt the fleeing masses. One soldier's cloak burst into flames. Another blast exploded above and a massive support beam came down like a thunderclap onto the steps between Roderick and Jacob.

"My lord, the men!" Gotard shouted.

"If we don't stop the scathen we'll all die! Die, you hear? We'll all die! They will not have him!" Brimstoke raved as he hurled bolt after bolt of fiery rain.

Kendall rushed over to Roderick. "Madness has overtaken him. Save the motley. We must flee this place before the shadows take us or Virinian kills us all!"

287

Blazing embers cascaded around the dais, lighting into the hair and clothing of one of the four men still holding with Gotard. Flames leapt up from the huge beam separating Roderick and Jacob as well.

"After the prisoners!" Gotard shouted.

Kendall turned to face Gotard and his men. Nagan and Portia moved in and out of the shadows to either side of the Savant, getting themselves into position to flank the soldiers.

"We must have him," the dark voices cried from within the swirling, shadowy storm.

Airy tentacles closed in on Jacob, but the mad, scarred baron stepped in front of them, hurling powders and globules and phials at it, emptying his robes in an alchemical frenzy. Green, black, and purple clouds of smoke covered the room, but the winds shot right through them and encircled Jacob, wrapping him in a dark, ghostly embrace. He disappeared inside the smothering strands. The hideous faces streaking through the wind contorted with twisted glee.

"We have it. We have the feyglimmer at last!," cried the insidious voices.

Ignoring the black gusts, and the flames licking the fallen beam, Rodrick leapt towards the dark mass surrounding Jacob. A chorus of shrieks assaulted his ears when he landed inside the current. The dark fury stormed over him in icy blasts. For a moment the winds threatened to push him back into the wall of fire he had just leapt through. He fought the currents for every inch.

"Mortal flesh is weak and frail. You cannot stand against us," the winds taunted him.

He strained forward, not even knowing if Jacob was even still there. His hands went numb. But then he caught a glimpse of glowing diamonds through the darkness. With the last of his strength, he thrust his hands forward and grabbed hold of Jacob. He pulled him close, wrapping his arms around him.

Though he now had hold of Jacob, the winds refused to let go. The shadowy storm had them both now.

The black wind pulled them off the ground, spiriting them back towards the glistering glass. The scathen were dragging them into their dream world.

The faces of Bethany and Aisha flashed into Roderick's thoughts. Would he ever see them again? Was there a way back from wherever it was they were taking him?

You've got to protect him, he could hear Beth say. *It's the right thing to do.*

Yes, he could do this. For her and Aisha as much as Jacob.

"Adonai, protect them,," he whispered.

He doubled down on his grip, though his arms were going numb from the chill. His weight slowed their progress, but the winds dragged them ever closer to the dark portal.

"It is ours!" howled the voices triumphantly.

The noise of the tempest consumed the chamber. All was clamor, tumult, a thousand instruments splintering into a symphony of affliction. To hear was to know pain, but Roderick dared not cover his ears.

The Baron fell in a gibbering heap.

"No more!" a resounding voice cut through the screaming winds, bold and strong above the maelstrom.

Aldin stood over his brother, holding his little trunk in his hand.

"I can stop the scathen, but you must promise to let the child go," he said.

"Never!" Brimstoke cried. "The motley must die!"

"Please, brother. Do not force my hand," Aldin looked as ancient and feeble as ever, but his eyes glittered with determination. He stood erect, like one of the statues of the ancient emperors in Evenspire. Whatever else he had been in life, he looked noble then, bearing himself with dignity and grace.

"Out of my way, you pathetic fool, only I can stop them!" the Baron snarled, rising and reaching into his robes one last time. "Behold my power! Behold my glory!"

But before he could unleash another ball of fire or fling more powder, Aldin pulled a white ball from his trunk the size of his fist. He flung it at Brimstoke's feet. An explosion of searing, incomparable light consumed the two brothers. A second later, a blast wave rocked the chamber, toppling chairs and sending Roderick and Jacob backwards down the stairs and onto the floor.

As the light faded, a breath of warmth passed over Roderick and feeling returned to his limbs.

"Fear not," a wise and ancient-sounding voice whispered in Roderick's ear. *"The shadows will not come by this path again."*

There was something familiar about the voice, but Roderick had no time to puzzle it out. The black wind had vanished and fire no longer rained from above. Aldin and the Baron of Brimstoke were nowhere to be seen. On the dais where they had stood, only empty, blackened stone remained, as if a great fire had burned there and then been swept clean. The glistering glass lay shattered in a thousand pieces. Tendrils of faint purple smoke drifted up into the air from its shards.

Gotard and his men lay unconscious at Kendall's feet. Portia and Nagan stood on either side. Nagan had his foot on top of one of the soldier's chests as if he alone had bested the Baron, the soldiers, the scathen wind, and all.

Jacob lay beside Roderick, silent and unmoving on the charred flagstones.

33

FRESH AIR

acob, oh Jacob…" Roderick propped him up in his arms.

Jacob's eyes remained closed, but Roderick could feel his little chest rising and falling. *He was still alive.*

Roderick shook him gently, but he did not stir. His skin was icy to the touch. He had a new yellow diamond glowing by his ear, but he did not appear to have suffered any wounds or burns.

Portia knelt beside him.

"Is he all right?" she asked.

"He was near the end of his strength when I found him." Kendall said, coming up along with Nagan.

"Master Kendall," Roderick said. "Can you help him? The shadows, I think they might have done something to him."

Kendall bent down and felt Jacob's arm and forehead. "When Virinian attacked him, it awakened the magic again. In his weakened state it was too much for his fragile constitution. I believe he will recover, but we cannot stay here until he awakes. The guards will return soon. Come, we must flee this place."

"For once I agree with the old quillscratch," Nagan said. "Do you think you're up for carrying Patches, Roderick? Your wrestling match with that wind didn't seem to go in your favor."

Roderick did have the beginnings of some nice bruises from being tossed down the steps by Aldin's blast, but they didn't bother him in the least. All his thoughts were of Jacob.

291

He certainly hoped Kendall was right about him. He wrapped the child in his arms and struggled to his feet.

"I'm fine," Roderick said. "Jacob is my responsibility. I can manage."

"All right," Nagan said. "But let me know if the little fellow gets to be too much."

Portia placed a hand on Jacob's head. "He's a tough little one. How ever did you find him, Kendall?"

"I am a Savant. Tracking the motleys is our business. Now hurry, let us be gone." He set off towards the back of the room. The others followed, skirting the blasted area and slippery pools of alchemical goo.

"I see what you mean about the danger of magic," Portia told Kendall. "That was even worse than when they came after us in the wagon. Somehow I thought the Thaumaturge would be able to control such things, or at least stand against them."

"Thaumaturges do not possess true magic," Kendall said. "Their evil may surpass that of other men, but it is nothing when compared to the scathen. Virinian was a fool to think he could stop them with mere alchemy."

"The old buzzard certainly had a common sense cramp." Nagan said.

Columns lined the back wall, spaced every few feet. Kendall pushed a stone in one of them and it sank in. The column slid silently into the floor, revealing a winding stairway leading down. Kendall fixed the lantern on his staff and lit it.

"This way."

The stairway soon let out into a small square room where four guards lay asleep on the floor.

Nagan froze, but Kendall walked right through their midst.

"What if they wake up?" Nagan whispered.

"There's no chance of that. I put them to sleep with *sarance*. They will not stir for quite some time."

At the opposite end of the room stood an open door. They passed through it and into another spiral stairway which led

both up and down. Again they headed down, and this stairway was much longer. It spun round and round the central
column until they emerged into a large cavern. Here the stairs
became one long flight that hugged the side of the wall.

Jacob's body began to warm in Roderick's arms. That was
an encouraging sign. Perhaps there was no correlation, but he
seemed to be getting heavier, too. Roderick told no one. He
just gritted his teeth down the last hundred or so steps until
they reached the flat ground.

"I need to rest," he said at last, breathing heavily.

"There is no time," Kendall said firmly. "Let the Gitano
take the boy, at least for a while."

Roderick did not want to let go. If Jacob woke up, what
would he think about being carried by the "burglar"? But
Roderick lacked the strength to continue. He passed Jacob
over into Nagan's arms.

"Oh my," Nagan said. "He is heavier than he looks. 'Must
have iron teeth', as my old mum used to say."

The smooth, damp cavern floor forced them to slow their
pace. The faint sound of waves crashing against rocks drifted
through the dark expanse. The smell of salt lingered upon the
air.

"We're near the ocean?" Roderick asked.

"Yes," Kendall said. "I borrowed a fisherman's boat and it
is waiting for us at the end of this tunnel."

"You 'borrowed' a fisherman's boat?" Nagan snickered.
"You better watch out or the Anciano might recruit you to
join him in the Tamber."

"Nonsense," Kendall said. "All the fishermen along this
coast are the Baron's serfs, so all the boats belong to Virinian.
Besides, it was the only way I could reach the secret entrance
to Brimstoke. But if you're suffering from a sudden case of
conscience you're welcome to stay behind in the castle."

"Stop pestering the fellow, Nat," Portia said. "Just be
thankful he came back at all. Not many would."

Nagan mustered an apologetic shrug.

The cavern narrowed until only two could walk abreast.

"I could use some fresh air after being trapped in the bowels of that castle," Portia said as they made their way down the tunnel.

The briny drafts grew steadily stronger and a glimmer of light appeared up ahead. Encouraged by the sight, they quickened their pace until they emerged onto a little shelf of rock with a pathetic, beaten up row boat beside it. The waiting craft was tied to a large rock jutting out from the surface of the shelf. Beyond the shelf, lay the wide, nocturnal sea. Brisk midnight breezes nipped at Roderick's ears and nose. Moonlight shone softly across the waters, stretching off into a great gulf of darkness, as beautiful as it was immeasurable, as mysterious as it was deep.

Nagan passed Jacob back into Roderick's arms once he got in the boat. There was just enough room for all of them to fit, but the craft rode so low that, from the moment they untied and pushed off, water lapped in over the sides and from the back. The warped sides made it look about as sea-worthy as the raft they had thrown together on the Fallowing.

"Are we going to go all the way to the Isle of Rinn in this old chicken crate?" Nagan asked. He and Portia did their best to keep the sad little vessel moving.

Kendall produced a cup from his bag and began scooping out the water. "Of course not. I managed to secure some horses as well. They are waiting for us about a mile north up the coast."

"Will it be safe to travel over land?" Roderick studied Jacob's face, shielding him from the wind. He was breathing more deeply, but until he awoke, Roderick's worries would not abate.

"We have no choice. We lost too much time in Virinian's castle. We ride for Iddlmar now. We shall attempt to hire a boat from there."

"But I thought you said we were going to find a ship from Davinsmoor," Roderick said.

"Castle Brimstoke is far north of Davinsmoor. If we headed back, we would only lose more time."

"You seem to know your way around these lands fairly well," Portia said. "And from the way you talked with that crazed Baron, it seemed like you've been here before."

"I was thinking that very thing," Nagan said. "Were you and the old shillelagh mates back at the Grand Academy in Evenspire or wherever it is you scholarly types do your learning?"

Kendall ceased bailing water momentarily and gazed back at the decrepit castle in the distance. "Yes, Virinian was my teacher at one point. But that was many years ago."

"Was he as cracked and crazed then as he is now—or was, I suppose?" Nagan asked.

"No, Virinian's descent into madness has been long and slow, though some say all Thaumaturges share a touch of madness."

"Power warps the mind," Portia said. "Even in the best of men. Trust me, I know."

"And can you believe that other fellow was his brother?" Nagan said. "I mean, the Baron was off his mark by six and a three score, but to keep your own brother locked up like that seems a bit much, even for a mad wizard."

"Aldin told me he was one of the Savants," Roderick put in.

"Yes," Kendall said, continuing to bail. "I knew of Aldin's work, though I had never met him personally. He taught many of the Savants, including Master Jareth. I think Virinian must have kept him locked up so that he could do research for him. He was always envious of his brother's skill with alchemy."

"Such a pity," Portia said. "He seemed like a good man."

"He gave his life for us," Roderick said, holding on to Jacob all the tighter. He would never forget the kindness Aldin had shown Jacob in the dungeons, nor in saving him from the scathen. *Why did it always have to be the good ones who got taken away?* He was reminded again of his mother and father.

"Sometimes sacrifice is the only path." Kendall's voice broke into his thoughts. An unusually large wave broke over the prow, spraying the Savant with flecks of foam.

As they continued on past the breakers, the boat began to take on less and less water, but the sea still rocked the vessel from time to time. Roderick had never been out on the open water before and based on this first encounter with it, he hoped it would be some time before he had to return. He scanned the shore as they made their way along the rocky coastline, hoping to see signs of Kendall's horses, but high, jagged cliffs formed a forbidding wall which offered no harbor. Eventually the cliffs gave way to rocky shores strewn with enormous boulders. Then the boulders gave way to smaller rocks and eventually sand. Shortly after, Kendall directed Portia and Nagan to row towards shore. Soon they spotted a little swelling hill with a few meager trees clinging to it. Four large horses grazed contentedly near the top, their sleek flanks glistening in the moonlight.

The boat lurched to a stop on the beach, and the party disembarked. As Roderick set foot on the blessed shore, Jacob's eyes fluttered open at last.

"Where are we?" he asked.

A warm tide of gratitude washed over Roderick at the sight of those beautiful green eyes. They lit up the night as if two sparkles had leapt off the water and onto his face.

"We're near the ocean. Away from that dark castle."

"Good." Jacob rubbed his eyes and sat up.

"Do you feel well enough to stand?" Roderick asked.

"Yes."

Roderick set him down.

"Good to see you awake again," Kendall said. He handed Roderick Jacob's bag. It had a surprising heft to it. "I took the liberty of restocking some of our supplies while we were separated."

Roderick flipped back the flap revealing dozens of pieces of dried fruit. "Ah, you're a double blessing, you are, Master Kendall. Here, Jacob, see what our dear friend has brought you." Jacob dug into the bag like a squirrel unearthing a stash of nuts, pulling out several apple slices at once and promptly going to work on them.

"I met a man in the castle who gave me some fruit," Jacob said between smacks. Though Jacob did not normally speak with his mouth full, he seemed to have momentarily forgotten his manners. "He was very nice to me. I saw him sitting by you in that big room."

"Yes, he told me how he helped you," Roderick said. "Sad to say, he didn't make it out with us. He—he sacrificed himself to save us from that dark wind."

Jacob stopped chewing on his apple slice. After a moment he swallowed down what he had. "Maybe he's with my mother and father now."

"Let us hope that is true." Roderick spoke in the same low tones he would have used in chapel. A long silence swept the shore. Even the crashing waves seemed to diminish out of reverence.

Jacob stuffed the rest of the fruit back in the bag and headed for the horses. The others came along behind.

Nagan boxed Jacob lightly on the arm. "Well, we're glad to have you back, Patches, that's all I have to say. Are you up for a horse ride? Looks like the old scholar has found us some real beauties."

"Indeed." Portia eyed the massive flanks and noble faces of the four horses. "These are not of Caledonian stock. They're real farm-bred Haliconian stallions. Wherever did you find them?"

"You'd be surprised what you can find with enough coin," Kendall said. "The Sanctum gave me more than enough to ensure that we would make it safely to the Isle of Rinn."

The steeds stood grazing in the sandy grass. One was black, two were brown, and the other dappled gray. Kendall took the reigns of the black one and Portia and Nagan grabbed the browns so that the gray fell to Roderick and Jacob.

Roderick took the reigns with some trepidation. Visions of old Blandy throwing him flat came rushing back. The ride to Middlehelm had been fairly short, but this would be several day's journey over open terrain.

Kendall gave him an encouraging nod. "These horses are well-trained. Just hold on tight and your beast will follow the others."

Nagan helped Roderick up onto the great barrel of muscle and hefted Jacob up after him. Roderick gave the horse a nervous pat.

"It could be worse," Nagan whispered to Roderick. "You could have to ride with old Stiff-staff over there."

Jacob dug out a few apple slices and resumed munching as he watched the others mount.

"Are you going to be all right, Jacob?" Roderick asked, though he appeared quite content to be up so high.

Jacob ran his fingers through the horse's mane. "I get to ride a horse. And I get to ride it with you. That's all I need."

Roderick smiled to himself. *A horse ride. I suppose that would be a balm to any child's soul. Still, Jacob's resilience is a thing of wonder.*

"What's his name?" Jacob asked.

"Hmm, I forgot to ask," Roderick said. "Master Kendall, what's the name of this horse?"

"Liath," Kendall said.

Jacob stroked his mane some more. "Liath. That's a nice name."

Once all were mounted, they took off across the sand. Liath was indeed a masterful steed, but the horses were trotting much faster than Roderick had ever gone before. He held on equally tightly to Jacob and to the horse's reins, but in truth, he never came anywhere near to falling. After the first hour, his fears began to subside and he eased his grip on the reins. He had to admit, there was something enchanting about riding along the coast, the sea air washing over him, being carried along by the tremendous creature beneath him. He didn't even mind the cold, brisk currents in his face. At least not much.

"I like horses," Jacob said. "They make me feel safe."

"I like them, too," Roderick said. Perhaps when he returned home he would have to give old Blandy another go.

34

OF HEARTS AND RINGS

he company rode through the night, stopping for a short nap around midday. Judging from the position of the sun peeking through the overcast sky when Kendall roused them, they slept two hours at most. If Roderick's bones could have given voice to their torment, they would have cried out in protest. But as it was a world in which bones did not talk, they said nothing and neither did Roderick. Instead, he grudgingly mounted Liath with Jacob and resumed their journey.

The one saving grace was that the coastal breeze blunted the cold weather of these northern climes. It was still rather nippy, but it felt more like late fall in Briar's Glen than full on winter. The countryside consisted, for the most part, of rolling hills devoid of trees. Sparse patches of grass poked up through the sandy loam. No proper road existed among these forgotten lands, but the terrain was smooth enough that they did not need one. From time to time they lost sight of the western coast, but it always came back, like a watery guidepost pointing them ever northward. Near dusk they spotted a fishing village some miles off and swung wide to the east to avoid it.

Jacob came around nicely towards the end of the day. He and Roderick made a game of guessing the shapes in the clouds as they rode. Where Roderick saw flowers and pastries and men in hats, Jacob saw castles and knights and crowns. The one thing they both agreed on was that there were lots of animals. They saw sheep, cows, deer, squirrels, bears, eagles, and even a crane. Some of the animals which Jacob saw, Roderick had never even heard of: a lemur, an iguana, and something called a lorikeet which Jacob explained was a kind of bird.

"Where did you learn about all of these animals?" Roderick asked.

Jacob grew shy at that point. "I've seen them," he said at length.

"Seen them? Where in creation did you see such unusual things?"

It took even longer for Jacob to answer this question. When he did it was with a heavy sigh. "My parents...they liked animals."

Had the animals belonged to his parents? That did not make much sense. Perhaps the gypsies had shown them some. They were known to show off exotic creatures in some of their shows. Whatever the case, Roderick sensed that such questions would weigh heavily upon Jacob if he asked them so he went back to the cloud game.

By the time they made camp, the ocean was nowhere in sight, but the feel of it lingered in the air. A sort of tingling anticipation hung over the land. They took shelter amongst a clump of large, weathered rocks. The stones looked out of place amidst the grassy turf, as if some giant's child had left off playing a game of marbles long ago, leaving his toys to grow gray and rough with age.

The four adults took turns watching during the night. As was his custom, Roderick spent most of his watch praying for Jacob, who tossed fretfully, but calmed down by the time Roderick woke Kendall for his turn.

Rain soaked the turf off and on throughout the following day, which slowed the horses. They had hoped to reach the town of Iddlmar by nightfall, but long after the sun had gone down they were still in the saddle. They ventured on by what remained of the moon, a slender sliver now, no more than a tiny tear in the fabric of the night sky. Roderick stared out across the bleak northern lands expecting scathen or Iddlglim warriors to appear, but nothing stirred beneath the wide, restless clouds.

Roderick was nodding off in the saddle when at last he caught sight of a line of lights on the northern horizon.

He shook the sleep from his eyes. "Tell me that is Iddlmar."

"You've good eyesight for one half asleep," Kendall said.

"I don't think there could be a more precious sight in the three realms," Portia said.

"Do you really think they'll let us hire a boat?" Nagan asked, stifling a yawn. "Isn't that city populated by the Iddlglim as well?"

"No," Kendall said. "They consider themselves Caledonians. The people who inhabit the cities along the coast are close enough in blood to the Iddlglim that they live in relative peace with one another, but this city is not home to the same savage tribes now invading Halicon. Still, things shift quickly in war. We must be on our guard."

"Well, let's hop a little, then," Nagan said. "This saddle is chaffing my hind quarters something fierce. How I long to be rid of it!"

For once, they all agreed with Nagan.

The small city of Iddlmar was surrounded by a low, crumbling wall, more like a deterrent to unwanted wildlife than any sure defense from invasion. Several spots were little more than piles of fallen rubble. Three stubby watchtowers kept vigil along its length. Though no lights glimmered within them, and though the pre-dawn land was dark and quiet, they decided not to risk getting caught climbing through one of the broken down sections and instead headed for the nearest gate.

The guards there had lighter hair than most of the citizens

of the Halicon Empire, and they were taller too, but they did not look anything remotely like the way Roderick had imagined the wildmen to be. They wore padded armor and had long hickory clubs with metal bands on the ends. Their boots and leggings were reminiscent of those worn by the men of Garring Province in western Halicon, though a bit rougher and thicker. They asked a few questions about Kendall's business and appeared somewhat wary that he and his companions had traveled through the countryside during the night, but showed little interest in finding out much beyond that. They soon waved them through.

The city proper was composed of one and two-story buildings, most of which were small thatched affairs built from rugged limestone. The doors were painted in dark greens, reds, or purples, but aside from that, the city was rather drab.

A handful of folk were wandering the streets when they arrived. A few gruff faces stared them up and down, but no one said anything. The market and docks were closed at that hour so Kendall found them lodging at the first safe-looking inn they came across, an establishment called *The Hook and Anchor*, one of two inns within view of the docks.

"A cozy little abode—if by cozy you mean cramped, cluttered, and reeking of fish," Nagan muttered as they wandered inside.

The ceiling in the common room was strung with fishing nets and, not surprisingly, quite a few examples of hooks and anchors lined the walls. Four long tables with a smattering of homely chairs and a cold fireplace were the only other adornments.

There were only two rooms left and they rented both. Portia was given one and the men the other.

"Thank you kindly," Portia said, inserting an old iron key into her door and pushing it open. "Nothing against you fine fellows, but if there's one thing I learned growing up in the Tamber, it's that a lady needs her privacy. That may be the one decent thing my grandfather ever taught me."

None of the men objected, but with only one bed, two of them were forced to sleep on the floor. Kendall insisted that Roderick and Jacob share the bed since Jacob needed the most rest. Roderick was not sure how Nagan and Kendall would divide the narrow strip of floor between the bed and the door, but he was too exhausted to wait and find out. He went to sleep the moment his nose sniffed the pillow feathers.

By the time he awoke, Nagan was already up and pacing about. Kendall was nowhere to be seen. Jacob was resting peacefully, curled between Roderick and the wall.

"Where's Kendall?" Roderick asked.

"I have no idea," Nagan said. "Hopefully out getting us some food. I tried to get the innkeep to give us a few of last week's biscuits, but he's as 'greedy as a rake', as my ol' mum used to say. I wish Kendall had left us some coin. I tried telling that greasy proprietor that the old man would pay for our food when he got back, but he said he didn't trust me. Said I had a 'suspicious-looking face'. Can you believe that?"

Roderick's stomach gurgled rather loudly. He had a few biscuits of hard tack in his pack so he rummaged around and found a pair of them, offering one to Nagan. The Gitano took it, but not without a curl of the lip.

"I'm sure he'll be back soon," Roderick said. "Then we'll have a proper breakfast."

A knock came just then at the door.

"Must be the old scribbler now." Nagan went over to it. "Who is it?" he called out.

"Portia."

Nagan flipped the lock and opened the door.

The Gitana entered the room with a tray full of fresh biscuits, honey, butter, and dried sweet-nectar fruits.

"Well, aren't you a sight for hungry eyes," Nagan said. "Wherever did you get all this?"

"Oh, the innkeep," Portia said. "I told him Kendall would pay for it later."

"He didn't tell you that you had a suspicious-looking face?"

Nagan asked.

"No," Portia said. "Is that what you thought he would say?"

"Never mind," Nagan grumbled. "Let's eat before I waste away."

With some coaxing they roused Jacob. He sat on the bed blinking at them for several minutes until the sleep finally left him. Though he ate slowly, he finished every last bit of the sweet-nectar. It had an orangish meat to it and the shape and look of a small peach. It filled the air with a tangy aroma. Roderick had only ever heard of such fruit before and would have loved to try one, but he was more than filled by the biscuits and honey.

"Thank you, Miss Portia," Jacob said after wiping his mouth with a kerchief.

Kendall arrived as they were finishing up. They offered him the last biscuit, but he declined, saying he had breakfasted while about in the town. He informed them that he had successfully secured a ship which would transport them to the Isle of Rinn. It had not been easy, with many ships having been commandeered by the Iddlglim for use in the war, and also due to the lateness of the year. Few of the remaining ship's captains were willing to make the long journey to the Isle of Rinn in the winter, but Kendall had offered enough money to persuade one of them to take them on.

"And how much would that be?" Nagan asked.

"That is none of your business," Kendall said. "All that concerns you is that we set sail just after midday."

"Ah, well, that gives us a few hours to carouse the city and take in the sights," Nagan said happily. He was in a markedly better mood now that he had eaten.

"You'll be passing your time in this inn." Kendall pointed the tip of his staff at Nagan's chest. "None of you are to leave these rooms."

A veil of protest fell over Nagan's face. "But I'm a Gitano, we're famous for our stealth, we blend in wherever we go."

Kendall's expression hardened even more. "There are

worse things than constables and Iddlglim sympathizers and you, of all people, should know that. I, however, need to buy supplies for the journey. I'll come back when it is time for us to leave."

Nagan was about to say something more, but Portia caught his eye and he thought better of it.

"Breakfast has been paid for and I've arranged for lunch to be delivered to your rooms. Be thankful you have any food at all," Kendall said. With that he turned with the briskness of a finger snap and departed.

Portia returned to her room to catch up on her sleep. Jacob lay down and soon fell back asleep as well. That left Nagan and Roderick sitting in the room by themselves, Roderick on the edge of the bed, and Nagan on the floor.

Nagan was strangely quiet. Though Roderick would have preferred to rest, the look on Nagan's face aroused his concern.

"Is something troubling you, Nagan?" he asked.

"Hmm? Oh, nothing." Nagan stared sullenly at the doorknob.

"Well, it doesn't sound like nothing. Why the long face?"

"It's just—" Nagan cut his words short with a frown.

"Just what?"

"It's just that I had my heart set on visiting the market today, that's all."

"Really? Well, why didn't you ask Master Kendall? I'm sure he could have brought you anything you needed."

"No, he couldn't," Nagan said. "There was something I needed that only I could get."

"And what was that?" Roderick asked, hoping Nagan did not mean to return to thieving.

Again Nagan hesitated, his eyes drifting listlessly about the room. "A ring," he said finally.

"A ring? Whatever in The Glen would you want a ring for?"

Nagan's eyes strayed towards the far wall of their room, the one adjoining Portia's chambers.

Roderick took in a sharp gasp. He quickly recovered, attempting to hide his surprise, though he could not keep from letting an "Oh, my," slip from his lips. He knew that Nagan had feelings for the girl, but he had no indication things were that serious between the two of them.

"So you mean to pr—"

"Shh!" Nagan cut him off. "She might hear you."

"My dear Nagan." Roderick patted him on the shoulder. "I don't think you could have chosen a finer lady in all of the Tamber. Do you believe she shares in your affections?"

"No," Nagan said, sulking. "In fact, there are a thousand men more worthy of her. I'm sure she could pick any one of them over me and be perfectly content."

Nagan certainly had some rough edges, but he was not entirely devoid of merit. "Have you talked to her about these things?" Roderick asked.

"Yes, once—a long time ago, right before I was sent to Middlehelm."

"And what did she say?"

"She laughed in my face," Nagan said quietly. "Told me she could never marry anyone who hadn't 'proved himself a man,' or some such nonsense."

"So have you done that—proved yourself to her, I mean?"

"Well, I stole a ruby necklace from Barillio's treasury."

"And you thought that was what she meant by 'proving yourself?'"

"How was I supposed to know what it meant? I'm a Gitano, that's how we show our skill, by stealing things. It seemed a reasonable idea at the time, though looking back on it...perhaps it was not one of my best."

Roderick got up off the bed and sat down on the floor next to Nagan.

"Listen, Nagan. How long have you known Portia?" he asked.

"My whole life."

"Well, I don't know what she was like growing up, but from what I've seen of her over the few days I've known her, she doesn't seem all that fond of Gitanos, or thieves, or her grandfather's criminal ways. Do you think I am wrong in that assessment?"

Nagan scratched at the floor with one of his fingers. "No...I suppose she's always been like that, now that you mention it."

"In fact, there are many things about your Portia that remind me of my Bethany. They're both a bit headstrong, but in a good way, rather idealistic, the kind of women who speak their minds and won't settle for cheap talk and false promises —in short, fine, noble women who want a man who does the right thing, or at least tries to."

"Really?" Nagan stared at him, perplexed, as if he had just noticed something odd about Roderick's face. "You think that's what Portia is looking for?"

"I believe so," Roderick said. "I mean, look at me. I'm a simple tailor. I don't have much to offer a woman. But when Bethany saw that I was honest and hard-working, that I could look her in the eye and tell her that I loved her with my whole heart, that I would cherish and protect her all my days, well, that was enough. It wasn't easy, mind you. Took a good deal of courage to tell her my true feelings, to be sure. But if this country simpleton can win the hand of the most beautiful girl in Briar's Glen, I think there might be a chance for you and Portia."

"You do?" A hopeful smile flickered onto Nagan's lips. "You really think there's a chance?"

"I do. If you're willing to do things the right way."

"Hmm..." Nagan nodded to himself several times, understanding spreading across his face like the morning sun brightening through the window. "The right way..." he mumbled. "You know, I never thanked you for trying to vouch for me with Barillio," he said after a while. "It was a foolish thing to do, but you meant well. And it meant a lot to me, even though I never told you."

"Yes, I suppose it was rather foolish," Roderick agreed. "But you're welcome all the same."

There was another long silence between them. Roderick stretched his weary arms and legs. Perhaps there might be time for a bit of rest after all.

"I'm just curious, though," Roderick said as he got up and lay down on the bed beside Jacob. "How were you going to buy her a ring anyway, since you don't have any coin?"

Nagan shrugged, doubt returning to his face.

"I don't know," he said. "I suppose I was planning on stealing it."

"Oh, Nagan." Roderick let out a weary sigh. "I think you may still have a few things left to learn."

35

ᏖHE ᏖLEDGLING'S ᏖLIGHT

Ꮦhe harbor was larger than Roderick expected. Four jetties stretched out into the lapping waters. It had room for twenty or more ships, but the docks were mostly empty. Six small fishing dinghies bobbed anxiously in the emerald waves, dwarfed by a double-masted monster rising above the wharf like a movable mountain. The sixty-foot vessel boasted three square sails with a crow's nest on the main mast and two more sails of similar shape on the forward mast. Two triangular sails ran from the prow to the foremast and a slanted rectangular sail stretched out from the main. The unadorned, sand-colored canvas had been repaired in a few places, but looked more than sturdy enough to brave the northern winds.

"The Fledgling's Flight" was the name painted on her side. The wings of a large green bird had been carved and painted on each side of the prow, with a large beak making up the point. The ship's wheel was in the aft on a raised section, accessible via stairs on either side. The *Fledgling's* flanks were a black-brown color, but the deck was stained a brighter, tawny hue. The railings along the sides were painted white, though they had faded to gray in many places.

Despite knowing almost nothing about what went into crafting a ship, the sheer size, complexity, and majesty of the vessel cast a spell over Roderick, making him wonder why he had never gone to the docks in Evenspire before. To his unschooled eyes it looked like something that might have belonged to the Emperor himself. A thrill of anticipation ran through him.

I might just enjoy this trip after all…just maybe.

Despite his newfound enthusiasm for sailing, the journey did not commence as quickly as anticipated. The ship was still being loaded when they arrived. Though the crew hustled up and down the gang plank, their brows sprinkled with sweat, hauling sacks and crates and barrels of all kinds, their industrious activity failed to impress Portia or Kendall. The two of them exchanged harsh words with the captain over the fact that it was a quarter past noon and the ship had yet to be loaded.

Captain Kade was a burly fellow with bright red cheeks framed by even brighter red sideburns. He doubled Roderick in weight, but was not fat, merely big. He could have tossed the diminutive Portia into the harbor with one arm, but that didn't stop her from giving him several pieces of her mind. The captain did not fare well in his encounter with the fiery young Gitana. He kept adjusting the monocle he wore, sputtering and clamoring like a tea kettle that could not quite come to a boil. By the end of it, he somehow found himself apologizing and promising all sorts of extra benefits, reducing his fees, and making all manner of adjustments and assurances to placate the tenacious gypsy. Kendall was more than content to let Portia do most of the talking.

Once she had been placated, Portia quickly changed her tune, recruiting Nagan and Roderick to help the other thirty-three crew members load the last of the boxes. Two of them were older like the captain, but the rest looked much younger, and five of them looked to be little more than tall boys. Most were endowed with the same ruddy complexion as the captain, though their hair ran in tamer shades of blonde and brown.

Jacob watched the loading from the safety of Kendall's side. On account of his luminous skin, the Savant had purchased a thick wool scarf for him so that only his eyes showed out from beneath the cowl of his cloak. He got not a few odd looks from the crew, some of whom mumbled about the possibility of "bad weather" and "bad luck" on the upcoming journey.

With the ship loaded at last, they unfastened the ropes and launched *The Fledgling* into the harbor. The vessel creaked and groaned like an old woman awakened from a very long nap who was none too happy about it.

Roderick was more thrilled than he ever dreamed he'd be on a ship. Besides the privilege of sailing on such an impressive vessel, being out on the open waters meant that the scathen would no longer be able to follow them. As if that were not enough, the day was a particularly gorgeous one —the prettiest he could remember for some time. The clouds were large and white and friendly, respectfully keeping their distance from each other as they floated along. The sky was that particularly deep shade of blue which was Roderick's favorite, for it reminded him of the eyes of his dear Bethany.

Ah, what would Beth say if she were here? Oh, to see her face again.

The chalky green waters complimented the beautiful sky perfectly. Roderick had only ever seen such hues in the gems sold in Evenspire's markets. It comforted him to discover the ocean could clothe herself in such majestic colors. Perhaps she was not as perilous and capricious as all the tales made her out to be.

Nagan and Jacob stood on the opposite side of the deck watching gray seabirds with long black beaks diving into the Neverless Sea. The sight of the two of them pointing and laughing at the exploits of the birds gave Roderick no end of pleasure. Watching them, it wasn't clear who was the bigger child: Nagan or Jacob.

"So what do you think of our ship?" Portia asked, sidling up alongside him, still in an expansive mood from her victorious haggling with the captain. "Looks like she's seen better days, but finding a windjammer in that deserted harbor was a blessing for sure. The old scholar certainly always comes up smiling."

Kendall was below deck, resting after the long morning of finding a ship, negotiating their passage, and securing supplies for the journey.

"A windjammer? Is that what they call this? Well, I like it a good deal better than that boat we rode out of Castle Brimstoke," Roderick said after a moment's reflection. "Though one does feel a little exposed out here on the open water. The sea is awfully beautiful, but far larger than anything I'd ever imagined."

"I've no doubt the captain will keep us afloat. Still, I do fear we may be in for some rough waters before all's said and done." Despite Portia's tender years, her countenance bore the wisdom that comes from a life of suffering.

"You don't look fearful," Roderick observed. "You always seem confident and sure of yourself."

"I'm just stubborn," Portia said. "I haven't managed to shake everything I inherited from my grandfather, unfortunately."

"Well, you appear to have turned out all right despite your upbringing. I can only hope my daughter will become as fine and noble a lady as yourself one day."

Portia beamed. "Coming from you, that means a great deal."

"I'm not the only one who thinks highly of you, you know." He returned her smile and glanced over his shoulder towards Nagan.

"Oh, Nat?" Portia chuckled softly. "I suppose he does have a rather high opinion of me. Too high, if you ask me, and not a high enough one of himself."

"Do you know of his intentions towards you?"

"Are you a tailor or a matchmaker, my dear Roderick?" she asked playfully.

"Well, at the moment my needle and thread are unavailable so I thought I might try my hand. They both involve a little mending of sorts, one of fabric, the other of hearts."

Portia laughed out loud, attracting the notice of a few of the crew and Nagan as well, who eyed her with a mixture of curiosity and suspicion. She and Roderick ignored them, gazing out across the sea in silence for some time.

"Nat is a dear friend," Portia said. "But he's a scapegrace and a scoundrel like all the other Gitanos. At least, that's what I've always thought. I don't know, though. I have seen signs that he may be changing."

"So there is hope for him?" Roderick asked, encouraged for Nagan's sake.

"Did he put you up to this?" Portia gave him a measuring glare.

"No," Roderick said. "And I'm not saying he would necessarily be right for you just yet. I have questions about his character myself. I'm just advising you to keep your eyes and heart open, that's all."

Portia stared out over the horizon thoughtfully for a time and then offered him her hand.

"Fair enough." She smirked as the two shook hands. "I suppose everyone deserves a second chance, even Gitanos."

On the second day of the voyage, the seas grew rough and the trip far less idyllic. Roderick spent most of the afternoon leaning over the railings, ridding himself of all the delicious food he had partaken of the day before.

Jacob also took ill, though he did not join Roderick on deck. He remained in his cabin, overtaken by fever and chills. When Roderick was not topside being sick, he was down below praying in a constant vigil over the little boy he had come to love so dearly. In all their days and nights together, Roderick had never seen Jacob this bad off. He was restless both waking and sleeping, often muttering unintelligible things in the dark hours of the night.

On the third day, Kendall appeared in Jacob's cabin and asked to speak with Roderick. He followed the Savant back up on deck. Out in the open air, a chilling drizzle peppered the *Fledgling's* yawing deck and Roderick's face.

"How is he?" Kendall asked.

"Not good," Roderick said. "He hasn't taken any fruit all day, only a few cups of water. And his feverish episodes seem to be getting worse."

"I want you to remember this the next time you consider advising him to use his magic," Kendall said.

"You think the fever has some connection to the magic?"

"No one else on the ship has taken ill, have they? Perhaps I underestimated the reach of the scathen, or perhaps it is simply the magic itself, asserting control. Either way I fear something other than natural causes."

"Perhaps his time trapped inside that dark wind in Brimstoke had some sort of lasting effect on him." Roderick's stomach turned, but this time it was not from the motion of the ship. What sickened him was the thought that they would never be truly safe, that the shadows had found a way to torment Jacob even out here on the open seas. And there was no way for Roderick to be cured of that kind of sickness. Relief would only come at the end of the journey when the curse was lifted.

Kendall gazed out across the overcast waters, staring intently, as if he could see something which Roderick could not. "At Brimstoke it was Virinian who caused the magic to manifest, but from here on out we must do everything in our power to keep the motley from using it. Do I have your word that you'll keep him from using the magic for the rest of the journey?"

"Yes. I'll do what I can."

"That's not good enough. I need your word. The boy's life —all our lives—may depend upon it."

Roderick took a deep breath. "I promise," he said.

"Good. I'm trusting in you to get us safely through to the end."

Roderick returned to his cabin wondering if he'd be able to keep his promise. So far, it seemed like magic was the only thing keeping Jacob from being caught. And sometimes it seemed to work whether Jacob wanted it to or not. Still, it certainly did seem to be taking its toll on him, and he trusted that Master Kendall knew what was best.

When he opened the cabin door he was surprised to find Jacob awake and sitting up on the corner of the bed. He was still shivering from cold, but looked more alert than he had been in some time.

"Are you feeling any better?" Roderick wrapped the blankets around him.

Jacob shook his head. "Where did you go?"

"To speak with Kendall." Roderick sat down beside Jacob and put his arm around him. The cabin was too cramped to sit anywhere else, with only room for a nightstand beside the creaky old bed. Their things were stored in a trunk underneath it. Even if there had been somewhere else to sit, he wanted to keep Jacob warm. "He's worried about you."

"He doesn't want me to use the magic, does he?"

"No. He says it's dangerous, that it might be what's making you sick or that somehow the shadows are using it against you."

"I'm scared about what they might do to me if they ever catch me. The nightmares are getting worse." A fresh wave of shivers overtook Jacob's little body.

Roderick felt like shivering himself. "Well, I agree with Master Kendall. It would be best if you didn't use it."

"Sometimes it happens even when I don't want it, though, like when the light came over me in that castle or when I disappeared from the soldiers in the woods. I just get scared and then the magic takes over. I just want to go home." Two lone tears dribbled out from Jacob's eyes.

"I want that, too." Roderick swallowed back his own emotions, fighting to stay strong.

The tears came on hard for Jacob, though, like a sudden squall. Roderick rocked him back and forth, rubbing his back to keep him warm.

Home. What did Jacob even think of when he thought of that word? For Roderick it meant Aisha's laughter and Bethany's embrace, a blooming garden and kind neighbors, sunny days in the market, chatting with Old Tim at the end of a busy day. But what was Jacob longing for? What was home for him?

Roderick imagined the two of them sitting in front of the hearth, the warmth of a blazing fire reaching through the blankets to melt Jacob's chills, its bright light banishing the shadows from the room. A wave of joy tingled through his body. The longer he held that image in his mind, the more settled and natural it became. Jacob's home was meant to be in that little cottage as sure as green grass coming in the spring, as sure as the new sun rising over the oak trees on Old Cottage Road.

Roderick wiped away Jacob's tears. "Tell me something, Jacob." He turned him so they could look at each other face to face. "After we finish with the stone and the island and all this terrible business, and the magic is an old, forgotten memory, do you want to come and live with me and Bethany and Aisha in Briar's Glen and be a part of our family?"

Enormous tears splashed down from Jacob's beautiful green eyes. "Yes," he said. "I would like that, only…"

Roderick's heart hung in his throat with that terrible word 'only.'

"Only what, Jacob?"

"Only I'm not sure I'll make it back," Jacob sobbed.

"Oh, you will, Jacob. You will." Roderick hugged him tighter than ever and resumed rocking him back and forth. He prayed aloud that Adonai would bring them home safe and that all the shadows would be destroyed, banished once and for all, never to return. He prayed for a good long while, and somewhere in the midst of his prayers, Jacob cried himself back to sleep.

A mixture of joy and sadness seasoned Roderick's thoughts as he held that precious child in his arms. Joy at the thought of Jacob returning with him to Briar's Glen and becoming part of his family, but sadness at the thought of what lay ahead. For, like Jacob, he had no assurance that either of them would make it back from this long terrible journey. And this wonderful vision of home and family, bright as it was, seemed as fragile and precarious as a tiny boat cast adrift in the midst of the vast, Neverless Sea.

36

DRAGONS ON THE WATER

acob's fever broke sometime in the night. The next morning he asked to go above deck for breakfast, but Roderick told him it would be better to wait until he got more of his strength back so they ate together in the cabin.

As Jacob munched on dates and apples he peppered Roderick with questions about life in Briar's Glen. Roderick had never heard so many words come out of Jacob's mouth in one day, much less in a single hour. He wanted to know about Roderick's parents, about what kinds of games Aisha liked to play, what the weather was like, what Bethany did while he was at the market, and about Roderick's trade. How did he decide which clothes to make? How long did it take to make each piece? And why didn't he offer more colorful things?

Somehow they began talking about the various holidays celebrated year after year. Of course Winter's Rest had just passed, but then would come Spring's Yearning, followed by Summer's Delight, and finally Autumn's Feast. Though such holidays were celebrated all across Halicon, Jacob was unfamiliar with them.

"You really give gifts every day in the spring festival?" Jacob asked. "How do people have enough money for that?"

"Only for the first five days. On the final day there is a grand parade. But people mostly just make the gifts, so they're not that expensive," Roderick said. "Flowers and garlands are rather popular. We also give cheese and cookies. Simple things—trifles, really. Though one year I did splurge and bought Aisha her ball. It's a bit faded now, but I don't regret it. She plays with it every day."

"Maybe we can paint it when we get back home." Jacob's face lit up with a smile that outshone the glowing diamonds on his skin.

"Aye, that's a fine idea—" in the midst of Roderick's reply shouts broke out above deck, followed by the thumping, scurrying sounds of the crew. "Oh, buttons."

"What's wrong?" Jacob asked.

"Something's going on. I better have a look. You stay here," Roderick told him.

Jacob grabbed hold of his sleeve. "Please, let me go with you. I want to see, too."

Roderick hesitated, but the noises above were tugging at him to hurry. "All right, but only for a little while. I'm sure it's nothing."

Jacob wrapped his face in his scarf as they headed out the door. "Maybe it's a big fish. I always wanted to see a whale."

Cold, stagnant air prickled across Roderick's skin as they emerged from below. The sails fluttered limply. The sailors on deck were all talking at once. Not a few of them leaned over the railing, surveying the horizon.

Nagan, Portia and Kendall were there, too, staring out in the same direction.

"What's going on?" Roderick asked.

"Black dragons," Nagan pointed to three black shapes holding steady on the horizon. "At least that's what the lookout said. Never heard of them coming this far out, though."

"The ships of the wildmen?" A sting of fear pierced Roderick's chest. Though he had never seen black dragons before, these long, swift ships were known far and wide as terrors of the sea. They were said to be made from northern ash wood and then covered in tar to keep them afloat in all types of weather. Their name came from their black color and the massive rows of oars that would rise and fall on either side like flapping wings as they raced across the water.

"Savages," Portia muttered. "Don't they have a war they're supposed to be fighting?"

"We are at the mercy of the wind now," Kendall said grimly.

"What does the captain say?" Roderick asked.

The captain was at the rear of the ship, conferring with his first mate Jasper, a gruff, gray-headed fellow who was gazing out across the sea through a beaten spyglass.

"He has said precious little," Kendall said.

"I overheard some of the crew talking about selling us to the wildmen if it comes to it," Nagan said with one hand half covering his mouth.

"If we are boarded, it is unlikely they will be afforded such an option," Kendall said. "The Iddlglim rarely take prisoners at sea."

Roderick put his hand on Jacob's shoulder, half to steady himself at this news, and half to assure Jacob that everything would be all right. But Jacob wasn't looking out across the sea at the black dots. He was staring thoughtfully at the forlorn sails. Perhaps the fever had not entirely left him.

Captain Kade called for the crew to be quiet as he addressed them from the helm.

"You've all seen the black dragons," his voice boomed across the deck with no breeze to compete with it. "I'm not going to lie to you, lads. If this wind continues to play opossum, you'd best be sharpening your cutlasses and fingering your charms. By my reckoning we've got two hours at most before they overtake us. Until then, be about your business and carry yourselves like sailors."

The men hung their heads, some shuffling away slowly, others murmuring amongst themselves. Dark glances shot towards Roderick and his friends like the glimmerings of lightning in a faraway storm cloud.

Kendall slipped one hand into his robes. Whatever powders he had left would come in handy if the wildmen attacked the ship, but Roderick doubted it would be enough.

"How many wildmen will there be on each boat?" Roderick asked.

"Close to a hundred," Kendall said.

Three hundred wildmen against some thirty-odd sailors, a Savant, two gypsies, and a tailor. The *Fledgling's Flight* looked anything but majestic to Roderick now, her sails of no more use than a tailor's needle in a sword fight.

"I want to go back down." Jacob grasped Roderick's hand.

"Yes, yes, that's a good idea." Roderick's nerves would not hold up for two hours of watching the relentless approach of the wildmen. "Jacob needs his rest," he told the others.

"We will do our best to keep them from gaining the lower decks if it comes to it," Kendall said.

Nagan tapped Roderick on the shoulder. "Pray for us," he said, nervous sweat trickling down his brow.

"I will," Roderick promised. Nagan had never asked him to pray before. This was not a good sign.

As they descended the stairs, Jacob asked, "Do you think it's only bad men on those ships?"

"Yes. They're the same ones who attacked Middlehelm," Roderick said.

"I don't think they're going to catch us," Jacob said as they entered the cabin.

"Really?" It was unlike Jacob not to recognize danger. Roderick touched his head to see if the fever had returned, but he felt normal. "And what makes you say that?"

Jacob took off his scarf with a shrug.

Roderick closed the door. "Here, kneel with me," he said, bending beside the bed. Jacob followed his example. He looked up at Roderick with expectant, unblinking eyes. "You know, I haven't studied like Master Kendall, and I don't know how to steer this big ship like Captain Kade either, and I'm sure Portia and Nagan could best me in a sword fight, but do you know what I can do?"

"Pray," Jacob answered softly.

"That's right," Roderick said. "Adonai has helped you through the nightmares in your sleep, perhaps he'll help us now that we're having one while we're awake. Let's bow our heads."

"Wait," Jacob said, putting his hand on top of Roderick's. "I have a question. Do you think maybe it was Adonai who gave me the magic?"

Roderick thought for a moment. "Well, I don't know. It seems like a terrible gift by most ways of reckoning, but Adonai does sometimes let difficult things come into our lives for his purposes. It may be that he has an intention for your magic which we do not understand."

"Why would he do that?"

"Hmm...that's another good question. Perhaps it wasn't meant for a curse at the beginning. It may be that it was something meant for good, but got twisted somehow by those who dwell in this fallen world. I'm afraid I don't have the answer to that one, but that is often the way of things. Only Adonai knows. But I do know this. You can trust in his wisdom, and you can trust he will bring good out of it in the end, even when the wind fails and there are black dragons chasing you."

Jacob nodded, a gentle smile slipping onto his glowing face.

Roderick realized then what Jacob had done. He had allowed Roderick to reassure him about Adonai's providence not because he needed it, but because Roderick did.

"Okay." Jacob squeezed Roderick's hand. "Let's pray."

"And so, to you, oh, Adonai, we humbly entreat you to protect us from this danger. For we are but weak and frail vessels—"

They had been praying for a good half hour when cries broke out above deck once again. Roderick stopped his prayer in mid-sentence and opened his eyes.

After listening for several moments he said, "It sounds as if they're cheering."

"Yes. Maybe Adonai answered our prayers," Jacob's eyes danced with excitement, but his head nodded forward sleepily.

The thought that their prayers had been answered so quickly sent such a thrill through Roderick that he gave little thought to Jacob's tiredness.

"Let's go up top and see what's happening," Roderick said.

Jacob blinked in sluggish assent. Roderick opened the door to the shouts and acclimations of joy from above. He raced up the stairs, leaving Jacob to put on his scarf by himself.

A fierce wind smacked Roderick head on the moment he set foot on deck. A scene of raucous good-will awaited him. The whole crew was out and Roderick saw at once what they were cheering for: the sails were up! They were stretched full with the strongest wind *The Fledgling* had enjoyed since she left Iddlmar. The sound of the gusts whistled through the breeze and a flock of gray gulls squawked in complimentary harmony far off across the waters, as if they, too, were as grateful to see the *Fledgling* moving again as Roderick.

Jacob waddled up beside him, leaning against his side.

"It's a miracle!" Roderick exclaimed, lifting Jacob into the air.

"I knew you wouldn't let us down, Patches. This is your handiwork, isn't it?" Nagan said, coming over and wrapping his arms around them, chuckling with delight.

"Not this time, my friend. This blessing comes straight from the Lord of Heaven." Roderick joined in Nagan's laughter, finding the spirit of celebration on deck contagious. It infused his being like sunlight warming a rock. "But I must confess, even I did not expect him to answer so quickly."

Nagan pulled Jacob and Roderick over to the railing. They peered out across the waves at the dragon boats. Though they had closed about a quarter of the distance to the *Fledgling*, they were slowly being drawn back towards the horizon from which they came.

"The captain says he's never seen the like of it," Nagan

said.

"Indeed, I'm willing to bet he hasn't," Kendall commented as he and Portia joined them.

"It's a blessing, isn't it, Master Kendall?" Roderick asked.

"You tell me," Kendall said, gazing steadily at Roderick. "From where I'm standing it may very well be a curse."

"Ah, now, Master Kendall. No need to keep your book bound so tight," Nagan chided. "We've been saved from the Iddlglim. Can't you at least be happy for that? Even for a moment?"

"You're not saying this is magic again?" Portia asked. "It's just wind this time, like Roderick says, a blessing from heaven."

Kendall shook his head gravely, immune to the frivolity and cheer which had seized everyone else on board. "This is no ordinary wind."

"Oh, no, Master Kendall," Roderick said. "You see, Jacob and I were praying and—"

"Then why are the Iddlglim still rowing?" Kendall pointed at the distant ships. "Their ships have sails as well and yet they remain unfurled. Or do you think we're under the influence of some special, divinely inspired gusts?"

Roderick couldn't see well enough to confirm what Kendall said, but Nagan, after several moments of eyeing the boats, nodded in agreement.

"You've sharp eyes," Nagan said. "I hadn't noticed it before, but it's true. No wonder they're fading."

"But—" Roderick wanted to protest, but he didn't know what to say. If the Iddlglim ships really were without wind, what else but magic could be speeding them along now?"

"Oh, buttons." Roderick set Jacob down. Of course Kendall was right, as usual. And he hadn't even mentioned the gull song. It kept going on and on in the oddest way, far more beautiful than was typical for those birds. Why did there always seem to be music whenever there was magic about?

"I thought I told you to make sure this did not happen." The old scholar's beard bristled like tiny porcupine quills.

"I'm sorry—I didn't know," Roderick said. "Jacob? Is this true?"

Jacob's glazed over eyes stared right through him.

Kendall stooped down and tried to look Jacob in the eye, but the boy's head lolled to the side. "You must not use your magic again," he scolded. "Especially now that we are so close to the tower."

"Jacob, I thought we agreed to listen to Master Kendall on this," Roderick said.

Jacob pulled up his scarf, so that it nearly covered his eyes.

A low rumble bubbled up from Kendall's throat. Roderick's father used to make a similar sound when he was about to hand down a punishment.

But Kendall's voice was surprisingly gentle. "I am only trying to protect you," he said. "You might at least be honest about things."

Jacob let out a deflated little groan. He was no better at hiding his disobedience than Aisha was. His guilt was as clear as the colored squares on his forehead.

"Yes," he finally admitted, his whispering voice almost carried away by the wind.

"Did not Roderick tell you that you were not to use it anymore? Have you not heard me on many occasions warn you of its dangers?"

Jacob turned to Roderick, a puzzled wrinkle on his brow. "But I thought you said Adonai might have a use for my magic."

"Well, I…" Roderick faltered, seeing Jacob's disobedience in a new light. "I may have said something like that, but that's not what I meant—I didn't mean you were supposed to use it, only that Adonai might have had some purpose in giving it to you."

"What good is a gift if you don't use it?" Jacob asked.

"Because…" Roderick cast his gaze skyward, as if the heavens might grant him the answer.

"I think he might have you there," Nagan poked Roderick in the ribs, clearly enjoying his companion's flusteration.

Roderick took a deep breath and somewhere out of the cavern of his memory, something his father had told him came back to mind. "All I know is that there is a time and a place for every gift and when we use them improperly all sorts of bad things may happen. It's like fire in the hearth. If you keep it inside, it warms the whole house, but if you let the fire get out, the house catches fire. It's not safe to just go lighting fires wherever we want, you see?"

Jacob's gaze drifted out over the waters, his eyes gradually taking on a more repentant look.

"All right," he said. "I guess that makes sense. I'm sorry."

"Let us hope you mean it this time," Kendall said, crossing his arms.

Roderick pulled Jacob in for a hug. "I forgive you, Jacob. We all make mistakes."

Nagan leaned in close and whispered, "Thanks for the wind all the same, Patches. I would have done the same thing if I were you."

Jacob's eyes sprang to life at the Gitano's words. Roderick was sure he must be smiling under that scarf, but it was just as well that he had it on. Kendall might have locked him in his room and tossed the key into the waves if he had seen it.

The magical wind continued for several hours, never slacking. The gull song ebbed and flowed with it as well.

Roderick, at Kendall's behest, pleaded with Jacob to dismiss it, but he did not know how. Like the rest of his magic, it had a mind of its own.

But whatever the consequences might be for using it, for now at least they were safe. Soon the dragon boats disappeared off the horizon. The Iddlglim threat gone, the sailors resumed their murmuring, this time about the unusually timely gale. From the snatches Roderick caught, it was clear that Kendall wasn't the only one who had suspicions about the origins of the winds now carrying them along.

Even Captain Kade seemed more gruff and irritable than usual. "The sooner we get to that island the better. I should've never taken this job," Roderick overheard him say to Jasper.

Jacob spent the morning resting, but came up on deck for lunch. When Roderick went to get him, he noticed that more glowing diamonds had appeared on his face. In fact, only four spots remained that were not glowing, one each of red, blue, green, and yellow.

But he understands now, Roderick told himself. *He won't use it again.*

An hour past midday, the lookout shouted the two most joyous words Roderick had yet to hear on the voyage, "Land, ho!"

Though the land was little more than a bump on the horizon at first, it captured everyone's attention. The inconsequential shape grew as they approached, forming into a looming mass that was both inviting and intimidating all at once. A single mountain dominated the island, dark gray in color, with a rounded top. Finger-like lines of trees gripped its flanks, seeming to rise up out of the sea itself. Beyond the mountain, another large hill, completely blanketed with green, melded into the surrounding forest. Most of the coast was rocky, except for the southern portion where there was a little sliver of a beach with gray-white sand.

Roderick hoisted Jacob up in his arms so he could get a better view.

"It is on the further hill that the Tower of Tronas lies," Kendall pointed out the far rise to his companions. "If we make good time, we should be there within six hours of landfall."

"That means we won't reach the tower until after dark," Portia said. "Shouldn't we wait until morning?"

"Portia's afraid of the dark," Nagan said in a teasing

whisper for which he got a playful swat.

"Mind your manners," Portia said.

"Lady Portia's not afraid of anything," Jacob put in.

"That's right." Portia patted him on the shoulder.

"We shall be fine during the night," Kendall said. "The island is not large and I have been here before."

"What if the wildmen catch up to us?" Roderick asked.

"Yes. Do you think we'll be able to get in and out of this jungle before they arrive?" Nagan asked, casting a furtive glance over the empty horizon behind them.

"In point of fact it is not actually a jungle," Kendall corrected him. "It is a rainforest. And it's not the Iddlglim that I'm worried most about. I've instructed Kade to meet us on the far side of the island so that even if they continue their pursuit, they should not be able to find us. Jacob's use of the magic is our greatest danger from this point on."

Jacob pretended not to hear the admonishment, keeping his eyes fixed on the approaching shore.

An hour after spotting the shore, the powerful winds died away, replaced by a gentle breeze, but it was enough to push the *Fledgling* the rest of the way. The flock of gulls, which had followed them since the winds began, flew off as well, taking their odd squawking song with them.

"What kinds of animals are on the island?" Jacob asked Kendall as the group stood on deck, discussing their preparations for the journey inland.

"Quite a variety, actually. Due to some favorable coastal winds and the past presence of a volcano, it's quite a fertile place and not nearly as cold as the mainland would be this far north. Lizards, turtles, frogs, snakes, ducks, and herons all make their home on the Isle of Rinn. According to the histories, mountain lions once stalked this land as well, but I saw none during my visit," Kendall said.

Mountain lions? That sounded worse than wolves.

The island swelled in size as they approached, stretching for miles in either direction. There might have been a thousand places where predators could be lying in wait for them.

"But no people, right?" Jacob asked.

"No, Tronas made sure of that. According to legend, when the Null Stone was first placed here, it caused that mountain, Mt. Tenebris, to awaken as a volcano. It destroyed all of the settlements here. Those who did survive the catastrophe fled, never to return. But that was long ago. The volcano has been dormant ever since."

"Oh, bother," Nagan said. "Just my luck, I'll sneeze and set it off again, just you watch."

"Oh, Nat," Portia said. "Don't flatter yourself."

By the time they set anchor just off shore, the sun was low on the western horizon. The waters of the bay dimmed to a dark, sinister shade of blue. The sailors loaded a few supplies into a row boat and the five travelers headed for shore along with first mate Jasper and another member of the crew. Roderick had his doubts as to whether the crusty sea captain and his men would remain true to their word and meet them again on the other side of the island, but he did at least allow Nagan and Portia to borrow a couple of cutlasses to assist them in hacking a path through the forest.

The island hummed with the chatter of birds, insects, and other unknown animals lurking within the looming wall of vegetation which ran right up to the edge of the slender beach. As they waded onto shore, the sun surrendered into the sea, and purple curtains of cloud closed around it. Jasper and the other sailor rowed away, wagging their heads.

Once the companions reached the shore, Kendall placed something in Roderick's hand.

"Here," he said. "Take my carmine crystal. It can sense the Null Stone as well. It will lead you to the tower if we get separated."

"But won't you need it?" Roderick asked.

"I already know the way, remember?"

Nagan's head appeared over his shoulder, peering down at the glinting stone.

"Well, if you're handing out presents, I'd be happy to take

some gold valins off you to lighten your load," he joked. "Though that piece of jewelry doesn't look half bad, either. You don't happen to have an extra one, do you, Kendall old chum?" He nudged Roderick with his elbow and smirked.

As Kendall shot Nagan a testy stare, Roderick stuck the twinkling stone into the special compartment inside his cloak for safekeeping. Nagan's "reformation" seemed far from complete, and though the Gitano would probably not take it, he did not want to tempt him by wearing it openly.

"As a matter of fact," Kendall said, his expression softening into a smirk of his own. "Since I'm in a generous mood, here is a bit of flameroot for each of you. The wood in this place is not much for burning."

He handed out slender reeds to Roderick, Nagan, and Portia.

"Don't I get one, too?" Jacob asked.

Kendall's face morphed back into a wooly frown.

"I'm sure your glowing skin will give you more than enough light," Kendall said, and headed off into the forest.

Jacob let out a sigh, but, as usual, took the admonishment without comment.

"Don't worry, Patches," Nagan said. "When the time comes, I'll let you hold mine."

A stiff wind ushered them into the waiting tangle of trees. While at first the ground was almost completely overgrown with ferns and bushes, after a hundred yards or so the canopy of trees grew so thick it crowded out the undergrowth. While this made the going easier, it also brought the night upon them all the quicker. The slender tree trunks and dense foliage took on a menacing look in the dying light as dusk took hold of the forest.

The creatures of the forest paid little heed to the coming of night. If anything the croaking, chirping, screeching, and skittering sounds grew louder the further in they went. A sense of something primordial pressed in all around them, like the island was a slumbering giant which might awake at any moment.

Soon Kendall was forced to light his lantern so they could keep going.

"I thought you said this land was uninhabited," Nagan said in a low voice about an hour in.

"Yes, of course," Kendall said. "We're dozens of leagues from the mainland. No one has lived out here since old Mad Tronas himself."

"Then what are all those sounds?" Nagan asked.

"Nagan, even you must know what the word 'uninhabited' means," Kendall said. "Have I not already explained that this rainforest is teeming with animal life?"

"Begging your pardon, Master Scholar, but that doesn't sound like any animal I've ever heard of. Can't you hear it?" Nagan asked.

Seeing that he was serious, they all stopped to listen.

For a while, no sounds could be heard above the cacophony of wildlife. Then came a crunch, like something stepping on a fallen branch.

"Something's out there," Portia whispered.

"I think you are right," Kendall said quietly.

"Oh, please, don't let it be one of those lions," Nagan said with a whimper.

The air grew still, as if the forest were holding its breath. Then, in a great exhale, it released itself upon them. The noises Nagan had heard came crashing down around them as dark shapes rushed in on them from every side. The giant had awoken.

37

FLIGHT

he shadowy figures swarmed in from the trees. Kendall's lamp snuffed out. Jacob screamed. Portia and Nagan let forth battle cries, their cutlases flashing in the scattered moonlight.

"There are too many! Run!" Kendall shouted.

The air exploded with black smoke and everything went dark. Jacob's familiar hand latched onto Roderick's, and they bolted forward. Blind and blundering strides led them out of the smoke, somehow missing the figures rushing all around them. They clambered up a small slope, stealing past dark silhouettes. Were they men or scathen? Roderick was too disoriented and panicked to tell. The sound of clashing blades and furious cries filled the night.

Roderick took a step back towards his friends and the black smoke, torn as to what to do. His throat burned and his eyes watered. How could he hope to find them in that smoke?

"Where's the boy?" shouted a voice.

"That way!" came the answer. "I saw him heading up that slope."

Dark shapes staggered out of the smoke. Roderick did not wait to see if he was spotted. He ran over the crest of the hill. The night showed him nothing but dark blurs. His reckless flight was more like falling upright than running. He had no idea where he was going.

As he shot up another rise, the clamor of the battle died away behind him.

He listened for pursuit, but could not hear anything above

his heaving lungs and his crashing through the underbrush. He stepped into an unexpected depression and barely avoided a fall. As he righted himself and kept running, he wondered if Kendall and the others had gotten free. He hated to leave them behind, but he had to protect Jacob.

The terrain leveled off again and the normal sounds of the forest told him he was no longer in immediate danger. He allowed his pace to slow, but as he did so, a terrible realization told him that the fate of his friends was the least of his worries.

Jacob was no longer with him.

"Oh, buttons!" Roderick couldn't keep from uttering the exclamation.

He stared back through the forest. There was no sign of Jacob anywhere. He spun this way and that, looking for where he might have gone. Terror seized him by the throat. How would he ever find Jacob in these shadowy, trackless woods?

Was it safe to call out for him now, he wondered? He stopped to listen again. The sounds of the night were all he heard. There was no sign of Jacob at all. Had he run off?

"Jacob…" he whispered. "Jacob, are you here?"

No answer.

"Jacob…it's me, Roderick…"

The woods chittered back, but nothing more. Roderick walked in a daze, whispering for several minutes until the hopelessness of his situation pulled him under the battering waves of despair.

What was he to do? He had no idea where Jacob was. Somewhere in all this dark, sinuous mess, he was wandering alone and Roderick had no way of finding him. Or worse, what if he'd been captured? Or turned into a shadow? Oh, where could he be?

Think, Devinson, think!

But nothing came. He was just a tailor, after all. He wasn't a tracker or a woodsman. But he had promised to protect Jacob.

The only thing he could think of finally was to start shouting. He might attract the scathen or whoever was pursuing them, or maybe some beast of the island, but he didn't care. He had to do something.

He was just opening his mouth to call out when he felt something scrape against his chest. It must have been there for some time, but he had been too panicked to notice. He reached inside his shirt and pulled out Kendall's carmine crystal. It glinted with a few bright motes of reddish light.

Of course!

Kendall had given him the crystal to find the Null Stone, but it could also be used to find Jacob. How had he forgotten it? Roderick swung around in a circle, pointing it in every direction. It flashed brightest when he held it to his left. But was it pointing to the tower or to Jacob? He couldn't know, but it was all he had to go on.

He took off again, hustling through the darkness. The stone's light gave him a dim view of his immediate surroundings, but nothing more. At least it made it easier to avoid the trees.

Roderick called out softly to Jacob as he ran. Though all he got was the chirping, clicking, buzzing sounds of the forest, the further he went, the brighter the stone's light became. What if the glow alerted the men to his presence? Or attracted some other denizen of the forest?

He tucked the crystal inside his sleeve. From then on he only checked it now and then to make sure he was still heading in the right direction.

Soon he arrived at a place where the light failed to increase no matter which direction he went. He paced back and forth over the same spot, trying to decide which way to go. At last, sweaty and exhausted, his hopes drained away, he leaned up against a tree and prayed.

"Oh, please, Adonai, please help me find Jacob."

A whispering voice from above drifted down to him.

"Psst, I'm up here," it said, sounding a touch woozy.

"Jacob?" Roderick asked, his heart drumming inside his chest. "Is that you?"

"I'm sorry. I must have fallen asleep for a little bit. I didn't know you were down there." said the voice, a little louder this time. It was definitely Jacob!

"The enemies are gone, Jacob. Tell me where you are. How am I supposed to find you in the dark like this?"

"Look up. In the tree," Jacob said.

Roderick looked up, but all he saw was a web of dark lines. But as he raised the crystal, the light grew strong enough to make out Jacob's small form resting peacefully amongst the branches of a tree, some forty feet above him.

"Oh, my," Roderick said, relieved to have found him and simultaneously alarmed that Jacob had gotten up so high. How ever would he get him down? "How did you climb up there? There isn't a single branch on that tree for twenty feet."

"I didn't climb. I flew," Jacob said somewhat capriciously.

"You flew? But when did you—" Roderick was cut off mid-sentence when Jacob leaned forward and fell out of the tree. "Jacob!"

Roderick's heart clenched.

But Jacob didn't keep falling. At least not in the normal way. It was as if an invisible hand caught him and lowered him gently to the ground. High notes resounded briefly through the air, like a stiff breeze blowing through a wind chime.

"I did it!" Jacob's face danced with a mixture of fear and exhilaration.

Roderick let out a great huff. "Oh, Jacob, you scared me half to death! Kendall would not approve. I'm not sure I do either. But at least you're safe." He was too overjoyed and frazzled to waste time on a lecture. He wrapped Jacob in his arms and held onto him until his heart stopped racing.

"Master Kendall isn't here," Jacob said. "And everything turned out all right, didn't it?"

Roderick could not miss the hint of pride in Jacob's voice. That wasn't like him.

"But what about the shadows? Whenever you use the magic it seems to call out to them."

The glow had spread to two more diamonds on Jacob's face. Only two remained which were not shining, a red and a blue.

"I can beat them back with the magic. I've done it before." The note of confidence in Jacob's voice sounded more like Kendall than Jacob.

"I think we had better find Master Kendall now. If he escaped those men, he should be waiting for us at the tower," Roderick said cautiously. Something was not right. This island was not supposed to be inhabited. And Jacob was behaving oddly. The sooner they got to the Null Stone and were rid of the magic the better.

"But what if those men are there, too?" Jacob lowered his voice. "I've seen them before."

"You've seen who before? The things that attacked us? Where?" Roderick asked.

"They had white mountains on their clothes, like the men in the forest who tried to catch us before we crossed that big river, way back at the beginning."

"So they were men, not shadows? You got a good look at them?"

"I can see pretty well in the dark, especially lately," Jacob said.

So they weren't scathen, or even Iddlglim. But that made no sense. If they weren't northmen, who were they? The Baron of Brimstoke was dead, so they couldn't have been his soldiers. And his men wore the insignia of the hawk on their livery anyway, not mountains. But the biggest mystery, whoever they were, was why they were even here at all.

"I don't see how they could have followed us all the way from Briar's Glen," Roderick said.

"Maybe they got here before us," Jacob suggested in his usual, direct way.

Roderick shuddered to think what that would mean if it were true. Kendall and the Savants were supposed to be the only ones who knew about the tower.

Jacob took off his gloves and stared at the glowing diamonds on his hands. They were like two stained-glass lanterns. Their prismatic reflections lit up the surrounding trees.

"Everyone wants the magic for themselves," Jacob said in a low, frightened voice.

"Jacob, listen to me," Roderick wiped the sweat from his forehead. "We've got to get you to that tower."

"But what if they're waiting for me there? What if they know that's where I'm supposed to go?"

Roderick's head was spinning from the mystery of the soldiers, Jacob's flight, and being separated from their friends. He had no answers. Oh, what was the right thing to do?

He leaned his hand against the smooth bark of one of the trees and took a moment to think. "Jacob, you've got to trust me," he said at length. "We've come all this way. We've got to see it through. Don't you want to be rid of this curse? Don't you want to be a normal boy and come back and live with me in Briar's Glen, like we talked about on the ship?"

Doubt swirled across Jacob's colorful, otherworldly face. A thousand thoughts flickered behind his eyes as his gaze wandered between his glowing hands and Roderick.

Oh, please, Adonai, help him snap out of whatever spell he's under. Help him find his way home.

On impulse Roderick grabbed Jacob's hands. "I only want what's best for you, Jacob. This is the only way. You have to get rid of this magic before it hurts you or other people."

Jacob closed his eyes. His lips moved wordlessly. Roderick feared he might be summoning forth the magic again.

After a long time his eyes flashed opened and stared straight into Roderick's. Those beautiful green orbs were the only thing on his face that did not exude magic.

337

"All right," he said in that soft, shy voice Roderick was accustomed to. "Let's go to the tower so I can give the magic back to Adonai. It's the right thing to do."

Back to Adonai? Roderick wasn't sure where that came from. But it didn't matter. They were going to get to that tower with Adonai's help and end this curse once and for all.

The Thaumaturge glowered at his men, though all he could see of most of them were silhouettes.

"I thought I told you to kill everyone but the boy and his guardian," he shouted at the captain, a broad shouldered man who was longer on courage than he was on wits.

"We tried, but they spotted us before we could get the jump. We fought the gypsies, but they gashed four of the men and took off running." The captain crossed his arms in frustration, not daring to raise his eyes and meet the Thaumaturge's gaze. "We searched for them, but it was too dark and their ilk are crafty in the woods."

"Twenty men and you couldn't kill two?" The Thaumaturge planted his staff in the ground between the man's feet. To his credit, the captain only flinched slightly. "The next man who fails to fulfill my commands will find himself a permanent home on this island, is that clear?"

"Yes, my lord," the captain said. "I take full responsibility."

"Enough about your failures. Where are the horses?"

"Just over the rise. We cut a path to the tower like you told us to." The captain's voice regained a slight measure of confidence. "It shouldn't take us more than an hour to reach it from here."

"Very well." The Thaumaturge strode past the men in the direction the captain had indicated. "It is imperative that I arrive before the motley. You and your men will hide yourselves around the perimeter, but within sight of the tower. Allow the child and his guardian to approach, but no one else."

"As you wish, my lord." The captain bowed low.

Despite the setback, the Thaumaturge took in a deep, satisfying lungful of cool night air. The end was close. The magic would soon be his. He could almost feel its tingling power flowing through his veins.

38

STRAIGHT AND TALL

he trek through the forest was harder than any other part of their journey. The canopy thinned and the undergrowth grew thicker with each step. The vines and fronds and curly weeds clutched at Roderick and Jacob's feet like overzealous beggars pleading for alms.

Nagan or Portia's cutlass certainly would have been handy right about then. *Oh, I hope they're all right.*

They wrangled their way through the clingy undergrowth. The few times they happened upon a break in the endless tangle, the damp and muddy ground made the going even harder. The slopping, popping suction of the boggy terrain slowed them to a crawl. After the first couple of tries through such patches, they began skirting around them instead of attempting to slog through.

Jacob had given his carmine crystal to Roderick so that it would not mislead the seeker stone as they sought the tower. Without Kendall's crystal, they would have been hopelessly lost, but the glints inside the stone sparkled whenever Roderick held it in a certain direction.

Jacob walked stolidly behind Roderick. After an hour, he started to fall further and further back. The rough terrain was taking its toll on his little legs. He wandered in a half daze. Roderick asked him if he wanted to stop and take a rest, but he only shook his head and plodded aimlessly ahead.

It's more than just the forest. He's afraid of what awaits him at that tower.

After the third hour Roderick called for a rest. He needed

340

one, even if Jacob did not or would not admit that he did.

"Are you well, Jacob?" Roderick asked, handing him a piece of fruit from his bag.

Jacob did not even put the fruit in his mouth, but held it in his lap.

"I'm fine," he said, a faraway look in his eyes.

"What are you thinking about?" Roderick grabbed some hard tack and took a sip of water.

"The tower."

"Are you afraid of going there?"

"Yes," Jacob said in a dream-like voice. "But that's not why I'm thinking about it."

"What is it, then?" Roderick asked, nibbling on the tasteless wafer.

"I'm wondering what it will be like."

"I've been wondering about that myself. I've never been in a tower before."

"I have," Jacob's shoulders drooped like he was on the verge of tossing himself into the moss and letting the creepers grow over him.

Roderick moved closer in case he really did collapse. "You have? When was that?"

"A long time ago." Jacob closed his eyes, walking in a memory which Roderick could not see.

Roderick waited for Jacob to elaborate, but he just stared off into the darkness. "What was it like?" Roderick asked.

"Straight and tall." Jacob drew himself up with a brief glimmer of vitality, as if trying to assure Roderick that he was all right.

"And which tower was that?"

Jacob's shoulders wilted back down. "It belonged to my parents."

"Your—? Really, is that so?" Roderick delayed his next bite, attempting to determine whether this information was real or just the product of Jacob's exhausted imaginings. Perhaps he had gotten confused with a tower that belonged to one of the land owners Jacob's parents worked for. "So what happened to this tower, then?"

"I don't know. I just remember what my father said about it. 'You've got to be strong like that tower,' he told me. 'Straight and tall...'" His voice was steeped in emotion, somewhere between wistful and heartbroken.

"What do you remember of your father?" Roderick asked gently. "You don't have to tell me if you don't want to."

"He...he was a good father," Jacob said, his eyes gaining a measure of alertness. "He took care of me. He always gave me fresh fruit. And he hugged me a lot. That's what I remember. We used to live in a great big castle and that tower was just one part of it. But one day he said we had to go. And that's when they started working in the fields. I don't remember the castle much, though, just the tower."

"So your parents weren't always field workers?" Roderick vacillated between shock and skepticism. Jacob was of noble lineage?

"No. We used to have the fruit brought in by these nice people who smiled a lot. They took care of me, too, but I don't remember their names."

"I'm sure they all loved you very much, just like your parents." Roderick said

"But we went away from the tower in the middle of the night and never came back." Jacob's voice cracked softly, like a tea cup clinking.

"That must have been very difficult."

Jacob's face trembled. A tear escaped down one cheek.

"I'm sorry they're not here right now to help you through this, but I think if they were, they would want you to keep going and get to that tower." Roderick placed his hand gently on Jacob's shoulder.

Jacob looked into Roderick's eyes and appeared to gain a measure of resolve. "Yes, that's what they would want." Without saying anything else, he wiped his eyes, bit into his piece of fruit, and set off again into the forest.

The silhouette of the tower cut a dark shape out of the starry shroud above. Its lines were rigid and unforgiving, like a great pillar set in the midst of the island. There were other stoneworks around its base, but it was impossible to tell what they had once been, for they now lay in varying states of ruin. Many of them were overgrown and had already been reclaimed by the forest. In stark contrast, the great tower rose defiantly, unbent and unwavering, as if newly built. How it had stood the test of time, who could say, but the closer Roderick and Jacob got to it, the more unassailable it looked.

There was no clear path through the ruins between them and the tower so they picked out the best route they could. They clambered over broken down stones, slipping on the moss more than once and losing their footing in the rubble a few times as well. It took them almost half an hour to reach the relatively clear area around the tower.

Though it was too dark to discern exactly what sort of stone the tower was made of, it was a lighter color than the surrounding ruins. The blocks were seamless. Roderick had never seen finer construction. It was roughly fifty feet in diameter at the base and three times that in height.

So this was it. This was what they'd come all this way for.

The only opening was a large arched doorway at the base. Until recently the entrance had been covered over by a network of vines which extended up from the surrounding overgrowth, but bits of vegetation now lay curled and withered around the door. The doors themselves had been fashioned from immense slabs of wood, a full head taller than Roderick. They were shut tighter than a clothes line.

Embedded into the door frame and going all the way around, metal letters caught the feeble moonlight and glinted in the dark.

Jacob walked towards the door. As he did so, the glowing

lights on his skin began to pulse and dance. Roderick pulled him back, fearing some sort of magical repercussions.

"It's a message about the tower," Jacob said, oblivious to the change to his skin.

Roderick did not like the look of those symbols one bit. He glanced back over the ruins behind them.

Where was Master Kendall when he needed him?

"What does it say?" Roderick asked.

Jacob read aloud:

Through labors long and untold strife
These stones were laid in a fateful hour
Til that day when a dawning life
Should part the doors and ascend the tower
To him alone whose name was lost
The way shall open to the spire's peak
Though only he may pay the cost
Or else the power another seek
Pass not the threshold once he's through
Lest the magic find its place in you

Roderick stared at the jumbled letters in awe, waiting for something to happen, but the night went on ever as before, hissing and croaking out its silvan song. Inside his mind the words swung back and forth like a pendulum. With each swing their meaning became more clear.

"That was written for you," Roderick said.

"I think so," Jacob said.

"It must mean...at least, I think it means," Roderick began, but his throat seized up. He did not want to say what he was about to say. "I think it's saying that you are supposed to go through the door alone."

"No. I can't go in there by myself. I must have read it wrong," Jacob stared at the letters as if he had been betrayed. He recited the words a second time. As he re-read the words "Pass not the threshold once he's through," his sigh seemed to come from the soles of his feet.

Jacob's glowing face bunched up like a torch rag. "Why? Why do I have to go alone?"

"I don't want you to go alone either," Roderick said. A pang shot through his heart. That tower might be filled with scathen. Or magical traps. Or a portal like the glistering glass. He might be sending Jacob into the land of nightmares itself. The shadows might have put the letters there for all he knew.

"The Null Stone is up there, on top of the tower," Jacob said reluctantly. "I can feel it now. It's pulling at me. But I don't want to go alone."

Roderick had not brought Jacob all this way only to abandon him at the end. He stared at the impenetrable tower in exasperation. He was Jacob's guardian. He had promised to protect him. Curse these letters and their awful message! Why did it have to be like this? If only Master Kendall were here. He would know what to do.

Just then, his paralyzed mind broke free and he saw a possible way out of their dilemma.

"It might not matter what the letters say, Jacob." He ran his hand across the surface of the door. "There's no handle, so we can't open it anyway!" He allowed himself a sigh of relief, as if the curse itself had been lifted and they could all go back home to Briar's Glen.

Jacob went up and pushed against the door with his little shoulder, but it did not move at all. The only thing that happened was that the lights on his skin flickered faster.

Roderick gave it an earnest shove of his own, but it remained as still as stone.

"Wait," Jacob said. "It says the way shall open 'to him whose name was lost.'"

"Well, that makes no sense." Roderick was starting to see why the builder of this tower had been called Mad Tronas. "How can anyone lose their own name? It can't be meant to be taken for the way it's written."

Jacob went over and touched the letters. They shimmered brightly with the reflections from his scintillating skin. "I had a different name once. Maybe that's what it means," he said.

"When we left the castle, my parents took different names, too, and they started calling me Jacob. That was a long time ago. I almost forgot about it. But Jacob wasn't my name at first. It was…Ithanaeus."

"Ithanaeus," Roderick repeated. The name did not fit Jacob at all.

"Some of these letters feel loose, like I could push them in. My father had a chest like that. If you pushed in the right panels it would open and play music. Maybe I'm supposed to push in these letters and spell my old name."

Roderick would never have thought of such a solution on his own, but once Jacob said it, to his dismay, it made a terrible amount of sense. Except, wasn't this tower built a long time ago? How would Tronas have known Jacob's other name all the way back then?

"Well, it can't hurt to try, I suppose." Roderick said.

But now that Jacob had come up with the idea, he wavered.

"We've come all this way," Roderick said. "I don't want you going into that tower any more than you do, Jacob, but if the answer to the curse is inside, we have to at least try."

"Would you push them for me?" Jacob asked.

"If you wish."

Jacob pointed to a long slender letter. "That's the first one," he said.

Roderick pushed on the smooth cold metal. At first, nothing happened, and Roderick started to get his hopes up, but then came the sound of some mechanism moving inside the wall. The letter sunk slowly into the stone and, with a loud click, held itself in place.

"That was *I*," Jacob said.

He pointed to another letter. After it went in, he indicated which one Roderick should push next. Jacob informed Roderick which one he had pressed as they went in. "*T, H, A…N, A, E…U, S.*"

After he pressed down on the last letter, even more grinding and whirring sounded inside the walls. Then all the letters pushed themselves back out and returned to their former positions. The two great doors jerked inward and slowly parted to reveal a dark void beyond. A chill air crept out from the opening, wrapping them in its icy tendrils.

The darkness beckoned, as if an enormous pit awaited just beyond the threshold. It was no place for a young child to go alone.

"It's so dark," Jacob said. "How will I find my way?"

Roderick thought for a moment. "Wait, I have something that will help," he said.

He searched the pockets of his robe until he found the black flameroot reed which Kendall had given him. Carefully, since he had only ever watched Kendall do it, he pulled back the tip of the stalk around the top, leaving most of the outer layer intact so that there would be something to hold on to. The end of the flameroot glowed orange, revealing some of the chamber beyond.

Smooth flagstones lined the floor, made of the same dusk-white stone as the outer walls. The austere chamber looked as cold as the air issuing from it. The only real feature inside was a set of curved stairs running along the left-hand wall. They jutted out from the side of the tower, thick stone blocks with nothing below to support them.

Roderick and Jacob stood staring at the chamber, and particularly the stairs, for the longest time. Roderick shook his head slowly back and forth. It looked like Jacob was going to have to go in there after all. Alone. In the dark. Upon those naked stairs. With who knew what awaiting him at the top.

The glowing diamonds on Jacob's body danced threateningly, as if his skin would burst open from the light at any moment.

"Can't you go with me?" Jacob pleaded.

Roderick's insides turned sour. His mouth went dry as sand. He hadn't felt this heartsick since he knelt beside his mother on her death bed. There was not a more cruel word in all of language than the simple word, "goodbye."

He took Jacob's hand and led him away from the door so that the lights from his skin pulsed less and grew dimmer.

Every instinct inside Roderick told him not to let Jacob go, but those instincts were of no use to him now. Jacob had to be healed. He had to be made well. And if going into that tower alone was the only way, then Roderick had to do what was best for Jacob. He had to let him go.

"I'm sorry, Jacob," Roderick lugged the words up his throat like he was pulling up water from a well. He stooped down to Jacob's level. "I don't know how this magic business works, but if the words say you need to go alone, we dare not disobey them. You might miss the one chance you have to break this awful curse. I will wait here for you, though. That I promise. And when you've finished whatever it is you must do up there, I will be here to take you home. I will not leave this spot until you return."

Jacob gripped Roderick with all his strength, trembling.

"Straight and tall, remember?" Roderick said.

Jacob drew himself up. He leveled his gaze at Roderick, his eyes fierce and brave.

"Thank you." Jacob said. "Thank you for all the fruit and for fixing my cloak and my shoes."

"No, thank you," Roderick said. "I was supposed to be your guardian, but you've been the one protecting me all this time. I won't forget what we talked about on the boat. About coming back to Briar's Glen to live with me and Bethany and Aisha. I'm going to hold on to that hope. When you return we'll go back there and we'll celebrate holidays and have birthdays and you can play with Aisha every day. We'll paint her ball and even get you one of your own. And you'll know peace, and joy, and the shadows will never come again."

Roderick wanted to say more, but his throat collapsed around the words. Oh, how he wanted to hold on to Jacob and not let him go off alone in the dark, into the shadows, into whatever nightmares he might have to face at the top of that tower. But in the end he had to let him go. This was what he had come for. It was the right thing to do.

He passed the flameroot to Jacob.

"I love you, Jacob," Roderick managed to get the words out

before choking once again.

"I love you too," Jacob said. Those words broke Roderick's heart and sent it sailing all at the same time. Whatever else happened, Roderick would always have those precious words.

He watched Jacob turn and walk into the tower, step by tiny step, his skin pulsing to a sorrowful, frenetic beat.

As Jacob set foot on the first step of the stairs, something clicked and the doors slowly began to close. For half a moment, Roderick thought about dashing through while he still had the chance, but love held him there.

There are roads we cannot walk for all we should wish to.

He peered through the crack at Jacob until the last possible moment when the doors shut completely. Then, alone in front of the forgotten tower, he knelt on the broken stones and began to pray to the only one who could walk Jacob through to the end.

39

THE TAILOR'S NEW CLOTHES

hen Roderick opened his eyes from his prayer he saw an unexpected sight: Nagan rushing towards him through the ruins, wild-eyed, and out of breath.

"Nagan, you made it!" Roderick blurted out, rising to his feet.

"Yes, but—" Nagan sputtered between great gulps of air. "Portia fell behind—" He threw his head back in the direction from which he had come. "She couldn't—the shadows—they took her."

So it was the scathen after all. Roderick's spirits, already drowning, plummeted all the way to the bottom of the sea. "We've got to go save her, where is she?"

"No—no time—she told me—she ordered me…to…to go on without her—and then the scathen—oh they, they…" Nagan collapsed, no longer able to stand. His hair was run through with sweat. Nicks and cuts lined his face and hands.

"We can't just leave her—"

"You don't understand…We've got to save Jacob…The shadows are coming this way—once they finish with the soldiers…" Nagan gazed up at the tower, as if noticing it for the first time. "But there's more." He forced himself to his feet again with a grimace and a groan. "Where's Patches? Is he already inside?"

Roderick pointed at the cruel door through which Jacob had gone. "Yes, yes, he went in a while ago." So there were soldiers *and* scathen? The fact that Nagan was willing to abandon Portia to such threats sent a shiver of fear through Roderick. Something must have gone terribly wrong.

"Then we have to get in there—we have to protect him," Nagan's words came out practically on top of each other. He made it sound like the scathen were already inside somehow. "How do you open that door? Where are the handles? Was this made by gypsies? Who makes a door with no handles!"

"Calm down. We can't go inside. There's an inscription, a warning—"

"Listen to me, tailor. We *have* to get inside. Now do you know how to open the door or not?"

Roderick scanned the ruins for signs of the scathen. It was as dark and eerie looking as ever, but he saw no sign of the creatures.

"Just tell me how to get in!" Nagan shouted. Roderick had never seen him this determined. It was like talking to Portia inside Nagan's body.

"You—you have to press a series of letters, but it doesn't matter. We can't go in! We have to stay outside until the curse is lifted. Only Jacob is supposed to enter. It says so on the doorway. Please, Nagan, now what's gotten into you that you're so keen on finding him?"

Nagan stared hard at the letters around the door, as if he were reading the pronouncement of some great and impending doom.

"I don't care if you send me back to Brimstoke's dungeon until I grow swill for a beard, we've got to warn Jacob!" Nagan slammed his shoulder into the door. "Ugh, what are these made out of, bricks?"

An unnatural chill swept over Roderick's skin. *The scathen were near.*

"Warn him about the scathen? But what good will that do? He can't use the magic anymore. He went inside the tower to —"

"It's not the scathen he has to worry about," Nagan rammed the door again. "It's Kendall!" His eyes raced over the inscription written around the doorway.

"Kendall? What are you talking about? Have you seen him?"

"Oh, I've seen him all right. For the first time, you might say." Nagan turned from the door and scanned the ruins. The chill in the air was so deep now Roderick's hands and feet had begun to go numb.

"What are you talking about? What's Kendall got to do with this? Speak plainly," Roderick said. Nagan was hard to understand in the best of times. And this was certainly not one of those.

"Well, his name's not really Kendall for one," Nagan said. "It's Mekthelion. And he's not a Savant. He's a Thaumaturge! And he's in that tower, waiting for Jacob!"

A whoosh of dizziness rushed to Roderick's head.

"What? That's ridiculous. Kendall couldn't be a—and even if he was, I've been here since Jacob went inside. No one else has gone in." Roderick stared at Nagan, wondering just what had happened to him in the forest over the last few hours. He scanned his face for signs of fever, but aside from being flushed and sweaty, Nagan looked to be, perhaps more than any other time since Roderick had known him, completely genuine in what he was saying.

"Portia and I hid in the bushes after the men jumped us. We saw him talking to them. He told them he was going to do something to Jacob in the tower, I just don't know what. We've got to get inside." Nagan started banging on the door, as if expecting someone to open up and let him in.

Roderick's heart felt like it stopped beating. Kendall was a traitor? He could not bring himself to accept it. There had to be some other explanation.

"Are you sure it was Kendall? That doesn't sound—"

"There's no time! I'm telling you, we've got to get inside this tower. What letters did you push to get Jacob inside?"

"I—I don't know." Roderick couldn't think straight. His head felt like he'd been clobbered by those ruffians again. "It had something to do with another name Jacob had. But I don't remember which ones," Roderick said, still reeling from

Nagan's revelation. Certainly Kendall had been aloof at times, even harsh on occasion, but he had brought them all this way and saved them countless times.

"Jacob has another name? Ack! Could this get any more complicated?" Nagan paced before the door like a man sentenced to the gallows. "And you don't remember any of the letters?"

"No, I told you already. The only thing I half-way remember is the other name. Anaeus or Isthmus or something odd sounding."

Nagan ran his fingers over the letters. "We'll never figure out which ones to push just guessing," he said, anxiously. "We'll just have to try breaking it down."

"Don't bother. The doors are too thick," Roderick said, but Nagan ignored his words and rammed his shoulder against the door several more times. The only effect that had was to make Nagan whimper as he winced and rubbed his shoulder. Desperate, he took out his cutlass and began hacking away. But the door flung off the blade like it was made from stone. All he managed to do was to send a few tiny splinters flying into the grass.

A growing darkness seethed across the ruins. Cold drops of invisible dread pattered across Roderick's skin.

"Ithanaeus!" he shouted, suddenly remembering the other name.

"Wonderful!" Nagan said. "How do you spell that?"

A pair of flashing red eyes blinked into existence at the far side of the ruins, weaving in and out amongst the crumbled stone.

"I have no idea," Roderick said. "I can't read."

"And I can't spell to save my life," Nagan said. "Which, unfortunately, is more than just a figure of speech at the moment."

Another set of eyes flashed among the rubble, then another.

"Well, hang me for a fool!" Nagan let out a high pitched giggle that could have passed for one of Aisha's. Roderick began to worry about the man's sanity. "Let's try and see if Kendall's own magic can't be used against him!"

Now Roderick was convinced. Nagan's recent brush with the scathen had driven him mad. Perhaps his grief at losing Portia had flipped the latch on his mind and it had fallen clean out.

Without explaining what he meant, Nagan reached inside his vest pocket and pulled out a little pouch.

"I was always curious about Kendall's powders," he said breathlessly. "So I took the liberty of sampling a few one night while he was sleeping."

He grabbed a handful of powder and flung it on the door. It was some of Kendall's glitter. When nothing happened, he flung another handful and then another until the entire pouch was emptied. It sparkled in the dim light and stuck to the door, but otherwise nothing happened.

"Curse it, I should have known better than to think I could accomplish anything through alchemy," Nagan said.

"Wait." Roderick realized then that Nagan was not mad after all. "Kendall used his lantern to burn through the roots in that tunnel. If only we had some source of fire, but I gave my flameroot to Jacob."

"Hurrah then! I've got that one covered as well," Nagan's excitement bubbled down into his fingers as he fumbled in his vest again and he pulled out a stalk of flameroot. "How does this work?" Nagan scraped it on the stone wall beside the door like he was trying to strike a piece of flint.

"Like this," Roderick said, yanking it from him. Peeling back the top half, he waited for the glow to appear. As soon as it did, he pressed it against the sparkling door. Though the root produced no actual flame, Roderick soon felt the heat.

Dozens of sets of eyes swarmed behind them in the ruins. The shadowy forms they belonged to grew steadily larger. The threatening shapes coursed over the tumbled down stones.

At that moment, the wood of the doors burst into a fiery glow. The yellow luminescence spread across the door, consuming the massive slabs of wood like boiling water poured over butter. In a matter of moments, a giant hole gaped back at them in the center of the doors.

The first of the scathen burst into the clearing. A dozen more appeared behind it. Some looked like dark parodies of soldiers, others like twisted imitations of what must have been Iddlglim warriors.

"Get inside!" Nagan shoved Roderick through the opening.

The unexpected push caused Roderick to bobble the flameroot. It fell near the threshold, but there was no time to go back for it. The light kept the scathen at bay, but only for a moment. One of them kicked the glowing stalk into the corner. The effort caused the creature to writhe in pain, but opened the way for the rest of the shadows to burst through.

Roderick and Nagan were about thirty steps up by that point, taking them two at a time, but the winding stairway stretched up into darkness.

"We'll never make it," Roderick said. "We'll never outrun them."

Icy winds followed them up the stairs. As the scathen scrambled onto the stairway after them, Roderick missed a step. He twisted to the side and went over the unprotected edge so suddenly he had no chance to reach for Nagan. But instead of falling onto the hard stone as he should have, the fierce winds blew against him from the side and knocked him back into Nagan. He landed on top of the poor, unsuspecting Gitano who fell forwards onto the steps.

Nagan grunted in pain as Roderick rolled off him. Before Roderick could regain his feet, a radiant, purple light swept down from above and engulfed the tower, accompanied by deep bass note which shook the very stones of the tower.

The light flashed for a moment and was gone. But when it disappeared, everything changed.

Warmth tingled across every inch of Roderick's skin. He felt like he was sitting in front of the hearth, back in the cottage in Briar's Glen.

What was going on? Had he taken ill? Was this some new form of scathen power?

Looking down at his hands, he saw that they had been transformed. His usual olive skin no longer covered them; it had taken on Jacob's motley hues, albeit much more faintly.

"Oh, buttons," he mumbled.

Nagan's face and hands were covered in the same colorful pattern. But their skin wasn't the only thing that had changed; the air surrounding them glittered in mysterious, prismatic currents. The patterns shifted and swayed like light reflecting off a swiftly flowing river. Everything inside the tower was brighter than before, so bright that the ceiling was now visible, though it was still several hundred steps above them.

A laughing, impetuous melody filled the tower. Splashes of percussion run up and down the walls, first here then there. The notes bounced around like Aisha's wooden ball dribbling down the steps.

"Well, we certainly washed up downstream," Nagan said as they helped each other to their feet.

"I don't know what that was," Roderick said. "But we've got to get to the top of this tower and find Jacob."

Whatever strange phenomenon was afflicting them had also affected the scathen. Whereas the moment before they had been racing forward in the form of large, shadowy soldiers with menacing red eyes, they now looked like the amorphous creatures Roderick had seen back in the sewers of Middlehelm. The dim outline of their humanoid shape could still be seen, however, like an image projected on top of them.

The scathen had been knocked to the ground and were slow to get up. Their eyes, the one unchanged aspect of their appearance, shot up the stairs towards Roderick and Nagan.

"There!" one of them hissed in a grating, cankerous voice.

"They've been touched by the glimmer. Get them before it's too late!" The creature motioned to the rest of the twisted figures, who eagerly surged up the stairs.

"Run!" Nagan yelled, practically hurling Roderick onto his feet.

No sooner had he said the word than the wind rushed down again. This time instead of pushing Roderick towards the wall, it swept him off his feet and out into the empty air in the middle of the chamber. Roderick's stomach went off into orbit somewhere outside his body. A fall at this height would shatter his bones on the flagstones for certain. But instead of plummeting, he floated along in the center of the tower, carried by the wind.

The notes of the precocious melody of the tower became more staccato, more urgent.

The scathen racing up the stairs glared at him with fresh hatred, but there was no way they could reach him now. Instead, they rushed after Nagan.

Roderick willed himself back towards his friend. He had to get Nagan off the stairs, but he had no more control of the currents than he did of any other wind he had ever encountered.

"Nagan, jump over to me!" Roderick cried. "I'll catch you."

Nagan eyed the enormous gulf separating the two of them. "Are you mad?" He raced up several more steps as the winds pulled Roderick further away.

"Save yourself!" Roderick swirled about like a pinwheel from a midsummer fair. The music in the air no longer held together in his ears. It melted into a rush of noise.

The dark creatures closed the distance to Nagan, reaching out for him with their shadowy tendrils. He faltered and fell to one knee, instantly caught.

"Save Patches!" Nagan yelled as the amorphous shadows smothered him. He disappeared under a flurry of darkness.

Roderick, helpless to save him, cartwheeled towards the top of the tower, his world turned upside down in more ways than one.

40

SOMEONE HAD TO HAVE THE MAGIC

here was no time to grieve Nagan's loss. It was all Roderick could do to keep from heaving up the hard tack he'd eaten as the winds swept him towards the top of the tower in a dizzying rush. He hurtled towards the ceiling, arms flailing, desperately trying to find something to latch onto. They were helpless gyrations in a sea of air. Just before he smashed into the ceiling, there came a tremendous popping sound. The world disappeared for a moment. When it came back, he found himself above the tower, floating gently down onto the flat stone roof the same way Jacob had floated out of the tree.

His astonishment at having survived his reckless flight lasted only a moment. For there, in the middle of the roof was Jacob. He stood in front of a round stone pedestal. Greenish-yellow cracks of light criss-crossed its surface like some eerie, cracked lantern. Embedded into the top of the pedestal rested a translucent black gem nearly as large as Jacob's head. His hands touched the gem, which sparkled with an inner green light, like the carmine crystal only much, much brighter. Swirling torrents of ethereal purple mist surrounded it, filling the rooftop with their otherworldly strands.

"Jacob!" Roderick cried out, but Jacob's eyes were closed and he gave no indication that he heard.

Roderick started towards him, but the next moment the misty, purple web imploded in on itself and vanished. Jacob collapsed to the floor.

Roderick rushed to his side. He knelt and rolled him over, cradling his body in his arms. He let out a gasp at the sight of Jacob's face. It was completely normal. The checkered pattern was gone. In its place was healthy, fair skin.

"Jacob, are you okay? Speak to me, say something."

Roderick stroked Jacob's cheeks, trying to stir him awake. Though he appeared to be breathing normally, he did not respond.

"You need not worry about him any longer," came a voice from behind. It sounded both familiar and strange all at once. "You have fulfilled your charge. He is a motley no more."

Roderick rose to his feet, holding Jacob in his arms, and turned to face Kendall. The old scholar stood near the entrance to the stairway, leaning upon his metal staff. Gone was the skullcap. He now wore a dark, hooded cowl, which cloaked his face in shadow.

"You." Roderick eyed him cautiously. "Nagan said you would be here."

"I am sure he told you many things, though he's not known for his fidelity to the truth." Kendall started walking towards Roderick.

"Was he lying about you, Kendall? Are you really Mekthelion?" Roderick asked, finding he had to force the name from his lips. He searched Kendall's face for some trace of the faithful friend he remembered, but his expression was cold and hard. Even the air of wisdom he had always had was gone. All that was left was brute determination and a grim sort of clarity.

Kendall continued forward. It soon became apparent that the shadowy shapes on his face were not actual shadows, but the checkered pattern of a motley's skin. It was not as intense as Jacob's had been, but it was much brighter than Roderick's.

"Such things matter not. All that matters is what happens to the magic. It looks like we've both had a taste of it now."

Roderick noted that Kendall had neither confirmed nor denied Nagan's accusation.

"Somehow it seems like we've become like Jacob and Jacob

like us," Roderick said. "The curse hasn't really been lifted, has it?"

"The magic is only a curse to those who do not know how to use it. Unlike the child, you see, I have studied enough to know how to be able to use the magic's power." As if to prove what he said, he began to float off the ground. His robes fluttering about him in an invisible breeze, he quickly covered the distance between them, landing in front of Roderick. "And just as he was unfit to use it, so are you."

A ravenous look shot from the old man's eyes, like flames licking at dry kindling. All Roderick's doubts about Nagan's claims vanished with that look. This was indeed Mekthelion the Thaumaturge. The man Roderick thought he knew was no more.

"Put the child down and place your hands on the stone," Mekthelion commanded.

"This is what you wanted all along, then," Roderick said. "But why? Why go to all this trouble to pretend to be our friend? Why not just capture Jacob like Virinian?"

"The magic would have protected him if he thought I was his enemy. Virinian only wanted to kill Jacob. I had other plans. I needed to bring him here so that the Null Stone could take the magic from him and give it to me—a goal which is nearly complete save for the small amount you syphoned off when you entered into the tower uninvited."

"So, Jareth and the other Savants—they were lying to us as well?" Roderick took a step back, but Mekthelion lunged forward and grabbed him by the arm.

"Witless fools, just like you. Now put the child down." The edge in his voice was like a knife at Roderick's throat. Roderick was in no position to defend himself while holding Jacob, so he lowered him to the ground.

"Good. Now place both of your hands on the stone. You didn't absorb much magic so this shouldn't take long." Mekthelion dragged him towards the pedestal. His grip was like iron, far stronger than it should have been for a man his age.

If Roderick was going to do anything to stop him, he

would have to do it now. He wasn't sure he really should stop him, though. Jacob was free of the curse. What did it matter if someone else took the magic? But the murderous look in Mekthelion's eyes told Roderick that once the magic had been drained from him as well, he and Jacob would be in greater danger than they ever were from the scathen.

"No," Roderick said quietly. "I won't do it." He dug in his heels and pushed back against Mekthelion's hold. The Thaumaturge shoved him forward with overwhelming force. Roderick's efforts amounted to nothing more than a symbolic protest. He might as well have been pushing against a wall.

"You will do what you are told or I shall make your death long and painful," Mekthelion said.

Please, Roderick prayed silently. *Adonai, stop this man.*

For the first time in his life, Roderick heard an actual voice inside his head in answer to his prayers.

"Use the magic."

There was something familiar about the voice, but Roderick could not quite place it. Somehow it was too earthy to be the voice of Adonai. It made him think of warm spring mornings, and quiet rain upon a meadow, of cool breezes rustling through the trees and light falling gently upon the waving grass. Then it came to him. It was the voice from his dream in Castle Brimstoke, the one with the river of many colors. Should he trust it? And if so, how was he supposed to use the magic anyway?

"This is your final warning," Mekthelion said. Waves of heat wafted across Roderick as flames flickered out from one of Mekthelion's hands. Two colored diamonds, one on the wizard's cheek and another on his hand began to glow.

Pushed by Mekthelion's irresistible strength and fear of the flames, Roderick's hands inched towards the glimmering gem. He concentrated with all his might on making fire come into his hands in the same way as Mekthelion's. His hands grew warm, but instead of fire, a torrent of hot water jetted out from them like a fountain. The steaming blast slammed into the pedestal. The force of the jet sent him flying backwards into Mekthelion and knocked both of them to the ground. A clashing din blazed through the night, like a pile of instruments falling into a pit. It plinked and squeaked and trembled and buzzed and gurgled and pealed all at the same time. The water continued to spray everywhere, creating puddles and cascading showers all around them.

Roderick was only mildly dazed from the unexpected collision. He rolled away from his captor and got to his feet before his opponent could recover, but the water ceased gushing a moment later. The cacophony of music died as well.

A fiery burst leapt from Mekthelion's fingertips and struck Roderick in the chest. Normally, his cloak might have burst into flames, but it was so damp all it did was hiss and smoke.

"You don't have enough magic to face me," Mekthelion taunted, rising to his feet. "And even if you did, you wouldn't know how to use it." His words were followed by another shot of flame. This time Roderick ducked and all that got singed were the hairs on the side of his head, filling the air with an awful smell.

Roderick flung his arm towards his adversary and willed a magic blast into existence, but all it did was sprinkle Mekthelion with water from his sleeve.

"Fire was my master's specialty," Mekthelion said. "But even he could never control it like this." He extended both his arms and twin jets of flame shot out. Roderick dodged one, but the other caught him on the arm, singeing him badly. He cried out in pain as the flames hissed and smoked and blackened his clothes.

Mekthelion only laughed, relishing his newfound abilities in his own dark way. Two more diamonds glistened to life on his forehead.

Come on, work, Roderick urged the magic. Hadn't there been music? Surely that must have meant he was on the right track. And come to think of it, he never heard any music with Mekthelion's magic. It was silent. Maybe there was hope for Roderick after all. He sprinted around the back of the pedestal to put something between himself and his opponent

362

and give himself time to think.

Flaming blasts erupted on either side of him. He felt the heat, but it did not burn him this time. He panicked, remembering that Jacob was on the other side. He tried to take a quick peek around the edge of the pedestal to see if Jacob was all right, but instead found himself launched into the air. He flew through the night as out of control as he had been inside the tower. A racing, disjointed melody chased him wherever he went, desperate to keep up.

Mekthelion cursed, firing bolt after blazing bolt up into the sky. But Roderick tossed about so erratically that the darts whizzed harmlessly by. He felt like a stringless kite gone astray in the midst of a fireworks display.

"You're not the only one who can fly," Mekthelion shouted. He raised his staff and launched into the air. He swooped towards Roderick's wind-tossed figure. All Roderick could do was throw up his hands to shield himself from the impact. Mekthelion collided into him, grabbing hold of him once more with his iron grip. The yellow light burning at the back of his enemy's eyes reminded Roderick of the malevolent gaze of the scathen. A green diamond lit up the side of Mekthelion's nose.

The two of them plummeted back down to the tower, but at the last moment, Mekthelion stopped and let go of Roderick. He crashed helplessly onto the unyielding stone, landing hard on his left arm. The bone snapped under the weight of his frame.

A flash of agonizing heat shot through his arm and into his side. He tried to get up, but the pain pulled him back down. Roderick's flighty song ended in a loud burst of noise and a wave of darkness washed over his vision, but it lasted only a moment. Mekthelion landed beside him, reached down, and pulled him up by the collar, eliciting screams from Roderick.

Roderick gathered all his strength, pawing at Mekthelion's arm. "I don't care what you do to me, I will not let you hurt Jacob."

Mekthelion grabbed him under the shoulders and hoisted him up to a standing position in front of the pedestal. Roderick's screams filled the night.

"I'm really not as cruel as you think," Mekthelion said, jerking Roderick's broken arm up and placing his hand against the Null Stone. Roderick nearly fainted from the pain. His knees buckled and he would have collapsed if Mekthelion had not propped him up. "All my life I've sought knowledge: to know, to understand how the world works. But with all my learning all I could ever do was mix a few powders, blend a few herbs. And now I have a chance to bring back actual magic, power over the natural world beyond anything learning and study could ever hope to accomplish if I had a thousand lifetimes. Do you think I it would be right to give that up simply because of the opinion of a mere tailor?" He pressed Roderick's other hand against the stone and pinned both of them down with his bony hands. "Someone had to have the magic, you see. Don't you think it should be someone who actually knows how to use it?"

The same comforting warmth Roderick felt when he first received the magic surged through his body and rushed into the stone, momentarily dulling the pain. A purplish cloud swirled around him like a hunted animal, looking for refuge from its pursuer. The heat and light flowed out of him and into Mekthelion. The magic's escape lasted several seconds and then, as suddenly as it came, everything faded. The color on Roderick's hands vanished along with the magic.

The magic drained, Mekthelion dropped Roderick onto the ground next to Jacob. The motley pattern on the wizard's face had grown brighter, but it was still not as intense as Jacob's had been.

Roderick gritted his teeth and fought through the pain to roll over and look at Jacob. He was resting peacefully, as if he were merely taking a nap. Though it caused him even more pain, Roderick worked himself into a sitting position with his back against the pedestal and, with his good arm, dragged Jacob into his lap. It took every last bit of strength he had to keep from passing out, but holding Jacob gave him some small measure of comfort.

"You don't know how long I've waited for this moment." Mekthelion's face reflected the light from the Null Stone like light going through a broken window. "At last I have it all."

But Roderick saw something over the Thaumaturge's shoulder. "Are you sure about that?"

41

WHAT CAME UP THE STAIRS

towering shadow shot through the opening in the floor behind Mekthelion. It looked like a tormented, ebony version of Nagan, only stretched to horrific proportions. It was twice as tall as the Gitano had been. Dozens of scathen poured onto the roof behind it. They no longer looked like amorphous creatures inside shadowy outlines, but semi-solid shadow men, as before.

A cold buffer of air preceded the darkened Nagan, announcing his presence on top of the tower. If not for that, Mekthelion would have been caught in the creature's embrace. Instead, the Thaumaturge launched himself into the air before the giant arms could reach him.

The giant shadow looked down at Roderick with flickering, hate-filled eyes, but quickly turned his gaze upon the flying figure.

"Give us the magic." The creature's voice was as deep as it was tall.

The shadow swiped at the air below Mekthelion's feet, but he was well out of reach.

"Doomed spirit, I see you now for what you are. You are Strath, the once great leader of the underdwellers before the curse fell upon you. It is such a pity to see you chained to these shadowy forms."

"I will not stay chained for long. Give us the magic!" Strath thundered.

"If you serve me, I will use the feyglimmer to release you and restore you to what you once were."

More scathen crowded in behind Strath, dozens of pairs of hate-filled eyes all fixed upon the floating Thaumaturge.

"We have heard such promises before," Strath cried out, his voice a bubbling cauldron of spite. "We do not need the help of any mortal to be free, only the feyglimmer."

"If you will not serve me, then you will perish. I care not," Mekthelion said.

"You cannot hold on to the feyglimmer forever. And the more you use it, the more it will seek to break free. It was not meant for the race of men." The other scathen howled and screeched at Strath's booming words. There were so many on the roof now that the chorus was almost deafening. They packed in around Roderick and the pedestal, but paid him no attention. The cold aura surrounding them sent pain-inducing shivers through Roderick's frame.

"The glimmer!" shouted the hulking Strath. "We must have it!"

From the stairway came two man-sized shadows. In their wispy claws they carried the body of Nagan. His skin was still checkered, but the colors had faded now, into shades of gray.

"No!" Mekthelion shouted from above. He dove for Nagan, launching darts of fire into the mass of scathen, but the ones carrying Nagan moved with dizzying speed, and Strath moved in to shield them with his giant frame. Strath's body writhed in torment as the bolts lit into him, but Mekthelion dared not come within his reach. The other scathen brought Nagan before the pedestal.

Roderick clung all the more tightly to Jacob as the mass of scathen pressed in close, a great glacier of darkness which towered over him.

Two scathen placed Nagan's hands upon the stone. Strath's gigantic hands enveloped Nagan's, along with the stone. The familiar purple mists drained the pattern from Nagan's skin like water spilled on a charcoal drawing. It flowed into the gem and back through the outstretched arm of the colossal shadow.

Strath contorted with delight as brightness coursed through

it. He grew more solid and less dark as the light spread. By the time the purple smoke faded, the creature no longer looked like a nightmarish version of Nagan. It was more like a faceless statue made of smooth, dark sand. Its body was thicker and stockier than before, but it had shrunk several feet.

The scathen let Nagan's body fall to the ground. They withdrew a few steps back, like an ebbing, sable tide.

"Yes!" Strath howled, his eyes burning bright. "Solid again! And closer to my true form. The feyglimmer is stronger than I remembered. This small taste is enough for me to call forth the rest of our brothers still trapped in the Dwimmerkell!"

The scathen sizzled and buzzed with excitement.

More incendiary streaks from Mekthelion lit into Strath's transformed body, leaving darkened burn marks. The sandy figure shrank back, bellowing in rage, but shook off the attacks.

"Come to me my brothers, forgotten and betrayed," Strath shouted. Ignoring his blackened wounds, he made a wide circle in the air with one of his club-like hands, just above the flagstones. The motion ripped a hole somehow through the curtain of the night. The opening looked strikingly similar to the one in the glistering glass, only without the surrounding frame. Through it lay the same terrifyingly beautiful landscape which had been visible in Virinian's castle, but this time the window was looking through the portal, from the other side of the gulf. The translucent bridge was gone and the dark chasm once again separated a massive crowd of scathen from reaching the portal. Silvery mists and stardust drifted through the air.

As had happened at Brimstoke, a plane of gossamer light began stretching across the chasm. It bridged the gap between the opening and the gathering of scathen on the other side. They rushed across the newly formed bridge, straight towards the portal.

Roderick shrank away from the opening instinctively, forgetting his broken arm. Fresh waves of agony sliced through his mangled limb.

I've got to get Jacob out of here. The scathen are going to overrun the tower.

But what about Nagan? He could not abandon his friend, and with only one good arm, he wasn't even able to take Jacob.

"Jacob," Roderick said, as loudly as he dared. "Wake up." He shook him hard. This time his eyes opened a crack.

"What happened?" Jacob stared at him blankly.

Before Roderick could respond, Mekthelion lanced more fiery blasts at Strath. They engulfed his entire upper body and also caught some of the surrounding scathen. Heat blanketed the pedestal. The half dozen or so creatures caught in the flames withered and disappeared in slivers of ash and smoke, but aside from blackening his sandy body and enraging him further, the fire had little effect on Strath.

"Kendall isn't a Savant," Roderick told Jacob. "He's a Thaumaturge and he's taken the magic and he's using it to destroy the scathen. He's throwing fire everywhere. It isn't safe. We have to go."

"That's not what was supposed to happen," Jacob mumbled in a bewildered tone.

Strath reached over to the side of the tower and carved a barrel-sized chunk out of the wall and hurled it at Mekthelion. The Thaumaturge barely dodged in time. The stone went sailing past him out into the rainforest below.

Roderick tried to spy out a path through the scathen to the stairway, but the tower was covered in shadows. "We've got to get away from here before you get hurt—" he said.

Jacob cut him off. "No, I mean, that's not what the words on the pedestal said."

Roderick was about to ask him what words he was talking about when a jet of white energy shot past them. Though he couldn't feel any heat this time, he shielded Jacob instinctively. The sudden movement sent pain shooting all down the left side of his body.

Mekthelion swooped in low, just out of reach of the

scathen. He left a fiery trail wherever he passed. Several of the scathen leapt at him, only to plunge into the stream of light, incinerating in a burst of nothingness. Unlike Mekthelion's other blasts, these persisted, forming a network of blazing walls six or more feet high, criss-crossing the roof.

Strath hurled more chunks from the wall, but Mekthelion was moving too fast now. Some of the massive stones landed on the tower, crushing several of the scathen. They simply reformed a moment later, seeping out from under the rock.

"The usurper has built a wall around the gate," Strath cried. "He must be destroyed!"

He plunged his sandy fists into the ground. In response, stones erupted from the floor, spitting out a shower of rubble. The rocks burst into the air, hurtling dozens of feet above the tower before plummeting back to the surface in a stony rain. The deluge pummeled Mekthelion, sending him flying over the edge of the tower. The scathen shrieked with delight, but the glowing barriers surrounding them remained, holding them fast.

"Stay away from the luminous walls, brothers, or you shall be banished to the everdeath," Strath shouted at the scathen. "My power is not strong enough yet to dissolve them. I must have the rest of the feyglimmer first."

But the tower was too crowded for the scathen to avoid the flames entirely. Any shadows near the brilliant, translucent sheets of light, shriveled into oblivion.

The scathen near the stairway turned and fled back down the way they came.

"Come back, you cravens!" Strath shook the stumps of his arms at them. "I cannot free you unless I get the feyglimmer."

His orders were met by terrified howling. None of them came back, however, or even slowed down.

At the same time, scathen began emerging from Strath's portal. Mekthelion had shrewdly placed a wall of light directly in front of the entrance. The newly arrived creatures ran headlong into the barrier, annihilating themselves the moment they emerged from their world.

"No!" Strath yelled towards the gate, "Stay back until I've dealt with this fool!"

The shadows inside the portal, heedless of his warning, kept coming.

The scathen which had not fled the roof huddled around Strath in the only significant pocket of darkness left, fifteen feet from Roderick and the Null Stone. Strath kept his arms extended to either side. He appeared to be somehow holding the light at bay. His dark, sedimentary form shook beneath the terrible strain.

The shadowy horde hurtling through the magic gate kept vanishing, like water pouring down a drain.

At that moment Mekthelion rose up from below the tower, looking unfazed by the battering he'd suffered from Strath's stony rain. His face was lit up with glowing diamonds so that only a few patches of normal skin remained.

"You underdwellers are far more dim-witted than the legends claim. I'll finish off your entire race in a single night." Mekthelion flew off after the scathen fleeing towards the stairs, spitting out more and more fountains of light, dispatching the inky forms like dry leaves blown into the hearth. When all the scathen around the exit had been destroyed he disappeared into the stairwell. Squelching hisses echoed up from within the tower.

Roderick thought once again of escape. He wondered if it would be safe enough to crawl through the walls of white flames to the exit. At this distance they gave off no heat. Perhaps they were only harmful to scathen. He tried shaking Nagan back awake, but he simply would not wake up. He looked so pale Roderick feared for his life.

"I thought the stone would fall away when it got all the magic," Jacob said, staring up at the glittering gem.

"What are you talking about?" Roderick asked.

"The stone was supposed to fall and then I was supposed to throw it in there," Jacob pointed at the gate to the realm of the scathen. Less than half of the shadowy horde remained, but the more their numbers dwindled, the more rapidly they came on.

Strath's arms buckled as the light from the luminous walls inched towards him, consuming a half dozen more scathen in disintegrating puffs.

"Throw it into the dream world? What makes you think that?"

Jacob pointed at a series of glittering shapes on the pillar as if it should have been obvious what he was talking about. What Roderick had at first taken for cracks of light he now realized were glowing letters and words.

"Those appeared when I got close to the stone," Jacob said.

"I can't read, Jacob," Roderick reminded him.

The scathen continued to howl down below and up on the roof.

"We are trapped, brothers," Strath said. And for the first time the rage faded from his cavernous voice. He sounded afraid. "He has too much of the glimmer. I underestimated his power. I fear we are doomed unless the winds of magic shift in our favor."

The scathen near the pedestal shivered and shrieked in dismay.

Jacob read the words on the pedestal aloud over the mournful, malevolent din.

When all that glimmers fills the stone,
And the underhall crafts are unmade
Then shall fall the ebony stone
And the shadow's power at last shall fade
Then shall darkness sound her reply
And open the way to Dwimmerkell
Then through the gate the gem must fly
And the dream arise from whence it fell

"Agh, more verses. But what do they mean?" Roderick asked, wincing. The panicked moaning of the scathen and the waves of pain from his broken arm made it difficult to concentrate on poetry just at that moment.

"The glimmer—that's what they call the magic—I gave all I had to the stone, but it didn't fall."

"I think Kendall and Nagan and I took it before it could get inside," Roderick said.

Down below, the screams of the scathen at last went silent. Strath and the others grew quiet as well.

"He will return to finish us off," Strath warned. "While our blind brothers flee the Dwimmerkell to their deaths. A curse upon me for ever opening that portal!"

As the last of the onrushing scathen melted in the luminous wall before the Dwimmerkell gate, a dark, misshapen thing emerged from the stairwell. At first it looked like another great shadow, for it was over ten feet tall and as dark as night. But it did not have the same glowing red eyes as the other scathen. Instead they were a ghastly yellow, like some sort of diseased feline. And the monster's body was far too solid to be a shadow. Its slate black skin looked distinctly reptilian, and yet, snakelike as it was, there was something familiar about the face. It walked like a man on two legs, but hunched over; its long arms dragging along the floor. And in one of its clawed hands it held Mekthelion's metal staff.

42

THE LAST GLIMMER

he creature with the staff spoke, its voice primitive and husky, but carrying a note of all too human pride. "You." it pointed a taloned finger at Strath. "You knew this would happen, didn't you?"

Strath laughed, a rumbling, groaning, stony sort of sound. Cruel confidence returned to his voice. "The fey were never known for their constancy. The glimmer controls you as much as you control it. Your fate will not be different than that of all the other motleys."

The creature that had been Mekthelion raised its long scaly arm. "I could blast you from this world once and for all!"

"Are you certain the glimmer will obey you if you try? Perhaps it will transform you into something worse," Strath mocked.

Mekthelion let out a throaty croak into the night, like some reptilian wolf howling at the moon. The white fire around the scathen flared higher. Strath's outstretched arms quivered under the encroaching light. The scathen pressed in close to their leader, huddling around him like frightened children. Only ten remained.

"All right!" Strath shouted. "If you banish these flames I will tell you how to use the feyglimmer."

"How do I know I can trust you?" Mekthelion asked.

"You don't," Strath said. "But how do I know you won't just blast us from existence once you regain control of the glimmer?"

"Fair enough," Mekthelion said. He lowered his jet black

hands slowly and the glowing barrier died down, but only the one surrounding Strath. The walls blazing around the Null Stone remained, as did those in front of the portal.

Strath let out a low, cruel chuckle. "I will tell you the truth of the feyglimmer. The secret to transforming back into your own form is never to use the magic in the first place."

"What?" Mekthelion screeched. "Deceiver!" He cast his staff upon the floor in anger, shattering it to pieces. He rose to his full height, raising his clawed hands as if to hurl more magic.

"I wouldn't if I were you," Strath cautioned mockingly. Mekthelion froze with his hands still above him. "You have used too much already. Any further attempts will only increase its hold upon you."

"You lie. The reason I can't transform is because I lack all the magic. Once I possess that which you have stolen, I will show you that I am indeed the master of the feyglimmer." Mekthelion threw his hands forward and a column of white fire exploded from them. But it only traveled a few feet before dissipating harmlessly in the air. "No..." he muttered, his sickly eyes going wide with shock.

"Kill him!" Strath bellowed. "The glimmer will be ours!"

The scathen cackled and hissed with delight. They sprang forward and Mekthelion prepared to meet their charge. Once again his body began to change. He shrunk several feet and shed his reptilian skin, revealing a shiny black coating beneath. It didn't look like skin at all. It undulated and moved like dark oil. The details of his face became lost in the shifting, changing form which he now possessed. His talons bloated, becoming blunt and paw-like.

The scathen rushed on. Two of them pounced, sinking their shadowy claws into the aqueous body. But instead of succumbing to their attacks and falling into shadow, Mekthelion howled in rage and tossed them to the ground.

Two more shadows leapt on top of him, but the monster beat them back with its sludge-like arms. He batted them in the direction of the flames surrounding the pedestal. More scathen joined in the attack, but their claws deflected off the slimy black hide. Each time they got up and sprang at him again he pummeled them closer to the flames. In their frenzy to destroy the Thaumaturge they failed to notice the danger they were in until it was too late. The monster bashed them into the luminous walls where they burst into ashen clouds and disappeared.

"No!" Strath cried out, his own lumbering frame lagging behind the others. "Stay away from the light!"

The shadows turned to regard the white flames, but it was too late. With sweeping blows from his trunk-like arms, Mekthelion battered them into the glowing barriers.

Only five scathen remained. All except Strath scattered and fled before the towering figure of Mekthelion.

"The shadow has no power over me anymore. My magic is too strong," he gurgled in a watery voice. "I care not what happens to me. I will see your kind consumed in the fire even if the magic destroys me as well."

He waved his arms and white sparks shot out towards the scathen. Though most of the sparks fell at his feet, a few lit into the bodies of the fleeing shadows. The scathen writhed in pain, black wisps smoking from the places where they had been hit.

Then Mekthelion changed again. He grew larger until he loomed over Strath. His skin hardened and turned stony gray. His neck thickened and disappeared. His arms thinned and elongated and his legs melded into a single giant column several feet in diameter. He looked like an enormous stone pillar with hardened ropes for arms.

Though Mekthelion could no longer move about the roof, his two arms were so long he could lash out at the scathen no matter where they fled. His flailing tentacles struck two more shadows and dragged them into the glowing light. Then snatched another one and sent him to the same fate. Only Strath remained.

"Now we shall see whom the glimmer will consume first," Strath growled. "You or me."

Mekthelion answered him with a whip-like blow to the feet, toppling Strath like a felled tree. Sand from the scathen's body flew everywhere, but he was too large for the ropey arms to restrain.

The slow-moving scathen arose only to be thrashed by another blow, which knocked him flat again. More of the shadowy powder which made up Strath's body scattered across the roof.

But Mekthelion overreached and his tentacles smashed onto the stone floor, sending a shudder through his monolithic form. Taking advantage of his adversary's momentary disorientation, Strath sprang up and hurled himself towards the giant figure.

Mekthelion recovered and jerked his tentacles back for another blow, but Strath slammed into his body before he could strike. The massive cylindrical form of Mekthelion hit the ground with a thunderous boom. The thick figure cracked in several places and failed to rise.

Strath pummeled his downed opponent with his sandy fists, but his blows glanced off the stony skin. The blows were damaging Strath more than they were Mekthelion. Great puffs of sand flew from his body with each successive blow.

The downed Thaumaturge wrapped his tentacles around his enemy and began to squeeze. Strath cried out in a raspy voice, a puff of dust issuing from his throat. Then his body collapsed altogether, only to reform a moment later outside the monster's arms. Strath was noticeably thinner, leaving behind piles of dark sand around Mekthelion's body, but he was free.

The scathen leader ran around to Mekthelion's side and, with tremendous effort, began rolling the pillar-like form towards the edge of the tower, pinning the tentacles underneath the roper's body like a giant spool. It was not clear how Strath intended to push him over the surrounding wall, but he never got the chance. Mekthelion began to change again. This time he did not grow taller, but wider. His tentacles disappeared. His body transformed into a ball of white lightning. A grotesque caricature of the Thaumaturge's face appeared within, spinning uncontrollably, like the swirls inside a giant rolling marble. His body was twenty feet in diameter now. Strath could not avoid him. The scathen screamed as the ball of light overtook him. He fell to the floor, the gray sand of his body singed and blackened through and through.

Mekthelion's cackle rang out like muffled thunder. He enveloped Strath's body, which began to disintegrate. The scathen's tortured screams echoed across the forest. The sandy exterior of his body burned away, leaving only a shadowy kernel beneath. But just when it looked like Mekthelion had finished him off, the swirling tendrils of Strath's body expanded. They shrouded the ball of crackling energy in shadow. Sparks flew from Mekthelion's body. It ejected spurts of white energy. Innumerable crackling sounds filled the night air. The ball of lightning pulsed once, twice, then exploded in a blaze of white brilliance.

Roderick and Jacob shielded their eyes.

When the glow faded, only the body of Mekthelion remained. He was a man once again. His skin still bore the marks of the motley, but he was not moving.

Strath, the last of the scathen, was nothing more than a heap of ash blackening the white stones of Tronas' tower.

43

A TAILOR'S CRAFT

deathly silence fell upon the tower. Even the chittering rainforest below grew still. The white walls of fire had all disappeared. Only the glistening portal remained, but it was empty of all the shadows.

"Strath's magic must have gone into the stone when he died. But Master Kendall still has his." Jacob pointed at the old man's slumped form. "We have to bring him to the stone to get rid of it."

Roderick knew it would cause him terrible pain, but Jacob would not be able to bring Mekthelion back alone. He bit back his cries and rose to his feet, every inch a lifetime's worth of torment.

Jacob held his good arm and did his best to steady him as they made their way to Mekthelion's fallen body. Sweat beaded out from every pore of his skin.

"Let's hurry," Roderick said.

Jacob reached down and grabbed one of Mekthelion's arms. "Yes, let's hurry."

Roderick took the other arm and they started to drag him back towards the stone. The old man was not heavy, but with only one good arm and the excruciating pain which even the slightest movement caused, Roderick felt like he must surely pass out before they ever got there. Bit by painful bit, they pulled Mekthelion along, until at last they had him propped up against the pedestal.

Roderick took a moment and leaned against the stone, his lungs pulling in shuddering, painful breaths.

"We have to place our hands against the stone," Jacob said. "So the magic won't come back to us."

Roderick took another moment to steel himself against one last surge of pain. "What about Nagan?" he asked, remembering how the magic had come to him as well on the stairs.

"He's in the dream lands," Jacob said. "The magic can't reach him there."

"Very well." Roderick hoped they had not lost Nagan forever.

They pressed their hands upon the stone together. It was ice cold and it burned like ice, too. Jacob placed one of Mekthelion's bony hands between theirs. A purplish mist rose out of the aged skin. It seemed to take forever for all of it to flow out. Roderick quivered from the effort of keeping his hand on the stone, but he pushed through the pain until the last of the otherworldly smoke had disappeared. The translucent gem shone so brightly now that it was hard to look at.

They let Mekthelion's pale hand fall to the ground. The motley pattern had vanished from his skin. Roderick slumped against the pedestal, his chest heaving, as he tried to recover. Pain saturated his body, like a sponge that could absorb nothing more.

All around them, the top of the tower glittered with the ghostly light from the stone.

"What now?" Roderick asked.

"The stone is supposed to fall out so we can throw it in there," Jacob pointed at Strath's shimmering portal.

Jacob pulled on the large stone, straining, but it just sat there, as solid as ever, encased in the glowing pillar.

"What did the inscription say, exactly?" Roderick asked.

Jacob read it again:

When all that glimmers fills the stone,
And the underhall crafts are unmade
Then shall fall—

"Wait," Roderick said. "What's that part about the 'underhall crafts'? What does that mean?"

"I don't know."

Roderick struggled to think through the pain. "…If the glimmer is the magic, it should be filling the stone, I suppose. But have the crafts, then—whatever they are—been unmade?"

"I don't know what that means. I don't know what the underhall is," Jacob said. "But crafts are things that are made, so maybe it means magical things?"

Roderick stared at the glittering stone. As his eyes slowly became more accustomed to its brightness, he was struck by the fact that there was something familiar about the glow inside, something he had seen before.

"The carmine crystals!" Roderick blurted out. "I remember now. Back in the cave at Bald Hill Kendall told us they had been formed in the underhalls according to the legends. I wonder if there is magic trapped inside there that needs to fill the stone as well?"

"That could be it," Jacob said excitedly "Do you still have them?"

"Yes," Roderick said, momentarily forgetting his pain. "They're right here in my—" Before he could reach inside his cloak, a bony hand shot up and grabbed him by the wrist.

Mekthelion sprang to life like a man possessed. He was on top of Roderick in an instant, rifling through his clothes. His knee hit Roderick's broken arm and Roderick screamed in agony. Bright, sparking lights burst inside his head. His vision dimmed.

Jacob's frightened scream shocked him out of the haze of pain.

Mekthelion knelt over the inert body of the child. He had his back to Roderick.

"Where are the crystals?" he bellowed.

Roderick didn't know what to do. Even without a broken arm, he wondered if he could have stopped someone as ruthless and obsessed as Mekthelion. But the thought of what this cruel man had done to the child he loved made his body quake with anger. With his good hand, he whipped out the small knife from his belt and staggered towards the Thaumaturge.

"Get away from him!" Roderick shouted.

Mekthelion spun to face him. His eyes were sunken, surrounded by dark shadows, but the malice within burned brighter than ever. He looked ten years older and none the wiser from his recent battle with the shadows. He meant to have every last bit of magic if it killed him.

"Give me the crystals," Mekthelion demanded, extending his hand and stepping towards Roderick.

"I'm warning you," Roderick said. "If you have hurt him in any way—"

"You'll what?" Mekthelion sneered. "Cut a thread or two from my cloak with your tailor's knife?"

The old man took a quick step forward and kicked out with his foot, striking Roderick's hand and jarring the weapon loose. It skittered across the rocks. Mekthelion closed and pressed his foot upon Roderick's broken arm, near the place where the bone had snapped.

Roderick wailed in agony.

Mekthelion stooped down, observing the writhing figure beneath him with all the fascination of a child watching a bug caught beneath his finger.

"I told you the gift was not meant for him. Nor was it meant to be banished from the world altogether. Think of the potential that would be wasted! All my long years of study and labor to master the powers of true magic will not be taken away by an unlettered commoner. You could not even use it properly when you had a small taste of it. It feeds off the will and you lack the mental fortitude and guile to seize opportunities when they are presented to you."

"Then why..." Roderick thrashed about, pawing at Mekthelion's leg, trying in vain to push it off. Every movement was a drop of pain in a waterfall of agony pouring over his body. "Why doesn't...your magic..." Torturous burning erupted from every inch of his flesh. "have any..." Pulsing fire ripped through his mind. "music?"

Mekthelion pressed down harder, grinding his foot into Roderick's flesh and bone.

"You're babbling. Music? What are you talking about?" he spat out the words. "You're weak, tailor. If you had really wanted to protect the boy, you should have stabbed me just now when I had my back turned to you."

Roderick could only respond with more screams.

"And that is why someone like you can never defeat someone like me," Mekthelion gloated. He gave Roderick one last spiteful glare and reached into the tailor's cloak.

"Where are they?" he demanded, fishing violently around, but he could not unravel the trick of the tailor's secret compartment nor spy out the clever seams concealing the crystals. He seized Roderick with both hands by the collar and shook him.

Pain flooded Roderick's vision. He was drowning in waves of it, drinking in salty gulps of agony, but in the midst of his thrashing he caught a glimpse of Mekthelion's face. His anger at that leering visage and all the evil behind it helped him focus just long enough to gather his strength for a single moment. That was all he needed.

He brought the fist of his one good hand around for a blow to Mekthelion's face. As his strike connected, it was as if he toppled the massive wall of anguish, shadow, and despair which had hounded him all throughout his long, arduous journey. For one brief, merciful moment Roderick's pain subsided.

His enemy slumped and rolled off him, momentarily stunned by the unexpected blow. Roderick reached into his secret pocket. Pulling out the carmine crystals, he shoved himself up against the pedestal. With his one good arm he heaved the stones across the roof with all his might. They struck the base of one of the crenellations and shattered into a thousand pieces.

Mekthelion rolled over and cast his gaze in the direction of the fragmented stones. A few shards glinted in the moonlight. As he watched in horror, two tendrils of purplish smoke rose up from the ground and rushed towards the Null Stone. Mekthelion reached out for them as they passed by, as if he could catch them in his hands, but they slipped through his fingers and disappeared into the stone.

"No!" Mekthelion shouted.

The huge gem began to glow with an effulgent light, stronger than ever before, brighter than a hundred thousand fireflies trapped in a jar.

They had done it. The curse was finally lifted. The magic was gone—all of it—forever.

In the midst of the awesome brightness, Mekthelion's maddened face appeared above Roderick.

"You should have killed me when you had the chance!" Mekthelion raged. "I will not make that same mistake." His entire visage radiated hatred. He staggered over to where the tailor's knife lay on the pavement. Roderick tried to scramble away, but nearly passed out from the effort.

Mekthelion rushed back and latched onto Roderick's good arm, holding it down. With his other hand he reared back, raising the knife to strike at Roderick's heart. But his malevolent expression froze in place, as did his hand. The knife fell from his grip. His eyes rolled back in his head and he fell forward, landing on top of Roderick, the hilt of a dagger buried in his back.

Behind the slain Thaumaturge knelt Nagan. The Gitano stared back at Roderick, quivering, his face pale with shock.

"Nagan!" Roderick exclaimed.

Glancing down at the fallen old man, Nagan said, "He—he's dead isn't he? I can't believe I—oh, Roderick, are you all right?"

Roderick's stomach lurched at the sight of the spreading stain of blood on the Thaumaturge's back, but a swell of joy pushed back his revulsion. Nagan was alive!

"You came back!" he said. "Thank heaven you woke in

time."

"You should thank Portia as well," Nagan said.

"What do you mean?"

"She—wait, what's going on?" Nagan's brow furrowed in confusion.

Roderick followed Nagan's gaze towards the glowing stone. The top of the pedestal beneath it glowed a molten, yellowish green. The Null Stone was sinking slowly down into it. Soon the surrounding rock dribbled away and the glimmering stone pitched forward and fell to the ground.

"Quick, see if Jacob is all right," Roderick said. He tried to move towards him, but the effort caused him to fold back in pain.

"He's fine," Nagan said. "Took a nasty hit on the head, though. Drained the patches right off his skin, looks like. Looks…unnatural." Nagan gently shook Jacob awake.

Jacob clutched the swelling welt on his forehead and looked warily about.

As Nagan helped him sit up, the flagstones surrounding the Null Stone began to glow as well. The gem started to sink through the floor.

"Look!" Roderick exclaimed. "The stone!"

Jacob leapt to his feet and grabbed it before it sank all the way through. The light from inside grew brighter by the moment, swallowing up Jacob's form so that only his outline was visible.

"Careful, Jacob," Roderick warned.

"It's all right," Jacob said. "It doesn't hurt."

"What are you going to do with it?" Nagan asked.

"Put it back where it belongs."

Jacob walked over to the shimmering portal. He cast the stone into the opening as if it were nothing more than Aisha's little ball. It flew into the silvery lands beyond and rolled down to the foot of the bridge crossing the great chasm. The mist along the ground surrounded it and the stone sank beneath the smoky tendrils. The portal shimmered and swirled in a panoply of colors, the whirlpool of a hundred sunsets. Finally, the gate itself vanished in a puff of purplish smoke and with it their connection to that strange, glimmering world. The three of them were left staring at the stark island sky.

"The magic is finally gone, isn't it?" Nagan said, his face grim and very much unlike the Nagan of old.

Jacob walked over to stand at Roderick's side.

"You saved me," he said, "I knew you would."

Roderick gulped back a surge of pride that welled up within. He looked up at Jacob, marveling at the way he looked now that the strange patterns had left him once and for all.

"You stayed straight and tall." Roderick grabbed Jacob's hand. "And now you're free. Your parents would be proud of you."

"I hope so."

"And I'm proud, too. So very proud."

Jacob gazed out at the dark silhouette of the forest which blanketed the island.

"I feel safe now. I don't think the shadows will come back. Not even in my dreams."

"I think you're right," Roderick said.

"Well, there is one thing I'll miss," Nagan said. "I won't be able to call you Patches anymore. And that's a shame, really. I was rather fond of that name."

Roderick let out a chuckle which caused him no small amount of pain, but it really couldn't be helped.

44

A LONG WAY FROM BRIAR'S GLEN

It took them some time to set Roderick's arm and descend the stairs. Nagan used strips of fabric from Mekthelion's cloak and the remains of his staff to wrap the injured limb and fashion a crude sling. Roderick had to remove his cloak for this, and since he could no longer wear it, they used it to cover Mekthelion's body. Seeing his shrouded form lying there, abandoned and lifeless, filled Roderick with sorrow.

"All that learning, and what did it get him?" Nagan said.

"I don't think he ever heard the music." Roderick said.

He had no words to add. The betrayal was still too fresh, too unfathomable. Somehow he could not altogether separate Kendall from Mekthelion in his heart.

As they made their way out of the tower, they found the stairway covered in ashes, all that remained of the scathen hordes. It was a long, silent trek to the bottom. Though Roderick was anxious to be rid of the place, they went slowly on account of his arm.

They were down to the last few steps when Portia came running into the tower, spent and out of breath. A huge smile erupted across her face when she saw them.

"Jacob—Roderick, you're alive! And free of the curse! Oh, this is beyond wonderful." She rushed up the steps and gave Jacob, who was in front, an enormous hug. "Look at you!" she gushed.

She did the same to Roderick, not noticing his injured arm. He bit down hard on his lip, but he was too happy to see her to complain.

"And what about me?" Nagan asked. "Am I just so much flotsam and jetsam?"

"Of course not." She gave him a fierce hug as well. She looked at Nagan in a different way now. Admiration shone in her eyes for the first time. Letting go of him, she finally noticed Roderick's arm and the joy fled from her face.

"What happened to you?" she asked.

Then Roderick explained everything that had occurred on the roof of the tower: his battle with Mekthelion, the appearance of the scathen, and how the magic was now gone forever. Jacob filled in a few details of his own. Portia's face shifted from one emotion to the next as she took in each turn in the tale. Though her face had glowed with pride to hear of Nagan's role in saving them from Mekthelion, she leveled a particularly displeased glare at him once the account was finished.

"You should not have moved Roderick like this with such a serious injury," she scolded.

"Well, I was in a bit of a rush," Nagan said. "I was worried about this lovely girl I'd left behind."

Portia's expression failed to soften, but she offered no more criticisms. Instead she went about re-setting the cast on Roderick's arm and reworking the sling.

"So you got to use a bit of the magic, eh?" Nagan remarked with a sigh. "I would have liked to have given it a go as well, but I never got the chance."

"It was not all that wonderful. A bit frightening, really. But tell me, how is it that you escaped the land of the scathen, Nagan?" He winced as Portia removed Nagan's handiwork.

"Ah, well, that's another tale now isn't it?" Nagan said. "I felt you trying to wake me up, but I chose not to come. I had just found Portia in the dream world, or whatever you want to call that place, and we were being chased by the shadows. I dared not leave her behind, though every moment in that place filled me with terror. Those dark nasties were everywhere. We fled through rainbow rooms and shimmering corridors, but we could not escape them. Then, just when it looked like they had us cornered, it was as if a ripple went through the whole realm and they all fled. Not knowing what else to do, we followed them into this enormous cavern, the one with the shining bridge, just like we saw in Castle Brimstoke. The portal was there and the shadows started going through. We guessed it must be the way out, though we couldn't see what was on the other side. We waited until the last of them had fled and then we waited a bit longer hoping that by then they might have cleared out from whatever was on the other side. Then we both dove through. But instead of coming back into Brimstoke or some other land, I came back into my own body again. Only I wasn't on the stairs, I was on top of the tower. And just at that moment that scurvy parlor magician was going at you with the knife and I didn't have time to think. Thankfully, like any decent Gitano, I had my boot knife hidden away and so I put it in that old false-heart's backside and that was that. I'm glad I was able to save you and all, and I'd do it again if I had to, but between you me and the trees, I hope I never get put in such a spot again."

Portia finished her work on Roderick's arm. He certainly felt less pain than before, but heading back out into the forest was hardly a pleasant experience. All of them were in desperate need of sleep, but they did not want to risk missing Captain Kade so they set off at once towards the rendezvous point where the *Fledgling's Flight* was to meet them.

With Roderick's broken arm and the uneven terrain, they had to take their time venturing back through the rainforest. Of the four travelers, Jacob was by far the most enthusiastic about the midnight trek. He walked with such a spring in his step, Roderick wondered if he did not leap back up into the trees again. As dawn's light caressed the botanical bounty surrounding them, Jacob took in everything with awe and wonder, gasping at every new bit of foliage they encountered or whenever he caught sight of some lizard or bird just before it darted into the trees. It was as if he was seeing the world for the first time.

"Look! A rainbow lorikeet! It looks just like I used to," he said, upon spotting a majestic, multi-colored bird. Tiny as it was, it lit up the morning forest with its brilliant feathers.

When they stopped for a rest and a bite to eat, Jacob surprised everyone by asking if he could try some of their hard tack.

"What—no fruit?" Nagan asked, baffled by Jacob's request.

"I think it's time I tried some new things," Jacob said plainly. "And I'm very hungry. I think I need something a little more filling."

"Well, I dare say hard tack is a sorry substitute for fruit, but it's nice to see you broadening your horizons." Roderick handed him one of the biscuits.

Jacob made a curious face when he bit into it, but then smiled and proceeded to devour not one, but two of the awful things.

As Gitanos are generally at home in the woods, even unfamiliar ones, Portia and Nagan had little difficulty finding the beach on the far side of the island. They skirted their way around the great mountain and reached their intended destination about midday, at last catching sight of the *Fledgling*. And what a sight it was. Her tawny deck glimmered in the sun like a golden wheat field and the green wings and painted beak on her prow glistened like a beacon, beckoning them on. Roderick was even more excited to get into the ship than he had been back in Iddlmar. When he finally set foot once more on the sturdy deck, he felt as content as if he'd come back to the cottage after one of his long journeys to Evenspire.

The captain showed only a passing interest in their tale. In fact, he frowned throughout most of their conversation, especially at any mention of magic or monsters.

He's afraid of such things, just like the rest of the sailors.

Roderick might have reacted the same way before he met Jacob, but that now seemed like so very long ago.

They ended up rushing through the tale and Roderick didn't mind one bit. All he wanted at that moment was a place to sleep.

After informing the captain that Kendall would not be making the return journey, the little band of travelers descended to their cabins in the lower part of the ship.

As Roderick turned into his room, Nagan handed him a leather pouch.

"I went through Kendall's, er, Mekthelion's, things before we left and found that," he said. "You may find it useful. It's a bit of that sleeping powder."

"*Sarance*," Roderick said. "Thank you."

Portia came shortly thereafter and brought him a cup of hot water to mix the powder in. He drank about half before curling up in bed beside Jacob. He was not two winks under the blanket before he fell headlong into a peaceful, dreamless sleep.

Roderick's arm was slow to heal, but it did get better during the voyage.

Portia, promising to double the captain's payment, persuaded him to travel all the way to the port of Farrinhill to avoid having to travel home through Iddlglim lands. Roderick wondered how they would be able to pay such an enormous fee, but soon found out that the powder was not the only thing Nagan had lifted from the deceased Thaumaturge. Nagan had come into a surprising amount of coin at Mekthelion's expense, but as it wasn't really stealing this time, and the Savants had given it to Kendall anyway to aid them in their quest, Roderick did not object.

Wintery winds buffeted the *Fledgling* throughout much of the return journey, but Roderick and the others mostly stayed below and slept through the worst of it. It took them nearly two weeks to arrive at Farrinhill, which was about half-way down the coast between Davinsmoor and Evenspire. After settling accounts with captain Kade and his crew, they were at last free of the seafaring life. Warmth flooded over Roderick as he stepped back onto his native land of Halicon once more.

Portia found them a room at a lovely inn overlooking the bay, *The Cracked Conch*. They spent the better part of two days there, gathering supplies for the long overland journey. Roderick visited a kindly old physik and got his arm properly wrapped. After that, he and Jacob spent most of their time resting and watching the seagulls dive and squawk on the white sand beaches, listening to the flutter of the waves roll in and out. By the time they left, Jacob could skip a stone practically out to the horizon.

Farrinhill was a sizable city whose many graystone buildings were mostly of recent construction. Colorful orange flags with a black horse stitched into them lined most of the major streets, giving the city a festive air. Being a seaside settlement, the winter weather was milder there than most of the rest of the Halicon Empire.

Though it was the capital of Garring Province, for years Farrinhill had been little more than a seaside retreat for the Emperor to escape the demands of the court. Recently it had grown into a thriving port in its own right. Roderick had heard a great deal about it, but had never had occasion to visit. He found it even more charming than it had been described. Unlike the central market in Briar's Glen, most of the merchants there had individual shops, and their glasswares, especially, were the finest he had ever seen. Nagan indulged him with the purchase of a milky blue flower vase for Bethany and a little glass dolphin for Aisha.

From the innkeep, they heard news that the war between Halicon and Caledonia had ended as abruptly as it began. Rumor was that the Iddlglim barbarians had only been goaded to war through the influence of some powerful warlord. Some said it was a Thaumaturge, others a man who was half bird, and still others a giant, shadowy wolf who could speak. But whoever it was, he had apparently been killed shortly after the war began. No one could account for his disappearance since they weren't even sure this mysterious leader had ever existed in the first place. But whether real or not, the wildmen lost heart for the battle and returned to the Woaden Heath to lick their wounds, but not without first sacking Middlehelm and several towns and carrying off a great many spoils of war.

Jacob's appetite continued to expand during their stay. He tried honey rolls, potatoes, radishes, collard greens, mint wafers, milk, and several kinds of fish. Whatever he tried he liked, and he never seemed to get full.

"Are you a horse or a boy?" Nagan asked during one of their meals.

"I think he's out-eaten the both of you," Portia said. And indeed, most meals he did.

Delightful as their time in the city was, they did not tarry longer than necessary in Farrinhill. With each passing day, the ache in Roderick's heart for Bethany and Aisha grew and Nagan and Portia sympathized with his desire to return home as quickly as possible. So, after they had acquired three stout horses and loaded them up with all the supplies they could possibly need, they took their leave of the fair seaside city and headed out onto the open road.

They first traveled to Havensward, the capital of Brackenland province. Unlike Farrinhill, this city was full of narrow streets and unfriendly people. Nagan, especially, was nervous about spending the night, for the Baroness of Hapshire was known to have had a home there.

Thankfully, they did not cross paths with the Baroness, or hardly anyone else for that matter, for they spent the afternoon and evening inside their rooms at a well-worn inn near the edge of the city, *The Minstrel's Song*. They left early in the morning to overcast skies and a slight drizzle and set off once again into the countryside.

The main road out of Havensward went south to Evenspire, but they took the trail to Divet instead. It was slower going, but they met fewer travelers and this suited them fine.

They ran into a light snow as they left Havensward, no more than a dusting really, but Jacob's face broke out in a wondrous smile at the sight of it. He made a game of trying to catch the flakes on his tongue, a game he kept on playing as long as the snow continued to fall.

Roderick and Jacob spent a good deal of their time on the road talking about what their life would be like once they got back to Briar's Glen. Jacob, far from the shy, reticent boy he'd been for most of the journey to the Isle of Rinn, wanted to know the name of every single person in the town, what their profession was, whether or not they were friendly or mean, and what clothes they had bought from Roderick.

Nagan and Portia laughed and joked with each other often. In the evenings they took long walks alone through the countryside. It may have been winter in the land, but it was spring time in their hearts. It was during this time that their love truly began to blossom. But Nagan's response to this blessed change took Roderick rather by surprise.

At some point between Divet and Massing, Nagan drew Roderick aside while Portia and Jacob were busy preparing the evening meal. The young Gitano wore an uncharacteristically solemn expression on his face. Roderick suspected he meant to announce that he and Portia would be taking their leave soon. They were well past the path to the Tamber Forest by that point and no doubt his two companions were anxious to get on with their lives. Instead, Nagan asked rather pointedly about what sort of fortunes a man could hope to make in a small town like Briar's Glen.

"You mean you'd like to settle down in The Glen?" Roderick asked, guessing what Nagan was getting at. "Well, that's a curious question. Do you think Portia would get on in a place like that?"

"It was her idea, actually," Nagan said. "But I think it might be just the place to start a...well, for two road-weary Gitanos to settle down."

Roderick smiled as broad as a sunbeam.

"Hmm, I suppose I could offer to train you in the tailoring trade, but I don't know as that there's all that much profit to be made from it. You might be better off trying your hand at farming. That's how most folk in The Glen make their living and there is ample land to be had. My neighbors, the Tullums, are getting on in years and never had any children. I'm sure Farmer Tullum could use a strong young hand like yours. He could show you the ropes until you got on your feet and found a place of your own. You won't find a better teacher when it comes to planting, harvesting, and tending the good green things that grow in the land."

"Farming, eh?" Nagan mused, scratching his chin. "Well, perhaps I would look rather fetching traipsing behind a plow. And I suppose it is good honest work, isn't it? How long do you think it would take me to earn enough money for a ring doing that sort of work?"

Even after all their travels, there was still plenty of coin left over from Kendall's sizable stash. Roderick knew Nagan did not really need to earn the money to pay for a ring, but it pleased him to no end that his friend wanted to earn his future wife's wedding band by his own hand.

"So, she's actually agreed to marry you?" Roderick asked.

"Don't look so surprised." Nagan smiled proudly, barely able to contain himself.

"You'll make a fine husband," Roderick said, amazed at the change in Nagan during the few short weeks since they'd met.

And so, after that day, as they headed on to Massing and then Talance, their talk turned more and more to the upcoming marriage. Roderick promised to sew Portia the most beautiful wedding dress in all of Vinyon province, and Nagan kept going over and over his calculations about how much he would have to make and how long it would take him to earn a "proper" ring for a woman as lovely as Lady Portia. Even Jacob got excited at the prospect of participating in the ceremony as the ring-bearer. From time to time he would practice his (very stately and somewhat comical) "walk" holding the imaginary ring on its imaginary pillow as they walked.

"Ring-bearer," he said gleefully. "I like the sound of that."

Then the last bend in the road was turned, the last hour of waiting passed, and they arrived high and happy at Briar's Glen. It was evening when they first caught sight of the sleepy little town. A real, honest to goodness snow had fallen the night before, and it lay several inches thick over the rooftops and lanes of the village. The snowy blanket absorbed all sound, bathing the streets in a blessed hush. It felt like the town was holding its breath, just waiting for his return and with each quiet clop of the horse's hooves, his dear and precious family drew that much closer.

They passed through the whisper-quiet town, unheralded and unsung. A chilly breeze wafted its way down the lane, but the moon shone like a pearly button on a nobleman's coat and to Roderick's mind, the light was as warm as the noonday sun.

They dismounted at the cottage, but no lights shone within the windows and not a hint of smoke escaped the chimney. To top it all off, the house was locked and Roderick, to his chagrin, had no key!

"Well, buttons," he muttered.

"No worries, stitch," Nagan said. "Looks as dark as old Brimstoke's dungeon in there anyway."

Portia grimaced. "Don't remind me of that place."

"It looks wonderful to me," Jacob said, bouncing at the window on the stoop, like the house was a present he could not wait to open.

"I guess the cottage will have to wait. They must be over at the Tullums'" Roderick said. "Don't worry, it's just down the road."

Arriving at the Tullum's farmhouse, they found light

streaming out from the foggy windows and music wafting from inside. They tied up the horses and made their way up the steps. Roderick, every inch of him fluttering with anticipation, knocked brightly on the door with his customary seven beat rhythm. Portia adjusted the little ribbon she had tied in her hair for the occasion and nestled close to Nagan, who whistled nervously. Jacob's eyes glowed with anticipation and never left the door, as if all the treasures of the Emperor lay beyond it.

The music died down and farmer Tullum's familiar face appeared in the open door. His red crinkled cheeks parted in wonder. His old eyes did a fair jig as he drank in the sight of Roderick and his road-weary companions.

"Oh, well I never!" he exclaimed, displaying more emotion in his old weathered face than Roderick had ever seen. "Bethany, Aisha, come quick!"

And, just like that, there they were, his lovely bride and beautiful daughter.

He could only embrace them with his one good arm, but that was enough. His tears flowed freely, as did Bethany's. Aisha was all smiles and laughter. She started jumping around and doing capers as joy seized her little frame.

"I knew you'd make it back in time for my birthday!" she said. "I knew it, I knew it! I knew it!" she went on and on.

"Oh, my, what day is it, then?" Roderick asked, having completely forgotten such details during the long journey.

"The seventeenth of Winter's Day," Tullum said.

"Why so it is!" Roderick answered back, laughter tickling his sides.

"We prayed you would make it home in time," Bethany said. "Adonai is indeed most gracious."

All eyes turned then to the transformed little boy. Bethany remarked how handsome he looked, but Aisha said that she didn't see anything different about him except that his cloak needed a washing. Jacob's countenance fairly shone with color. If he'd had glowing diamonds reflecting off it, it could scarcely have been more radiant.

"Welcome home, my son." Roderick ushered him into Bethany's waiting arms. Then Bethany cried even harder.

Aisha clapped her hands together and said in a sing song voice,

"Jacob's home…We'll have such fun…Now we get to play and run…"

Poor Nagan and Portia were getting lost in the reunion so Roderick stepped back and introduced them, telling everyone what kind and dear friends they had become. And then another figure appeared in the doorway.

"Master Jareth," Roderick said. "Thank you for watching over my family." He went over and pressed his hand warmly into the Savant's. The two apprentices, Evan and Rand, both holding fiddles, waved their greetings from behind.

"It was my privilege. I dare say it's been a quiet winter. We've heard nary a rumbling or rumor of the Thaumaturge since you left. But what news of Master Kendall? I do not see him among you. Did something happen to him?" he asked. His skullcap dipped into his wrinkled forehead.

"He did not make it," Roderick said.

From Jareth's pained expression, Roderick saw that the poor Savant had no idea of his friend's true identity. But Roderick didn't feel comfortable coming right out with the truth in the midst of all the happiness of the occasion. "Perhaps we should go inside and everyone should sit down while I tell you our tale."

"And we finish celebrating my birthday!" Aisha squealed. "Mrs. Tullum made caramel cakes!"

As they all came in off the porch, Roderick remembered the vase and the little glass dolphin he had acquired in Farrinhill. His wife and daughter were of course delighted with their gifts. Aisha even forgot about the cake and sat down next to Jacob to play with the tiny figurine.

The rest of the company gathered around the hearth. There were just enough chairs for everyone, but Roderick remained standing. And then, for the first time he could remember, he told a story to his family. Only this one was not made up. Though it no doubt lacked Bethany's skill and flare in the telling, everyone in the room was so caught up in the tale, not a word was spoken during all the long unravelling of it. Aisha ceased playing with her dolphin, and Master Jareth sat spell-bound, as if Roderick were unveiling some long lost legend of antiquity. Even Nagan, Portia and Jacob were silent, though they had been as much a part of it as Roderick. They seemed to understand that this was his tale to tell, and tell it he did, and well at that.

When at last the account was finished, those gathered around the fire had many questions. Roderick, Nagan, Portia, and Jacob went long into the night in answering them. As they spoke, the travelers partook of their fair share of the fine caramel cakes and birthday cheese. Bethany took special delight in Jacob's newly expanded palate.

"I dare say he's the exact opposite of before," Roderick said. "I don't think he's tried a single dish he hasn't gobbled up on the spot since we left the tower. The challenge now is keeping him full!"

The chatting, the laughter, and the tears went long into the night until Aisha began nodding off. At that point Roderick and his family reluctantly took their leave and headed home.

Nagan and Portia stayed at the farm with Master Jareth and the apprentices, for the Tullums had plenty of room to spare. Roderick promised to return and breakfast with them in the morning.

Once they reached their cottage, he stood for a long moment in front of the hearth, arms wrapped around his family, now for the first time four instead of three.

Then Roderick prayed and it was the best, most pure prayer he had ever prayed. He took pride in many things in his life. His work, his home, his reputation as an honest craftsman. But the honor of being a husband to Bethany and a father to Aisha, and now Jacob, well those were honors beyond estimation, and it's fair to say he was never more thankful for the privilege of those blessed responsibilities than in that hour. And all of his gratitude he offered up to the Giver of all good gifts.

As long as the journey had been, when he finished the prayer, Roderick did not feel the least bit tired. His heart was so full at that moment, his only care was where to expend such a surfeit of blessing. If that day could have gone on forever, he would have been equal to the task.

But days were not meant to last forever and so they brought the children to their room and to tuck them in.

Jacob gasped at the sight of his very own bed next to Aisha's. Farmer Tullum and the Savants had made it while they had been on their journey. It was nothing special, the same size as Aisha's only with newer wood and unfaded blankets, but from the light on Jacob's face it might have been the Emperor's castle itself.

He leapt onto his bed, forgetting to remove his dusty traveling cloak, but no one seemed to mind.

Aisha crawled much less enthusiastically under the blankets of her own bed. She smiled blissfully through droopy eyes and muttered about her "perfect day."

"Welcome home," Bethany said, kissing Jacob on the forehead.

"Thank you for taking me in." Jacob said. His eyes shone like sunlight on the grass. "And for being my new mother and father."

Tears filled both Roderick and Bethany's eyes, dropping down onto the multi-colored, patchwork quilt which covered Jacob's bed.

It was a strange way to begin a family, but then, every family has a story to tell, Roderick supposed. And all of them are mysterious and fantastical in their own unique way.

ℰPILOGUE

acob lay asleep in his wonderful new bed. He had not had a single dream, much less any nightmares, since he came to live with his new family. The weeks since returning back from the tower had certainly been the happiest of his young life.

But on this night, many hours after drifting off to sleep, while the moon was drained dry and the land was as dark as the pitch on a black dragon boat, he had another dream.

In it, he saw a silvery landscape, glittering with lights, as if he were walking amongst the stars themselves. A tender melody beckoned him along, a song whose gentle notes plopped like stones in a stream, allowing him to cross the great river whose name is Beauty, which flows through the heart of every child. He walked for a long time, feeling quite peaceful, enraptured by the music's spell, until he came to an actual stream. Its water was silver as well, but it shone with a light that was even brighter than the stars.

A voice began to sing softly to the music, but Jacob could not make out the words. It was a voice that was both high and deep all at once, both fragile and strong, as unbreakable as sunlight and as tender as the rain. As Jacob ventured further along the stream, the song grew in power and intensity until, at the height of its majesty, a figure appeared out of the mist.

Jacob knew at once that this was the source of the song, but the sight still gave him a start. For though the figure had the outward shape of a man, it was a shadowy being and looked more like a hole in the air than any sort of actual creature. It was not as twisted and unstable looking as the ones which had come out of his dreams to try and capture him, but it was a shadow nonetheless and for that reason he froze where he stood.

"*Do not be afraid,*" the shadow told him. Its voice sounded as if it came from far away. It did not sound quite human, but there was something familiar and even comforting about it.

"Who are you?" Jacob asked.

"*My name is Aladelrin,*" the voice answered. "*And I have come to say goodbye.*"

Jacob struggled to place the voice or the name, but he could pin down neither. "We've met before, haven't we?" He stared at the shadow, trying to make out any details, but it was like staring into pure blackness, only glowing faintly around the edges.

"*No, not in the way you are thinking of. But I was with you all along, helping you control the feyglimmer.*"

"Oh, it was your voice I heard, then, when I was using the magic. Yes, I recognize it now."

"I made a promise to someone long ago to protect you. There were many others I tried to help, but I could not save them."

"So you are a good kind of shadow then?" Jacob asked, at the same time wondering if such a thing were even possible.

"*There is only one of whom it is proper to use the word 'good.' I am but his servant.*"

Somehow that answer made Jacob more certain of this being's goodness than if he had claimed to be good on his own merits.

"Well, thank you for helping me. I'm sure I would not have made it without you."

"*But still my help was not enough. You needed the tailor, and even the Gitanos. And there were others, those who opposed you. Without their greed and evil desires, you would have failed.*"

"You mean the scholar and those shadows? They helped

me too?"

"*Yes, albeit unknowingly. And there was another, one who passed from this world long ago, but whose lies nonetheless inflamed the hearts of men and watered the seeds of malice sewn there.*"

"And who was that?"

"*Some call him Gloam, though he did not always go by that name. Through treachery he caused the magic to enter the world as something it was never meant to be. But that is a tale for another time. Perhaps one day you shall hear it, perhaps not. Either way, I must leave you now.*"

"I see. Does that mean you won't be protecting me anymore?" Jacob asked.

"*No,*" the voice answered. "*You no longer have any need of my protection.*"

"Will I ever see you again, then? In my dreams at least?" Jacob felt rather sad that he had never gotten to know this good shadow, though he had apparently done so much for him.

"*You will see me one last time. But that day is very far off yet by your reckoning of time. Between then and now you have much growing and learning to do.*"

"And what about the magic and the stone? Will they be safe here? This is where I put them, isn't it? In the land of dreams?"

"*The Null Stone has cracked and the glimmer inside it will never return to your world in its corrupted form. But with the destruction of the stone the glimmer is free to leave the Dwimmerkell and spread itself abroad in the land. For Adonai's will was that your race, the race of men, should know and use this gift, though I and my brothers doubted and because of that, the feyglimmer ran wild and much harm was done.*"

The voice had grown sad and soft, but now it brightened once again.

"*Now that the magic is free, it may touch men through their dreams, both in waking and in sleep. In this way, Adonai's gift is more powerful than ever before, for it shall touch not just one man or a few, but all who bend their thoughts and wills to this place.*"

And saying those words, the shadow began to fade. Jacob

did not want him to go. He felt it would be like watching a sunset disappear, or as though some immeasurable beauty were fleeing the world, never to return. He started after the shadow, but it moved away too fast for him to catch. As it disappeared, it carried the silvery stardust of the dream world with it and Jacob found himself cast out of that shining realm and back in the cottage once again.

He sat up in bed. It was the middle of the night. Aisha slept quietly in the bed beside his.

When the magic had first left, it was as if a tremendous burden had been lifted from him and the world had become new again. But even in the gladness that followed, Jacob had always wondered in the back of his mind whether or not the power might come back and call forth whatever shadows might still be hiding in the forgotten places of the world. Now, he felt at last that he was truly free. He could cease to worry and live in peace, enjoying the new life he had been given.

And he found, as he grew older, that what the voice in his dream said was true. Though he no longer carried the magic inside of him, in some mysterious fashion, it, or something like it, was still at work in his life. Through his hopes, his dreams, and wonderings, a kind of magic was still present, only this kind did not force itself upon him and did not change the color of his skin. It did not cause things to glow or catch fire, but was simply there, waiting to inspire him whenever he needed it most.

In truth, this so called magic waits for any and all who might choose to listen to Adonai's call to create something beautiful, or speak the truth, or invent something good and useful which brings joy or eases another's suffering. Sometimes it even works its way into stories and books.

There is still a kind of magic in the world that moves and inspires us through our dreams, Jacob realized. And that magic, when it can be found, is a very good thing, a very good thing indeed.

Other books by DJ Edwardson

THE CHRONOTRACE SEQUENCE

INTO THE VAST
AWAKENING THE SENTIENTS
ASCENT OF THE NEBULA

ABOUT THE AUTHOR

DJ Edwardson traveled a lot when he was younger. Now he's busy crafting exotic destinations of his own. Although he has written both Science Fiction and Fantasy novels, he likes to say he writes in the "genre of imagination".

He has a degree in English from Cornell College where his emphasis was on the works of Shakespeare. He's tried his hand at both acting and directing in the theater, but these days is happiest with a pen in hand. He lives in Tennessee with his wife and three children and a rather large collection of board games. His family often gangs up on him so that he doesn't win, but he has fun anyway.

For more information about DJ Edwardson's writing please visit: *www.djedwardson.com*

19660667R00234

Made in the USA
Middletown, DE
06 December 2018